JAC
COL

JACKIE COLLINS

THE STUD

THE BITCH

THE LOVE KILLERS

INDEX

This edition produced by Carlton Books Limited
by arrangement with Pan Macmillan Limited, London

This edition published in 1995 by Index
Unit 1, A1/M1 Centre, Garrard way, Kettering, NN16 8TD

1 3 5 7 9 10 8 6 4 2

INCORPORATING:

The Stud
Copyright © Jackie Collins 1969, 1984

The Bitch
Copyright © Jackie Collins 1979, 1984

The Love Killers
First published in Great Britain in 1974
under the title *Lovehead*
Copyright © Jackie Collins 1974, 1989

ISBN 1-85868-037-9

Printed in Great Britain

Contents

The Stud

1

TONY

LONDON 1969

There is something very exciting about the beginning of the evening—well, the beginning of my evening, usually about ten-thirty, eleven o'clock. Every night at 'Hobo' is like a party—a great party where everyone knows and likes everyone else.

They start coming in slowly. First the ones that want to be sure of a good table, then the watchers. Usually this whole group is stacked neatly out of the way on the wrong side of the room, or if they are really rough, in the back room. We've got a closed membership, but a few manage to find their way in. Then everyone sits around waiting for the swingers, and about twelve-thirty, one o'clock, they start arriving. Golden-haired girls in cowboy outfits, Indian gear, boots, backless topless see-through dresses. The wilder the better. Their escorts varying from the long-haired mob of rock groups to the latest young actors. Elegant young debs in full evening dress, with chinless-wonder escorts. The older society group. The rich Greeks. The even richer Arabs. An odd movie star—an odd M.P. or visiting senator. Anybody famous who's in town. Young writers, dress designers, photographers, models. They all come to look and be looked at, and to see their friends. It's like a building excitement—reaching a breathless climax at around two a.m. when the room is so jammed you couldn't get anyone else in except maybe Frank Sinatra or Mick Jagger.

It seems ridiculous that six months ago they would hand me a couple of quid and wouldn't recognise me if we passed in the street. Now they can't wait to grab hold of me—'Dahling'—kiss—kiss—kiss—'Who's here tonight?' Sly grab if the boy-friend or husband isn't looking. 'Please don't give us a lousy table like last time'—affectionate squeeze and promising look. Then husband or boy-friend steps forward—firm handshake, few masculine chummy words, and I hand them over to Franco, swinging head-waiter supreme, who whisks them off to whatever table their position rates. The watchers on one side of the room, the doers on the other. All very neat, the duds with the bread tucked firmly away in the back room.

Yeah, I'm very popular now, everyone wants to know. Funny thing, isn't it? I'm the same guy, talk in the same voice, the clothes are a little more expensive but that's about the only difference. You wouldn't believe it though, the ladies practically fight to climb in the sack with me. You would think I was doing them a big favour, and listen, the way things have been going I think I am!

I tell you it's a great life if you don't weaken.

I suppose you're wondering how this all came about, how a guy like me, Tony Shwartsburg from somewhere near the Elephant and Castle, turned into Tony Blake—man about town, friend of the stars, host at the most 'in' discothèque, 'Hobo'. I have exchanged confidences such as 'Where can we get some pot?' and 'Got any birds?' with some of the most famous in the land. 'Tony can arrange anything' is a well-known catch phrase around town.

Well, to begin with I had the same useless tough life as most of the kids in my neighbourhood—fighting in the back streets, watching in on the fights at home. My parents, Sadie and Sam, were a nice old Jewish couple who hated each other. Sam couldn't care less about me, but to Sadie the sun shone out of my left ear. 'Learn a trade like your cousin Leon,' she would say, 'let the family be proud of you.' I got laid at thirteen, just before I got barmitzvahed. If the family knew they'd sure as old harry be proud of me. It was all good clean fun. The girl, she was a few years older than me, gave me the crabs, and I spent about six months alternatively trying to get rid of them and passing them on to any girl who got lucky! Eventually I passed them on to the wrong girl and everyone found out. Sadie had hysterics and Sam patted me on the back and bought me some ointment.

At sixteen I got caught pinching petrol from a car. It was a good racket while it lasted. You hosed it out into a can, and sold it back to the garage where it had probably come from in the first place! Anyway, they shoved me on probation and that was the end of my criminal tendencies.

I got a variety of jobs, delivering papers, sweeping up in a factory, usher in the local cinema—I got fired from that when the manager found me making it with a bird in the back row of the stalls. It was his best usherette and he was screwing her at the same time, so he was a bit choked. Unfortunately I knocked her up and there was a family scandal, but seeing the manager wanted her back, as good usherettes were hard to come by, he paid for her to get unknocked up and everything was all right.

By this time Sadie and Sam were getting a bit fed up with me, and who could blame them? Sam stopped screaming at Sadie and started on me. It was a good job someone thought of Uncle Bernie.

Uncle Bernie was the success of the family. He owned two delicatessens and had sort of cut himself off from the rest of his clan. Anyway Sadie felt that as she was his only sister he owed her a favour, and she dragged me down to his place in Great Portland Street and insisted he gave me a job. He wasn't too thrilled at the prospect, but knowing he wasn't going to get rid of Sadie any other way, he agreed.

He had a daughter, Muriel, a big strapping girl with lots of thick black hair—everywhere—you name a place, Muriel had thick black hair there. She wasn't bad apart from that, a bit sexy looking. Big tits and a thin crooked nose. I suppose I shouldn't have, I mean she was my cousin and all, but one day the opportunity arose, and if the opportunity arises who am I to put it down? Of course Uncle Bernie found out and there ended my career in a delicatessen. It was all too much for Sadie, and even Sam wasn't pleased about it.

Life at the Elephant was becoming a drag anyway, and having got as far as Great Portland Street, I thought why not go a bit further. I got a job as a dishwasher at the Savoy, and a room in Camden Town. Life was great. I entered my twenties a happy man.

I met a girl, Evie, a pretty curly-haired blonde, she was a

11

hostess at a clip joint. She fixed me up with a job as a waiter and I discovered the world of tips. It was great, taught me a lot about people. Taught me the right way to milk a pound from a drunk whose intention was to leave nothing.

I was making twenty quid a week. I branched out to striped Italian suits and pointed shoes, then dated girls with a bit more class, hairdressers, shop assistants and all that group. Not bad, I felt like a king! Visited the Elephant on Sundays, and handed Sadie a fiver. Of course she never took it, she always came out with a speech about how I should save my money, settle down, look for a nice Jewish girl and get married, be like cousin Leon—in my opinion a real schmuck.

I left the clip joint and started as a busboy in a high-class restaurant, not so much bread but a road to better things. And the better things were all around me. The birds that came into the place Beautiful! Furs, jewellery, expensive smells.

From there I became a waiter in another high-class place and I became involved with Penny, daughter of the owner. Penny was something else. Red hair, she was very neat, small and compact. I suppose I fell in love with her. Couldn't make it, that was probably why. Looking back on it now, I reckon she was undersexed, but at the time it bothered me a lot. She was the first girl that I had wanted and couldn't have.

I don't want to sound conceited, but imagine a taller Tony Curtis with a touch of Michael Caine and Kris Kristofferson.

Anyway Penny and I wanted to get married. Her father of course was furious, but she got round him and since he didn't want his daughter marrying a waiter he opened a new place and put me in charge—sort of a de luxe head-waiter.

It all started there. That's where I first saw Fontaine.

Of course everyone's heard of Fontaine Khaled, she's sort of like a national institution, though not so old—around thirty-five I would say, even now I still don't know the truth.

Fontaine looks very haughty upper-class English. Beautiful, of course, with chiselled cut bones (by nature or cosmetic surgery no one knows), a fine parchment skin, an angular boney body which lends itself to fancy clothes, and long blonde hair worn pulled back.

When I first saw her I couldn't take my eyes off. Here was a lady. Sounds corny I know, but there was no mistaking the fact. She had been a world famous photographic model, and had retired to marry Benjamin Al Khaled, billionaire. She was always in the papers, jetting here there and everywhere, showing us around her house in Acapulco, her castle in Spain, her town house in London or penthouse in New York.

I read the columns a lot. In my business it's always good to know who's who, so as soon as she came in I knew it was her. She was with three men and two women all of the same social scene but not in the same class as her. I led them to their table personally, a thing I had stopped doing when I took over the place. I even referred to her by name just to let her know I was around. But she didn't give me a glance. So much for the instant impact of Tony Blake.

There was no Benjamin Al Khaled with her, and I didn't think she was anyone's date, very square the fellows with her, typical no balls types, with loud public school voices.

She was wearing what I thought was a rabbit coat, but later I discovered during a course of intensified education that it was chinchilla. I thought I was pretty hip then, but I didn't even know a Gucci handbag from a Marks & Sparks.

I hovered around the table a lot, but not so much as a look.

I eavesdropped, 'St Moritz is becoming a terrible bore'—'Did you know Jamie broke his leg in Tibet?'—'Do you *believe* St Laurent this year?'

Pretty dull snatches of conversation came my way.

The one that paid the bill left a nothing tip.

Two nights later she was back, this time with her husband. He was much older than her. They were with another old guy. She threw me a brief smile on her way in, which startled me, and after that they came in a lot whenever they weren't flying round the world.

Penny was causing me problems. Since her father had promoted me, so to speak, I was having a fair amount of success. Customers liked me, I remembered their names, saw their food was just right, and became casually friendly with some of them.

13

The place developed a good reputation, people were disappointed if I wasn't there. They liked to be greeted by name and made to feel important.

Penny's father realised I was good for the joint and I realised Penny was no good for me. It was not a good situation. She started to get very narky and jealous, accusing me of all sorts of things, which were true. Well, I don't know if she thought I was jerking off or what, but I certainly wasn't getting any action from her. I moved to a small one-roomed flat off the Edgware Road and she caught me there one day with a red-haired croupier—female of course!

What tears and scenes! She even offered me her virginity but, by that time, I didn't even fancy it. So we parted bad friends.

Needless to say it was a matter of time before her father and I also parted company. I had my eyes wide open for another job. By that time I had had the waiter bit, I wanted to move up in the world, progress. The ideal situation would be to get my own little place, but for that one needed bread, and who had any?

I cast my eyes around and one memorable night they met squarely with Fontaine's. It was one of those looks, her cool aquamarine eyes clashed straight on with my moody dark stare (many's the bird who's told me I've got a moody dark stare) and that was it. We both knew something had to give.

She went to the powder-room shortly after and I was waiting when she came out.

'Tony,' she said, she had a deep very English clipped accent, 'you're wasting yourself here—why don't you drop by and see me tomorrow, I have an idea that maybe you can help me with.' She handed me a small hand-engraved card with her address and added, 'About three o'clock will be fine.'

I nodded dumbly, to tell you the truth I was knocked out by the whole thing.

I must have changed my outfit ten times the next day—was a casual look best or should I go for the slightly formal Italian gear? I finally settled for a pale lilac shirt with a stiff white collar, and a black silk suit.

I arrived half-an-hour early at this knockout pad she had in

Belgravia. It was too much! I found out it was an ex-embassy. They even had a swimming pool.

A butler settled me down in what I suppose was the living-room, but it turned out to be a mere waiting-room. It was all expensive with crazy carved furniture and jazzy old pictures on the wall. Some of them were rather sexy—there was one with three birds and one guy that was a bit strong, but just when I was studying it a bit closer Fontaine came in 'Are you interested in art, Tony?' she asked.

She looked great in a long sort of silk robe and her hair all loose.

Man, I can still remember how nervous I was. This was real class.

'Let's go in the study,' she said. 'Would you care for a drink?'

I asked for a sherry, I figured it was the thing to have.

'You don't look like a sherry man to me,' she said, her eyes cool and amused.

I started to get excited there and then, and in the tight black trousers I was wearing, this was no joke. I approached her warily, she didn't back away, in fact she came towards me. I put my arms around her, she was tall, I could feel her bones through the thin robe. She fastened her arms about my neck and pulled my mouth on to hers.

It was some kiss, she was like a hungry animal pushing and probing with her tongue, biting and sighing. I think I can safely say I gave back as good as I got.

'Let's go upstairs,' she said at last, and added, 'It's all right, Benjamin is away.'

I followed her to a small elevator and we pressed closely together as it started up. She unzipped my trousers and rubbed me with her long talented fingers. Man, I was ready to shoot off there and then!

Suddenly the elevator stopped and she shrugged off her robe.

I stared at her lean body. She had tiny breasts with pale extended nipples. 'Are we there?' I asked foolishly.

'No, but we soon can be,' she replied pulling at my trousers.

The elevator was small, gave you a touch of the claustrophobia, but she managed to get me down to my bare skin.

I must say in all my dealings with birds I've never had one behave like *this*.

'Tony, you come up to all my expectations,' she muttered. 'Sit down, I'll show you how to do it in a lift.'

Oh man! What an experience!

Thinking back I didn't get a chance to do much because she did everything. Of course I rose to the occasion magnificently. I was out of my depth and knew it. I just let her have her way, I wasn't going to blow this set-up.

She dug her nails deep into my back and twisted her long white legs around me. She didn't moan or cry out. She muttered, 'Screw me you bastard, keep it hard.'

Well, I'd never had any problem doing *that*.

Afterwards she was all calm and businesslike. She stood up and put her robe on. She waited for me to struggle into my clothes, then the elevator took us back to the study.

I was destroyed. I flopped into a chair. She rang a bell, and the butler appeared with tea.

She chatted away in her high-class tinkly voice and who would have thought that half-an-hour earlier she'd been frothing and raving about in the elevator.

'I want to open a discothèque,' she said. 'Something different, something chic, somewhere to go that's fun—something mad and exclusive.'

'Yes?' I was all interest. Here came my big chance.

'You could manage something like that, couldn't you?'

She chatted on about how there was nowhere to go that was chic. 'All these places now are filled with scruffy little nothings—don't you think this town needs something different—somewhere for grown-ups like Paris has, or Rome?'

Her line of chat killed me. Somewhere for grown-ups yet! However I nodded seriously. I was looking for an out from the restaurant—this could be it.

'You start looking for premises, Tony,' she said, 'money's no problem. My husband will finance the whole thing. We'll pay you a good salary and five per cent of the profits. How's that? Of course you'll be running the whole show, does it appeal to you?'

16

Did it appeal to me? You bet your ass it appealed to me.

She stood up, smoothing her robe down. 'I have to get dressed now. Start looking and keep in touch.' She turned at the door. 'Oh, Tony, in the lift, that was nice, very nice, let's do it again soon.' Then in the same cool voice she added. 'The butler will show you out.'

It was all too much. This was a real cool lady and a raver to boot. I had a feeling I'd fallen in the right direction.

I set to work, started getting up early in the mornings and hanging around the estate agents, saw a lot of lousy joints. I had a feeling for what she wanted (ha ha) and I kept right on looking until I found it. It was a rooftop restaurant that had gone bust—bad neighbourhood everyone said, impossible to park—but baby, you get the right doorman and nowhere's impossible. To me, it was just right. Not too big, not too small. Different because instead of creeping down to some cellar you went up and you had windows and a view. I called Fontaine right away, and she came gliding over with a chauffeur in a Silver Cloud Rolls. She loved it too. We were in business.

We had tea at Fortnums. I hadn't seen her since the day at her house. She was wearing a silver mink coat and hat, and everyone turned to take another look.

She stared at me with those cool eyes and I knew the look. 'Benjamin's home,' she said, 'but I have another place.'

'Well, let's go,' I said, gulping down dainty tea sandwiches and feeling pretty good.

She dismissed the chauffeur and we took a cab to a small apartment building in Chelsea. It was one room luxury, a big bed covered in white fur, rugs, mirrors everywhere, louvred shutters to remove the daylight and red-tinged lights. A few erotic pictures on the wall, a lot of dirty books in a built-in bookcase next to the bed.

'This is my whore's room,' she said with a small tight smile. I didn't know what to say, I'd never met anyone like her before. She took off her clothes and stretched out on the bed. I fumbled with mine, I mean, well, I was embarrassed!

I finally got them off and started some action. She just lay there

17

very stiff, smiling slightly. Very different from the last time. It was rather exciting really, took me off guard so to speak. I mean, I was expecting it to be like the last time.

It didn't take me long before I was through—wowee! I rolled off her and studied our bodies in the mirrored ceiling.

She said very slowly, 'Tony—how would you like to learn to be a good lover?'

I sat up on one elbow and stared at her. Was she kidding? I mean I was all there you know, I'd never been lacking in *that* department.

As it happens, looking back on it now, I suppose she did teach me a lot. Little tricks she'd picked up in Beirut, Tangier, South America. You name it, she knew it. She was a great teacher, very detailed. I grew to look forward to our little classes more than anything. Of course I was knocking off another bird on the side. Fontaine didn't know about it, but it was useful, gave me a chance to do my homework so I'd be in good shape for Fontaine.

Lana was a stripper, a bit of a scrubber but a knockout when it came to practising my lessons. In fact, she added a few ideas of her own. She had the best pair of knockers around, a big full juicy bird. I mean Fontaine was very classy and all that jazz, but a bit lacking in the tits and ass department. A man likes his steak rare, but he needs his bread and potatoes too.

Life was really good. I left the restaurant and started organising the new place. Interior decorators, waiters to find, members' lists, ordering stock. There were a million and one things to do.

Fontaine chose the name, 'Hobo'. It was good, although Benjamin offered the suggestion of calling it 'Fontaine's'. She said that would be tasteless and vulgar. She was right, she was usually right.

And so eventually we opened. Big party, lots of publicity, all the right people. They all came, they always turn out in bulk for anything free. Fontaine personally supervised the guest list and I think that's what started the whole thing off, her guest list. It was such a wild mixture—from rock groups to movie stars to high society to hookers (international ones of course!). It was great. It all just happened, and within a few weeks 'Hobo' was *the* place and all of a sudden I was *the* person to know.

It's wild really, I still sort of expect the bubble to burst. But here I am, Tony Blake—ex-nothing, ex-waiter, now great host, lover and friend of the stars.

Great me!

2

FONTAINE

I have always enjoyed waking late and breakfasting in bed. Benjamin says it's because bed is my favourite place. He's right actually. He gets up at the unearthly hour of seven a.m., so I lie awake with my eyes closed and listen to him cough and belch and fart! Delightful! Benjamin Al Khaled in the mornings—I wonder what the society gossip columns would make of an exclusive like that! I've begged him for separate bedrooms but that's one thing he won't surrender to. He likes his nightly ashes hauled, and maybe in the middle of the night too if he feels like it. So the communal bedroom stays. It's worth it, he's very very rich. Even I don't know how many millions. He's sixty-one years old and randy as hell.

Bed is delicious. I can lie here and think and relax and not have to do anything. At eleven my maid wakes me. She brings breakfast and the papers, runs my bath and lays out the clothes I tell her to. I can have anything I want. Benjamin will give me anything except actual cash.

We have been married for five years and both of us were married before. His ex-wife is a bitch. Plain and dreary with two hulking great children by him—Alexandra and Ben junior. My ex-husband is somewhere in California now, basking in the sun on the money that Benjamin had to pay him to agree to a divorce. Paul was always lazy. When we were married he never did a stroke of work, just lived off my hard-earned modelling money. He was rather beautiful though, and very virile. It was a shame to have to divorce him, but I was bored with modelling, and one doesn't grow any younger, and there was Benjamin offering me a title and all that divine money. Well, really, I had no choice.

Being married to Benjamin is rather like a part-time job. He works so hard and travels so much that I hardly ever see him. That's why he said I could do the discothèque, somewhere for me to go, 'a little interest' as he calls it. 'Little interest' indeed. It's making a fortune! Benjamin would have a fit if he knew, he hates me to have any money of my own. He thinks it would make me independent of him. Isn't that silly? As if I would be independent of all his millions.

Benjamin thinks I'm faithful to him. He told me. He thinks that if I'm well looked after at home I won't want any more. For a man of sixty-one he's really very naïve, especially since he's away half the time. As if I could be satisfied with that withered old thing!

Fortunately I have arranged my life rather well, and I have occasional exciting affairs. In London the current one is Tony. He's really rather divine. Very obvious looking, but tremendously sexual. Tall and strong, he has a body rippling with hidden muscles, and a black hairy chest which is *very* exciting. His face is an open invitation to bed. What an innocent he was when I got hold of him, and look at him now. Of course, basically he'll always be a head-waiter, but I think I've improved him beyond recognition.

The first time was a disaster. Of course he had an animal charm, a sexy walk, but that was about all. In bed he had a marvellous body, but he had no skill. For someone so well endowed it was a shame. I thought to myself, he is very attractive in a basic way. If he appeals to me he will probably appeal to lots of women. That's why I decided to use him in the discothèque. I needed someone, and as it turned out he's just the right person. Of course I know he's having an affair with everyone in sight now, including my best friend Vanessa. He thinks I don't suspect. Isn't that silly?

20

I mean I don't mind, but of course I must pretend not to know, pretend a little touch of jealousy, otherwise his manly pride would be hurt. Vanessa and I laugh about it, 'Tony the stud' we call him. It's great fun comparing notes. He thinks he's the best lover in the world. He's not bad, but if he wasn't so well endowed he would be disastrous. Poor conceited Tony.

I'll never forget the first time he came to see me at my house. The clothes he had on—unbelievable! A cheap black silk suit with trousers so tight his pecker shone through like a beacon! I decided I had to take a look. Benjamin was away, so I took him in my lift and enjoyed him there. Well, I mean to say there is nothing more dreary than always doing it on a bed. When I got his clothes off I thought 'Not bad', but after it was all over I knew there was a lot to teach him.

The best lover I ever had was this great big black zulu. I was doing a swimsuit lay-out for one of the glossies deep in the heart of nowhere—and we took a break for a cigarette and he grabbed me behind a tree and gave it to me quickly. Delicious! I'll never forget it, his timing was perfect, he brought me to the most beautiful climax ever! Unfortunately we moved to a new location the next day and I never saw him again. I often think about him, usually when Benjamin is sprawled on top of me huffing and puffing.

Vanessa says Tony is awed by me! Can you imagine! I suppose it's being married to a billionaire and everything. Rather useful, brings people to their knees, lots of respect and all that. Fame, money and titles that's all people really care about.

I don't want children. What for? They ruin your figure, give you a lot of boring trouble, and then leave you. I don't need children, I don't have what I suppose is called the maternal instinct. Personally, I like being free. My God, my mother never gained any advantages by having me. A woman should be strong, I've seen too many marriages fail because the wife was weak. Vanessa has three children and she never sees them. They live with their nanny on the fourth floor and she never goes up there. They might as well be in Siberia. Isn't that silly? She doesn't look too bad, a bit saggy. Saved by that pretty pretty face. One day I'm going to tell Tony I know about him and Vanessa. He'll have a fit! He thinks he's being so clever. He's like a little boy, hates being found out. I don't care, as long as he's got enough left for me he can do what he likes. He's really an idiot, a sexy idiot stud! It's that lower class mentality of his, he'll never change. He's useful though, definitely worth keeping on the leash. And so eager to learn. Always asking me where by bag came from, and what perfumes was I wearing, and who made my clothes.

Think I'll give him a call, pop in before the hairdresser...

3

TONY

Tonight's going to be good. Two big parties in town and everyone will be coming along after. Fontaine nearly caught me today. Fast asleep in bed with this bird—Janet something or other, and her ladyship phones. 'I'm coming over.' Charming! Wake up Janet, she complains, horrible whiney voice, long sloppy black hair, ugh! I must have been well stoned. She struggles complaining into a dress hardly long enough to cover her ass, nice ass. I shove her out the front door, five minutes later Fontaine comes wafting in. I hardly had time to hide the sheets!

Sometimes she's like a witch, very cold. 'I have to go to the hairdresser,' she announces, stepping out of her Rhavis skirt, Gucci shoes and Dior stockings.

At times I hate her, I'm not a machine. She remains standing with her suit jacket still on, her hair hidden in a mink turban. She leans obscenely against the wall. She wants it standing up. I think of her husband. Poor guy, he's working his ass off while she's handing out the action. Never trust a woman that's what I always say. She looks like a high fashion model top half and a dirty photograph bottom half. The thought excites me and I manage to accommodate her. Oh man, I can imagine the scene if she'd caught me this morning!

She dresses briskly, her legs are getting thinner, she diets too much. 'I'll see you tonight,' she says zipping up her skirt, 'keep my table for seven—we have a French diplomat and his wife with us.' Then she was gone, leaving a cloud of Hermes 'Caleche'.

It was a good thing when it started. Fontaine Khaled and all that jazz. But she's kinky, she's definitely kinky and I don't want to be used the way she uses me. Her whore's room and her strange preferences.

What about her old man? He must be a right idiot. Now I've got all the crumpet I want. High class crumpet galore. But she's got me by the balls, 'Hobo' is hers, if I want out of screwing her then I'm out, period. It's not really fair, I built the whole place up, worked my ass off until five every morning, and all I get is peanuts compared to what the joint is making—and I've yet to see my share of the profits. I have no contract, nothing. I just work for her. She's a pretty cool bitch—a pretty clever bitch.

'Franco, bring me a scotch.' Franco's a great head-waiter. Probably I could grab him if I left here and opened up somewhere else. But with what? I've got no bread. People have offered to back me in a new place—women—it would be the same scene all over again. I was casting my eye around for a guy to promote a new joint, one of the rich Greeks would do. Got one in mind, but I'll have to play it cool, make it seem like his idea.

'Hallo, Tony darling.' This bird threw her arms round me, I swear I'd never seen her before.

'How are you?' I said beaming with pleasure, winking. The well-known Blake charm churned forth.

'I'm fine, this is Chicky and this is Robin and this is Henry.' Three nonentities strained forward to give me greetings. The evening was starting.

There are certain regulars who always congregate at the top table. It's called the top table 'cos it's at the top of the room in the best position for seeing everything, and it's where I sit, *when* I sit, which is about twice a night. I always make sure it's available for any visiting celebrities in case there's nowhere else. The regulars

23

can always be shuffled around. If I have a date she sits there. Oh, I'm allowed to have dates as long as it's not the same girl too often. After all, they just sit there by themselves all night.

The regulars are all guys, a varied selection, my friends. There's Sammy—small, wiry, dark-haired. A hat manufacturer —crumpet mad—always chatting up different birds. Likes them tall. I should really get him and Fontaine together, but she thinks he's revolting and he says she's a rich old bag. Any female over twenty is an old bag to him. Sammy's a sweet guy, but a lot of people don't understand him.

Then there's Franklin, quiet, young, good-looking and shy. Sits there drinking Coca-Cola all night. We all reckon he's a virgin.

Next Hal—an American promoter, constantly stoned, a wow with rich old widows. Fortyish, attractive if you like the Dean Martin type. He has a big heart, every bit of honest bread he makes he sends to his kid brother in New Jersey and that's the only thing he doesn't brag about.

Lastly, Massey, a singer. Good-looking in a black is beautiful way. Great dancer.

When there's nothing better to do and if none of us have dates, we sit there and discuss the talent. 'I'd like to screw that!' is a constant cry from our table.

Fontaine hates them all. 'Why do you always have that motley group around?' she questions. But they pay, so there's nothing she can do.

They all suspect about Fontaine and me, but no one actually knows. I like the regulars, they're a good group of guys.

Franklin came in first tonight. With a girl, surprise, surprise. His father is a big guy in the film business. The bird he was with was definitely too hot for him, probably thought he'd put in a good word with dad. She had those pouty lips and jaded eyes that all would-be movie stars have. Too much screwing and not enough fresh air! Franklin was treating her like a lady, all proper and polite. He's a nice kid, but a schmuck. Treat them rough if you want to lay them. She had lots of long thick reddish hair and she gave me the well-known come on look.

24

'Janine James—Tony Blake,' Franklin said, 'Janine's over here doing a film.'

'Hi,' she simpered.

Ugh, sometimes American broads turn me off, that horrible nasal twang. I gave her my angry knowing stare, that usually gets them. She responded with what I took to be a sexy look. Poor Franklin, he didn't have a chance with this one.

The next of the regulars to bounce in was Sammy, friendly, Cockney, pussy-crazy Sammy. As luck would have it he had no date, and he immediately launched into a line of chat with Janine. Franklin sat silently, I could see it was going to be one of those nights.

Fontaine's usual table was next to ours. I had explained to her a hundred times that she couldn't have the top table because it was the only table that could be made easily available in an emergency. This bugged her, but she settled for the next best. After all, she certainly wasn't there every night. Maybe six nights in a row then not at all for two or three weeks while she was on her travels. The places she went made me dizzy. Benjamin had his own private jet which was useful. She never came in with less than five or six people. She had this girl-friend Vanessa, blonde, pretty, a bit plump, but with huge bouncy knockers. Married to the son of the owner of a very famous chain store. Worth a fortune. Got three kids. Vanessa was a mess. She idolised Fontaine and copied her faithfully. It was only fair that I should knock her off. She practically begged me. I went to her house one afternoon while hubby was at the office and the kids were out with nanny. I don't think she knows about me and Fontaine, anyway she promised she wouldn't tell anybody about us. I hope to God she doesn't. It's all very risky. Anyway she's a lousy lay, but these unbelievable tits! I could just stay playing with them for hours, they smother you, all big and soft, very mumsy. Vanessa is usually in Fontaine's group with or without hubby who isn't bad—a lot better than Benjamin. I hear he's got a girl tucked away in a neat little flat. In my business you get to hear most things.

Fontaine and party made the grand entrance about one-thirty. She was covered in white mink to the ground. Her hair was piled high and secured with the gleam of diamonds. Husband was by her side, shorter than her and fat. She looked fantastic. Who would have thought that in the morning she had been leaning against my bedroom wall with her pubics on show! I had an insane desire to shout out—'I've had that!' but instead I went into the whole greeting routine. All the kisses and nice to see you's and all that bullshit.

Vanessa and hubby were naturally present. She looked her usual pretty mess. Whispy hair, boobies flopping in a chiffon dress. I gave her an unseen tweak on the nipple when I kissed her cheek. She blushed, I shook hands with hubby. 'How's Veronica?' I was tempted to say, Veronica was his girl-friend.

They had an elderly French couple with them, another youngish man and this girl. She stood back from the others and was quite obviously embarrassed by all the loud greetings. She was plainly dressed in comparison, a simple wool dress slightly too long and a single strand of pearls. She had long shining auburn hair pulled straight back and secured with a plain pearl slide. Very little makeup, in fact she wasn't that pretty—but there was something about her that gave me a jolt I could feel right in the pit of my stomach. She had these wide brown very innocent eyes, they stared at me with slight contempt. She certainly wasn't some little ding-a-ling obsessed by who to lay next, or how short her shirt could get. She was quite young, about seventeen or eighteen. All in the space of seconds I knew that I had to have this one. This one was special.

They were all sitting down. Wasn't anyone going to introduce me? Fontaine was busy ordering champagne, her cool aquamarine eyes darting around to see who was in. She waved at a few people and then Vanessa's husband took her off to dance. If there's one thing Fontaine's lousy at, it's dancing. It's good to know there is at least one thing she can't do. She's got no rhythm, sort of jerks around like a skinny puppet.

I smiled at the guy with the auburn-haired girl and extended my hand, 'I'm Tony Blake,' I said, very friendly like.

The girl didn't even glance at me, she stared off into the middle distance, looking bored. The guy was a creep. Square suit, short back and sides, a real nothing.

26

Benjamin joined in, 'Oh, Tony—don't you know Peter Lincoln Smith?'

The name rang a bell. I had met his father several times. He owned half of London.

'And this is my daughter Alexandra,' Benjamin finished proudly, 'just arrived home from Switzerland today.'

His daughter Alexandra! My mouth must have hung open for at least five minutes. His daughter!

She threw me a sulky 'How do you do.'

The French couple butted in then, and I had to chat to them. It seemed their daughter came in all the time and they had heard lots about me. I knew their daughter, ugly little blonde nympho who wore Paco Rabanne dresses and thought she was the knock-out of all times. I hadn't actually been there, but Sammy had, and his verdict was thumbs down.

Benjamin was now urging the creep to dance with Alexandra. She was blushing and saying she didn't want to dance. Peter Lincoln Smith was caught in the middle and didn't know what to do, to please Daddy or daughter. Daddy won, and a reluctant Alexandra was led off to the dance floor. There were hints of a great body. The dress wasn't showing anything, but it was there, hidden underneath.

I didn't know what to do, I was caught up with this girl, don't know why. I hadn't even spoken to her, she was probably a spoilt rich bitch. I fancied her like crazy, man, this was going to be tricky, dare I take the risk?

Fontaine came back to the table, breathless and slightly hot in all that white mink. The whole room had seen it, so she slipped it off, revealing a black body-moulding backless sheath. She certainly knew how to show herself off.

I took myself back to the regulars' table and ordered a stiff scotch. Massey had arrived with a thin angular model girl called Suki. Her hair was cropped close to her head, her skirt close to her ass and she wore a weird white makeup with huge clown-like eyes.

Massey was his usual cool self. 'Hey, man,' he said sitting down beside Sammy, 'what's the action tonight?'

'Same old action, everything's swinging,' I replied.

27

He was wearing a white suit, very smart. I thought I might get myself a white suit.

I spied Alexandra on the dance floor. Amongst all the movers she stood quietly holding her boy-friend at arms' length doing a sort of nothing shuffle.

I grabbed Suki and took her off to dance edging my way near to Alexandra. The only reaction she gave was a slightly incredulous look at Suki. Shit! What could I do to make the rich bitch notice me?

Suki was a very stylised dancer, religiously studied every new step, and wouldn't be caught dead doing anything that was out. She and Massey made a great couple. Me—I did a sort of wild shake and that was it.

'I bet this is different from Switzerland,' I yelled above the din of the music, an inane grin on my face.

Alexandra just ignored me. Either that or she didn't hear me.

Suki said, 'What?'

'Nothing,' I muttered, dragging her back to the table.

An Italian actress, Carla Cassoni, was making an entrance, surrounded by three attentive men.

'Wowee,' Sammy whistled through his teeth, 'How about that?!'

She was beautiful, black hair, olive skin, a body edging on being plump, but ending up merely voluptuous. Her new movie had just opened in town. Something about a peasant girl who gets raped by an army—I could understand the army!

I hurried over to give greetings, shaking hands warmly, meeting crystal-clear green eyes, a throaty accented voice. Ordinarily I would have become Charlie Charm, dancing attendance, but tonight my mind was elsewhere. I saw she got a good table, and left her with the three guys.

Miss Rich Bitch was sitting at her table. Peter was being led off to dance by Fontaine. I nipped in quickly, Vanessa was dancing with her husband and Benjamin was talking to the French couple. I sat down next to Alexandra and we both stared off into space. She was drinking plain orange juice. 'How do you like it?' I asked.

'How do I like what?' her voice was soft and very precise.

28

'The club,' I waved an expansive arm around.

'Very nice,' she said, stifling a yawn. I noticed her nails were cut short and painted a buff colour. Most of the girls or women I knew had either long red talons, or short chipped bitten ones.

'Would you like to dance?'

'No thank you.'

No thank you indeed! Most girls would give their false eye-lashes to dance with me! We sat there with nothing else to say until Fontaine and Peter returned.

The club was filling to capacity. The music was getting louder and louder. Time to take off the records and put on the group. Time to circulate around some tables, give them the chat. Time to give the waiters a blast.

I got up, silly little cow, she wasn't even that pretty, and man, like I could have the prettiest. I grabbed my scotch, gulped it down and wandered around the joint. People liked me to sit down at their table, it showed they were really 'in'. I tell you this is such a phoney business; maybe that's why I dug Alexandra sitting there so bored and unimpressed.

I joined the table of the Italian star. She was with her 'Producer'—fat—good-looking, didn't speak a word of English; an English actor, and his stunt-man boy-friend. Carla Cassoni was very lovely, with this incredibly throaty accent. The producer kept a firm hand on her thigh, but she winked at me and flirted, safe in the knowledge that he didn't understand one word.

'You are very attractive,' she purred, 'such a lovely body, but no money huh? It ees beeg shame,' she laughed a deep sexy chuckle. She was a smart cookie.

I asked her to dance, she shook her head, 'Ee is veree jealous,' she indicated the producer, ''ee don't like me to dance with other man.'

Nobody wanted to dance with me, it just wasn't my night.

Suddenly Franco rushed over, stared bug-eyed at Carla and whispered something in my ear. It seemed some black chick had come in wearing a topless dress, and what was he to do? Should he ask her to cover up, or what? He pointed her out, she had just sat down, and the top of her dress which was all fringe, parted as she

29

moved, revealing firm dark brown breasts. It was tantalising, now you see them, now you don't. The guy she was with was old, suited, obviously out on a jaunt. She was a wild chick called Molly Mandy—part-time dress designer. What the hell, there was no law against topless dresses. I told Franco to leave her be. A few people had noticed and a lot of staring was going on; then she got up to dance and the staring really began. The old guy didn't care, he got up there with her, proud as punch. She started on a slow shake, titties hardly moving, then suddenly she started to go and the fringe swung and the titties swung, and baby *she* swung.

Everyone stopped dancing and made a hand-clapping circle round them. The guys all loved it, some of the birds looked a bit choked. I saw Fontaine rush over to the side of the dance floor with Vanessa to get a better look. It was a wild scene. Then the Greeks joined in, threw some glasses to start it off, then a couple of them shouldered the old guy out of the way and started dancing with Molly. One of their girl-friends, not to be outdone, ripped off her blouse unhooked her bra and joined the scene. Everyone cheered.

The time had come to stop it otherwise we'd get the police. Charming! I pushed my way through the crowd just a little too late. One of the mad Greek shipowners had grabbed hold of a brown tit and the old guy attempted to punch him and ended up flat on his back.

A lot of screaming started, but Franco had his waiters in there so fast, and the old guy was carried out, and the Greeks were persuaded back to their table, and Molly sat down at our table saying 'Shit, man, what's all the fuss?'

It was action like this that made 'Hobo' the only place in town.

I glanced over to Fontaine's table, she was just sitting down, laughing. Alexandra and escort had gone, probably left during all the confusion. Just as well.

'Hey, Molly baby, don't come here like that again,' I said.

She smiled at me, rows of white pearly teeth plus a few gold fillings. 'What's the matter, Tony sweetheart, don't you like my boobies?' She shook her shoulders and the fringe parted giving me an eyeful.

30

'You know I like them—but not in here, you'll cause a riot, come on, I'll take you back to find your boy-friend.'

She made a face, 'Man, that old fart's out cold, I feel like fun tonight.'

I was getting irritated, what did she expect—to tag on to me? I didn't even fancy her—I looked to Sammy, but he was busy chatting up Janine.

I took a grip on her arm and led her to the reception area, the old guy was laid out in the office at the back. He was just coming to when we got there.

'I'll arrange a cab, you take him home,' I hissed at her.

She pouted, 'O.K., but maybe I'll come back, isn't it about time you and I had a scene?'

I gave her a shove towards the old trout and got out of there. I think it was the gold fillings that turned me off.

Fontaine summoned me with the imperial wave when I was back inside. I knew the gesture well—she raised one long thin arm high and sort of clicked her fingers at me. Charming! Sort of a—come here serf!

I went. After all she was the boss.

'Tell us about it,' she said, excitement gleaming in her eyes. The others all leaned forward too, anxious to hear the story. 'Who was that pathetic little man with her?' Fontaine went on, 'I mean, really, they made a ridiculous couple.' She gave me a sharp kick under the table, her signal that she wanted me to ask her to dance.

I obliged. I hated dancing with her, talk about looking ridiculous. Is there anything more ridiculous than an elegant-looking lady jumping and squirming around like a seventeen-year-old? Especially when she's got no sense of rhythm. I gave my secret signal to Flowers—the disc jockey, to put on a slow record. He launched into a medley of Tony Bennett, making a face, he was strictly a Motown man.

Fontaine held me tight. 'Did you touch her?' she asked licking silver-coated lips.

'Did I touch who?'

'Oh, you know who, she looked straight out of the jungle!'

I ignored that. Fontaine had a poor opinion of anyone who

31

wasn't in her set, she was also very bigoted, and was for ever trying to get me to get rid of the black waiters and Flowers. In bed one time she had gone on about how they made her feel uncomfortable, and then she had got very excited and given me a few scratches on my back I'll probably have for ever. I can't imagine anyone making Fontaine uncomfortable.

I would never get rid of Flowers, he's the best D.J. in town. A tall thin black guy with freak out hair and pale blue eyes. Usually stoned out of his mind. But he can feel a room like I can feel a woman.

Fontaine was dancing very close. I glanced over at her husband. He was talking with the French couple.

'Hello, Tone,' a girl greeted me. She was dancing alongside us. I smiled at her.

Fontaine dug me in the ribs and said with an amused smile, 'You love it don't you, all these little dollies after you?'

I must admit I did love it.

Wouldn't you?

4

FONTAINE

I arrived at Tony's shortly after phoning him. A horrible little scrubber with long black hair came yawning out of his apartment. I waited a few minutes before ringing the bell, it would never do to let him know that I knew all about his little 'affaires'. One would think he would show a degree of taste, but no, he would sleep with anything, studs usually do.

He greeted me with a kiss. What a sloppy habit, I have a great distaste for kissing, especially when his mouth has the lingering odour of someone else.

32

Immediately he started fumbling with my clothes, and getting my skirt off, he pinned me to the wall.

I must admire him, he's never at a loss. He took me like that, quite exciting, though only momentarily of course.

The awful thing about Tony is that he's a terrible bore. He has nothing even remotely intelligent to say. After sex I really have to get away from him.

I dressed again and told him I was late for the hairdresser. Of course I wasn't, so I popped in to visit Vanessa.

Vanessa reminds me of a big blonde jersey cow. Placid, slow, always churning children forth. What on earth Tony can see in her I really can't imagine. Probably that big mother earth bosom.

In my position it's difficult to acquire friends, I mean it's got to be someone on the same social level, otherwise they're just absurdly jealous. All my friends from before became impossible after I married Benjamin. Each new mink coat or diamond ring was greeted with tight little smiles, they just couldn't stand it. Vanessa of course has no need to worry, I suppose her husband is nearly as rich as mine, although to look at her you would never guess.

I love having beautiful clothes and jewels and being envied and stared at. I suppose I always knew that I was destined for this kind of life.

I was a very plain child with a very plain mother and a bastard of a father who made mother's life a misery. Felicity Brown of Bournemouth. I grew up very quietly, went to the best girls' school, decided I would like to be a vet, and knew nothing about sex except what the other girls whispered. All nice little English girls want to be vets, it's part of our tradition—well it was then anyway. At sixteen I was allowed on my first outing with a young man, none of this 'raped at thirteen' business in my past. He was nineteen, the local doctor's son and a nice quiet boy. We got along fine, held hands, had a few furtive kisses and decided to get married. I was a good chaste Bournemouth virgin engaged to be married, with a sweet marquesette ring, and stars in my dull little eyes. We decided, along with the help of our middle-class parents, that we would marry when he was twenty-one and I was eighteen.

33

My future was cut out and planned. He went off to finish his medical studies and I enrolled in all sorts of activities, such as sewing and cookery classes. I really didn't know any other boys and I thought I loved Mark. What a situation! I had no idea what love was all about.

At cookery class I met a girl called Marcia. She was pregnant and unmarried and people whispered about her. My mother called her 'fast' and 'shocking', and my father said it was a disgrace she was allowed to join the cookery class. But join she did, and she was the first breath of fresh air I had encountered in all my nearly seventeen years.

We became friendly and I told her about Mark and my plans.

'What's he like in bed?, she asked.

I looked at her blankly.

'Oh, no,' she started to laugh, 'don't tell me you haven't?'

I had to admit that I hadn't, what's more I wasn't going to because it wasn't what nice girls did, was it?

This made her laugh even more, and then she got very serious and said, 'How on earth can you marry someone if you don't know if you like each other in bed. It's very important, you *must* do it.'

Of course she was no walking advertisement for sex, with her belly swollen out and no visible husband, but I did think she was right, I *should* try it.

I waited anxiously for Mark to come home on holiday, half excited, half terrified at what I planned to do.

He was allowed to borrow his father's car and we went to a film and he held my hand and afterwards we went to one of the big hotels for dinner.

It's very difficult when you're a nice quiet virgin suggesting that your equally nice quiet fiancé make love to you, especially when he's never attempted anything along those lines.

I said, 'Let's drive down to the beach, it's such a lovely night.'

'Oh, Felicity, I'm tired.'

'Please, Mark.' I was quite determined to get the beastly deed done.

'All right,' he reluctantly agreed.

34

We parked somewhere along the front and sat there, he made no movement towards me.

After a few moments of silence, I said, 'Mark, if we're going to get married don't you think we should get to know each other?'

'What are you talking about, Felicity?' he replied crossly.

I moved closer to him, 'You know what I mean.'

He was genuinely shocked and pushed me away, 'If I want that type of girl there's plenty around.'

I was very excited by this time, the first moment in my life I had been sexually excited, and Mark—the man in my life, was pushing me away. I was furious.

He drove me home in silence and I refused to ever see him again.

The next night, still determined to find out what sex was all about, I went to a local coffee bar, and there met a tall leather-jacketed boy called Ted. I had seen Ted before around town, and I decided that he would do to initiate me into the mysteries of life. We started to talk and when he invited me for a walk I accepted readily.

We strolled along making our way towards the beach, and then he grabbed me, kissed me, pushed his hands up my skirt, and we both fell down on the sand. I was ready for him without any preliminaries. He forced his way into me and the pain was exquisite and I clung to him and begged him for more, and as he was finished and went limp I wouldn't let him go. He was trying to get away and I was hanging on to him. It was wonderful. We fought silently and he called me a bitch and said I was hurting him! *Me* hurting *him*, that was a delightful statement.

A new Felicity Brown had emerged. I loved it! I tried everyone and everything. A whole new life had opened up for me and soon Bournemouth wasn't big enough and I left for London. My father by this time was pleased to see me go. My mother shed a few tears I think.

I arrived in London, tall, skinny, with mousy hair, but plenty to offer. And by the time I was twenty-two I was Fontaine—top model. Beautiful—a few changes here and there, blonde, a girl with London at her feet.

35

I was making lots of money and lots of men, and then I met my first husband, Paul. He was very attractive. Lean and lazy with smoky green eyes and a beautiful body. He was a sometimes male model, sometimes actor, but mostly enjoyed living off some lady. He was divine in bed. His gymnastics nearly matched up to mine. He was the first man who really satisfied me and saw I stayed satisfied.

So one day we got married amidst a blaze of flashbulbs, and he sat back while I worked, and life went on. He gambled, drank, and was unfaithful, but we stayed together, because I suppose I must have loved him.

Everyone told me I was mad but there was still a little bit of Felicity Brown left in me somewhere, and I wanted my marriage to work.

At twenty-nine I looked in the mirror and took stock. I had been a top model for seven years and that's a long time to have been at the top in any profession. How much longer could it last? Paul used up all my money, soon I would be thirty, and how many more magazine covers lay ahead?

Also I was exhausted. Modelling is not an easy job as people seem to think, it's back-breaking work, a constant grind of hairdressers, make-ups, blinding hot lights, and anatomically impossible poses.

I certainly wasn't faithful to Paul any more, after six months of marriage we both agreed it was ridiculous to confine ourselves to each other. As a matter of fact, we had rather a lot of fun with 'group parties'. Very interesting.

I finally decided Paul was a luxury that would have to go and I cast my eyes around for someone more substantial to take his place.

I met Benjamin in St Moritz. I was doing a fur show there for one day and he was with his unbelievably dreary wife and two ghastly children. We met in a group and I knew who he was. We managed a few words alone, 'Can I see you in London?' he asked. He reached a little past my shoulder in height. I gave him my phone number.

It took exactly five weeks for him to offer to divorce his wife. I played my game very carefully, I gave him everything but, and I had him mad for it. There's a ghastly expression Tony uses—'I'm hot for you, baby,' and that just about sums up how Benjamin felt.

It was no problem getting rid of Paul. Benjamin paid, and he took. Benjamin's wife was also easy. She agreed to divorce him with no argument. Of course she got a fortune and also the children. We have never spoken, but I am obliged to see Ben Junior and Alexandra sometimes. They are really very dreary. Young Ben·is twenty and an even shorter version of his father. Alexandra is just plain, no sparkle, like her mother I suppose.

So that's my story. Benjamin and I got married, once more in a blaze of flashbulbs, and we honeymooned on a new.yacht he bought for the occasion.

He buys me whatever I want, I have my occasional stud and I'm happy—I suppose.

Whatever happened to Felicity Brown?

Vanessa was not dressed when I arrived. Her big breasts were flopping about in a blue dressing-gown and she was eating toast and honey and reading a gossip column.

It's very important in our circle to see your name quite often in print. If Vanessa hadn't been very rich she would have been a real slut. I knew that Leonard, her husband, was keeping some tramp in a flat, but I hadn't told Vanessa, what was the point?

We greeted each other warmly, and I ordered a champagne cocktail from their Filipino houseboy and sat down and relaxed.

'What's new darling?' Vanessa yawned.

I slipped off my jacket, 'Nothing much, just had a little session with the stud.'

We both laughed. 'Was he in good running form today?' Vanessa asked with more than a touch of interest.

I have a feeling she has a secret crush on Tony, offhand as she may try to be.

'Yes,' I replied, 'when is he ever not?'

Vanessa was a bit bored at that, she had to wait for Tony to approach her, *I* had a far different kind of relationship with him.

The houseboy brought my cocktail. It was cold and delicious. A

37

good champagne cocktail really sets you up for the day.

'What are you wearing tonight?' I asked.

Vanessa shrugged, 'I haven't really thought.'

Hadn't really thought indeed, I planned my outfits months ahead. No wonder she always looked such a mess.

We chatted a while longer and then I went off to the hairdresser.

Alexandra arrived at our house fresh from Switzerland at seven. She dislikes me and I can't stand her, but of course Benjamin fails to see this. She looked as dull and plain as ever. It always amazes me how in this day and age a girl can look so utterly dowdy. Her hair scraped back, no makeup, uninteresting little wool dress. She's seventeen and yet manages to look years older.

Benjamin greeted her warmly. She's polite to him, but I'm sure she hates him for deserting 'Mummy'. He has a huge trust fund for her when she's twenty-one. She sipped an orange juice, and soon the others arrived—thank God!

I wore my new full-length white mink, and Vanessa loved it. I have no doubt she will shortly appear in a bad copy, she copies everything I have, but invariably it just doesn't suit her to wear my style, we are completely different types.

Dinner at 'Annabels' was fun. Lots of friends there. It was a terrible bore having Alexandra along, she was always looking at me with a sort of disdainful half smile. I wish she would stick with Mummy in the country instead of bothering us. Now she's talking of sharing a flat in London with a girlfriend, and Benjamin is insisting she come and live with us. How dare he! Thank God she's declining the invitation. Stupid child is starting a job as a secretary. What's the point with all her money?

Dinner lingered on. I danced with the old French goat who held me too tight and breathed garlic in my face. Delightful! I danced with Leonard, he's not bad although Vanessa's description of his activities in bed are very dull indeed. He probably saves it all up for his little popsie on the side. It's quite amazing how the most unimaginative of husbands can turn into a real Casanova in someone else's bed.

We finally set off for 'Hobo'. I simply love it there. Such a marvellous mixture of people, always something going on. And Tony, well, Tony at work is a real sight. Absolutely everyone's best friend!

I must admit, it's when I like him best. He's king of the whole place, everyone wants him at their table, all the women want him.

He has a very sexy animal walk, almost as though he has a hidden erection. I wish he had as much confidence in bed, after all I've taught him his tastes are still a little on the suburban side, he can't seem to project any originality. To be a good lover you need a constant source of inspiration.

Of course his friends are unbelievable. They gather at his table like a clutch of male rejects. What a motley group!

The records are fabulous, so loud you can't even hear yourself think. I love dancing. The whole room is staring at my coat—one little dance in it won't be too hot. Let them all get a good look before I slip out of it.

Alexandra sits like a ton of bricks. I really can't stand her. Benjamin is so proud, he thinks she's so lovely. And as for the little bore he has fixed her up with, why his father's got more life in him than he has. Actually, he's just right for Alexandra, two dreary non-personalities together!

Oh no, he's not going to ask me to dance. Yes he is. Oh, how awful. Rich men's sons are all the same. Real smug little bores. This one's probably about the same age as Tony—only he's got about as much sex appeal as a flea. It's no use rubbing yourself up against me, sweetheart, you just haven't got what it takes.

'Let's sit down, Peter dear, it's so hot.'

He looked disappointed. I'd be disappointed if I had to go back and sit with Alexandra. Why, she wouldn't even dance with him. I must say, I love to dance. So lovely and uninhibited, Tony can't wait to dance with me and show me off to the whole room.

There was some sort of commotion going on at the dance floor.

'It's some black girl completely nude!' Vanessa said excitedly. We both jumped up and rushed over. Mustn't miss a good show.

After, Vanessa and I went back to our table. 'You didn't say goodbye to Alexandra,' Benjamin said crossly.

'I didn't even know she was going,' I replied, delighted she had left.

'She had a headache,' then relenting he added, 'Perhaps you'll phone her tomorrow.' He squeezed my leg under the table. His hands were sweaty. He had grey hair, bald in patches, like moth-eaten fur.

Tony was coming back in the room and I called him over. He looked very sexy tonight, God, those trousers he was wearing didn't leave much to the imagination!

He asked me to dance. Slow music was playing and he held me very tight.

'Aren't you being a little obvious?' I said indicating Benjamin, but he just held me tighter and I felt him and I wished we could do it there and then in front of everyone. Oh what bliss! But tonight is impossible. Benjamin is in town and *he* will probably want to do it. What an utter bore! Sex with Benjamin is so utterly dreary. I like young strong bodies, not old tired ones. He huffed and he puffed like he would never quite finish the show. Dear Benjamin was so monotonously the same in bed, he was unlovely and un- interesting.

Fortunately he was quick.

We left 'Hobo' soon after and once in the privacy of our bedroom I flopped on the bed exhausted. What a day!

Benjamin announced he had to leave for Paris the next after- noon. Did I want to come? Well, I wanted to come, but not to Paris. I decided I might pop over to New York to our flat for a few days. I adored the shops over there and I supposed I should visit Ray. He is an adorable looking hairdresser whom Benjamin has set up in his own salon there. I haven't spent time with Ray for ages. A few days with him might be fun.

Benjamin was pulling at my dress. He knew I hated that, I got up quickly and he backed away. Oh, poor old Benjamin, I'd frightened him. He was always frightened I'd say no—but of course I never did.

I peeled off the dress and hung it up carefully, then I lay flat on the bed, the way he liked me to and waited for him.

I closed my eyes and thought about Tony and Ray and Paul and it wasn't too bad. In fact, if he wasn't so goddamned fast it might not be bad at all.

He washed himself after, a habit that drives me to distraction. I took off my makeup and put on my sleep mask. He was reading now. Oh, for separate bedrooms. What a joy!

5

TONY

Sammy said, 'Watcha dancing with that old bag for?'

Sammy Schmuck! What did he know about class.

'I mean I know she owns the place but—'

'I think she's fantastic,' Janine interrupted, 'really fantastic, did you see that coat she had on?'

'What's a coat if there's nothing but skin and bone underneath?' Sammy chuckled at his own joke. 'Now that Italian number's not bad, nice pair of boobies.'

I should remark that Sammy has no conversation except about women. We have all heard clinical descriptions of every bird he's ever laid.

'Come on, darling, I'll do you a favour,' Sammy dragged Janine off to the packed dance floor.

Franklin looked miserable. 'Listen, long face,' I said, 'that's not for you, let Sammy have her, she's a pig.'

Massey said, 'I've got a beautiful little bird for you, Suki's sister—wouldn't she be great for Franklin?'

Suki nodded wide clown-like eyes. 'She's only fifteen but lovely.'

I had heard it all before. Everyone was always fixing Franklin

41

up, but nothing ever worked out. He was too shy to make it with a bird. To get Franklin laid was one of our group projects. He would sit and listen to all our chat about women and agree with us when we told him he should blow his cherry, but nothing ever happened.

The evening was at its peak.

The place was so jammed that some tables' occupants had to take it in shifts to dance because there wasn't room for them all to sit down at the same time. It was always dodgy dancing at this time anyway. For one thing the tiny dance floor was so jam-packed you couldn't move, and for another you took a risk of losing your seat altogether.

I looked around with satisfaction. It was one of the more star-packed nights. There was a good sprinkling of top talent from most professions.

'The Must', current top rock group were all present. Long hair, tighter than tight clothes. They were nice boys, stoned out of their heads, but harmless, with their flaxen-haired girl-friends who all looked the same. It's a funny thing how in the rock world it's important to all to be on the same wavelength—you know—the long hair bit. They all look like out of the same mould. They try to be different from everyone else and bingo—there you go—all the same.

More people were crowding in. I got up and did the greeting bit. I wandered round a few tables having a scotch here and a scotch there. The world was starting to buzz. I could fancy something cuddly. Fontaine had left me with a sour taste in my mouth. As a matter of fact, I could fancy Vanessa, but that was impossible, there she was with hubby. I must remember to give her a ring, sneak in while nanny and the kidlets are out!

I kept on thinking of Miss Rich Bitch—she was so sort of different from other birds, she had this kind of aura of class. I wondered if I'd see her again. Probably not, she looked like she hated it here.

Flowers grabbed hold of me—'Got to see you, man,' his eyes were distorted and nervous. He was flying on pot, probably needed more bread, that was always his problem. He was living

42

with Tina, our Swedish receptionist. What a couple they made—he, dark and wild, she, white and quiet. There was a song there somewhere!

I lent him five pounds, listened to his bullshit about how grateful he was, and made a mental note to get it back from his next week's salary—otherwise I'd never see it again.

Miss Italian Movie Star and party were leaving—'Bye, Bye, Tonee,' she purred slowly through pearly white teeth, 'not long before we shall meet again huh?'

I loved her voice, it was a real turn on. 'Yeah,' I gave her the sincere stare. All the Italian waiters were going mad, hovering around to get a closer look. 'S'long, Tony, old boy,' the actor said. 'Bye, Tone,' the stunt-man said. They all wanted to know me, be my friend. The Italian producer muttered some Italian, gave me a dirty look, gripped Carla by the arm and they were gone. Good. I quickly had Franco put a visiting senator and party at their table.

So the evening reached its peak, and slowly around two-thirty it started to thin out, and by three-thirty only super swingers and odd-balls were left. Franklin said he was going and Janine said she wanted to stay, and they argued quietly and then he left.

I caught him at the door. 'Listen, kid, we'll get you a date with Suki's sister. O.K.?' He shrugged. A waiter came at him with his check and I grabbed it. 'The cokes are on me tonight,' I said.

'Thanks, Tony.'

Back at the table Janine seemed to fancy me, and in spite of Sammy's frantic efforts she didn't want to know. She asked me to dance, and tossed the sad starlet's mane of red hair, and wriggled the sad starlet's curvy body, and the accent twanged.

We ended up in my flat. I just don't like going home alone.

I was loaded and she didn't stop talking. I heard all about the movie she was doing, some bit part in a B film no doubt, and how Franklin was very sweet but such a baby, and how she loved London, and 'Hobo' was such a wild place, and just as I got it in, she said, 'Can I have a free membership?' So I gave it to her.

That's life.

6

ALEXANDRA

It's simply terrific to be home.

Madelaine and I flew back together. Her father and brother met us at the airport. Michael, her brother, is super. Of course I've known him for ages, we were all children together, but lately he has become *so* attractive.

I daren't tell Maddy what I think of him because she wouldn't understand. I mean him being her brother and everything she most likely sees him in a different light. We always discuss boys together, not that there was too much chance in Switzerland, our school was run like a convent. However, Maddy had this huge crush on the school gardener. I used to unlock the hall window at night and she would sneak out to meet him. We'd probably have both been expelled if we'd been found out. Anyway, she had a lovely time, he was quite old—about thirty, and they used to neck and once she let him take her sweater off *and* her bra. But she said he went a bit berserk after that and used to try all sorts of things, so she didn't meet him any more. It was just as well because I didn't think he was much at all. Rather dour really.

On our last vacation we went with Maddy's parents to Monte Carlo and I met a gorgeous boy who sort of looked after our beach. He was so brown. He took Maddy and me dancing one night and kissed me goodnight. It was awful, he stuck his tongue in my mouth!

Anyway, here we are out of school at last. It's like a wonderful dream. No more school!

Madelaine and I have a plan. She's going to work on her parents and I'm going to work on my mother and we're going to share a flat. In London!! In Chelsea!! We decided Chelsea was the best place, sort of swinging and everything. We'll both get jobs and have a terrific time. After all, I've been seventeen two whole months now. I'm practically old. And nothing exciting has ever happened to me—nothing!

We went back to Maddy's house, it's in Virginia Water, and she's always lived there, with both parents. My parents are divorced. My father went off with an awful woman who lured him away from Mummy. I think it was really selfish of him. We were all so happy before, and my mother is great fun. Very sensible. I wish she wasn't so sensible, then perhaps she would have held on to him. I must admit that Daddy's new wife is quite glamorous. She hates me, I can tell. Not that I care because I can't *stand* her, and fortunately I don't have to see them very much, only on occasions like tonight when I'm on my way home from school.

Maddy's father's going to drive me into town tonight for an evening out with Daddy and Fontaine, and then tomorrow morning I'm getting the train down to Mummy's. We live in a house near Newmarket, Mummy, my brother and me. We moved after the divorce because although Daddy would have let us stay in our old house it was too big, and anyway I don't think Mummy was very happy there any more.

Our new house is splendid, and has stables, I have my own horse. We have a swimming pool, although of course it's never warm enough to swim in. But somehow it's not the same. Anyway, the last year I've been in Switzerland and before that boarding school, so I really haven't spent that much time there. I'm sure Mummy will let me come to London, she's so understanding, and I'll be with Maddy so I don't see how she can object.

'What are you wearing tonight?' Maddy came into her room wrapped in a towel. She always took ages in the bath. I had been waiting to get in the bathroom for half-an-hour.

'I'm not going to dress up,' I replied. Actually I didn't have anything to dress up in if I'd wanted to, 'cos we mostly lived in sweaters and skirts in Switzerland. Both Madelaine and I had to get ourselves kitted out, our clothes were awful and old-fashioned.

'I don't blame you,' Maddy said, 'I certainly wouldn't get dressed up for *her* either.'

We both shared a mutual loathing for Fontaine, although of course Maddy had never met her, but knew all about her from me.

I bathed, brushed my hair, and put on the cleanest dress I could find.

Maddy supplied some makeup. I didn't put on much, because quite frankly, I wasn't very good at it. I needed practice.

'Have a glorious time,' Maddy said when I was ready, 'see you later.' I was coming back to stay the night.

I went downstairs to find Mr Newcombe. He was going to a business dinner in London. He really is a nice father, I liked him awfully, and I wished *my* father was like him.

Oh good! Michael's coming too. He's very good-looking, tall, with lovely longish hair. He lives in London. I'm sure when Maddy and I get our flat in town we'll see lots of him. Anyway, I hope so.

He sat in the front of the car with his father, and I was in the back, so there wasn't much chance for talking on the way.

My father lives in a big house in Belgravia. Mummy says it's in very bad taste. It has a lot of white statues balanced about outside, and inside it's huge and not at all comfortable. There is even an awful indoor swimming pool which is in a sort of glass room, all dark and depressing, with hundreds of vines and plants growing around it. It's creepy. I loathe it.

I said goodbye to Mr Newcombe. Michael smiled at me.

I said, 'See you soon.'

Maybe he likes me too. Maddy was always talking about how he has heaps of girl-friends, maybe I could be one of them or *the* one.

I mused on this as the butler let me in, and took my coat.

Fontaine came bearing down on me. 'Alexandra darling, how wonderful to see you.' She kissed me on the cheek. I knew she was only doing it for Daddy's sake.

He hugged me. He seems to have grown shorter and older. Suddenly I felt a warmth towards him and I hugged him back. Oh, if only he'd stayed with Mummy! Everyone knew Fontaine just loved him for his money.

'We're going to have a lovely evening,' my father said.' How was school? Tell me all about it.'

We sat together on the sofa, and I wanted to cry because he did look so old and tired. I had seen him four months before and he had looked fine, but now—oh my goodness, what had she done to him?

'Are you well, Daddy?'

'Of course I'm well. Working very hard but that's what I like. I was never one for sitting about.' He glanced over at Fontaine, but she was taking no notice of us. She was sipping champagne, and reading a fashion magazine. 'How's your mother?'

'I haven't been home yet, but I spoke to her tonight and she sounds fine. She said she just got a letter from Ben and he's having a marvellous time.'

My brother Ben was at a University in America.

'Wonderful woman your mother, very strong . . .' He tailed off.

I could still remember the day Mummy told us he was leaving. She hadn't cried or anything, but I knew he was breaking her heart. My mother is a pretty woman, about fifty. When she was young she had been gorgeous. In their wedding photos she was petite, with golden curling hair and a dimpled face. I knew that she had married my father long before he was rich.

'I'll give Mummy your love,' I said, and wondered if that was the right thing to say. But it was all right because he just smiled, and patted me on the knee.

'I'm going to come and live in London,' I blurted out, 'I'm going to share a flat with Madelaine and get a job.'

'When did you decide all this?'

'Maddy and I have been thinking about it for ages. Actually it's not all set yet, but I've written off for three jobs and I've got interviews next week, and Maddy's got two flats to see. Don't you think it's a good idea?'

My father frowned. 'But if you want to come to London you can live here, you don't need to get a job. Fontaine and I would be more than delighted to have you here.'

'No, Daddy, you don't understand. I want to be independent and free. I'm eighteen now and I know at twenty-one I'll have heaps of money from my Trust. Well that's why I want to keep myself, sort of support myself for a few years. I don't just want to be a rich man's daughter. I want to think for myself and work for myself and then at twenty-one I'll be able to accept the responsibility of my money. I don't want to "come out" and be a deb. I want a few years as just an ordinary girl.'

There! I'd said it. The speech I'd prepared for my mother.

Father beamed, 'That's my girl,' he said, 'that's my little girl. But I could help you find a nice job, you could take your choice.'

'*No*, Daddy.'

Some more people arrived, and my father joined Fontaine in greeting them.

'Alexandra, I want you to meet Peter Lincoln Smith. He's kindly agreed to escort you this evening.'

My face burned. *Kindly* agreed to escort me! Oh, my father was *so* embarrassing. I didn't want to be fixed up, it was so awful and old-fashioned, and my father hadn't even mentioned it to me.

Peter Lincoln Smith had a mean thin mouth and a limp handshake. I didn't like him, and I don't think he liked me.

There were two other couples, much older people. We had a long, dull dinner at 'Annabel's'. I wished I was with Michael, then it would have been wonderful.

Fontaine never stopped talking all night. I really don't know how my father can stand her, she's so loud.

Afterwards they all wanted to go to a discothèque and Peter and I had to go too. I don't think we had exchanged more than six words all evening.

I felt embarrassed trailing in behind Fontaine. Everyone stared. It was awful. At one point the manager sat down and tried to be nice to me, for Daddy's sake I suppose. He asked me to dance and I said no. Honestly people are such phonies. Just because of my father they think they have to be nice to me. Well, they jolly well don't.

I felt very tired. It had been a long day and I had the ride back to Virginia Water. I asked Peter if he'd mind putting me in a taxi.

There was some commotion on the dance floor and Fontaine had rushed over to see what it was. So I said goodnight to Daddy and thankfully left.

Peter had a red M.G. which he had driven me to the club in.

'I'll run you home,' he said.

'Oh no, it's much too far and much too late.' I didn't want to face another hour of Peter's company.

'Nonsense,' he said, suddenly linking his arm in mine. 'No traffic at this time of night, won't take long.'

So I was stuck. I climbed in and we set off in silence.

Peter drove fast and I leaned back in the seat. I soon fell asleep. I must have slept for ages, because when I awoke we were parked in a country lane and Peter was kissing me.

I didn't know what to do, he had taken me by surprise and I didn't want to offend him. After all, he had driven me all this way. So I sat quietly while he kissed me, waiting for the right moment to push him away.

Oh no! Suddenly I felt his hand on my breast. Well, I certainly wasn't going to just sit there now. I moved his hand away, 'Please stop that, Peter,' I said firmly.

But he didn't, and soon I found myself really struggling.

His hands were everywhere. 'Don't fight me,' he said, as I managed to push his hands away again, 'just lie back and enjoy it.'

I hated him! He had one hand up my skirt now, and I swung my arm at his head with all the force I could muster.

He stopped at once, clutching his mouth where my blow had landed. 'You little bitch!' he exclaimed in surprise.

Well honestly! I couldn't wait to tell Madelaine.

I jumped out of the car and ran off into the night. It was awfully dark, it wasn't a main road at all, and I had no idea where I was. Men are really disgusting, all they think about is one thing.

Suddenly I heard a car. It was Peter's, headlights full on, he was coming to find me. Maybe he wanted to rape and murder me! I mean things like that *do* happen, you read about it all the time. On second thoughts perhaps he was scared I would tell Daddy and wanted to take me home.

I didn't know what to do. Should I duck down and hide, and hope he wouldn't see me. Or should I climb in his car and demand he take me home.

It was cold and spitting with rain. I was completely lost. I stood quietly by the side of the road, with dignity I hoped. The car stopped beside me and Peter leaned over from the driving seat and flung open the door.

'It's all right, I'm not going to rape you,' he said as though reading my thoughts. 'Get in.'

I climbed into the car. The least he could do was apologise.

As it happened we were only about five minutes from Maddy's house and we both maintained a stony silence on the short drive. I climbed out as soon as he stopped the car. 'Goodnight,' I said coldly.

'Goodbye cock-teaser!' he yelled, and drove away.

Oh! Oh! I was *so* furious.

7

TONY

A week has passed. I saw four movies, had dinner at Trader Vic's, lost twenty-five pounds at roulette—bought three new shirts and got laid every night.

Fontaine has gone, taken off on one of her trips. She never tells me she's going, just buzzes off. I suppose she thinks it's good to keep me in suspense.

Janine has sort of moved herself in and I can't seem to get rid of her. 'The Twang' as I call her, seems to think she's here to stay. She comes to the club every night and sits with the gang and then she comes home with me and rushes off to the studio a few hours later, then she's back at seven—just about when I'm getting up. She's not a bad bird after all, very accommodating. But she'll have to go. I haven't had a chance to call Sadie this week.

It's Saturday, big bright Saturday, busiest night of the week. It's eight p.m. and I'm seriously thinking of getting up. 'The Twang' is still asleep. Well, I mean she's knocking herself out, poor little bird. Not so little, she's built like a brick shithouse.

I would like a new flat. This pad I have now is very small. When Fontaine gets back we're going to have a serious talk about money. I need more, I deserve more. Every night except Sunday from ten p.m. till four a.m. is no joke.

I think I shall wear the black silk turtle neck and new black slacks tonight. That's where all my bread goes—on gear. Well, I like to look smart, keep up an image. It's important in my business, no use looking like one of those long hairs—dirty and all that. I reckon I've got a good look and I'm going to stick with it.

I mean I don't have short hair—not by any means. It sort of curls around the back of my collar—just right.

If I'm lucky, I can get out of here before 'The Twang' wakes up.

I wasn't lucky. She caught me at the door. 'Babee,' she squealed, 'wait for me, where are we going?'

Oh shit! that meant she expected me to buy her dinner.

I waited while she wriggled her starlet's body into a too-tight white dress and back-combed her hair and put on her eyelashes. She was definitely becoming a drag.

I called Sammy, he had a date, so we joined up with him at a little Italian bistro and dined royally on spaghetti and meatballs.

Sammy's date was fifteen if she was a day. He had picked her up at a bus stop. One of Sammy's habits was to cruise the streets in his secondhand E-type looking for likely birds. He never copped out, always came up with something. I guess they liked secondhand E-types. One of his favourite stories was of how he followed a bus from Baker Street to the Elephant and Castle because he fancied some little darling on it, and according to him he made it at the end of the ride!

One of these days he was going to get himself into a lot of trouble. Some tough father was going to ram a fist down his stupid throat. Anyway, until that day came, he was happy.

After dinner we went to the club. I liked to get there early on a Saturday. It was too soon for anyone to be in, Flowers was playing a few far out sounds. Franco was screaming in Italian at his waiters, Tina was polishing her nails.

51

'The Twang' and the fifteen-year-old went off to the ladies' room where they stayed at least half-an-hour.

'What do birds do to their faces that takes so long?' Sammy said, ''Ere, what's with you and this American bit, going a bit strong, isn't it?'

'Sammy, Sammy, you know me better than that. As a matter of fact I wondered if you wouldn't mind stepping in.'

Sammy shook his head sadly. 'She had her chance, anyway she's a bit old for me.'

Janine was all of twenty-five.

To tell the truth, I felt rather bad about Franklin, I knew he was choked about her latching on to me. I wish I could talk her into showing him the ropes—in other words, get him in the sack with her. He was a great-looking kid, some lucky girl was in for a thrill. I mean he'd been saving it up for a long time.

They started to come in. As usual, the ones who weren't too sure of a good table first. It always reminded me of a show. The audience files quietly in, sits down and waits, then here come the performers. Yelling greetings, kissing everyone, wearing maxis, minis, caftans, flowers, bells, you name it, they wear it. The beautiful people. An assorted group of high frequency talent, and every one of them my friend.

On Saturday you get the 'one night out a week' group too. Dressed to kill, they make a lot of uncool noise and most of the regular clientele send them up. However, they have the money and run up the really big bills, so you have to put up with them.

Here comes a group of them now. Hymie Verne Blatt, dress manufacturer, and his heavily jewelled wife Ethel Verne Blatt, with Jack Davidsonly, coat manufacturer, and even more heavily jewelled wife Bessie Davidsonly. What a group! Every time the wives went away, which was often, Hymie and Jack would appear with au pair ding-a-lings—proud as punch.

Meanwhile, from what I heard, Ethel and Bessie were making it with a couple of Spanish beach boys in Majorca!

However, tonight they were all a happy family. Neither couple had ever been known to appear anywhere alone, there were always the four of them, or the two guys or the two wives. Did they fuck together? We all wondered.

What a greeting I got when I went over to their table! You would think I was their closest dearest friend. These were the same four people who wouldn't look at me sideways when I was a waiter, many's the time I've seasoned their salad.

'Who's coming in tonight, Tony doll?' Ethel asked anxiously, she was the blonde one, Bessie was dark, they obviously thought they were a hot team together, appealing to all types.

I gave her a kiss on the cheek, standard procedure, 'You'll see, you'll see.' I had four types of greeting routines. Big stars I didn't know, firm handshake, sexy look. Big stars I did know, kiss kiss. Ding-a-lings and swingers (female or male) hug and a kiss. Everyone else a kiss on the cheek.

The evening was starting to swing. It was going to be a good one. On a Saturday night we could do with a hundred more tables and fill them all. Who would have thought that people would fight and struggle to get into a hot smoky crowded atmosphere with deafening music, but they did and loved it.

Franklin arrived girl-less and sad-faced. He sat and stared at 'The Twang'.

Hal arrived with an American widow to whom he was showing the sights of London. What an operator! Always dressed to kill in the best Savile Row had to offer, hand-made shoes, Turnbull and Asser shirts, and a lot of gold from his fillings to his cufflinks.

Meanwhile he was flat on the heels of his ass, busted out, broke. His last fifty pounds had gone to the kid brother in New Jersey.

He lived in the best hotels, promoting here, promoting there, and there was always some rich old bag to bail him out. This one tonight was a real horror. From the blue-rinsed hair to the sagging body. Oh boy, Hal certainly had to work somewhere along the line, and I didn't envy him.

Franco was patting me on the shoulder, we were reaching jamming up point and there were only a few emergency tables left. Someone at reception was asking for me. Shit! He knew I never went out front on a Saturday night. Too embarrassing turning people away. He muttered something about friends of Benjamin Khaled's. Well, they could go screw. No room, not on a Saturday baby.

On second thoughts, maybe I should give them the bad news

myself—people never said they were friends of Benjamin's, it was always—'Fontaine insisted we come by'—and then they would be shocked when they got a bill.

I went out front, there were two young guys, a sandy-haired girl, and another one talking to Tina.

'I'm sorry,' I said, 'but we just don't have a table—you know it's—'

My stomach did a somersault. It was Alexandra. She gazed at me with wide brown eyes and tentatively smiled. She had a gorgeous smile.

'Hello, do you remember me?' she said softly.

Did I remember her—ha!

'Of course I do.' What should I call her? Alexandra? Miss Khaled? What?

She said, 'Couldn't you squeeze us in somewhere? Daddy said it would be all right.'

As if I would turn her away, even without the threat of 'Daddy'. She looked different, prettier. Her auburn hair was loose, kept off her face with a green head band, and she wore a matching green sweater and tweedy slacks. Nothing flashy but she looked great.

'I'm sure we'll find room for you. How many? Four?'

She nodded, well pleased, and attached herself to the arm of one of the fellows. I hated him.

It was then I had a sudden flash of inspiration and decided to jam them all on to my table. What a great idea!

I led them in and told Sammy, etc., to move over. They all looked choked. The table was crowded as it was. But I managed to get the four of them seated. Then I offered them a drink and was shocked when Alexandra agreed to have wine with the other three. I had sort of imagined that she didn't drink.

They chatted amongst themselves while I hovered by the table. Sammy pantomimed a face at me as much as to say—what the hell is this?

I really don't know why I had flipped for this girl, but I had, and this time I wasn't going to let her get away.

I studied the schmuck she was with. Casually dressed, slightly long hair, much too good-looking in a boyish way. He had an arm around her and was tapping her shoulder in time to the music This was certainly no creepy little Peter Lincoln Smith. This was probably the boy-friend. Well, we would soon find out.

'The Twang' suddenly yelled at me across the table, 'Can we dance, sweetie?'

I froze her with a grim look. Stupid loud-mouth. Got to get rid of her. 'Franklin, dance with Janine,' I said pleasantly. Silently I said —For Christ's sake give her a grope and get her interested in you.

They went off to dance. That was a start. I sat down. I stuck out my hand to Alexandra's boy-friend, forcing him to take his arm from around her. 'Tony Burg, glad to see you.'

Alexandra said, 'Oh, I'm sorry—this is Michael Newcombe'— then she indicated the other two, 'Michael's sister Madelaine, and Jonathan Roberts.'

We all shook hands.

'Super of you to squeeze us in,' Madelaine said, 'we didn't believe Alex when she said she could get us in. Michael's been trying to come here for ages!'

That made Michael out to be a right idiot.

'I hope you like it,' I said. 'Saturday night's a real killer.'

Sammy leaned over, his cockney accent cutting the air, ''Ere— take a look at that.'

We all turned to see Massey and Suki come in. She was wearing the shortest dress ever, split under the arms to below the waist at the side. It was a good job she was flat-chested. Even then, it was some dress. What with her huge made-up clown eyes, her mannish haircut and white face, she looked like she was in fancy dress.

Massey was cool as ever. 'Hey, man.'

They squashed down at the table and I could see Michael giving Suki a stare. Good. I performed introductions and soon everyone was talking.

Alexandra had one of those classless beautifully spoken voices. She really was a knockout, and she was nice. She wasn't a stupid little rich bitch as I had thought. Her friends of course were a bit on the square side, hadn't been around much I reckoned. From the conversation I gathered that Madelaine and Alexandra had been at a finishing school in Switzerland together.

Michael hadn't taken his eyes off Suki and I could see Alexandra getting a bit edgy. What an idiot he was to stare at a freak like Suki with a girl like Alexandra by his side. Still it was just as well, what did he know, he was your typical well-educated student type. I willed him to ask sweet little Suki to dance. Sweet little Suki indeed. She was your typical bony angular model girl, all legs and no tits. Massey and she had been going together for a few months on and off, and though they both appeared regularly with other dates, they had a nice scene going.

Bingo. Michael, the jerk, was asking her to dance. I thought for a second the dumb face was going to refuse, but no, she couldn't resist the opportunity of wriggling her backside. She got up. Michael got up. Alexandra frowned.

Madelaine looked embarrassed and started to chatter loudly. I grabbed my opportunity like a sinking diver, 'Come and see round the club,' I said directly to Alexandra.

'Super,' Madelaine replied.

Alexandra shook her head, 'I think I'll stay here.'

I glared at Madelaine who had got up, and then to cap it all Jonathan asked Alexandra to dance and off they went.

Have you ever been choked?

I caught Franco's eye. I said to Madelaine. 'We'll have to take a rain-check, I'm wanted out front.'

Tina was patiently turning people away. She smiled at me, she looked tired and pale. I guess it was no joke living with Flowers, he probably never quietened down.

'How's it going?' I gave her a pat.

'Fine, Mr Blake.' She brushed a lock of blonde hair off her forehead.

I felt sorry for her. 'Go home early tonight, you look tired— I'll get Franco to bring one of the boys out front.'

'Oh, thank you, Mr Blake, I don't feel too good . . .'

I went back inside and hovered by the dance floor. Alexandra was making an attempt to move. She wasn't very good at it. I studied her body partly visible through the folds of clothes. A nice full bosom, slim waist, small hips and long legs.

Was she or wasn't she? Did she or didn't she? I had a hard on to find out.

Madelaine was dancing with Sammy, and his teen-age wonder was nowhere to be seen. Probably back in the ladies' room.

Franklin and 'The Twang' were sitting down.

'Hi, Tony,' a girl I knew on her way back from dancing. She was very pretty. She squeezed my arm, 'When am I going to see you?'

I honestly couldn't remember if we'd made it or not. Some nights I was so loaded I wouldn't have known who it was wriggling about underneath me.

She was with a well-known singer, Steve Scott. One of the new breed, trying to project the sexy Englishman image and not doing a bad job. She was a dancer, a swinger, I did remember her. Her name was Carolyn something or other. I went over and sat with them and bought them a drink.

'Want to come to a party tomorrow?' Steve asked. 'My place, all you need is a bottle and a bird.'

'Yeah,' I was half catching glimpses of Alexandra dancing through the throng.

'You must come, it will be great,' Carolyn said. She jotted down Steve's address which I absentmindedly stuck in my pocket. Who needed parties on a Sunday anyway?

Flowers was launching into some slow soul sounds and when I glimpsed Alexandra again she was clutched in the schmuck she was dancing with's arms. Well, Flowers could forget that. I rushed over to him and made him change mid record to something fast. Automatically Alexandra and partner jerked apart. I noticed happily that Suki and Michael didn't.

Massey noticed too: 'Think I've lost her,' he joked when I sat down. 'Always knew she'd go off with the first white cat that came on strong.'

Now—how about Massey and 'The Twang'? No—she didn't like spades unless they were stars, and he didn't like busty chicks. Oh well . . .

Alexandra was coming back to the table. She looked flushed. 'It looks like we've been deserted, Jonathan,' she said with a wry grin to schmucko. I took her arm which she politely but immediately pulled away.

Oh God, her skin felt like velvet.

'Listen, I want to make you (should I add the rest of the sentence) a member. Let's go to the office.'

'Now?' she looked surprised. 'It's very nice of you but I don't think' . . .

I didn't let her finish, 'You've got to be a member, it will only take a minute and then you can come here anytime without having to go through the whole bit.'

'O.K.,' she got up. 'Come on Jonathan.'

He got up too and fast thinking I said, 'You stay here, otherwise the table will jam up and there will be nowhere for you to sit when we get back.'

He sat down. I had her.

This time I took a firm grip on her arm and propelled her through the crush. She was looking over to the dance floor to see Michael and Suki. I got her out to reception and then down one flight of stairs to the office. It was quite dark and only the faintest sounds of music reached us. I unlocked the door and switched on the light. It was a bare room with filing cabinets, a desk and a couple of chairs, very unromantic.

She stretched and yawned, her breasts taut against her sweater.

I had a mad urge to grab her, strip her clothes off and make violent love to her. This little bird had really got under my skin. But it would never do to rush things. To get her out of my system I had to have her, and to have her I had to play it cool.

I lit a nervous cigarette and she sat down, tapped impatient buff nails on the desk and said, 'Who's that awful girl Michael's dancing with?'

I sang a few off key lines of an old song 'Jealousy'.

She glared at me. 'I'm not jealous I can assure you,' she stuck her chin out, a gesture I immediately loved. 'But she's just ghastly. Who is she?'

'Some dopy model. Is Michael your boy-friend?'

'Oh no,' she flushed. 'Actually, we've known each other ages,

58

him being Madelaine's brother and everything, but this is the first time we've been out together.'

The scene became clear, schoolgirl crush, fancied him since she was a little girl bit. Well, we would soon get rid of him.

I found a membership form and doodled on it with a chewed pencil that was on the desk. She looked at me expectantly, wide brown eyes, beautiful eyes.

'What's your address?' I asked. You know, this bird made me nervous.

'I wonder if I should give you Mummy's address,' she mused aloud, 'I shall probably be there every weekend and it is my proper address.'

I didn't want Mummy's address. I wanted her improper address.

She licked her lips, they were very full and shiny with some kind of lip gloss, very sexy. 'No, perhaps I should give you my address here although I don't know how permanent it will be.'

Was she a virgin? No, impossible. There are no virgins left over the age of fourteen in London, even Sammy hasn't come across one yet.

'Madelaine and I are sharing a flat,' she said, rather proudly. 'Can Madelaine be a member too? The address is 14 Dundee Court, Chelsea.'

Chelsea yet! What did she want to go and set herself up amongst all that mob for? Oh well, at least she was in London and not living either with Mummy or Daddy. 'Phone number?' I asked, silently rehearsing what I would say the first time I phoned.

She gave me the number and I said, 'That's great, we'll send you the card this week and then I expect to see lots of you.'

She blushed. There are actually girls that still know how to blush.

'I doubt it,' she said standing up. 'I start my job on Monday, and I have to be there by nine every day.'

'Nine in the morning?' My voice was incredulous. Nine in the morning was ridiculous.

She smiled, 'That's right, I'm a secretary.'

Was I going mad, or was there a definite note of pride in her voice?

A secretary indeed! Could this possibly be Benjamin Khaled's daughter? I was choked, but so what, I still fancied her even if she didn't have any money. The old bastard, making her work. Fontaine was clad from head to toe in mink, and this poor little bird had to go out to work. What a game.

Still it was just as well, if she'd had money everyone would have thought I was after that.

She was at the door, anxious to get back to see what Michael was up to, no doubt. I stayed sitting at the desk like an idiot.

'Shall we go back?' she said politely.

Didn't she realise I fancied her? Couldn't she tell? She treated me like I was nobody special. I mean, I don't want to sound big-headed but I do run the place and everybody likes me. And I do have a good look, and she should bloody well pay me *some* attention. Running after some little long-haired student, the girl was mad.

We went upstairs and Tina gave me a knowing smile.

At the table Sammy said loud-voiced as ever, ''Ere, where you bin?'

And then 'The Twang' had the nerve to say, 'Tony babee, you're neglecting me, let's dance.'

That was the end of her. She had gone far enough. She could pack her false eyelashes and hank of hair and go.

Alexandra said, a trifle irritably, 'Is Michael still dancing?'

Madelaine nodded and looked embarrassed. I seized the opportunity and grabbing Alexandra before she could sit down said, 'If you can't beat 'em, join 'em,' and I whipped her off to the dance floor.

I vaguely heard 'The Twang' shrieking in astonishment, 'Sonofabitch!'

Alexandra let me hold her at a discreet arm's length to the beat of 'Jimmy Mack'. I signalled Flowers to put on some slow sounds and she said, 'Your girl-friend's furious.'

'My girl-friend.' I looked amazed. 'I've never seen her before tonight.'

She smiled, that insane innocent smile, and I pulled her a little closer as Flowers switched to 'Groovin' and she struggled a bit but I had her in a tight grip and I wasn't letting go. She smelt of clean hair and toothpaste. I could feel her full breasts against me and her narrow waist was firm against my hands. She felt every bit as good as I'd expected her to.

'Isn't that Steve Scott?' she asked suddenly. He and Carolyn were wrapped casually around each other close by.

'Yeah – why? You like him?'

'Oh yes,' she was like a little schoolgirl, 'I always buy all his records, I think he's a terrific singer.'

Any second I expected her to produce an autograph book. She was a real sweet innocent.

Suddenly I had a great idea, 'I'll tell you what I'll do for you since you're so nice.'

She looked at me with those big brown eyes.

'How would you like to go to a party at Steve Scott's house tomorrow?'

'Really? You mean I'd actually meet him?'

'Sure, I'll take you. How's that?'

She pondered a bit, 'Have you been invited?'

Oh, this girl was too much! I nodded seriously. 'Of course. We'll go, O.K.?'

'Can Madelaine come?'

Fuck bloody Madelaine, I was getting good and fed up with her. 'That might be a bit tricky, but we'll go anyway.'

She made a snap decision, 'All right, but I can't stay out late.'

Had I made a wise move? Steve's parties were always a bit of an orgy. Well, that was O.K. We could always leave and go somewhere else—a nice romantic little restaurant, or my place, my sumptuous gaff off the Edgware Road. I kept on meaning to move, but who had the bread.

Flowers gave me a freaky look as we danced by, 'Man, who is the disc jockey tonight?' he muttered, rolling mad eyeballs. Sometimes he got very temperamental. He would go on kicks of playing far out sounds that nobody knew and then when he was told to play something a little more 'in' he would sulk for days. At other times he was so stoned he didn't even know what he was playing. But when he was good, forget it. He could make the room move like nobody else. He was great.

Alexandra said, 'What shall I wear?'

All birds are for ever asking that question and you know they already have the whole outfit planned.

'Nothing dressy, whatever you fancy.'

Perhaps she would fancy something with a long back zip that I could get her out of in next to no time.

I must say I had been neglecting the club since Alexandra had arrived, but it suddenly came to my notice that a great struggle was going on in the corner, and all I could see was the backs of three waiters and a worried-looking Franco. Alexandra felt so good I didn't want to let her go, but there was always tomorrow. Business was business. I gave her a gentle push in the direction of our table, 'Be a good girl and go sit down. I sense a little trouble.'

Stewart Wade, bum drunken actor, was sitting on the floor screaming four-letter words at the waiters while they answered angrily back in Italian. They were trying to pick him up and he was landing a drunken punch anywhere he could.

'What's the trouble?' I asked Franco.

He waved his arms around excitedly. 'The punk, 'ee no wanna pay 'ees bill, 'ee broke one of my boys' noses, 'ee say 'ee never pay bill anywhere.'

I pushed through the waiters.

'Come on, Stew, baby,' I said, 'let's not cause a scene. On your feet.'

'Ah, Tony,' he had one of those booming Shakespearean voices. 'Tell your frigging morons to leave me alone.'

'Come on, sweetheart, let's go and talk about it outside.'

'I want to stay here.' He sat there, all two hundred pounds of him with a childish drunken smile. 'Fuck the lot of you,' he shouted gleefully. 'I'm Stewart Wade, *the* Stewart Wade, I never pay, so fuck you.'

The waiters were muttering angrily amongst themselves.

'Pick him up and throw him out,' I said. I'd had enough. Customers like him we didn't need.

Happy in their work, the four waiters grabbed him by the legs and arms and proceeded to carry him out bodily while he bellowed—'I'll get the frigging police,' and then he passed out cold. A large scrubber in a micro-mini with legs like a football player scurried out after him.

Franco and I looked at each other and shrugged. You get used to anything in our business.

Back at our table Michael and Suki had finally returned. Alexandra was saying she wanted to go, and so were Madelaine and Jonathan, but Michael was saying nothing, just looking a bit glassy-eyed in Suki's direction as she studied her face in a Mary Quant make-up box.

'I say, could we get the bill?' Jonathan asked.

'That's all right,' I looked at Alexandra who was looking at Michael, 'it's on me.'

'Oh, that's awfully nice of you,' Madelaine said. She wasn't bad in a debby sort of way. A suitable room-mate for Alexandra, not flighty, a bit plain and plump.

They all got up and exchanged goodbyes around the table. I walked them out front. I managed to pull Alexandra to the side, 'I'll pick you up around eight p.m.'

'Oh fine.' She looked like she had forgotten all about it.

They piled into the lift and left. The last glimpse I got of her she was staring accusingly at Michael. She opened her mouth to say something, but the lift doors closed.

I stretched in anticipation of the following night. I would soon have her forgetting all about Michael.

It was two a.m., peak time. Flowers came strolling out, the group had just gone. 'Just going round the corner, man,' he said. Off to get high, at least he had enough sense not to smoke in the club.

Hal appeared with his blue-rinsed bag. I had to admire him, he certainly had a lot of style. 'We're going to play a little chemmy,' he announced giving me the wink. That meant *he* was going to play a little chemmy with *her* money. He was a mad gambler and sometimes won a bundle which he would immediately blow on new gear.

She smiled at me, rows of nicotine-stained teeth, 'I just love your little old club, honey.'

Hal said, 'Mamie's got a girl-friend coming in next week if you want to make up a foursome.'

A girl-friend yet! She was about sixty! I shook my head seriously, 'I'm engaged.'

'Oh, what a shame, honey, she would have loved you.'

He was a bum. He knew I didn't go for the rich old widow scene, yet he never gave up, he was always trying to recruit me.

'You and I as a team, Tony, we'd destroy them,' he would say.

Fontaine was enough for me, thank you. I could just about make it with her, although it was becoming more and more difficult.

Fontaine—I had forgotten about her what with her being away and all. But I glumly supposed she would be back soon. How would she feel about me and Alexandra? I pondered on this fact and decided she wouldn't like it at all. It was a tricky situation. If I had any sense I wouldn't go near Miss Alexandra Al Khaled with a barge-pole. But I had flipped for her, she had really knocked me out. So let's face it, I wasn't playing it too smart, but so what? Fontaine would never find out, and Alexandra and I could have a fast affaire, then bye-bye. 'Schmuck,' a little voice kept saying in my ear, but I ignored it.

'Well, baby, I guess you and I can call it quits,' a furious voice said. It was 'The Twang', all quivering, sexy five foot five of her.

I wanted to say, 'Yes, you're right,' but Alexandra had put me in the mood, and 'The Twang' was there and ready, and there didn't seem to be much else available stock around. One more night with her wouldn't be too much of a hardship. I patted her sexy bum, 'Customers, my lovely, I've got to be nice to the paying people.' She pouted, and I put my arm around her, 'Let's dance.'

8

ALEXANDRA

What a week! It has rushed by, and *so* much has happened. Maddy and I are sitting here in our *own* flat, in *Chelsea*! And on Monday I start a *job*! And tonight I've got a date with Michael!! I feel *so* lucky. Mummy was first class about the whole thing. She gave me money and came to town to look at the flat with Maddy and me before we took it. We had lunch at Fortnum & Mason, and she bought us a tea-set and some cutlery.

Maddy and I have thoroughly discussed the Peter Lincoln Smith incident and we came to the conclusion that he behaved like a pig. Maddy said I should tell Daddy. But I don't think so.

We have both made up our minds that with the right boy sex would be all right. Actually we have both decided that we *should* sort of—well you know—*sleep* with the right male. Being a virgin is definitely out of date.

I have secretly decided that Michael and I should have an affair. Maddy and I discussed birth control for hours. Maddy says we should find a nice old doctor to prescribe us the pill. It certainly sounds a lot easier than all the other undignified methods. I mean they all seem so *complicated*.

Between us our sexual experience is very limited. I have been kissed by three boys, including Peter, and Maddy about the same, although, of course, she has been sort of semi-stripped when the school gardener got her bra and sweater off. We talked about that a lot. Maddy said she felt all sort of weak-kneed, and he had kissed her there, and sucked on her nipples like a baby. But then he had been angry when she wouldn't let him go any further.

Maddy has small breasts. Mine are bigger. I feel all embarrassed when I think of Michael looking at them.

'I wonder what Jonathan Roberts is like,' Madelaine suddenly said. 'Isn't it funny that Michael wants to be your date.

65

Maybe I'll have you as a sister-in-law!' she giggled.

I blushed. 'Don't be so silly. He's just being nice to us I expect because we don't know anyone in London.'

'Huh! Michael's never been nice to me before. In fact, he's very selfish. *I* think he's after your body, your pure white virgin skin.'

Honestly, Madelaine could be infuriating at times.

Michael had telephoned the day before and said that he and a friend of his were going to take us out. Maddy had answered the phone and I was trying to listen. 'Do you want to go?' she had whispered to me.

'Yes,' I whispered back. 'Of course I do.'

So it was settled, much to my delight, and they were picking us up at eight.

Michael had instructed his sister that we were to wear something casual. I had rushed down the Kings Road and found a Jaeger shop where I got some green tweed slacks and a matching sweater. There were lots of other shops with incredible clothes in the windows, but Mummy had always said, 'Buy quality' and I knew Jaeger was quality.

Michael and his friend Jonathan were half-an-hour late. I felt sure they had forgotten all about us.

Jonathan seemed quite nice, and Madelaine looked pleased.

Michael said, 'Well, girls, we're going to show you the town.' He looked terrific in a yellow roll-neck sweater and black trousers. Honestly, he is *so* good-looking!

We all piled into Jonathan's Mini, Maddy and me in the back. They took us to a very small cellar restaurant, jammed with people, and we sat at a corner table, scrubbed pine with a black candle in a glass holder. *Very* romantic, but rather noisy.

I was sitting opposite Michael and he leaned across and said, 'You don't look too bad tonight. London suits you.'

Oh, what a wonderful evening!

We drank red wine and ate chicken casserole. Madelaine got on awfully well with Jonathan, and Michael was really nice to me. In fact, the best thing was when he said to me at the end of the meal, 'You know—for a girl you're quite intelligent.'

It was past twelve when we left, and Michael held my hand. I felt marvellous.

'What shall we do now?' Jonathan said to Michael, 'Want to pop into "Judie's" and have a dance?'

'Can't stand that place, it's always filled with such a grim crew.'

'How about "Hobo"?' I ventured. It hadn't been much fun for me before, but with Michael it would be different.

'I'm not a member,' he said, 'and they're very sticky about letting non-members in.'

'That's all right,' I said, 'my father sort of has money in the place. I'm sure we'll get in.'

'Not on A Saturday night,' Jonathan said, '"Hobo's" the hottest place in town.'

'I'm *sure* it will be all right,' I felt rather proud of the fact that they all seemed to think the place was so exclusive. I tried to remember the name of the manager. Tony something—Beard, Bird—I wasn't quite sure.

'Look, if Alex says it's O.K., let's go,' Madelaine said.

'It will be a wasted trip,' Jonathan said, 'that place is impossible. You've got to be Marlon Brando at least.'

'Come on, Marlon,' Michael said with a grin, squeezing my hand. 'Show us the impossible!'

By this time I was a bit nervous. What if I couldn't get us in? I wished I hadn't said anything.

Outside the club cars were double parked all down the street. Jonathan dropped us and we waited outside while he went off to park.

A beautiful girl arrived in a black sports car. She left it smack in the middle of the road and strode into the club. Michael turned to stare at her. I felt a pang of jealousy.

Soon Jonathan got back and we all marched in, me at the front.

'Yes?' a blonde girl behind a desk questioned.

'Er, we're friends of 'er—Benjamin Khaled. He said it would be all right.'

'Did you book?' she asked.

'Well no, but—'

'I'm sorry,' she shrugged, 'if you didn't book I can't help you.'

67

'I told you,' Jonathan jeered. 'Come on, let's go.'

'Just a minute,' I said, determined not to be embarrassed. 'Is Mr Bird here?'

'Mr Who?' the girl behind the desk said.

'Mr Tony Beard.'

'Oh, you mean Mr Blake.' She pressed a buzzer on the desk and a waiter appeared. 'Luigi, tell Mr Blake—*if he's here*—that there's some people who say they're friends of Mr Khaleds.' The girl smiled at me sympathetically. 'Saturday night you *must* book,' she said, 'and also a member has to sign you in. If I were you I'd talk to Mr Khaled.'

I heard a voice behind me say, 'I'm sorry, but we don't have a table.'

I turned quickly. It was the Manager. I smiled, 'Hello, do you remember me?' Oh thank goodness, he's smiling back.

'Of course I do,' he said.

'Couldn't you just squeeze us in somewhere? Daddy said it would be all right.'

I waited with a tense smile. How awful if he turned us away! But it was all right. He said he would find room for us somewhere. I grinned triumphantly. We followed him in.

What a terrific place it is, with the loud music and frantic dancers. How super to be here with Michael.

We were crowded on to an already full table and I was jammed next to Michael. He took my hand and said slowly, 'Very, very good.'

It was all great until some awful girl appeared and started ogling Michael, and then he danced with her practically all night.

It was just too bad. The only good thing that happened was that I saw Steve Scott—in the flesh!! And Tony Blake invited me to a party at Steve Scott's house!

I was very quiet on the drive back to our flat, and then Jonathan parked the car and he and Maddy started talking in low voices. I was trapped in the back seat with Michael.

He said, 'Well, little Alex, we'll have to do this again.'

Little Alex! I was furious!

'Maddy,' I said in a loud voice, 'we've been invited to a party at

Steve Scott's tomorrow night. Tony Blake's going to take us.'

She squealed. 'Oh, marvie! How did you manage that?'

Michael said, 'You can't go out with Tony Blake.'

'Why not?' I asked, my heart fluttering.

'You just can't,' he said. 'Two little kids like you, he'll eat you for dinner!'

Honestly! 'Come on, Mads, let's go'. How dare he call us kids. 'Thank you for dinner,' I added, and then rushed into our entrance, not even waiting for Maddy.

Tears sting my eyes.

I think I am in love!

9

FONTAINE

New York is cold. The people in the streets and shops are boring. They all seem to discover you're English and to them this means instant friendship, they think they can chat to you for hours about their dreary grandma in Scunthorpe. Today a perfect stranger came up to me in 'Bendels', and demanded in a deep Southern drawl where had I got my dinky chinchilla. Why, she practically ripped it off my back with her eyes. However, they *are* chic, the very rich women.

Ray has become the darling of the society set. They all pop into him for their comb-outs. Actually, he's become a bit effeminate, I'm shocked! He who was always so virile. Maybe it's my imagination, but I'm not usually wrong about these things. He hasn't even approached me about going to bed together. Success has definitely gone to his head. I shall have to talk to Benjamin about him, take the salon away or something.

After a week here I find myself thinking about Tony. A week of nothing sexually, only a short two-hour affaire with the husband of a friend of mine. Nothing special, rather boring actually.

It would be rather amusing to have Tony come over for a few days. Show the sexy animal off. I could tell Benjamin I wanted him to see New York, to find out what he thinks about opening 'Hobo' here. Tony would love it. I could buy him some clothes, show him the city.

Yes, I shall call Benjamin tonight and have him arrange the whole thing. Tony could be here by Monday and we can fly back the following weekend together.

I dressed carefully. Lunch with Sarah at '21', wife of the man I'd had the two-hour affaire with. I knew she wanted to tell me about her latest lover. The gossip around town said he was a Chinese waiter. Well Sarah has always been kinky, so I wasn't surprised.

Sarah would adore Tony. She's a very well educated society matron in her thirties, thin and beautiful, we used to model together. She married a Texan oil millionaire, then a Californian property millionaire, and now Allen, attractive unsuccessful writer. She has loads of money and Allen spends it well. They both have affaires and neither seems to mind. Actually she would be rather pleased if I told her about Allen and me. He wasn't very good though, a disappointment.

Sarah looked divine. If ever I decided to turn lesbian she would be my choice. Thin slavic face, jet black hair dramatically plastered down with a centre parting. She wore yellow, this year's Dior, I was a little more avant garde in Yves Saint Laurent.

We started with champagne cocktails and ordered melon and steak. Life is a permanent diet.

'Tell me all,' I demanded.

She smiled dreamily, 'Fontaine, my darling, if you haven't tried the mysteries of the East you haven't lived.'

I smiled back, 'I like my men a little—shall we say taller?'

She giggled, 'It's the quality not the quantity.'

'Give me quantity, to hell with quality!'

It was a pleasant lunch, I always enjoyed being with Sarah. We are alike in many ways.

Later I called Benjamin, 'Darling, I've got a marvellous idea.

70

What about a "Hobo" here? Yes, here in New York. Can you arrange to have Tony Blake sent over for a few days? Now, immediately, tomorrow if possible. You're wonderful, of course I miss you. Yes, darling, have your secretary call me back with the details. Yes, of course I'll be home soon. I love you too, 'bye.'

Poor old Benjamin. He really believed I loved him. I mean how could he? Didn't he ever look at himself?

Oh well, a party at the Sidwells tonight. Better dazzle them with the new Courrèges. Soon I would be dazzling them all with Tony. Quelle fun!

10

TONY

It's four o'clock in the afternoon and there's no getting rid of 'The Twang'. It's her day of rest and she's making the most of it. Fast asleep like a lump of clay, unmade-up face hidden beneath a tangle of hair. In the daylight it's orange and quite revolting, she says it photographs fantastically. She's very ambitious. I'm also ambitious, ambitious to get her out of my bed and on her way.

I gave her a gentle tap on the shoulder, she snuggled down in the bed and snored softly. Oh man, the only thing that was going to wake her was something I didn't feel like giving her this morning.

I went in the bathroom and had a wash. She slept on. I made coffee and turned the telly up loud. She didn't stir. I gave her a shove. She sighed and stretched out tarantula arms. I ignored them. She opened sleep-filled eyes and said, 'C'mon back to bed, baby.'

Really, she and Sammy would have been great together.

'Get up, Janine,' I said, 'my mother's coming to visit.'

'Your mother,' her eyes snapped wide open and she sat up revealing full orange-tipped boobs fresh out of the centre spread in *Playboy*.

'Yeah, my mother, she takes it into her head once a year to come—today's the day.'

'Oh shit,' Janine twanged and got up.

She was built. Although without makeup her face was puffy and washed out. It's amazing what makeup can do for a girl.

She stomped into the bathroom and closed the door. I congratulated myself on the mother bit, and tidied up. I could go out, get something to eat and then get ready to pick up Alexandra. I wanted the pad to be in good shape in case she wished to view it.

Janine emerged an hour later, face in place, figure in sweater and too short skirt. Her kind of figure didn't go with mini-mini's. She was playing it cool, trying to look like she didn't care too much. I had gathered her things together in case she hadn't twigged.

She smiled at me coolly, 'Bye, sweetheart,' she said, 'see you around.' And exit 'The Twang'.

I phoned Sammy.

'What a night,' he moaned, 'the little raver wouldn't leave me alone.'

'You want to grab something to eat?' I asked him.

'Yeah, pick me up.'

I pulled on old gear, and drove over his place five minutes away. I was driving some decrepit old car that a girl-friend had left with me to look after while she did a dancing tour of the Far East. I wondered if Sammy could be conned into lending me his E-type for tonight. Very sexy the E-type, a low slung roaring phallic symbol.

Sammy looked terrible, still in his dressing-gown, unshaven and seedy eyed. 'I'm giving up the young ones,' he announced, 'too much bloody energy.'

We went to a little salt beef hangout nearby and I listened to the tale of Miss fifteen-year-old's sexy acrobatics.

'And to top it all,' Sammy concluded, 'she pinched a fiver from beside the bed when she left. Liberty!'

By this time it was half past six and I wanted to get home and changed for Alexandra. 'What are you doing tonight, Samuel?' I asked.

'Going to bed, I'm knocked out.'

'Can I borrow your car?'

'What for? You've got the mini.'

'Oh, come on, Sammy, I've got an important date, I can't take her in that.'

'Who is it?' Sammy was like a nosey old woman.

I kept my voice casual. 'You know, the bird from last night, Alexandra.'

'She's not your style,' Sammy said in surprise. 'You like flashier models than that.'

'I like her,' I said shortly. 'Can I borrow it?'

'Sure, only I've got to 'ave it by eight tomorrow morning.'

He tossed me the keys and I gave him the keys of the mini. He was all right Sammy was.

At home the phone was ringing and under my door was a telegram. I picked up the receiver and flipped open the buff coloured envelope.

'Mr Blake?' a crisp efficient bird's voice. 'This is Alice, Benjamin Khaled's secretary, I've been trying to get you all day but your line's been out of order.'

I always take the phone off the hook when I'm asleep.

'Yeah,' I said. Maybe Fontaine had had an accident.

'Mr Khaled requires that you fly to New York to investigate the suitability of opening a "Hobo" there.'

'What?' I was stunned.

'Mrs Khaled suggests you leave immediately, I actually had you booked on the eight p.m. flight, but I shouldn't think you'll make that now. Of course if you rushed—'

I interrupted, 'I can't go tonight, death in the family you know,' I always have been an exaggerated liar.

'Oh,' the crisp voice paused. 'Well, how about seven-forty-five tomorrow morning?'

What the hell was this? What was all the urgency? Of course I would love to see New York, but what was the panic? I scanned the wire quickly.

'Need you here. Benjamin will explain. Make it fast. Fontaine.'

'How long am I supposed to go for?' I asked Alice.

'A few days I believe. Is the seven-forty-five all right?'

'Yes, that's O.K.'

'Fine, a car will pick you up at six a.m., everything will be taken care of this end, a car will meet you on arrival. Bon voyage!' Alice's crisp voice hung up.

I sat back a bit stunned. New York. I'd always wanted to go there. What about visas and everything? I thought it took months. What should I take? 'Hobo' in New York. What a scene *that* would be!

There was no time to waste, I didn't want to be late for Alexandra. I'm off to New York in the morning—sounded good.

I sorted out some things to take, counted my money, only twenty quid, well I supposed Fontaine would take care of that. Then I dressed. Best-casual clobber. Groomed the barnet. I was ready.

Alexandra and Madelaine lived in a big grim block of flats. I rang the bell of No. 14 and waited. I was shocked when Madelaine's brother Michael answered. He was unconcerned at seeing me, and invited me into an old-fashioned large living room. Madelaine bounced in next, dressed in a flouncy blue dress, she said, 'Is it going to be all right for me to come too?'

I looked sad. 'Sorry, darling, absolutely not. I warned Alex.'

'Oh,' Madelaine's bounce sagged a bit, but she lit a cigarette and choked. Then she brightened. 'Well, Alex can tell me about it anyway.' She wasn't a bad little bird, certainly understanding.

Michael offered me a drink. He acted like he lived there. Then, enter Alexandra. She looked lovely in one of those Victorian-type dresses with frills everywhere, her hair was tied back and she really looked so young and pretty. I was knocked out.

Michael said, 'You've got everything but the kitchen stove on.'

She glared at him and replied, 'Better than wearing the minimum.'

Rather clever I thought. I said, 'You look great,' and she smiled triumphantly at Michael.

I was getting fed up with the whole thing between her and the

74

idiot, so I quickly downed the weak scotch he had given me and said, 'Come on, we can't be late.'

Then followed a whole explanation about why Madelaine couldn't come too. I was in trouble if Steve Scott blew his big mouth off about open house.

Finally we got out of there and she admired Sammy's E-type, I forgot to mention it wasn't mine, I mean why confuse things? And then we were off.

It suddenly struck me we were much too early to go to the party. I mean nine-thirty would be the earliest we could appear, and then we'd probably be the first anyway.

A nice cosy drink somewhere was the thing. I decided the rooftop bar at the Hilton was suitably romantic. London shimmering and shining below us was a good scene. Or maybe I should destroy her with one of those wild drinks at Trader Vic's.

She was sitting demurely, the ribbon tying back her hair gave her a real little girl look. To tell the truth, I was worried about taking her to Steve's. His parties got very wild, plenty of booze and birds and everyone turning on. I don't go for the pot scene myself—cannot see what all the fuss is about—it doesn't do anything for me. Just give me a few scotches and I'm all right. Of course, in my business, to certain people, I have to pretend I turn on—otherwise they would think I wasn't cool, and you've got to keep a hip image going. Fontaine and friends smoke occasionally. It's like a gang of children having naughty fun. They think they are so decadent. I have found that the really cool pot smokers just get on with it and don't make a whole group scene. Hal was always high, but he never discussed it.

'It's a shame Madelaine couldn't come,' Alexadra said.

'Yeah, sorry about that. Listen, I thought we'd grab a fast drink, we're early for the party.'

'Oh, what time does it start?' She fiddled with a few of her Victorian frills.

'About nine. Is the Hilton O.K. for you?'

She nodded. 'I've never been there.'

I was amazed, I'd never met anyone who hadn't been in the Hilton.

75

I took her to the rooftop bar. If she'd never been there this was something she had to see. The view was a knockout.

I could see she couldn't decide what to drink so I ordered her a champagne cocktail and I had a double scotch and coke. We attacked the nuts and she giggled a bit and said. 'What a super place!'

'Have you really never been here?' I was still surprised.

'No,' she shook her head. 'Actually I haven't spent very much time in London at all, Mummy hates it, so we never came. But now I've finished school I wanted to come so much and Mummy simply had to agree to let me share a flat with Madelaine—you see Madelaine's mother and mine are best friends.'

'What about your father?' I asked.

'Oh, Daddy,' she shrugged. 'Well, since he married that awful woman we haven't really spent much time with him,' she stopped, then rushed on, 'I suppose I shouldn't call her an awful woman, but she is.'

If she had stuck her tongue out and added—so there—I wouldn't have been surprised.

I wondered what Alexandra would have said if she'd known about the affair Fontaine and I were having.

She sipped her champagne cocktail and I gulped my scotch. Her dress didn't reveal any flesh at all, even her arms were covered and the skirt wasn't particularly short.

As if she sensed me thinking this she said, 'Now that I'm in London I must shorten my skirts. I feel like an old frump. In Switzerland we had to wear a regulation skirt length and that was that.'

'You don't need your skirt any shorter,' I said quickly. Quite frankly, I was fed up to the teeth with all the birds around practically exposing their knicks. On a clear night in the club you could see for ever. I didn't want Alexandra joining the ranks of the ass flashers. Really a very short skirt only looks good on a seventeen-year-old flat-chested girl with great legs (thin) and how many of those are there around? Not many I can tell you.

Alexandra finished her drink, 'What time can we go to the party?' she asked brightly.

I glanced at my watch—one of Fontaine's very few presents—Roman numerals, black croc strap. It was nearly nine, so I figured it would be all right.

Just as I asked for the check, a loud voice yelled, 'Tony, honey pie,' and arms were thrown around me. It was Molly Mandy. Just what I needed. She was wearing a multi-coloured jersey dress cut out everywhere, and as I tried to disentangle myself from her I noticed Alexandra's look of —well—amazement I guess.

Molly finished her greeting, flashed very white teeth in a friendly smile at Alexandra, winked, said, 'Have a ball,' laughed, and swung off back to her escort, a soberly dressed old man, her speciality. God knows where she found them and God knows why they wanted to be seen out with her.

'Who's that?' Alexandra asked breathlessly.

'Just a girl that comes into the club, a dress designer. Come on.'

I took hold of her hand, she went a bit stiff, but didn't pull away. We set off for the elevator. Oh, if Fontaine could see me now.

I thought I had better cover my tracks. 'Listen, you know your father might not approve of my taking you out. I work for him in a roundabout way and he might not like it, so I think it's best not to mention it. Right?'

'All right,' she replied, a bit surprised.

'I'd like to see you a lot more,' I added quickly. 'What do you think?'

I was making a right berk of myself. Never acted so stupid with a girl. The right way to go about it with someone you like is at the end of the evening to mumble casually, 'I'll call you' and then don't call for two weeks. That always gets them going. But I thought this girl was wonderful and sweet and warm and I wanted her to know how I felt. We were outside. 'Party time,' I said, and helped her into the car.

I was right, we were too early. Steve lounged to the door in his underpants and a sweater.

'Come on in,' he said. 'Just finished boffing, where's your bottle?'

I'd forgotten he'd said to bring a bottle.

Carolyn appeared wrapping a pink dressing-gown around her.

77

She had nothing underneath and I noticed the firmness of her small breasts and I remembered the night we'd had together. She was a right raver.

'Tony, you're so bloody cheap,' she said, 'no bottle indeed, I suppose you forgot.' She smiled at Alexandra. 'Hi, I'm Carolyn.'

Alexandra smiled back and I noticed her eyes wandering to Steve's crotch. I started a slow burn.

'Make yourselves at home,' Steve said. 'We're going to dress. Answer the door if it rings.'

'He's terrific,' Alexandra whispered when he'd gone.

'Yes, I could see you liked him,' I replied drily, but it was lost on her.

I fixed her a vodka, all I could find. She made a face, but sipped it all the same. I couldn't see any food. Steve was the one that was cheap.

Soon the mob started to arrive. All the familiar faces. What a small town London really is. I spread the word I was off to New York to open a joint. Everyone was suitably impressed. Steve's parties were O.K. when they started, it was only after a couple of hours that they went to rack and ruin.

Alexandra seemed quite happy sitting with her vodka (third one, I aimed to get her smashed).

Steve said to me. 'Who's the pussy cat?'

Dirty bastard—I hadn't thought she would be his type. He was chatting her a bit and I was choked. I didn't leave her side, and then who should walk in but 'The Twang'.

'Ooh, Tony, is that your mother?' she asked in her loud nasal voice. I could have killed her. 'You're a lousy sonofabitch,' she said in a lower voice, 'I could take my choice, you know—I don't need you.'

Well, why didn't she leave me alone then?

I figured it was time to go. I didn't want Alexandra involved in the scene that was starting.

'Come on,' I said, 'the time has come to find food.'

'I feel awful,' she said, 'sort of buzzy.'

I got her up and she leaned on me. I realised she was loaded, my fault.

Janine said, 'Bye-bye, lover boy.' She really had a big mouth.

Outside the cold air hit Alexandra like a ton of bricks. She clung to my jacket and said, 'I feel sick.' Then she was sick, narrowly missing my jacket by inches. Then she started to cry and I felt like the world's worst shit.

'Please take me home,' she moaned.

So much for an evening of fun.

I got her in the car and she huddled miserably on her seat, 'I'm so embarrassed,' she said weakly. 'I've never done anything like that before.

'Don't worry about it,' I said, 'it happens to everybody. You just had a little bit over the odds, you'll soon feel better.'

'I'm so sorry.' She really was in a state.

'I'll tell you what, we'll go back to my place and I'll fix you some eggs and you can rest up a bit.'

She made a face, 'I couldn't eat, ugh! I just want to crawl into bed and hide.'

Didn't she realise that's just what I had in mind? 'Well, how about some coffee then, nice strong black coffee?'

She nodded and I headed the phallic E-type in the direction of my pad. I switched the car radio on, a touch of Aretha Franklin at her most soulful—very nice. Things were looking up.

We arrived and Alexandra said. 'Where are we?'

'My place, going to make you some nice hot coffee.'

'Oh, Tony, I'm being such a bother. I can make coffee, you don't have to go to all this trouble. Just drop me home, and I'll be off your hands.'

Was she very smart or genuinely an innocent?

I got out of the car and helped her out. 'It's no bother.'

She looked pale, but being sick had obviously done her good. We stood by the car.

'I'd rather go home,' she said, 'I'd feel much happier.'

'Don't be silly,' I was determined to get her to my flat, 'you'll feel better after some coffee.'

'No, really, Tony, I must go home.' She started to climb back into the car.

Well, I couldn't stand there arguing all night. Mummy had

79

probably warned her about going to big bad men's apartments, and Mummy was dead right. I got into the car too.

She smiled at me, 'You're being very kind.'

How could I resist those liquid brown eyes? I took her home, saw her to the front door. Shook her hand (her idea, not mine), kissed her on the cheek (my idea), said goodbye and promised to phone her as soon as I got back from New York.

'Super,' she said, and was inside her flat with the door closed in my face quick as a flash. Charming!

But she was a lovely little bird, and I could wait.

11

ALEXANDRA

Madelaine and I discussed it. I was forced to tell her how I felt about Michael, because I had to tell someone, and since she was his sister and my best friend perhaps she could help.

She roared with laughter when she heard. 'Soppy old Michael! You're joking, I hope.' But then she could see that I wasn't, and she got very serious and said. 'Alex, he's terrible with girls. He just wants them for one thing and then drops them.'

I didn't see how Maddy could know that. After all, she had been away at school with me for most of the year. Anyway if he wanted one thing he could have it.

We sat up late on Saturday night talking and Maddy came to the conclusion that the best thing to do was make him jealous. 'I think he quite likes you,' she said, 'only I don't think he looks on you as a potential girl-friend. After all, you've known each other since we were all kids together.'

'He still thinks I am a kid,' I said miserably, 'he said so.'

'We've just got to make him realise how gorgeous and desirable

80

you are.' Maddy's eyes were gleaming, she loved organising things. 'Tomorrow night, when Tony comes to fetch us—we'll get Michael to be here. and you'll sweep past him looking absolutely fantastic and sort of act very cold and off-hand with him.'

'How do I look absolutely fantastic? I haven't got anything to wear.'

We went through my wardrobe and the only thing remotely glamorous I possessed was a frilly terylene dressing-gown.

'You can wear that!' Maddy exclaimed. 'Put a belt around it and no one will know.'

I tried it on, and with shoes and a belt it really did look quite good. So I decided I would wear that and we finally got to bed at three a.m. I was exhausted.

Maddy phoned Michael the next morning. Actually it was about twelve o'clock as we both overslept.

'We're in frightful trouble,' she wailed, 'we've blown a fuse and I can't work the television, and the stopper's jammed in the bath.'

'Christ!' Michael complained. I was listening on the extension. 'All right, I'll come over when I get up.'

'We've got to pop out now. Do you think you could make it about seven?'

'Seven. Where the bloody hell are you going?'

'We have to go and see Alex's father. Is seven O.K., then?'

'Yes, I suppose so, but I can't take you for dinner if that's what you're getting at. I've got a date.'

'That's O.K.,' Maddy said sweetly, and hung up giggling. 'All fixed,' she declared. 'Now you've got to really devastate him.'

We spent the afternoon in preparation. I washed my hair and Maddy set it. I washed the dressing-gown and Maddy ironed it. It was fun having a flat of our own. We had bacon sandwiches for lunch, and pears and cream for tea washed down with heaps of Coca-Cola. What a thrill to be able to do anything you want!

When Michael arrived I was shut in the bedroom with my hair in rollers trying to do a proper makeup. My hand shook and I smudged the eyeliner, so I had to take it all off and start again.

Maddy was ready. She had promised to keep Michael busy until Tony arrived. I wasn't supposed to come out of the bedroom until

Tony got there, then I was supposed to just glide out and practically ignore Michael.

I was only just ready by eight. I heard the doorbell and counted a slow sixty as arranged (it felt like six thousand and sixty!). I then walked casually (my heart was beating so loud I was surprised no one mentioned it!) into the living room. Michael was sprawled in a chair.

'I can't come,' Madelaine wailed, 'Tony said he tried to get me invited too, but it's just not possible.'

'What a shame.' I didn't really want to go without Madelaine, especially now.

'Sorry, girls,' Tony said, 'just one of those things. Come on, we can't be late.'

I looked at Michael. Was he just going to let me walk out of here with a comparative stranger to a wild pop star's party and not say anything? Apparently he was.

'Goodbye,' I said.

Madelaine smiled half-heartedly, and Michael said, 'Don't forget to get his autograph!'

Tony had a very nice car. Actually he was being sweet to me. I wonder why he's bothering. Because of Daddy. I suppose. Lots of people are nice to me because of Daddy, him being so rich and everything. Mummy always says. 'Having money doesn't make you any better than the next person.' I think she's right.

Tony said, 'We'll go to the Hilton for a drink first.'

It was rather fun and I drank champagne.

Tony seemed awfully popular. He joked with the barman and kept on saying hello to people. He made me feel very comfortable and he was funny. I wished Michael could be as nice as him.

I suppose a lot of girls would consider him good-looking. He has lovely black curly hair, but he's really not my type, and I'm sure I'm not his!

'What time can we go to the party?' I asked.

The champagne had made me feel good and I was determined to forget about Michael and have a terrific time.

When we left, Tony held my hand and said that Daddy might not approve of his taking me out and would I please not tell him.

Well, that confused me. I mean I had thought that *was* the reason for his taking me out—to sort of get in Daddy's good books. 'All right,' I said.

Steve Scott's party was fantastic. We were the first ones there and he answered the front door practically naked. Then he and his girl-friend went off to dress and Tony gave me a drink, I don't know what it was but it tasted vile. I swallowed it down, anyway.

Tony stayed by my side most of the evening and I felt so sort of light-headed and witty. I felt I could talk to anyone, I even knew exactly what I would say to Michael if he was there.

Steve Scott was wonderful. Once, when Tony was fetching me another drink, he sat on the arm of my chair and said, 'I bet you've never had it.'

'Had what?' I replied.

'Oh baby,' he laughed, 'I could show you a thing or two. You and I could really fly.'

Then Tony came back, and Steve said. 'Who's the pussy cat?'

Tony said, 'Hands off, lover boy.'

Then Tony's girl-friend appeared and started yelling at him, and I drank some more of my drink, it was about my fifth, and Steve said, 'What's your phone number, sweetheart? Little girls like you are far too rare.'

So I gave him my phone number, and Tony came back and said we should go. Just when the party was getting to be fun. I couldn't wait to tell Madelaine that Steve Scott had asked for my number!

As soon as I stood up I felt horribly sick.

Tony put his arm around me and helped me outside, and then—talk about being embarrassed—I *was* sick and could have died! Why didn't the pavement just open up and swallow me!

'Please take me home,' I begged, hardly daring to look at him.

He kept on talking about going for coffee and food. Ugh! I couldn't face food. Really I couldn't face anything, I just wanted to get home and into bed.

He drove somewhere and stopped the car.

'Where are we?' I asked.

'My place, I'm going to make you some nice hot coffee.'

He got me out of the car and I got back in and insisted it was too much trouble and I *had* to go home.

He was very nice about it. I don't expect he really wanted to be bothered making me coffee anyway. After all, he was off on a trip to America the next day and probably had to get up early.

Oh, the relief of saying goodnight to Tony, dashing into our flat, and throwing up again.

He was probably glad to be rid of me, anyway.

12

FONTAINE

The thought of struggling along some crowded freeway with a talkative chauffeur is an utter bore.

I did want to see Tony, and although I hadn't planned to go to the airport, I suddenly decided it might be fun. So I cancelled lunch with friends, managed to sit through the boring drive to Kennedy International, and here comes Tony now. I can see him through the glass standing in line for Customs. He has a cheap suitcase—nothing worse, a give-away immediately. I must take him into Gucci.

He does look attractive, rather white in the daylight, he has an eerie night-club pallor which makes an exciting contrast to his jet black hair. What a shame he's not a bit more intelligent, though if he was he wouldn't be wasting his life in a discothèque.

Poor Tony. Poor stud. What will happen to him when his hard body and curly hair are gone? Who will want him then?

At last he's through Customs and hurrying towards me smiling. He's not subtle, I can see he's going to kiss me, so I fend him off with a handshake—stupid boy, there are always photographers lurking.

'How was your trip?'

'Great,' he yawned, exhibiting his tonsils to America. 'Saw a movie, boozed a bit, what's this all about anyway?'

I shrugged, 'Just an idea of mine.' It was best not to tell him I wanted to see him, it would go to his head and he would become impossible.

'Have you got a location or what?'

'Oh no, we're not that advanced, I thought I would hear your opinions and see what you think. We can visit all the competition and you can decide if it would be a good idea.'

He laughed, he had good strong white teeth, 'You mean all the panic was just for me to look around?'

'Yes, actually it was, I thought you would be thrilled to see New York.'

'Yeah—but did I have to leave like a shot out of a gun?'

'Really Tony, I'm surprised at you, you wanted to come while I was still here, didn't you?'

We were in the car by this time and I told the chauffeur to go to my apartment. Alice had arranged a room for Tony at a hotel, but he could damn well accommodate me before going there.

I laid my hand lightly over his, 'How's "Hobo"? Have any of my friends been in?'

Tony shook his head. He didn't look as delighted with this trip as I had thought he would be. He was probably tired from the journey.

'What about Vanessa and Leonard?'

'Haven't seen them.'

'Not even her?'

He looked at me, guilty as hell, probably been screwing the life out of her.

Oh well, *I* had him now.

I certainly wasn't going to force the conversation, let him be uncommunicative and sulky.

I leaned back in the car and closed my eyes. Tony Blake should be kissing my feet. I found him. If it wasn't for me he'd still be a waiter, bowing and scraping all over the place, full of phoney smiles and running for a tip. The trouble with people is that they never appreciate what you do for them. Tony probably thought he would still have been successful without me.

I mean, *really*, 'Hobo' was *my* idea. I could have taken any one of hundreds of good-looking studs, and each one of them would have been as popular as Tony.

'This is wild!'

Oh goody, the great oaf was finally talking. We were entering the city and he was window gazing at the tall buildings, rushing people and general din. Big dirty New York, the city of fairy tales and garbage cans, society balls and riots. You can get anything or do anything here, as long as you have the money of course.

'I thought I'd take you to my apartment first, and then the chauffeur will take you to your hotel. I've got all sorts of exciting things planned for tonight.'

'Great,' his voice lacked enthusiasm. Tony was definitely not himself.

Benjamin had done rather well for me in the Big City. I suppose you could say I have one of the best apartments in town. Of course Tony's eyes fell out as soon as he saw it. It's one of my favourite homes, small—only three bedrooms—but with this marvellous four-sided terrace which goes all around, alive with rose bushes, winter flowers, and an adorable lemon tree. Very pretty. Adamo—our Vietnamese man, takes care of it. He bowed us in and produced martinis.

'Lunch is laid out in the blue room, Madam,' he spoke like an English butler, perfect. All my friends were trying to steal him, but he liked working for Benjamin and me, after all, we are hardly ever here.

'Fine Adamo, you may go, I'll buzz if I need you.'

'Very good, Madam.'

He lived in the basement of the building, very convenient, easy to summon and easy to get rid of.

Tony was prowling around. 'This is fabulous,' he said, 'I've never seen anything like it, this view is the end.'

'How about this view?' I unbuttoned my dress.

One thing I'll say for Tony—he knows his part—and tired or not, he'll play.

We embraced very slowly and then he pushed me to the floor and took off the rest of my clothes.

'Welcome to New York,' I whispered.

He *was* a stud.

13

TONY

I don't think I've ever met a girl like Alexandra before. She's so sort of innocent and girlish and pretty and soft. She looks great. Clean and tidy and young, I really like her, I really do. Even the thought of New York doesn't turn me on too much and Fontaine doesn't turn me on at all any more. In view of the close relationship involved I'd be much better off to avoid Fontaine completely. (Impossible) My only chance is to get away from 'Hobo' and open up on my own. But there's that old problem—money.

I fancy the hostess wriggling up and down the aisle in a tight skirt. I bet she's got something waiting for *her* in New York. Sammy says he's made it on a plane, on a night trip to the South of France. According to him, he had it off with the hostess in the loo—bit crowded I bet.

'Can I get you anything?' She smiled at me, ignoring the old lady in the seat beside me.

'Yeah—but I don't think it's on the menu.'

She giggled, getting the message immediately. These air-hostesses weren't slow.

'Do you wish to see the movie?' She smoothed down her tight skirt.

'Any other suggestions?'

Another giggle. 'Well, some of the passengers come and sit at the back if they have already seen the film.'

There's no doubt about it, I'm irresistible to women! 'I'll come and sit at the back then.'

'Good.' Another smile, and then wiping it off, she leaned across to the old lady and said briskly, 'If you care to see the film there will be a slight charge!' I got a whiff of perfume—cheap but sexy.

We had only been in the air an hour, but I reckoned I was going to be all right.

After a decent interval of three minutes I followed Miss Tight Skirt to the back of the plane. She was busy with another girl getting tin foil trays of cold roast beef, congealed potato salad and hard-boiled eggs that had seen better days.

'Need any help?' I asked, trying to squeeze into the tiny kitchen.

'Sorry, you're not allowed in here.' She smiled to take away the sting. 'You can sit in any of the back row seats if you like. I'll be free when the movie starts.'

The other girl grinned at me too, she had a suntan and freckles. It looks like being a jolly afternoon.

I sat down near the window, viewed the grey expanse of sky and sea, and fell asleep.

I was woken up by Miss Tight Skirt sitting beside me. I kept on thinking of Sammy's experience. 'Ever done a night flight to Nice?' I asked casually.

'Why yes, as a matter of fact I used to be on that run.'

Oh no, it couldn't be true!

The movie was on and the plane was pretty dark. We were sitting on the inside two seats of a three-seater, and there was no one across the aisle.

'What's happening?' I asked.

'Anything you like,' she replied.

I mean, it had to be the same girl.

I thought of Alexandra so sweet and innocent. I guess I wouldn't be being unfaithful, because nothing had happened with her—yet. I put a hand on the hostess's knee.

'Oh come on,' she said, 'you can do better than that.' She pulled a big regulation rug across us. 'Shirley will warn us if anyone comes back to go to the loo.'

What a scene! Under the rug I fought my hand up the tight skirt. She wriggled down in the seat helping me. She had nothing on underneath, making things very easy she was! I unhooked her bra under her prim blouse, her breasts were small but nice, I wished I could see them but there we were all huddled up under the rug.

She unzipped my trousers and with a deft movement twisted herself towards me, and then I was up up and away!

'What about the pilot and stewards?' I asked. She was wriggling and squirming at a good pace.

'It's all right, they're all boozing up front,' she gasped.

Charming, the pilots were boozing up front, and the hostess was screwing at the back. I wouldn't travel on *this* airline again!

'Quick, someone's coming,' a whispered voice said. It was Shirley, and how right she was!

Oh boy—fun at twenty-six thousand feet, I was hardly finished when Tight Skirt pulled out and all in one movement was standing, smoothing her skirt down, and smiling at the passenger who was on his way to the loo.

'Everything all right, sir?'

He nodded. 'Er, I'd like a whisky and soda, is that possible?'

She winked at me, destroyed under the blanket. 'Everything's possible on this airline, sir.'

She deftly hooked her bra as he carried on to the john. 'I don't know your name,' she said to me, 'but I hope you'll fly with us again.'

I went back to my seat, there seemed no point in hanging around.

The old lady smiled and nodded to me. 'Lovely trip,' she said.

'It certainly was!'

'I beg your pardon?'

'Nothing.' I slouched down in my seat and watched the end of a silent Doris Day movie. A silent Doris Day is better than a talkative one. Man, I was tired, I fell off to sleep until Tight Skirt appeared pushing my shoulder and saying, 'Fasten your seat belt, please, we're coming in to land.'

She had freshened up and added a jacket and matching cap. Very smart and efficient.

I yawned and inspected the view. New York was spread out beneath me. What a sight! I wondered what Alexandra was doing now. Poor little chick getting sick like that. I scribbled her a fast postcard conveniently supplied along with a paper bag to throw up in.

'Dear A. Dull flight. Had any good vodka lately? See you soon—Tony.'

On the way out I handed it to Tight Skirt to post.

'What are you doing tonight?' I asked, more for conversation than anything else.

She gave me a wide grin, 'Going on the town with my fiancé, he's the pilot you know.'

Charming!

I went through Immigration and Customs. An emergency visa had been waiting for me at London airport, along with a vaccination. Money can buy anything.

Fontaine was there to meet me, wrapped in mink, shod in crocodile I was surprised, I didn't think airports were her scene. I forced a smile and set off in her direction. Everyone was taking a second look, she was that kind of woman.

She wanted me to kiss her, she offered that elegant chiselled face, but I wasn't going to fall for that with everybody looking our way. Benjamin could be having her followed or anything and I wasn't going to be the patsy. We shook hands and chatted about the journey. I was dying to find out what this trip was all about, but she was giving nothing away.

We rode in silent luxury to her apartment. She kept on questioning me about who had been in, but that was all.

What a great apartment! Huge and very modern on the top floor of the tallest building I've ever seen, surrounded by a wild garden with a not-to-be believed oriental butler dressed in flowing robes with an English accent. Too much!

It was the usual scene. Servant bowing and scraping, serving drinks and then vanishing. This one backed out of the apartment with such an inane grin on his face that I thought he would trip over his robe.

It was the same old Fontaine. He had hardly closed the front door when she was stripping off her clothes and making a grab for me.

'On the floor,' she whispered.

Oh no, after last night, and the trip, and her relationship to Alexandra, I didn't know if I could make it. But strength will tell, and I managed to do my best. I felt like a heel but what could I do? Alexandra wouldn't forgive me for this, but what *could* I do?

My mind was going in sixteen different directions, all the opposite way from the lady under me. *That awful woman* as Alex described her. And she *was* an awful woman. She had dazzled me at first with all her glamour and fame, but now I saw right through her. A social nymphomaniac, that's what she was.

'You're out of practice, Tony,' her voice was cold and edgy. I finished before she was ready, and she was choked. Little did she know she was lucky to get anything at all, what with the scene on the plane.

'Yeah, well what do you expect with you away and everything?'

'Oh, please, Tony, let's not play the innocent virgin with each other.' She shifted about on the floor, 'Finish the job for God's sake.'

I obliged.

This really is a wild city. Great hotel, fantastic T.V. in the room with lots of channels. Since the chauffeur brought me here two hours ago I've changed stations ten times. Take your choice—quiz show, old English movie, cowboys and Indians. It's all too much! And about room service, great! Club sandwiches I've only dreamed about. I've ordered three times already.

This is the life. I lay on a king-sized bed after a shower watching a blonde chick in a plastic raincoat announce the weather on T.V. Fontaine was picking me up at seven, I had an hour yet.

I wanted to phone A. But Benjamin would be paying the bill and I didn't want him checking through and finding phone calls to his daughter.

I tell you married women disgust me, they're all out for a piece of action away from their husbands. There's hardly one married woman I know that I couldn't truthfully say I could have if I

91

wanted. It makes a man think twice about getting married.

What was I thinking about marriage for anyway? It's not for me, not after all the things I've seen. If I ever did get married it would be to Alexandra. My lovely lovely Alexandra. And she had no money, so where would that be going?

Not that I minded about her having no money—I mean I did think it was a bit strong on Benjamin's part—but I had no money either, so I couldn't even think about getting married. Alexandra Blake. Hmm—not too lyrical but nice, very nice. I imagined Sadie and Sam's faces if I married a girl that wasn't—'a nice Jewish girl'. They would go mad, but so what, I was a big boy now.

The time had come to get dressed. Fontaine had plans for the evening's entertainment—she had reeled off a list of things we were going to do that made me dizzy. We were to start off with a cocktail party, and then go to some friends apartment, and then to dinner, and then a round of discothèques, and then there were a couple of other parties we might attend.

I chose my suit carefully, this would be the first time I had been out with Fontaine socially. I guess under normal circumstances I would be flattered, but things were different now, it all seemed a bit of a drag. It had been quite a day.

I decided on a pale lilac shirt from Turnbull and Asser, hand-made, of course. Actually it had been made for Hal, but he didn't like the colour, so I bought it from him. We took the same size in shirts which was useful. He had some great gear which he got fed up with in a hurry—then I would buy it from him at half the original price. He made bread that way 'cos some old dear had probably bought it for him in the first place. Good old Hal. The last of the great promoters!

To go with the shirt I had a toning polka dot tie. The suit was black, with it I wore pearl cuff-links and tie clip, black socks and shoes. Even though I say it myself, I look pretty damn good.

The desk rang to tell me a car was waiting.

Great—New York City, here I come!

14

FONTAINE

After Tony left and the chauffeur returned I went for my massage.
Bliss. Hot sweaty hands pounding and pummelling my white skin.
Then a delicious steam bath, followed by a soft massage with oil of
pine, its odours sinking into my body.

Oh, what luxury, almost as good as sex. Wrapped in pink
towelling I had my hair washed, then lay on a floating pink couch
while it was dried by concealed jets of air.

This is 'M'lady's Parlour', the very latest beauty house, and I
must say, very impressive.

Sarah dragged me here immediately I arrived. 'It's so divine,
darling, you'll come eighteen times.'

It's beauty in an aphrodisiac atmosphere. All the boys here are
queens, it's like a harem with eunuchs preparing you for the
night's fantasy.

Roger did my hair, small petite Roger with a mass of golden
curls and pursed bitchy lips. 'Darling, do you believe what
Clarissa wore to the premiere last night? She looked like a baby
yellow elephant! Ridiculous! My friend says her dress was a Rudi
Genreich, but I can't believe that Rudi would be so wicked!'

I smiled. The good thing about Roger was the fact that one
could relax and listen to all the gossip. His bitcheries could go on
for ever.

He continued, 'Saw a dreadful movie last night, I couldn't
believe the clothes though, terribly now. You'd look divine in
white satin with lots of fox fur. I think I'm going to do your hair
Grecian. Strand it with pearls and things.'

I felt so good from the massage, my body tingled. Oh God, if all
these little twits could see Tony they'd cream themselves!

He was getting a rather attractive quality of self-confidence.
With me he had always been so fawning and adoring. Now he
seemed to treat me in a slightly cooler fashion. Although of course
he was still a boy scout when it came to material things. Why the

way his mouth had popped open when he saw my apartment! The stud prowling around and sniffing the luxury!

Of course, I know eventually he will begin to flap his wings, but I'm sure this trip will cool him down and make him realise exactly who he's mixing with. After all there aren't many women like me around, and however many little affaires he has to indulge in, he'll soon find that out.

Roger did wonders with my hair, only two pieces and it looks marvellous.

'Have a lovely time,' he said, stepping back to admire his work.

I went home and phoned Sarah, we were all to dine together. I hadn't told her about Tony, I had just said a business associate of Benjamin's was joining us. I couldn't wait to see her face!

'What are you wearing?' she asked.

'I haven't decided yet,' I replied, although I was going to wear the black silk backless Cardin.

'Neither have I.' What a liar she was.

'We'll see you about eight, going to pop into the Carlton's party first.'

'What a bore. They're so show business, Allen can't stand them.'

Actually I knew that Sarah and Allen hadn't been invited, as Salamanda Smith, a Hollywood film star, and Allen had been a very hot item indeed the previous summer, and Peter Carlton, whom she had since married, was terribly jealous. Oh, the intricacies of the social set!

'Are the Bells and Sidwells meeting at your place too?'

'Yes, everything's arranged,' Sarah lowered her voice, 'I had a wonderful afternoon. Have you ever tried yoga?'

I didn't want to get involved in one of Sarah's sexual discussions, they always began with a lowered voice.

'Yes, darling, often. See you later.' I hung up.

Tony looked refreshed. He also looked flashy and a bit cheap, but I was prepared to forgive him that. It was the terrible tie he had on that did it, change that and he wouldn't look too bad. I slid the glass down between me and the chauffeur and said, 'Stop at

Saks.' They were still open. I smiled at Tony and said, 'Let's pop in a minute, I want to get you a little something.'

Everyone stared at us. Well, Roger had gone a bit avant garde with my hair, divine for evening but not quite suitable for a flit through Saks. People who say that nobody stares at you in New York are mad. They stare more than anywhere else. Blue-haired mink-stoled ladies with beaded handbags and plastic rhinestone studded shoes are the first to say, 'Oh ma Gawd, lookit her!'

In the men's department I picked out six divine imported ties and made Tony put one on. 'We'll come here tomorrow and do some more shopping.'

The salesman goggled at me and gave Tony the package.

'Didn't you like my tie?' He was surly.

'It was lovely, I just like this one better.' Oh God, don't tell me he was going to sulk. He should be delighted with six new thirty-dollar ties.

The party was a shambles, so many people. Salamanda, floaty in pink chiffon. Tony was impressed. He still got awed by meeting film stars.

She gushed over to us, 'Gee, so great of you to come, Mrs Khaled,' she held the smile for the hovering photographer.

What a dull pretty little face she had, not a bone worth anything in the whole structure. Her puffy eyes surrounded in caked mascara were studying my diamonds.

'Tony Blake, our hostess, Mrs Peter Carlton,' I said.

He beamed, 'I loved your last film,' he said almost stuttering. 'How did you manage so long in the desert?'

Oh God, save me from the film fan!

She blinked, 'Gee, it was O.K. Petey came down on the weekends.'

'All that way?'

'We made it just outside of Vegas—hey,' she started to laugh, 'wacha think, we, made it in the Sahara or somethin'? They wouldn't get lil ole me there, honey.'

I really think Tony is a cretinous bore. I can't imagine why I wanted him here. I left the two of them and looked around. The same old faces, oh God, sometimes *everything* is so boring.

95

15

TONY

Fontaine is the biggest put-down merchant of all time. Here I am, looking great, feeling great, ready to go, and she gives me one of those tight little smiles of hers and says, 'Tony, darling, we'll simply have to stop and get you a decent tie. You just can't go out like that.' I mean screw her, sitting there with her hair looking like a Carnival Queen. Who does she think she is? She doesn't own me, and pretty soon she's going to find that out.

She dragged me into some store and lumbered me with six of the dreariest ties you could imagine. Imported yet, probably couldn't find a buyer for them in their own country.

I put on the best of the bunch, to keep her happy, and silently fumed. Fontaine was a cow. An old cow. I contemplated telling her to take a running jump, but I had no money to pay the hotel and I'm sure if I did that, no job to return to in good old Blighty.

Fontaine Khaled had me by the short and curlies, and what was worse she bloody well knew it.

We arrived at the party, it was pretty jammed, but everyone turned to take a look at us. Fontaine hadn't bothered to tell me whose party it was, but I soon got the message when Salamanda Smith, *the* Salamanda Smith, came wafting over.

She was a gorgeous bird, curvy and blonde with a pair of bristols that fair knocked your eyes out. I'd just seen her in a wild desert movie, full of sex and sand type thing. She was bowled over by Fontaine, but I could see she had an eye (baby blue) for me, and we got to chatting about her last movie.

She had to go to greet some more people and Fontaine had done a vanish, so there I was on my todd. I scouted around and got hold of a scotch from a white-coated guy who called me 'bud' and was really loaded. Was he a waiter? The way he was acting I wasn't quite sure. But he picked up a tray, belched, and set off in the direction of some guests, so I guessed he was.

He weaved into a fake marble column, and it swayed, but stood its ground, then he staggered with his tray over to some people and hands stretched out like vultures, relieving him of the glasses. He came rolling back in my direction—'S'elluva party,' he mumbled, 'lotsa cooze.' Then he was off again towards Salamanda, and dropping his tray with a loud crash, he grabbed hold of her with one hand, and with the other unzipped his fly and said, 'Get a load of this, honey!'

There was a short silence while she struggled to free herself. Then three guys jumped on the waiter and he disappeared beneath a torrent of blows.

It was a funny scene really. Salamanda took a deep breath, smiled, and the waiter was dragged, blood dripping from his face, out of the room. Great! I counted ten knowing that Fontaine would appear at my side, anxious to hear all.

Fontaine—the last of the great gossips. She was there on the stroke of nine. 'What happened?' her silver-lidded eyes glistened anxiously.

'Just some drunk waiter, nothing exciting.'

'Oh,' she was disappointed, 'is that all?'

Salamanda was now retelling the story to a small group surrounding her, and Fontaine went over. I trailed behind. She was just saying, 'and there was his enormous *thing*! Just staring me in the face!'

Fontaine shot me a dirty look, I'd left out the best bits.

I wished I could phone Alexandra. I looked around for a phone, nobody would notice me making a quick call to London with this group. I strolled out of the door, looked about and found an empty bedroom with a shiny gold bedside model. I grabbed it quick. 'Overseas please—London England—a personal call to Miss Alexandra Khaled—8934434. No, I'll hang on.'

A beautiful girl came into the room, long straight black hair, long straight black body. She looked directly at me, 'You going to Marcellos after?'

'Who's Marcello?'

Her eyes were stony, unsmiling. 'You putting me on?'

'Nope.' I shook my head and winked. 'Who is he? I'm a stranger here.'

97

'Ah God almighty,' she smoothed down her long black hair. 'Marcellos is a restaurant, man, everyone seems to be going there, I'm looking for someone to take me. You interested?'

I was interested all right, but unavailable. 'I'm with someone. How about another night?'

Her eyes swept over me. 'Yeah, maybe.'

Just then the operator said, 'I'm putting you through now, your party's on the line.'

Then Alexandra's voice, clear and sweet, 'Hello?'

The girl was combing her hair at a mirror.

'Hello, baby, and how are you today?'

'Oh, Tony, how super of you to phone me all the way from America. I'm much better, thank you. I feel such an idiot about last night.'

A warm glow came over me, 'Don't give it another thought. It was my fault for taking you to a lousy party like that. What are you doing?'

'I'm in bed actually.'

I imagined her with brushed shining hair and a fluffy pink nightdress. 'That's the best place to be.' I glanced over at the girl, she was hanging around. I covered the mouthpiece of the phone, 'Write down your number,' I hissed at her. I said back into the phone, 'I miss you.'

I did miss her. The girl wrote Norma and a number on some book matches and threw them at me, then she went out.

There was silence from Alexandra. 'I said I miss you.'

'I know,' her voice was a whisper.

'Well?'

'Well, what?'

'Do you miss me?'

'I don't know. I mean, you've only been gone a day, and after all we don't know each other very well.' She paused. 'Yes, I do miss you.'

My heart did a little skip, 'I'm going to be back soon, then we'll get to know each other really well. Be a good girl.'

'Yes.' She had such a lovely accent.

'See you soon.' I hung up. It was good to be alive. I peered at myself in the mirror. I looked good but wished I had a suntan. Maybe Fontaine would fancy a few days in Florida.

I went back to the party and found Fontaine. She was holding court, her clipped British tones ringing round the room. When she paused for air, she noticed me. 'Oh there you are, we've got to be going.' She wasn't as friendly towards me as she had been. You never know with Fontaine, she blows hot and cold. Maybe she didn't like having me out with her, maybe she thought I wasn't good enough. All right for a fuck, but not for her friends. I scowled. She glared. We left.

In the car she said testily, 'You know, Tony, you shouldn't act so star-struck. I would have thought that by now you would have been used to meeting celebrities.'

Me—star-struck! I was choked! That was the *last* thing *I* was.

She tapped talon-like nails on her small gold (real, of course) handbag and added, 'You made a fool of yourself with Salamanda. You acted like a film fan. Don't you realise five years ago she was a stripper, and you—anyone—could have had her for ten dollars.'

I've learnt one lesson in life. Never argue with a woman when she's putting down another woman.

'Yeah, you're right,' I conceded. Who needed an argument?

She softened a bit. 'Just don't forget—you'll probably meet many big stars while you're here. Don't mention their work or anything about it, socially that's just not on.'

Silly cow! I yawned. 'I'd love to go to Florida.'

She ignored me.

We arrived at a big apartment house, and the doorman nearly broke his neck getting her ladyship out of the car.

'These are my dearest friends in New York,' Fontaine said, 'Sarah and Allen Grant, a wonderful couple. Don't embarrass me.'

I mean, what did she think I was going to do—pee on the carpet or something?

We went into a fantastic pad on the ground floor. Big dark, crammed with antiques, stuffed animals and tall plants. Very nice. What a scene you could have here!

This lady came to greet us, bony face, pulled back black hair and whiter than white skin. She looked like she was suffering from a touch of malnutrition. She and Fontaine kissed, summing each other's outfits up with their eyes. Then Fontaine said, 'Sarah, I want you to meet Tony, Benjamin sent him over.'

Man, she made me sound like a package! Sarah looked me over. She had wild black eyes that burned right through you. Her lips were thin and painted dark red. I guessed she must be about forty. If you like skeleton thin older chicks she was a knockout. Personally I don't. Her glance jumped between me and Fontaine, and she smiled slightly. 'Well, what a surprise.'

Fontaine smiled too, 'Yes,' she said, and they linked arms and walked over to the bar, leaving me standing there like a right berk.

There were four or five other people sitting about, and a guy got up and came over to me. He had what women's magazines would call a craggy handsome face. He wore a shapeless grey suit, 'Allen Grant,' he said, shaking hands and giving me an amused squint.

'Tony Blake.'

'Come and have a drink.' He took me over to the bar and fixed me a very large scotch on the rocks. He fixed himself an even bigger one and disposed of it in three hefty gulps. Then he made himself another and said, 'Who are you?'

Charming! I mean I love questions like that from a complete stranger. What do you say? The Pope—Gunga Din—'I'm over here for Ben Khaled, looking for—er—properties.'

'Oh. Are you having an affair with the lovely Mrs K. then?'

I mean was I supposed to hit him or what? Fortunately Fontaine came over. 'Allen, you naughty boy, what are you saying?'

She was flirting, a pose of hers that drove me mad.

He laughed. 'Nothing. How are you my sweet?'

'I'm fine.' Their eyes met in the sort of intimacy usually reserved for lovers. They probably were, that would just about be Fontaine's scene, knocking off her best friend's husband. I didn't care. My little Alexandra was tucked up at home in bed, and that's all I cared about.

Sarah took my arm, 'Come, Tony, I want you to meet the others.'

100

I racked my brain to find out where I'd seen her before. I pride myself on never forgetting a face, and I knew I'd seen this one somewhere. She hadn't been in the club, that I was sure of. She was certainly very striking, although as I said before, not my type at all. Her hand was brittle on my arm, skeleton fingers digging in. Suddenly it struck me where I knew her from. American Vogue three months ago, a big layout of her in Bermuda or somewhere modelling beach exotica. I told you I have a great memory. Sarah Grant—society bigwig—New York City.

'Fontaine never told me about you,' she said in a deep husky voice, 'you're divine.'

Instant lay, better watch out, didn't want to upset her ladyship.

I was then introduced to the others, your average rich couples—neither of the women could hold a candle to Fontaine or Sarah, and the men were balding and moved in a cloud of cigar smoke.

After some boring small talk we left, a convoy of chauffeured cars.

First stop was dinner, an exclusive restaurant off Fifth Avenue, with hothouse plants growing wild, and gold-jacketed waiters. I sat between Fontaine and Sarah, fighting a losing battle to taste my food against the fumes of their respective perfumes.

They both ignored me, making polite small talk around the rest of the table. I couldn't join in as I didn't know who or what they were talking about. I mean are you ready for 'Fleur met Itsy in St Moritz and they had a terrible fight and he ended up with Poopsie at Mooeys.' Allen was the only one who spoke to me. I had a feeling he was as bored as I was.

So this was New York—social circuit number one. You can have it and stick it. I wished I was with Norma at 'Marcellos', wherever that might be.

Dinner dragged on and on and I was getting a bad case of yawning. At last Fontaine said, 'I think we'd better get Tony to "Picketts" before he falls asleep on us.' She shot me a dark look to let me know she was furious about my yawning all night.

'Picketts' was the newest disco to open and make it big. I had heard about it, but all the same it was a shock. The whole interior of the club was like a huge monster's open mouth. Fangs and cobwebs hung from everywhere, and in a transparent tooth hanging like a light fixture from the ceiling, a near-naked female freaked out to the blaring sounds of James Brown. There was an assortment of waitresses dressed in flimsy bits of cobwebs, and lots of glimpses of a tit here, an ass there. Pretty wild, but not what I'd call a cool scene. I mean who needs gimmicks? The customers are supposed to make the fun.

Fontaine made her usual grand entrance, the guy running the joint nearly kissed her feet. He was small, dark and nervous looking. No competition there.

We were sat round a table shaped like a huge withered hand, and a little teeny bopper, happy in her cobweb gear, took our order. Champagne all round and a scotch for me.

'Why fight it,' Allen murmured. 'Why not get used to her habits?'

'I only drink scotch,' I answered.

'Come on, Allen sweetie, let's show 'em.' Fontaine was getting frisky as she dragged Allen off to dance.

'Shall we?' Sarah asked with arched eyebrows, already getting up without waiting for my reply.

I followed her to the dance floor. She was even more embarrassing stiff-assed than Fontaine.

What the hell was I doing here? Six months before I would have given anything to be involved in this scene with these people, in fact I wouldn't have believed it was possible. But now—well, who needed it? I had everything going for me in London, I didn't need this trailing behind Fontaine bag.

We stayed at 'Picketts' an hour, and then on to 'The Flower Mission', a wild mass of psychedelic symbols and freak-out light effects.

By this time the other two couples had dropped out and it was just Fontaine, Sarah, Allen and me against the world. We were all well smashed.

'Have you ever studied yoga?' Sarah asked me, black eyes piercing and probing.

'Er—no.'

102

'You should. You have a powerful body. I'm sure you would excel at it.'

'Tony,' Fontaine said excitedly, 'Allen's met a man here who can get us some cigarettes,' her voice lowered on the word cigarettes and I knew with a sinking feeling she meant pot. That's all I needed, one of her 'aren't we being wicked' pot-smoking scenes. I just don't dig it, it doesn't do a thing for me except make me go to sleep, and from the way Fontaine is carrying on, me going to sleep is not what she has in mind.

'We'll go to Sarah and Allen's, shall we?' Not so much a question, more a statement.

So we left and chauffeured all the way to the Grant pad.

Once there the two women disappeared and Allen made a beeline for the bar. He wasn't talking, just knocking back a large glass of brandy and looking hollow-eyed.

'What's the action?' I asked helping myself to a drink as he didn't seem to be offering.

'God knows,' he said. 'You're lucky, at least you're not married to yours.'

What did *that* mean?

I glanced at my watch, it was three a.m. I was bushed. I tried to calculate what time it was in London. Five hours difference but I couldn't remember which way.

Sarah came back in first. She had changed into a full-length brocade caftan, and her jet-black hair was combed straight down. She looked vaguely Indian.

Fontaine followed, her hair was still piled high on her head, but she had changed into a long white floating thing, slightly transparent, and I could see the outline of her small naked breasts.

'Allen,' Sarah said, 'why don't you and Tony put on these?' She handed us each a black silk sort of short Japanese kimono.

'Come on,' Allen said resignedly.

I followed him into another room, and he stripped off his clothes and put on the black kimono.

He smiled grimly, 'I know why I'm doing this, how about you?'

I felt well choked about the whole thing, but what the hell, in a way it was rather exciting.

103

I put on the kimono, the silk felt great. I wished it wasn't so short, it just about covered my balls!

We went back inside. Fontaine and Sarah were smoking already, taking long thin-lipped drags. I went to sit beside Fontaine but she motioned me over to Sarah. Oh boy—if the regulars could see me now!

There was some weird Japanese music playing, and Sarah offered me her cigarette. I took a drag. We were sitting on a sofa, and opposite on another sofa were Fontaine and Allen.

I handed the cigarette back to Sarah. She puffed and leaned back blowing little smoke rings to the ceiling.

My turn, this wasn't too bad, I felt a certain numbness creep over me and the music sounded fantastic. I put the cigarette back in her mouth, and she leaned over and put her hands under the kimono. Her fingers felt like burning tongs as they fled around my flesh.

I glanced over at Fontaine. She was lying against the cushions and Allen was peeling the white thing off her. I watched fascinated as her body came into view and he started to kiss her. Her legs were spread and she moaned softly.

Meanwhile Sarah's hands manipulated me. She took off my kimono, and man, I felt great! Then I started to fly and I was pounding into someone and when I looked it was Fontaine and then Sarah and then both of them were all over me. It was a kaleidoscope of faces and, man, for the first time I was really stoned.

16

ALEXANDRA

My first day at McLaughton & Co. was awful. To start off with I was late, unforgivable on one's first day; secondly, I felt dreadful, with what I supposed was my first hangover; and thirdly, according to Madelaine all Michael had said about me the previous evening was, 'What a ridiculous dress'.

I wasn't sure that I liked working. It was awfully dull just sitting at a desk typing. Perhaps I should have let Daddy help me to get an interesting job. I couldn't wait for five o'clock when I could rush home and have a proper chat with Maddy.

Fortunately five o'clock finally came and I took a taxi home. Maddy was lolling about reading magazines, the lucky thing didn't start her job until next week.

'What was it like?' she asked. 'Have you got a super boss who looks at your legs when you take dictation?'

'No, I've got a grumpy old man who doesn't even know what legs are!'

We both laughed. 'What's for dinner?' We had planned to take it in turns to organise meals, and today was Maddy's turn. It was fun actually as we could try out all the recipes we had learnt at school.

'Roast beef and Yorkshire pud, and to start, puréed Avocado pear, and to finish, crème caramel, and we've overspent on our budget and Michael and Jonathan are coming to dinner. I thought you'd be pleased.'

'Oh great! How did you fix that?'

'Easy. I just asked them. My brother's not one to turn down a free meal.'

I was delighted. 'What can I wear?' I wailed. Clothes in London were a great problem. I *had* to go shopping.

'Slacks and a tight sweater. Let him see your bosom, maybe *that* will attract him.'

I suppose my bosom *was* one of my best features.

I didn't have any tight sweaters, so I borrowed one of Maddy's. It *did* look good.

'Wow!' Maddy said. 'Are you wearing a bra?'

'Of course.'

'Take it off. Men find it more exciting if you're not.'

'I can't do that.'

'You want to get him in your evil clutches, don't you?'

I went back in the bedroom, took off my bra. and slipped the sweater back on. You could tell I wasn't wearing one, they bobbed a little when I walked.

Maddy prepared a really gorgeous dinner. Michael and Jonathan devoured every mouthful of the food, then watched T.V.

Michael said, 'How was the party last night?'

'It was very nice, but I got s—'

Before I could finish Maddy blurted out, 'She's got a date with Steve Scott. He's mad about her.'

I blushed. How could she tell such awful lies?

'You really are seeing London,' Michael said grimly, 'moving with the in crowd already. I bet your mother won't be too pleased with the company you're keeping.'

He was insufferable! They watched a bit more television and then left. I decided I hated him.

Madelaine giggled as soon as they were gone. 'It's working,' she said, 'I think he's jealous.'

'He's not, he's *so* sarcastic to me.'

'That's good. At least he's *aware* of you now, you're not a little kid he's known for ages any more. And he couldn't take his eyes off your sweater. You see, he'll ask you out.'

'Yes, I bet.'

We cleared up the mess—one bad thing about not living at home, the washing up! I was really exhausted. What with the hangover, the first day at work, and the dinner. I had a bath, brushed my hair and collapsed into bed. I was soon asleep, and dreaming a really awful dream where I appeared at work stark naked and lots of fingers were typing on my body, then my breasts turned into typewriters, and Michael came and looked at me and

106

turned his back in disgust, and a bell started to jangle louder and louder. I woke up. The telephone was ringing.

Maddy reached it before I did. 'It's for you,' she said sleepily, 'Tony Blake phoning from New York. Do you know it's one-thirty. You certainly made a hit with him.'

I took the phone and Maddy leaned close so she could listen. Why was Tony phoning me?

He was very friendly, wanting to know if I felt better and everything, then he said he missed me, and Maddy hissed, 'Say you miss him too.' So I did.

He said goodbye and I turned to Maddy exasperated, 'What did you want me to say that for?'

She smiled, 'If he's spending all that money phoning you, you may as well be nice to him. I think he likes you, actually I think he's rather divine!'

'You can have him then,' I said crossly, 'I don't miss him, and I wish I hadn't said I did. Honestly, sometimes I think you're mad.'

'You won't think I'm mad when I tell Michael about it, he'll be green if he thinks Tony Blake is after you *and* Steve Scott.'

'Maddy, let's go to sleep.'

'All right, but you'll see, you'll get your man in the end!'

17

TONY

I opened my eyes and I was in my room at the hotel lying on top of the bed with all my gear on. How did I get back?

That bloody bitch Fontaine was a real balls breaker, and her skinny friend—Miss No Tits society bag. All right, so we'd had a big scene and there wasn't a gun at my head, but how could I have done it? What about Alexandra? What about Sadie and Sam, my nice respectable parents? What if they ever knew, could see? I've always had this funny sort of thought that after you die you sit in a room and like watching a movie your whole life plays across the screen and all the people you know get to watch it. Charming! Last night's scene would make lovely viewing. Shit! Making it with Fontaine is one thing, but having a show with her so-called friends is another.

That faggot husband of Sarah's tried to sneak it in while the two women crawled all over me. But I caught him at that little game, thank you very much. I remember Fontaine saying, 'Let him do it, Tony, you'll love it.' Wow, she was *really* stoned. Bitch!

It was two o'clock and I was starving. I had a shower and ordered three eggs and a hamburger from room service. What was I supposed to do? Hang around until her ladyship decided to call me? I viewed television. Maybe I should call the club later. Maybe I should call Alexandra now. What the hell am I doing here anyway? It's a long way from the Elephant and Castle.

I guess I fell asleep again, 'cos when I woke up the T.V. screen was alive with sweaty teenagers and the phone was ringing.

'Yeah?'

'My, my. Aren't we American already!'

I glanced quickly at my watch, five-fifteen, and she was only just calling, 'What's happening?' I asked.

'Well, darling, all sorts of exciting things. Did you enjoy last night?'

'No.'

Her voice went very cold. 'Oh—why?'

'It's not my scene, Fontaine, I don't like threesomes or foursomes. What's wrong with normal sex?'

Her laugh was amused, 'Tony, you are *such* a suburbanite. It was fun. If you relaxed it could be a lot more fun.'

'I don't want to do it again, O.K.?'

Her voice was sarcastic. '*Yes sir.* We will not indulge in any more naughty little orgies.'

There was silence. I knew she hated being criticised, but God almighty, somebody had to tell her. It was bad enough screwing around on her husband, but this beat the band.

108

'What's happening?' I asked.

'I don't want to corrupt you, Tony dear, but I thought you might like to come over for an hour or so, then there's two parties and dinner with Sarah and Allen.'

Oh Christ! I certainly didn't want to face Sarah and Allen again. What were we all supposed to do—discuss positions?

'Look, I don't want to see them. I'll come to the parties with you, then maybe I'll roam around on my own, get the feel of things.'

'Tony, you can be such a bore! All right then, do that. Be here in half-an-hour.' She slammed the phone down.

How did I ever get myself into this?

It was too early to phone the club, but Alexandra should be home. Was it a clever move to risk a phone call? No.

I thought of her pretty wide-eyed face and her soft auburn hair. She was the sort of girl who would still look good in ten or even twenty years. When I got back to London I decided I would take her down to the Elephant and Castle and introduce her to Sadie and Sam. What a shock they'd get to see me with such a lovely girl. They thought I only ever went out with showgirls and 'tarty bits of fluff' as my Ma always said. How many times had they both said to me—find yourself a nice Jewish girl and settle down. So what difference Jewish smooish as long as she was nice. They would love pretty little Alex.

I got dressed. Polo-necked striped silk shirt, one of Hal's best buys, and my Dougie Hayward grey suit. I had to get some money from Fontaine. I was walking around with nothing. It was embarrassing, especially if I was going to take off on my own later.

On top of the T.V. with my comb and cigarettes were several book matches I had picked up at various joints the previous evening. I liked things like that, lay them around the London pad and people knew you had travelled. Scribbled across the front of 'Lorenz—eat in style' was the name Norma and a number.

Norma? I didn't know a Norma. Come to think of it I'd never been to a place called 'Lorenz' either.

Norma, Norma, Norma. Ah yes, the tall lady with the long black hair at the party last night. Rather beautiful, a definite raver, very cool. I dialled the number and a guarded tired voice answered 'Yeah?'

'Is Norma there?'

'Wait a minute, I'll see. Who is it?'

'Tony Blake, but she doesn't know my name, we met at a party we—'

'Hold it, baby, I don't want your life story.'

The guarded voice left me hanging on while I strained to hear the muffled conversation the other end. Then a voice identical to the first one said, 'Yeah?'

'Norma?'

'Yeah?'

'We met at Salamanda Smith's party last night.' Nothing like dropping a name. 'I was on the phone in the bedroom remember?'

'Yeah.'

She was a wild conversationalist. 'I thought I could see you later, like buy you a drink or something.'

'Sounds O.K. I'm having dinner with some guys, you can join us if you like.'

'Some guys' didn't sound too exciting. 'Look, if you're busy maybe another night.'

'Suit yourself. We'll be at "Marcellos" if you change your mind.'

She hung up. Friendly girl, couldn't care less if I came or not.

I didn't even have cab fare, so I walked the few blocks to Fontaine's. She let me in herself, her hair hanging smoothly down her back, her face a mass of white cream, but her eyes fully made up. She wore a thin silk dressing-gown.

'Come in the bedroom, I'm making up. Fix the champagne first, it's in the fridge.'

I went in the fully fitted oak panelled kitchen and opened several cupboards before locating the fridge, which was cleverly disguised as part of the wall.

I opened the champagne and took it in the bedroom. Fontaine was lying on the bed, the silk dressing-gown exposing her from the waist down so that the whole thing looked slightly obscene. She stretched her arms back behind her head.

110

'We won't need glasses,' she whispered, 'just bring the bottle, we'll drink it my way.'

I was excited in spite of myself. She repulsed me, but my body was responding to her.

I took off my suit and shirt, I certainly wasn't spoiling the outfit.

'Come on, Tony,' she said impatiently, 'I'm thirsty.'

When it was all over and the room stunk of champagne I lay on her bed watching her calmly get on with her makeup. I knew I couldn't make it any more. Oh, I could 'make it' in the physical sense, no problem there, but after—well, I get this kind of unclean feeling, this sort of feeling of shame. With other women there's always some affection—something—even if it's just a casual lay. But Fontaine is cold as bloody ice, it's almost as if she's using my body to suit herself. She's a bitch, and I've got to get away from her. Especially now with Alexandra in the picture.

'Can I shower?' I asked.

'Of course, you don't have to ask permission. Use the one in the guest-room.' She was painting her thin lips and didn't look up.

I showered the smell of the champagne off me and the smell of Fontaine, and then I just stood there turning the water on to icy cold. It felt good.

When I got back to London I was going to find someone to back me in a new club. It shouldn't be that difficult, I had a lot of connections, and me in a new club couldn't fail. I mean I'm not being conceited but 'Hobo' would never have made it without me. Maybe the new place could be called 'Tonys', or is that too obvious? I like it myself, sounds good. Find a location, find a backer, and kiss Fontaine Balls Breaker Khaled goodbye.

'Tony, are you ready?' She walked in wearing black satin and a lot of diamonds. She looked annoyed. 'What the hell are you *doing* in here?'

I got out of the shower quick, skin shrivelled by the cold.

'Come on, for God's sake. I hate hanging around waiting.' She swept out of the room.

I dressed quickly and found her on her terrace smoking.

'Listen, since we'll be splitting up later I'd better have some money,' I said. 'I was rushed over here so quickly I couldn't arrange any.'

'I see.' She looked furious. I knew she hated parting with cash. 'Why on earth didn't you ask Benjamin's secretary?'

'I didn't meet her. The whole thing was arranged by phone.'

She opened her small evening bag and extracted three ten-dollar bills. 'That's all I have,' she said, 'I'll make some arrangements for you tomorrow.'

Charming! Thirty measly dollars to see New York on. That wasn't going to get me very far.

We went to the first party. Held in a restaurant the crush was terrible. I stood by the door watching Fontaine waft around. I drank three scotches.

After half-an-hour she found me, gripped my arm and said, 'We're leaving. Do see if you can be a little more sociable at the next party. Klaus is coming with us.'

Klaus turned out to be a small gay dressmaker, dressed to kill in frills, with rotting teeth and beady eyes. He sat between me and Fontaine in the car, pressing his thigh close to mine.

'Klaus has taken New York by storm with his thirties trouser-suits,' Fontaine remarked.

Well, good for little old beady-eyed Klaus. He may have taken New York by storm, but he was going to get a punch on the nose if he pressed his leg against mine any harder.

The second party was even worse. A party full of queens. Droves of them. Scattered among them were the well-dressed ladies, and a few—very few—normal guys. At least they looked normal.

Klaus said, 'How divine. Everyone's here.'

Fontaine said, 'All the best designers in New York. You'd better stay close to me, Tony, I know how you feel about your precious ass!'

I hated her. So beautiful and elegant and bitchy.

I stayed there about ten minutes, but I was getting so many leers and coy glances I couldn't stand it any longer.

'I'm getting out of here,' I told Fontaine.

She brushed me aside with a cool, 'Bye-Bye,' and I wandered out into the New York night.

It was still early, before nine, and I tried to decide if it was too early to try 'Marcellos'. I was starving, with gnawing pains in my stomach. I walked into a hamburger joint and had three. That felt a lot better. What now? Seek out the wild Norma? There seemed to be nothing else to do. I hopped a cab and told him 'Marcellos', and he knew the place.

From the outside it looked all right. Small red and white awning, few steps down, pretty girl at reception desk. She smiled at me. 'You 'ave reservation, sir?' She was Italian. Should have known it when I saw those great big eyes.

'I thought I'd have a drink.'

'Certainly, sir—downstairs.' She smiled again. I smiled. If Norma didn't show I wondered what time this little darling finished.

Downstairs it was packed. The bar bordered the restaurant and every table was full. I ordered a scotch and looked for Norma.

She was easy to spot with her sleek black hair pulled back into a long plait and her huge horn-rimmed tinted glasses. She was at a table with three guys. I watched them a bit, before going over. She was a very striking girl, her features more Indian than black, her eyes big and soulful.

'Hi there,' she said. She was authoritative, and got a waiter to bring another chair with a snap of her fingers. She nodded round the table: 'Mark—Terry—Davey—this is Tony.' Two of the guys were white, the other a very good-looking black guy with a beard.

'Hi man,' the bearded Davey greeted me.

The whole thing was a very warm scene. I could relax. Norma surveyed me coolly through her tinted lenses. 'Hey, what were you doin' at that *awful* party? What a giant sized drag!'

I nodded, 'Somebody took me.'

'Yeah, somebody took you all right,' she laughed. 'First time in my goddamn life I ever got stood up. Some prize jerk supposed to meet me there, and the sonofabitch never showed!'

'That will teach you to go with stars, girlie,' Davey said, grinning.

'You can bet your ass on that,' Norma agreed. 'Now to beat the band, the sonofabitch's secretary—secretary yet—hasn't even got the balls to call me himself—phones me today and says—quote— Mr Nicholas is *so* sorry he couldn't manage last night. Can I confirm your address as Mr Nicholas wishes to send you a colour television set. Man, I laughed and laughed. Tell Mr Nicholas to take his colour T.Vee and shove it right up his rude white ass, I said.' Everyone laughed. 'That guy is too much,' Norma continued. 'He can only make it with us black girls. He has some kind of hang up, cannot make it with a white lady. Then the poor bastard thinks he has to pay. I've got a little news for him—If I was planning on getting paid, a colour T.Vee wouldn't go anywhere near covering the cost! I should never have balled him, but he's so goddamned beautiful—umm—that body—wowee!!'

Buck Nicholas is a very famous movie actor, mostly appearing in tattered Tee shirts and tight Levi's to show off his equally famous body.

'You know we met before,' Norma said, lifting her glasses, balancing them in her hair and staring at me.

'We did?' I couldn't remember, and I had a good memory.

'Yeah, "Hobo", London. You used to run the joint, all the little girlies creaming themselves over you.'

I was sure I could never forget meeting a girl like Norma.

'Yeah, I still run "Hobo". When was it?'

'Coupla months back—you wouldn't remember me. I was wearing a blonde wig. You came over. I was with Steve Scott.'

Bingo! Could I ever forget her. What a night *that* had been, with every guy in the place fighting to meet her and Steve playing it cool.

'Of course! You look completely different now.'

'Yeah—I use the blonde wig when I want to really knock 'em in the aisles. I was only in London two days, crazy city, I'm going back soon. What are you doing here?'

'We might open up "Hobo". I'm getting the feel of things.'

'Yeah? Great. Talk to Davey, he can *really* show you the town.'

She was right. After dinner (I just drank) Terry and Mark went off, and Norma, Davey and I saw New York. But I mean *really* saw it. We went all over in Davey's silver Porsche, uptown, downtown, Harlem, Chinatown. Norma was a wonderful girl. She talked in her laconic clipped style non-stop, and she danced like a mother, and she laughed a lot and drank a lot, and at six a.m. exhausted, drunk and happy we landed up at her apartment.

'Hey, you're O.K.,' she said laughing, undoing her plaited hair until it hung jet black and straight to her waist.

'You're pretty O.K. yourself,' I replied, putting my arms around her and pulling her close to me.

We were both loaded and both in the same happy mood. She was almost as tall as me, and I'm six one. She had on a clingy orange dress which I helped her out of. Underneath there was gorgeous brown skin and nothing else.

She laughed and moved out of my arms. 'Want a drink?'

'Yeah, great.' I watched her move about the room pouring two scotches and clinking the ice. She had a fantastic body, like a long supple panther.

I felt a little twinge of guilt about Alexandra, but this lady was so *beautiful*! A man can only take so much temptation. She came over to me and held the drink to my lips. I caught hold of one of her wild boobies. She took the drink away from me and put it carefully on a table.

'You want to swing, man—let's swing. I've got an insane bedroom. Only no hang-ups, huh?'

I covered her ass with my hands, 'No hang-ups.'

'O.K., let's go!'

She turned around and I followed her, my hands sticking to her backside, so high and round like a boy's.

Her bedroom was great. Leopardskin walls and a huge circular bed with a giant poster blow-up of Mick Jagger (Mick Jagger?!?) on the ceiling. She pressed a button and Ray Charles singing 'Eleanor Rigby' flooded the room.

115

I pushed her on to the bed and she stared up at me with amused black cat's eyes as I got undressed. I pinned her shoulders to the bed.

I started to kiss her, and we began to make it, and I could have sworn Mick Jagger's eyes moved!

To me New York will always mean Norma. What a girl!

I left her asleep at eleven the next morning and cabbed it back to my hotel. There was a message for me. 'Please be ready to leave on noon plane for London, Alice Clerk—secretary, for Benjamin Al Khaled. All tickets, etc., to be collected at Kennedy airport information desk.'

Charming! I was on the move again.

18

FONTAINE

Reflecting on the whole thing it was a dreadful mistake. I should have left Tony where he was, he is nothing but an embarrassment here.

From the moment he arrived three days ago he has been gauche, naïve, star-struck, and a bore. Of course there was that one rather fun evening when we all got high, but he had the nerve to lecture me the next day about how I shouldn't involve myself in orgies, and that he certainly wasn't going to do it again. I mean, really, as far as I can remember he enjoyed it more than anyone!

Sarah thinks he's a bore. 'All cock and no brains,' she says. 'Really, Fontaine, find yourself an oriental.'

She is right. The stud is a dismal failure in New York. I have arranged for him to leave on the noon flight and this time I am *not* going to the airport.

Benjamin is flying in anyway. Dear rich, randy Benjamin.

There are a lot of things I need at 'Tiffany's'. Also I have seen a beautiful sable coat. And Saks have some divine Rudi Genreich originals.

Benjamin is arriving at the perfect time,

The phone rang and I waited for Adamo to announce who it was.

'Mr Blake, Madam.'

'Tony darling,' I may as well say goodbye with charm, the poor stud was probably shattered.

'Look, Fontaine, I just received a message that I'm supposed to be leaving.'

'Yes, darling. Well, Benjamin's coming into town, and I think you've seen enough to form some opinions. There's no point in you being away from "Hobo" too long.'

'Yeah, well I suppose you're right, But, Jesus Christ, I mean I'm shuttled around like luggage. Why didn't you mention it last night?'

'Oh, don't be boring, Tony. I didn't know last night. Anyway, do give everyone my love, especially Vanessa. I'm sure you'll see Vanessa.' Oh God, he probably couldn't wait.

'Yeah. I'll see you in London then.'

'Ciaou, sweetie.'

That's got rid of him. Back to his little London dollies. He's so narrow-minded. After all I've taught him he still only likes one position! Stupid boy.

The phone again. 'Mr Grant, Madam.'

'Allen darling.'

'How about meeting today?'

'Where's Sarah?'

'Out. Well? Two o'clock the Plaza?'

'No, that's too late, Benjamin's coming in this afternoon. How about the St Regis at one?'

'Fine, I'll arrange it.'

'Allen.'

'Yes?'

'Bring your imagination.'

He laughed. Dear Allen wasn't so bad, not as equipped as

117

Tony, but passable. After the little *ménage à quatre* of the other evening, I was really rather fond of him. It would be a pleasant way to pass the day until Benjamin arrived.

19

ALEXANDRA

My second day at McLaughton & Co, was no better than the first. I can understand why girls become models and things, I mean just sitting here typing is worse than school. Mummy said I can take a modelling course if I want to, and if I wasn't so determined to pay my own way I would say yes. I don't suppose I would be a very good model anyway, I'm not thin enough, and my face is not unusual. But I don't think I can stick it at this job.

Maddy was all pleased with herself when I got home. She was a mass of Carmen rollers and face cream. 'I've got a date,' she announced, 'Jonathan phoned to thank me for dinner last night, and would I like to see a flick.'

'Great,' I said with as much enthusiasm as I could muster, 'what about Michael?'

She immediately looked guilty. 'Oh sorry, Alex, Jonathan didn't mention him. But I promise I'll pump him tonight and find out all the gen. You know, what girls he sees and everything like that. It will be very useful to know all those things.'

'Yes, very.' I was acutely miserable.

Madelaine spent the next hour doing herself up and singing and generally being far too cheerful.

'Stay out of the way when Jonathan fetches me,' she said, 'I'll tell him you're at some party.'

'Thanks,' I said, shutting myself in the bedroom with a tin of cold baked beans.

I heard the doorbell and a mumble of voices and then the door slammed, and I was alone. I phoned Mummy. I wished I was at home.

'Why don't you bring some friends down with you this weekend?' Mummy said. 'We could all go riding.'

'Perhaps I will. Can I let you know?'

I decided to invite Michael, whether Maddy thought it was a good idea or not. It was awful being in the flat alone. I suppose this is the bad thing about living away from home. I even felt nervous, sort of kept on hearing funny noises as it got later and darker.

I drew all the curtains, turned on the television and concentrated on a play. Then the phone rang.

'Is Alexandra Khaled there?' A husky mysterious voice.

'This is she.'

'Steve Scott. How are you?'

'Oh—I'm fine. How are you?' I felt myself blushing.

'All right. Sort of movin' along like a good boy. I thought you might want to come out.'

'Now?'

'I sort of thought tomorrow night, like dinner and that bit. You want to?'

'Yes, I'd like to.' Wait until Maddy heard about this!

'All right then, why don't you come round here about nine?'

'I'd love to.'

'See you then.'

'Oh, just a second,' I frantically searched for a pencil and paper. 'Could you please tell me your address.'

He did so, adding, 'Don't dress up,' and was gone.

How terrific! Although I would sooner it was Michael. I couldn't wait to see Maddy's face!

She staggered in looking awful. She reminded me of how I had felt on Sunday night. 'Alex, I think I'm going to be sick!' she announced. 'Too much wine'.

'For goodness sake, make sure it's in the bathroom.'

It was, and like me she felt better afterwards. She lay on top of her bed groaning and I made some tea.

'I think I'm in love,' she murmured between groans.

119

'What happened?'

'He tried to rape me in his mini. Of course he didn't, I pretended to faint and then he was *so* sweet, he even did my bra up and helped me to the door and kept on asking if I was all right.'

'How far did you go?'

'Far enough,' she replied mysteriously, 'far enough.' And with that she fell into a deep sleep, snoring loudly, with all her clothes on.

I managed to get her shoes and dress off but she was too heavy for me to get her properly undressed, so I pulled some covers over her and left her to her snores.

So much for my exciting news about Steve Scott. It would have to keep until morning.

'Don't look so nervous, I'm not going to eat you.' Those were Steve Scott's opening words as I stood at his front door.

I must admit to being nervous. After all he *is* a star, and *so* dreamy looking. Not conventionally good-looking, but exciting, with his long wild hair, and very bright blue staring eyes.

'Come in then, don't stand there with your mouth hanging open.'

I shut my mouth quickly. I must say he is rather rude. Madelaine and I discussed my date when she blearily opened her eyes this morning. 'Whatever you do you must sleep with him,' she had announced dramatically. 'It's so dull being a virgin, and it would be marvellous for you to be able to say your first man was Steve Scott.'

'What's new, pussycat?' he asked.

'Er—nothing,' I replied. He had on a denim shirt and tight jeans.

'You're a funny little thing,' he said. 'How come you were with the big bad Tony the other night?'

'He works for Daddy,' I stuttered, 'er—what I mean is my father sort of owns "Hobo".' I wished I hadn't said that, I sounded like some awful little rich girl.

'Who's Daddy, then?'

I didn't want to start boasting about Daddy. 'Nobody special, just a—er—er—businessman.'

'Oh,' said Steve, studying me with those bright eyes of his. 'What do you do, then? Model or actress?'

'Actually I'm neither, I'm a secretary.' That should stop any ideas he might have about me being rich. I hated people knowing I was rich, it embarrassed me.

'Great! Want to do some typing for me?'

'Yes—if you like.'

He laughed, 'I'm kidding. You know I think you're for real, a baby innocent.'

'I'm eighteen,' I lied.

'You're ancient,' he replied, still laughing. 'Where have you been?'

'I've been at school in Switzerland.'

He took my arm, 'You know for an eighteen-year-old bird you certainly manage to come across like fourteen.'

I was furious and pulled my arm away, but he gripped it again and said, 'Hey, I'm not knocking it, I like it. You don't know how unusual it is. Are you a virgin?'

I blushed.

'You are!' he said accusingly. 'I bet you are.'

How I wished I had never come. How could he ask me questions like that?

'Let's go and get some food,' he said, 'I want to hear all about Daddy and Switzerland and why you're still a virgin at your advanced age.'

He had a big old-fashioned Bentley, brightly polished. Everyone stared at us as we drove along.

Fortunately once we reached the restaurant he was descended on by various friends, and didn't have a chance to question me during dinner.

He drank an awful lot, and the language at our table was incredible. Maddy wouldn't believe it, even the girls swore. I couldn't wait to get away. Perhaps I could just sneak off to the loo and not come back.

'Hey listen, everyone,' Steve suddenly said loudly. 'This girl's a

121

virgin!' And he clapped his hand on my shoulder and everyone stared at me.

Oh floor, please open up and swallow me!

'That's nice for you, Stevie,' one of the girls said, 'makes a change,' and she giggled.

I blushed beetroot. 'I think you're a pig!' I hissed at him. 'Please take me home.'

'It's nothing to be ashamed of,' he said surprised, 'You're probably the only bloody virgin of eighteen in England!'

I gulped my coffee, and was just deciding to get up and leave when who should walk in but Michael, *my* Michael—with that funny-looking girl he had danced with all night at 'Hobo'—Suki something or other. She looked ridiculous in a silver tunic outfit.

She came over to say hello to Steve. Michael walked behind her, saw me and looked amazed.

'Hello, Michael,' I waved gaily, wishing Steve would put his arm around me *now*.

'Hello, Alex,' Michael returned my greeting. I could see he was impressed.

'See you later at "Hobo",' Suki said to Steve, and she and Michael went off to sit at a nearby table for two.

After a while, Steve said, 'So, what do you want to do? My pad? "Hobo"? Or there's a poxy party going on somewhere?'

'I think I'd like to go to "Hobo",' I said, hoping that Michael would follow shortly.

'Let's go then.' He got up, and without even saying goodbye to anyone we left.

In his car he lit a cigarette and offered it to me.

'No, thank you, I don't smoke.'

'That's all right, take a drag, it will put you in good shape.'

I gingerly puffed on the cigarette. It had a funny taste and smelt vile.

'There you go, little girl, you're turning on nicely.'

'I really don't want any more,' I politely handed it back to him. I suppose it was one of those 'funny' cigarettes, I'm not exactly as dumb as he seems to think.

We sat in the car silently while he finished the cigarette.

I know I'm in love with Michael. Here I am sitting next to Steve Scott and *all* I can think of is Michael.

'All right, let's go,' Steve said, more to himself than to me, 'Let us go out into the night and swing, little baby girl.'

I peeked quickly at my watch. It was nearly eleven-thirty. If this was going to be a late night how on earth was I going to get up for work tomorrow? I am one of those people who need masses of sleep.

'Hobo' wasn't very crowded. 'I like getting here early,' Steve said, 'you can feel it build that way.'

Soon we were joined by some of the people who had been with us at the restaurant, and others. I was determined not to get drunk so I stuck to Coca-Cola. I didn't really care how stupid Steve thought I was, I had decided that whatever Maddy said, I wasn't going to bed with him. He was much too personal and rude. I couldn't bear the thought of him seeing me without my clothes on. Honestly, the whole thing was going to be embarrassing enough without someone like him.

I watched the entrance, waiting for Michael, which of course was the only reason I was here.

'Come on, let's dance,' said Steve. 'You *can* dance, can't you?'

'Of course I can!'

On the dance floor after a few minutes he said, 'I thought you said you could dance.'

'I don't know why you wanted to take me out,' I said angrily, 'you've been rude to me all night.'

'Oh come off it, little Miss Virgin, I'm only kidding. Can't you take a joke?'

'I am *not* a virgin, and I *can't* take your sort of hurtful so-called jokes.' With that I went and sat down, surprising, even myself.

He followed me, laughing. 'Them there's fighting words, little girl. Want another coke or shall we go back to my place and see who's right?'

'Another Coca-Cola please.'

At last Suki and Michael came in. She headed straight for Steve. 'Carolyn's downstairs,' she hissed.

'Oh shit!' he said quickly. 'She's supposed to be working

123

tonight. Great!' He turned to me. 'See the trouble you're just about to get me in?'

'Why, what have I done?'

'Carolyn's my girl, she'll go mad if she sees me with another bird. Look, go over and sit with Suki. I'll see if I can get rid of her.'

'But—'

'Go with Suki.'

Honestly!

Suki giggled. 'Carolyn will scratch your eyes out. Come and sit with us.'

So to my complete embarrassment I had to go and sit with Michael and Suki.

Michael said, 'What's going on?' and Suki explained.

He wagged a finger at me, 'You're certainly getting around in your first week in London. How's the job going?'

'Fine.'

The three of us chatted a bit. Michael had his arm around Suki's waist and he kept on giving her little squeezes.

Oh, where was Steve? I didn't want to sit here playing gooseberry to the man I loved.

'Oh look!' Suki suddenly said. 'There's Jan and John, I must go and see them.' And she dashed off.

Michael said, 'Noisy here, isn't it?'

I nodded.

'Well, perhaps I'll take you to a nice quiet little place I know one night, that's if you can fit me into your busy schedule.'

'Oh yes,' I said weakly. 'I could manage tomorrow.'

20

TONY

On the plane back to good old Blighty I made several important decisions.

(1) Get out of 'Hobo' and into something else where I wasn't gripped tightly by the balls by a sex-mad nympho.

(2) Tell Alex how I feel about her (I do love her) and give up other girls.

(3) Save some money if possible, in case I should decide on marriage.

My mind was made up that a place called 'Tony's' would be fantastic. I had a lot of friends, and between them I could raise enough money—I didn't need one big backer. The new place would knock 'Hobo' right out. I could picture it now.

First thing tomorrow I'll be out searching for a suitable location. I think I can swing the whole thing for about ten thousand pounds. Now that shouldn't be hard to raise. If I can only get five people to come up with two thousand each. Sammy must have a couple of grand stashed away and Hal would be able to find it, and Franklin could talk to his old man. It was all going to work out great.

We landed about midnight and I decided to get a cab straight to the club. I only had one suitcase.

What a trip! I'd hardly even had time to take a pee before I was on the plane home again! Still it was good to be back. I would wait until the morning to phone Alexandra, she was probably deep in the land of nod. Poor little kid, having to work at some lousy nine to five job. Maybe one of these days I will marry her, and then she can spend her time looking after me. Oh boy! Mustn't think about her like that. I can feel myself getting horny. I think the high altitude affects me!

I took them all by surprise at the club. 'Flowers' was chatting to his girl-friend at reception—sonofabitch. He jumped up like he had a candle under his ass when he saw me. Franco was nowhere in sight. Inside a waiter was playing the records, and I couldn't see another waiter in the room.

I stormed into the kitchen where it was like an Italian wedding. Franco and the girl cashier were dancing—dancing yet! And the other waiters were slouched around watching. I can't leave the lousy place for a minute.

'Come on everyone,' I screamed. 'What the fucks going on here?'

'Meester Blake!' Franco reeled like a startled rabbit. 'Meester Blake—we wasn't expecting you.'

'Yeah, I can see that. Get back into the room, you lazy slobs. Let's have a little action here, get some drinks moving.'

The waiters milled around in panic and confusion, while Franco started screaming at them in Italian. The cashier slunk back behind her desk.

Franco got rid of all the waiters and turned to me crest fallen, 'Meester Blake, I—'

'Yeah, yeah, I know, Franco, you weren't expecting me.'

I went back inside. Flowers was at his stand, waiters were rushing around looking busy. We were back to normal.

I went over to the regulars' table. Sammy was there, arm around a horrific little black-eyèd teeny bopper. 'Tony me boy, wacha doin' back? What happened? Good to see you.'

'Yeah,' I replied. 'Have a drink, Sammy, I'm going to do the rounds, see you in a minute.'

I tell you 'Hobo' knocks spots off all those New York joints. It's got what I call classy flash—excitement—call it what you like, it's got it.

I bought a drink here, a drink there, shook a lot of hands, kissed a lot of faces, pinched a few bottoms. Then, wowee— pow! Alexandra sitting there as calm as you like. Pretty, she was very pretty, like a gorgeous cultured rose amongst a lot of dandelions.

What the bloody hell is she doing here?

I shook her hand, trying to keep cool. She smiled at me. She looked tired. She was with Ring-a-ding Suki and that schmucky student type. I sat down.

126

'Tell us all about New York,' Suki asked. Was she with the student or was Alex?

'How do you feel?' I asked my lovely Alex.

'Fine,' she said brightly. 'You certainly had a short trip.'

'Come on, darlin'—all fixed,' Steve Scott appeared. 'Hey, Tony, you back already?'

'Yeah, baby, I'm back.' We shook hands.

'Well, come on then,' he said to Suki, but Alex got up.

I watched, shocked as he took her by the hand and pulled her off to another table.

My Alex with that randy little singer—*my* Alex—*impossible*—there must be some mistake.

'What's she doing with him?' I asked the clown-faced Suki.

She shrugged, 'I don't know, I guess he's on another kick. You know, educated Miss Prim and Proper for a change.'

'You should be so bloody lucky as to be even a tenth as educated as she is,' I said burning. 'What is she—prim and proper because she doesn't screw on sight?'

'What's the matter, Tony, I only said—'

'I don't give a goddamn what you said, Suki. You're not fit to sit at the same table as her.' God, I was so angry. I got up and stormed over to Steve and his table of cronies.

'Tony, sit down, have a drink, tell us about the New York scene.'

I could have smashed his stupid face in.

'Alex, I want to talk to you,' I said, trying to appear casual.

'Yes, Tony?' She questioned me with her wide brown eyes.

'Leave her alone,' Steve said loudly. 'She's mine tonight.'

'You're talking to a lady,' I said grimly, 'and if you don't mind I'd like to speak to her.

Alex got up quickly. She was blushing. I took her out on the terrace and held her very gently by the shoulders.

'Look,' I said quietly, 'you can tell me to mind my own business, but a girl like you shouldn't be out with a shit bag like Steve Scott.'

She brushed her hair back with her hand, 'He is rather awful,' she admitted, much to my great relief.

'Tell him goodbye then, I'll take you home.'

'I can't do that. I mean he *has* given me dinner and everything, I can't be rude.'

'Listen, sweetheart, that animal doesn't even know what rude is.'

'It's nice of you to be so concerned, but honestly I can manage.'

I couldn't stop myself, I grabbed her tightly and kissed her. I pressed my mouth against her lips hard. Her mouth was dry and refused to open, but I pushed my tongue between her teeth and forced her to let me in. I put my hands on her breasts and felt their warmth and roundness through her dress.

She struggled and pushed me away. Her cheeks were flushed. 'Honestly!' She exclaimed, 'I thought you were warning me about Steve.'

'Can I see you tomorrow?' Young schmuck asking for date.

'I'm sorry, Tony, I'm busy.' She smoothed down her dress and looked at me in a funny way, 'I'd better get back inside.'

'Yeah,' I was destroyed, 'I guess you'd better.'

I felt like I'd been kicked in the stomach. First of all I was hot as hell after kissing her and feeling her fantastic body. Secondly, I knew I wasn't about to let Steve frigging Scott take her home.

I followed her inside. She sat down beside Steve and he whispered something to her. Bastard! I was going to fix him. I went over to Suki who was busy feeling up her student boyfriend under the table. God, Massey was well rid of this freak.

'Who did Alexandra come here with?' I asked.

She was mad at me. 'I don't know.'

I exerted a bit of the famous Blake charm. 'Come on, Suki sweetheart, don't be so touchy.'

'She came with Steve— and then Carolyn arrived downstairs looking for him—well, he must have got rid of her because that's when he came back and took Miss Goody Two Shoes off again. Why are you so interested anyway?'

I shrugged. 'She's only a kid, I'm keeping an eye on her.'

'Oooh!' Suki the Freak shrieked with laughter, 'Sir Galahad Blake!'

Michael butted in. 'I expect she can look after herself.'

I glared. Who asked for his ten cents worth?

Anyway I had a plan. I went downstairs to the office and dialled Steve's home. As I thought, Carolyn answered, she had been sent home to wait. I disguised my voice (I could have been a wild actor) 'Your boy-friend's at "Hobo" making it with another girl.' Then I hung up, went upstairs and waited.

Fifteen minutes later Carolyn came storming in, her wild red hair flowing, her eyes mean and narrow.

Steve didn't even see her coming. She gave him a whack across the face that made me wince. 'You lousy sonofabitch,' she screamed, 'what the *fuck* is going on here? Giving me some story about you had to show the head of Gloom Records around. Some fucking head.' She paused and glared at Alex who seemed quite cool and collected. 'It might interest you to know,' she continued, 'that this is my fucking husband you're sitting next to. We got married last week and I wasn't supposed to tell anyone because it might upset his fucking fans. So fuck off.'

Steve practically slid under the table. What a scene! But Carolyn wasn't finished yet, 'I'm three months pregnant too—so stick that up your jumper—you little cow!'

Alexandra had gone visibly pale in the dim of the club. She stood up. 'I'm so sorry,' she said quietly, 'I didn't know,' and with that she made for the exit.

She certainly had class, lots and lots of class.

I caught up with her outside. She was crying. I wanted to wrap her up in my arms and carry her somewhere safe. Silently I handed her my handkerchief and she blew her nose.

I called a cab and we got in. I gave the driver my address. This time I wasn't letting her escape. She didn't say anything until the cab reached my place, and then we went through the same old discussion:

'Oh, Tony, it's simply much too late, I must get home.'

'Just one quick brandy, you need it.'

'I hate brandy.'

'Well, a coffee then.'

'It will keep me awake, please take me home.'

The cab driver sat there, his ugly hawk face listening to every word.

'Look, just five minutes, we'll have a quick coffee, a chat, and then I promise I'll take you right home.'

She sighed. 'All right.'

I paid the cab and he winked and muttered, 'Enjoy the quick coffee, guv.' Lousy dirty old man.

My flat smelt horrible, all the windows had been closed, and something had gone off in the fridge. I let some air in and stuck the kettle on. It was a horrible little pad. I had to move.

Alexandra sat on the sofa and I put on an Astrud Gilberto album. Now that I had her here I didn't know what to do with her.

'This is a nice flat,' she said in her best polite voice. 'Have you lived here long?'

'A few months, it's too small. I want to move, get somewhere nicer.'

We lapsed into silence until the whistle of the kettle boiling. Coffee was a mistake, I should have given her a drink, got her more relaxed.

'How about an Irish coffee?' I asked.

'I've never had that.'

Not that I had any cream or brown sugar or any of that jazz, but I could put a slug of whisky in it, better than plain coffee. 'You'll love it.'

Astrud was singing. 'The Shadow of Your Smile'. If I had been with any other bird by this time we would have been stripped off and hard at it.

'Did you have a nice time in America?' she asked.

'Yeah—great.' I finished the coffees and handed one to her. It tasted good—personally I don't think you need all that sugar and cream shit.

'You know, Alex, I've got a lot of things to tell you.'

She sipped her coffee and stared at a picture of me taken the opening night of 'Hobo'.

'Do you want to go to bed with me, Tony?' she said politely, as if asking what time the next bus home was.

I was stunned. I practically spilt my coffee. 'What?' I stuttered like an idiot.

She was blushing now and biting her lower lip. 'Well, *do* you?'

This wasn't exactly the way I had the whole thing planned. I had figured on telling her how I felt, maybe kissing and cuddling her a while. 'Yes, of course I do,' I said lamely. She had really caught me off guard.

'All right then,' she said calmly.

We sat and stared at each other for a bit, and I noticed her hand was shaking as she drank the coffee.

I went to her, took the cup out of her hand and kissed her. This time her lips parted and she gave a little sigh.

I ran my hands around her body, feeling her squirm under my touch. She was wearing a brown woollen dress, high-necked with small buttons down the back. I started to undo them.

'Can we go in the bedroom?' she asked. 'Perhaps I can go in first.'

'Yeah, O.K.' She had me so excited I didn't know where I was at.

'I'll call you when I'm ready.'

She trotted off and left me in a state of shock. Wowee—I had thought she was a little baby innocent. I still loved her though, in spite of the fact that she had obviously—well—been around.

I wondered should I strip off? I wished there was time to take a bath. I felt hot and sweaty from the plane trip.

'I'm ready, Tony,' a little voice called. 'Please don't turn the light on.'

She was in my bed, covers up to her chin.

I took my clothes off clumsily, throwing them on the floor. I kept my pants on and jumped into bed beside her.

She had velvet skin, I swear to God her skin was actual velvet. I could only see her faintly in the darkened room, she had drawn the curtains and wouldn't let me pull the covers off her.

I felt her slowly. Her breasts were very high and full, her waist narrow and her hips curved out, all covered with this wild velvet skin. She lay on her back, her body tense, her hands gripping the covers.

'Relax, baby!' I whispered. 'Take it easy, enjoy it.'

Her body hair was sparse and silky like a fine down, she tightened her thighs when she felt my hand there.

131

I rolled on top of her and forced the covers out of her grip. She was shivering. I stood up over her and took my pants off. She shut her eyes and I came back on top of her and worked to get her legs apart.

'Tony, I'm a virgin,' she suddenly said after a short silent struggle during which I couldn't shift her legs open.

I felt myself go down like a punctured balloon.

She opened her eyes quickly, 'You don't mind, do you?'

Mind? Mind! I was delighted. Only it put another aspect on everything. She was a virgin, and she wanted to go to bed with me, which could only mean that she must love me.

'You silly kid, of course I don't mind, I think that's wonderful, perfect.'

'Oh good,' I felt her relax.

I rolled off, gathered her in my arms, and held her.

'You see I don't know what I have to do, I don't know how not to have a baby or anything. It's—it's the first time I've ever seen a naked man.'

Well, they say that if you wait long enough, everything comes your way. I felt like a giant! A king!

We lay there for a bit. I was perfectly content just holding her beautiful body. I shut my eyes. I was a bit knocked out by the plane trip and everything.

'Tony, is everything all right? You're not disappointed or anything?'

I opened my eyes quickly. Wow—I was so comfortable and happy that I must have dropped off to sleep for a second.

She had escaped from my arms, and was kneeling on the bed holding a sheet in front of her.

'Of *course* it is, baby. Come back here.'

'I just mean—well, if you are disappointed and you don't want to, well—I quite understand.'

'You're kidding!' I pulled the sheet away from her and she quickly lay down. I kissed her face and stroked her hair and felt her unbelievably perfect breasts. She started to make little soft noises, like a kitten.

I had this funny sort of choking feeling. Christ! I loved this girl

132

so much. It wasn't even sex, I wasn't so sure that I wanted to make love to her. She was so pure and innocent, and maybe she should stay that way.

But she wanted me. She wanted to belong to me. She smelt so sweet, like summer flowers.

I was on top of her and showing her what to do. And she was gasping and biting her lower lip and staring at me with those wide brown innocent eyes.

Oh God! I pulled out just in time. It was fantastic! Then she rolled away from me and lay on her stomach.

She was mine.

21

FONTAINE

It is such a relief to be rid of the stud. I have learnt a little lesson, never take people out of their natural surroundings. My God, look at the zoo, all those poor animals locked up in cages neurotic as hell.

In London in charge of 'Hobo', Tony is a man. Here he is nothing.

I spent a very entertaining afternoon with Allen. He has a lot of possibilities, and he *did* bring his imagination! He told me some absolutely shocking stories about himself and Salamanda Smith. *Très risqué!* I shall look at the vapid blonde movie queen with new eyes.

Benjamin has arrived and is showering, cleaning his teeth, and gargling. God know what else. Benjamin is immaculate. He washes his short round body at least three times a day. Whenever we make love he showers first *and* after, an infuriating habit, although very hygienic. He changes his underwear and socks twice a day—sometimes three times. As a businessman Benjamin is a genius. But as a husband he is an infuriating, irritating bore!

Unfortunately only the Body Beautiful can really interest me, that and money of course. Benjamin and I have very little to say to each other. Social gossip doesn't interest him, and financial and business talk drives me to distraction. His children bore me to tears, and he hates discussing my clothes. Actually we are very rarely alone together.

Once he asked me if I would have a child. I told him that at his age it was a ridiculous idea. I don't like children. I find them time-consuming, dirty and noisy. Apart from which, they destroy your figure. Look at Vanessa, big cow-like Vanessa.

Yes, I must say, I am quite happy with my life the way it is. I really have everything.

It's so exciting finding new studs and watching their progress. Tony is a prime example—from waiter to my lover to—well, what exactly is he? A host I suppose one could call him.

There comes a time in every relationship I undertake when a man's body is not enough. I think I have reached that time with Tony. I think he must go. I'll throw him to all the little dollies who may not want him when he's no longer at 'Hobo'.

I must remember to get Benjamin to arrange to have him fired when we get back.

Of course what I really need is a *rich* stud, with all the things that Benjamin has. Then I could divorce Benjamin and *really* be happy.

I don't think I've ever come across a rich stud, they just don't seem to exist. All the men with *real* money and position are old, fat, and desperately boring—like Benjamin. Poor old Benjamin.

'Did you have a nice shower, darling?'

'Yes, very nice. Is my secretary here yet?'

'I don't know, I'll buzz Adamo. I've arranged dinner with Sarah and Allen. He's Sarah's latest husband, a writer, I'm sure you'll like him.'

'You know I can't stand Sarah.'

'Darling,' I went to him and started to pull off his bath towel

134

which was tied round his middle. He looked ridiculous with his white hairy legs peeping out.

He turned away, 'Not now, Fontaine. My secretary should be here.'

Well, well! Independent Benjamin, after any separation he was usually rarin' to go.

Deliberately I stepped out of my negligee and stretched. 'I think I'll have a bath while you're with dear old Miss Clerk. Do you think I'm getting too fat?'

I knew there wasn't an ounce of fat on my entire body. I knew the sight of my body excited old Benjamin like hell.

'No, you're not getting fat.' His beady little eyes flicked over me, and then abruptly he turned away for a second time.

Was he getting senile at last?

I rang Adamo on the intercom. 'Is Mr Khaled's secretary here?'

'Yes, Madam.'

Benjamin was busy getting dressed. 'She's here. You *will* be finished by six, won't you? I promised the Sidwells we would drop by for a drink.'

He grunted. I stretched my naked body, blew him a kiss, and went off into my bathroom.

After all, if the poor old fellow can't get it up, well what can one do?

22

TONY

I can remember when I was a kid seeing all those wild Hollywood movies where there would be some kind of great love scene—and then the hero (usually Gene Kelly) would say goodnight to his girl and rush off into the street singing and dancing it up a storm.

Well that's exactly what I feel like doing now. Man, I feel like Gene Kelly ten times larger than life.

What if I burst into song and dance in the middle of the Kings Road? I'd probably get nicked for being drunk!

I took my little Alexandra home in a cab. She was very quiet after, very lovable, very shy. In fact, she didn't say a word. She dressed in the bathroom while I snatched a quick kip, then she shook me awake and said please could she go home.

I didn't know what to say to her, I was so sort of knocked out by it all. So we both sat quietly in the cab, and then I dropped her off and let the cab go, and here I am in Chelsea. It's three a.m. and now I'm wide awake, starving hungry, and feeling great.

I picked up another taxi and rode over to 'Hobo'. They never learn—this time there was nobody out front.

I raged inside, grabbed a frightened Franco and said, 'Where the hell is Tina?'

'Meester Blake—we wasn't expecting you back.'

'Yeah, baby, you're not telling me anything new.'

'I think Tina no feel good, she go home early.'

'Great Franco—great. So if you let her go home why not put someone else out front?'

'Of course I deed, Meester Blake. Frederico is there.'

'Frederico ain't there.'

Franco looked shocked. 'I keel that Frederico, I told 'im 'undred times to stay out front.'

I felt too good to argue any more. I just had to be there, that was all. Franco was fine when I was around.

Flowers was playing Lou Rawls. The place had that nice relaxed atmosphere at the end of a good night. There were about thirty people left in the room.

Sammy was still sitting with his juvenile wonder. He grabbed me. 'Where you bin? You missed all the excitement. It's a good job I was 'ere, I straightened things out a bit.'

'What happened?'

'That Carolyn's a mad bird. She started picking everything up in sight and throwing it at Steve, and 'e's trying to 'ide under the table, and the f-ing and blinding that was going on is nobody's business! So anyway, I grab a hold of 'er, and then she starts to cry, and 'e goes running out of the club, and then what do you know—the bleedin' newspapers arrive—some joker must 'ave phoned 'em. What a barny!'

I shrugged. I wasn't sorry I'd missed it all, because if I had stayed I'd probably have smashed that half assed pop singer to pieces.

Sammy's bird sat gloomily in the corner chewing on her thumb. 'Can we go?' she whined.

'In a minute, don't be so anxious, I'm going to give it to you.' Sammy replied, winking at me and mouthing—'a raver'!

Sammy was still chasing scrubbers. Why didn't he look around for a nice decent girl?

'Hey, Sammy, while I was in New York I was thinking.'

'Ye gods—'e's thinking yet!'

'No, Sammy, seriously. I've got this great idea for opening a new place.'

'A new place? Watcha want to do that for? What's wrong with 'ere?'

'Well, you know, Sammy, I'm the last one to ever see any bread out of this place, it's making a bomb and I see about tuppence.'

'Yeah? Well, you're a schmuck, aren't you? Watcha want to make yourself a lousy deal for?'

'Because I wasn't in a position to make *any* deal when this joint opened. Anyway—who knew it was going to take off like it did?'

'Yeah, well—why doncha get 'em to pay you some more? You work 'ard enough—*when* you're 'ere, that is.'

'Why let them put *more* money in their pockets? This place is *me*—without me they'd be finished in a couple of weeks.'

'Hold on, boy, you mean a lot to the place, but it still managed very nicely while you were in New York.'

'Aw, come on Sammy, let's go,' said the whiney-voiced scrubber, 'I'm fed up with sitting here all night.'

'Yeah, you go Sammy, I'll talk to you tomorrow.' I could see that I wasn't going to get much out of him.

'Meester Blake,' Franco was at my elbow. 'There ees Meester Ian Thaine outside with a party of ten, they want to come in, but we cannot serve any drinks now and 'ee is screaming 'bout that.'

'O.K., Franco, I'll handle it.'

Ian Thaine was a pain in the neck. He had made a fortune in so-called 'swinging London' gear—clothes, souvenirs, old uniforms, posters. He had 'Thaine' shops everywhere, and he made Sammy look like one of the aristocracy. He was about my age, thin and weedy-looking, out to better himself socially but never making it. I knew he hated me, because he saw me chatting to all-comers—film stars, lords, politicians. It killed him. He wanted to be someone. In fact, the rumour had it that he hired a permanent press agent to try to get his name in the gossip columns alongside the élite. I suppose he was worth a few million at least. He was usually with a motley crowd.

Tonight it was a couple of last season's debs, three members of a scruffy rock group, a once glamorous sexy actress with her nineteen-year-old 'Manager', a bit part actor, and two wide-eyed teeny boppers obviously culled from the streets of Piccadilly.

'Ian, m'boy,' I gave him the brotherly firm sincere handshake.

'Tony,' he sneered at me, 'is that right we can't get a pissing drink?'

'Sorry, Ian, that's right, got to think of our licence.'

'Balls to your licence,' he said peevishly. 'We want drinks.'

I smiled pleasantly, 'You'll just have to go somewhere else then.'

Ian bit on his lower lip, 'Oh, all right, we'll suffer on Coca-Cola then. I can see I'm going to have to open a place of my own in this town before I can get a drink.'

Bingo! Lights flash. Ian Thaine. Why hadn't I thought of him before?

'Come on, Ian,' I put my arm around his shoulder, 'I'll buy you all Coca-Colas myself.'

My mind was working quickly. Ian was perfect for the set-up I had in mind. He would jerk off at the thought of owning a successful joint. All I needed was a little sweet talk. He had the

138

money, plenty of it. We could go fifty-fifty. He to put up all the money, me to put up myself.

'Hey, Ian,' I said, 'I've been thinking . . .'

23

ALEXANDRA

Maddy was asleep. It seems whenever I need her she's huddled in an immovable ball beneath her covers. I gave her a push, but she groaned and vanished under her eiderdown. The most important night of my life, and she doesn't even want to hear about it.

I feel strangely weak at the knees, but studying my face in the mirror I really don't look any different. Perhaps a little more sophisticated?

What an evening! First the terrible time with Steve Scott, then his *wife* appearing. I could have died with embarrassment. And Michael being there witnessing the whole thing. I must have looked such a fool.

Anyway, at least Tony was very nice coming after me and everything. He was so sweet and kind that when we were in the taxi outside his flat I suddenly decided that if I was going to go to bed with someone, *he* would be the perfect person. After all, he's the only one who seems to pay attention to me.

I think he was a bit shocked when I asked him if he wanted to make love to me. *Me* approaching *him*! I don't know how I did it. But I had decided I was going to lose my virginity and I was determined.

Michael likes women of the world. Am I a woman of the world now? It wasn't much fun. I mean I just sort of lay there while Tony climbed on top of me. He was awfully heavy and it hurt. I don't know what all the fuss is about if that's all you do. And it's so messy—ugh! I didn't enjoy it at all. I can't *ever* imagine Mummy and Daddy doing it. Did they? I suppose they must have.

I shook Maddy again, but she refused to budge. I'll never get to sleep until I tell *someone*.

Of course, the most exciting thing is the fact that I have a date with Michael! A date! Just the two of us. He must like me if he wants to take me to a quiet place for dinner.

I don't know how I'm going to face going to work tomorrow.

Oh, Michael, have I done the right thing? I only did it for you.

What if I get pregnant? Tony said he'd been careful but how do I know? What does he think of me? I don't know if I can face him again. Surely it was better in the old days when a man was supposed to want his wife to be a virgin. Now the whole thing has changed, and it's dumb to be a virgin. I feel so confused.

'Maddy, wake up!'

24

TONY

Ian Thaine was easy. I couldn't understand why I hadn't thought of him before. He was craving to be a big man, dying to be friends with everyone, and what better way than to own a club?

I chatted him and he responded like a baby. I'd hardly ever given him the time of day before, because he was an obnoxious sonofabitch, but talking to him I realised just how much he wanted to be liked.

After an exhausting hour of costs and profits and all that jazz we shook hands.

'It's a deal,' Ian said.

Beautiful! He would put up all the money. I would do everything else and get a salary plus forty-nine per cent. I struggled for fifty, but Ian wasn't budging on that.

'We'll call it "Ian's",' he said.

'Yeah,' I muttered. We could argue about that later.

It was all too good to be true. It was late and the waiters were looking mutinous. Ian and party were the only customers left. One of the debs came and plonked herself on Ian's knee. He slid his hand up her skirt. The aged actress was in a tight clinch with her young manager. Nobody looked like budging.

I stood up. 'I think it's bedtime.'

Ian stood up, the ex-deb sliding in a furious heap to the floor. 'Yes, let's go.' Ian was now my friend.

To the waiters' relief the whole party got itself together and we all left.

Downstairs the three rock singers piled into a Ford with the two teeny boppers and roared off. The actress, her manager and the bit part actor got into a taxi. The two ex-debs, Ian and I were left. He was driving a white Lincoln Continental with gold fixtures and maroon upholstery.

'Where's your car?' he asked me.

'Er—in the garage being fixed.'

'I'll drop you then.'

'No, that's O.K., Ian, I can take a cab.'

'I said I'll drop you.' He took me to one side, 'Besides I want you to take Diana with you. You'll like her.' He whispered her speciality.

'Look, Ian, I don't want to get involved.'

He ignored me. I climbed in the back of the car with Diana. She was horsey-faced, tall and skinny. I couldn't have fancied her on the best of nights.

'Where to?' Ian asked.

I told him. How the hell was I going to get out of this? I mean he obviously thought he was doing me a big favour. The best thing was play it by ear.

He dropped me off and Diana clambered out with me.

'See you at my office at three,' Ian said. 'Have a good time.'

Shit! He drove off and Diana and I stood there. 'Where do you live?' I asked her when the car was out of sight.

141

'With Ian,' she replied slightly surprised. 'Why?'

It looked like I was lumbered. Why was I such a jerk? Why hadn't I just taken Ian to one side and explained? I suppose because I wanted a deal, and if accepting one of his tatty girls was going to please him, well, I guess I would just have to accept her.

'Come on,' I said wearily.

Please forgive me, my wonderful Alexandra, but I'm doing it for us.

25

FONTAINE

Benjamin is not himself. Surly, bad-tempered, and positively rude to Sarah and Allen. I am absolutely furious. I've never seen him like this. Of course I know he's a monster in business, but, with me he has always been placid and polite, and never verbally attacked my friends, which he did quite viciously last night, calling poor Allen 'a lily livered, poor man's Tennessee Williams'. Well, I mean really! I didn't know he'd even read anything of Allen's.

Sarah was livid. I have rarely seen her angry, but last night her eyes were flashing and the words practically spitting from her lips. Needless to say we all parted outside 'Le Club' simply dreadful friends. I haven't spoken to Benjamin since. How dare he think that he can insult me and my friends!

Allen says he knows all about us. What nonsense! How can he possibly know? I'm always very discreet.

On top of everything else we have the added thrill of beastly little Ben junior joining us tonight. Alexandra is bad enough, looking down her nose at me all night, but Ben junior is impossible. Mutual hate abounds.

God knows why Benjamin insists I have to see his children.

They're *his*, not mine. I want no part of them.

What I would actually like to do is go back to London. I expect I am missed there.

I have decided to wait a few weeks before having Benjamin fire Tony. After all, he is different in London and I may as well make use of him until I find another London stud. I must say I feel quite nostalgic about Vanessa and 'Hobo' and all the little intrigues.

Oh God, I suppose I shall have to make peace with Benjamin. Why the hell *I* should make peace I don't know, but I *do* want to buy that sable coat today and it *is* twelve thousand dollars. I'll put on my white mink over nothing and go and wake him.

Benjamin, of course, is already up and at his office. It is noon and he always rises at seven.

Adamo remained impassive at the sight of me wandering around in my coat. Dear Adamo, the perfect servant.

Benjamin wouldn't appreciate me turning up at his office in my mink and nothing else. The erotic secret of being naked underneath is very exciting. But of course Benjamin is much too staid to enjoy it.

I phoned Sarah. 'Darling, I'm sorry, I'm just too upset for words.'

Sarah's voice was acid. 'I'm sorry for *you*, sweetie, *you're* married to him.'

'That's all right, darling. He's full of remorse today. I'm just off to get a new sable.'

'They're more chic in Paris this year.'

Sarah was a bitch, but I could out-bitch anyone. 'Why don't you buy Allen one?'

She laughed coldly. 'You're so amusing, Fontaine, maybe I shall.'

We said our goodbyes, and I phoned Benjamin at his office.

'Yes, what is it? I'm busy.'

Oh my god, he was impossible. It crossed my mind to forget the coat and let him beg my forgiveness. But a sable coat *is* worth a slight effort.

'You're not still angry?'

'What is it, Fontaine? I'm busy and can't discuss things now.'

'Well, darling, I need some money.'

'Talk to my secretary, she'll send over what you need.'

'Twenty thousand.'

There was a pause. 'Twenty thousand dollars?'

'Yes, darling, I've seen a gorgeous sable coat, and I have to get a few other bits and pieces.'

'But I just bought you the white mink.'

'I know, darling, but I *need* a new sable.'

'No, Fontaine, we'll talk about it later.'

'What do you mean, no Fontaine?' I was shaking with fury.

'Goodbye,' he hung up on me.

I phoned back at once. 'Mr Khaled is in conference, and can't be disturbed,' an embarrassed secretary said.

'But this is Mrs Khaled.'

'I'm sorry, he said I wasn't to interrupt him for anyone.'

I slammed the receiver down. How dare he! How dare he! He would pay a lot more than a sable coat for this.

26

TONY

I think I'm a right bastard. What I should have done was told Ian Thaine to take his messy little ex-deb home with him and screw the fact that it might louse up our deal. If our deal depended on me knocking off one of his birds, then to hell with it—who needed it?

I did. Who even knew if he was going to come up with the money anyway? So far it was all conversation.

I really felt bad. Diana had gone, I had to force her to go. She was disgusting. And I was disgusting too, laying back and letting her slobber all over me. Well, at least I hadn't touched *her*.

I have definitely decided I'm going to marry little Alex. It's a big

144

decision, I know, but I love her, I truly love her. I think I would kill any bastard that tried to touch her.

The whole situation is very dodgy. I've got to get away from Fontaine and 'Hobo'. Christ, if Alex ever found out about me and Fontaine it would be all over. She's a girl of principles, so sweet and kind, and that body! Wowee! I've never seen such a gorgeous body, so shy, and a virgin. I can hardly believe it, and she's mine, all mine.

I think what I'm going to do is get up, dress, and maybe take little Alex for lunch. Of course, I don't have her office number. I should have asked her last night, but maybe her girlfriend is home.

I dialled their flat, but there was no reply. Shit! I couldn't even remember the name of the firm she worked for. It's twelve o'clock, which means I've got to wait until five-thirty or six before she gets home.

I had to meet with Ian Thaine at three, that would pass the afternoon. Maybe Sammy would fancy a bite of lunch.

I couldn't track Sammy down, but I found Hal and Franklin in our favourite coffee bar, a nice little place where you could sit all day and watch the American tourists go by.

Hal said, 'Listen, baby, I've got a beautiful deal going. You remember Mamie? Well, her old man invested in this film company in Rome before he died, and now the company's going bust and she's putting up a lot more bread and I'm taking over. We're leaving for Rome tomorrow. Beautiful huh? If you're a good boy I'll put you in a movie, you're pretty enough!'

Hal came up with a deal like this every so often, but something always ballsed it up, usually him.

'That's great, Hal, you're going to be a big man.'

'Baby, I'm always a big man.' His smokey eyes surveyed two American ladies struggling with their mink stoles. He was always on the look out. 'So what's new, Tony baby? How was my town?'

'Great, Hal. I had a ball.'

'Yeah, one of these days I'll go back. I'm waiting for my bookie to die! Got to be a success in that city baby, otherwise you're nowhere—but nothing.'

My favourite waitress came scurrying over. 'Morning Mr Blake. Same as usual?'

'Yes, pretty. Make sure the eggs are nice and firm.'

She dimpled a smile at me. 'I see your club made headlines today.'

'What?'

Hal said, 'Yeah, baby, didn't you see it. A load of shit about Steve Scott.'

'Oh,' I patted my waitress on the bottom. It felt like she had nothing on under the flimsy blue skirt and white apron. 'Be a darling and grab me the papers.'

'I'll try, Mr Blake. We're awfully busy just now.'

She returned in two minutes flat with three morning papers. I scanned them quickly. Steve Scott was on the front page of all of them. The headlines screamed about his secret marriage. I read the first one.

'Steve Scott (23) disclosed at London discothèque "Hobo" last night his secret marriage to actress and dancer Carolyn England (23) some time last week. Steve Scott found fame two years ago when his record "Laurie Baby" shot to the top of the charts. Since then his records have stayed consistently in the Top Ten. He has just finished recording his own Weekly T.V. Show and is due to start work shortly on his first film "MUD". Miss England has appeared countless times on your T.V. screens and was only last year voted "The girl with the longest legs on T.V." The news was broken when Miss England surprised her new husband at "Hobo", where he was enjoying a quiet evening of fun with Alexandra Khaled, eighteen-year-old daughter of billionaire Benjamin Al Khaled. The new Mrs Scott also announced the fact that they are expecting an addition to the family. The Steve Scott fan club hung a black flag from its windows early this morning. Steve Scott has no comment on his surprise marriage.'

There was a big picture of Carolyn leering sexily in a black fishnet cat-suit, and a small picture of Steve having his shirt ripped off by a band of fans.

I was really choked. Where the hell had they got their information about Alexandra? Why should *her* name be brought up?

Lousy newspapers. They all carried more or less the same story.

My poor Alex would be upset if she saw it. Well, it would teach her a lesson for going out with the randy little bastard in the first place.

I attacked my eggs.

'Hello, mind if I sit here?'

It was Suki, dressed for the day in a thigh-length Indian shift and fringed jacket.

Franklin said, 'Where's your sister? You promised to fix me up.'

'Oh yes, sorry, I've been busy. I forgot about it. I'll talk to her.'

I don't understand Franklin. He's a good-looking boy with every opportunity to chat up all the birds at the club, but he never makes a move. Now he's hanging his hopes on Suki's sister.

'If you promised him, do it,' I said. 'Get your sister for tonight.'

'She might be busy,' Suki replied, producing her compact and studying her freaky face. 'Anyone seen Massey lately?'

Under all the piles of weird makeup she was probably quite pretty.

'What do you want to know about Massey for? You've got your little student now,' I said.

'I just wondered if anyone had seen Massey, that's all,' she replied defensively, 'I thought he might be here today.'

I finished my eggs and ordered some cheese-cake. Eating is one of my favourite pastimes, but I never get fat. I stay in great shape. Twenty-five push-ups a day. My stomach's hard as a rock.

Just then who should walk in but Massey. Cool as ever in a white suit and brown polo-neck sweater. He's a great-looking guy.

'Tony,' he clapped me on the shoulder, 'good to have you back. Hello, Suki—Franklin—Hal.' He sat down at our rapidly expanding table.

Suki snapped her compact shut and put it away. 'Mass, can I come back?' she asked.

147

'No,' he said quietly, 'no, baby, you stick with your little white boy.'

Her clown eyes filled with tears. 'Oh come on, Mass, let me back.'

'I said no, Suki.' And he turned to talk to me about New York.

Suki sat there a few minutes, then with two black tears hovering in her eyes, got up and left.

I ate her open cheese sandwich, which she hadn't touched.

'She thinks she can just come walking back to me when she gets a little bored with her sweet little white boy,' Massey said grimly. 'Well, she can just sweat it out.'

I think Massey was actually jealous.

I hung around until it was time to meet with Ian Thaine, then I walked the short distance to his office.

He sat on a black leather throne in front of a huge antique desk in a red room hung with pictures of himself. His opening words were, 'I told you you'd get a good job done, didn't I? Those little convent-educated bints are the ones.' His face was evil and his eyes thin yellow slits.

'Yeah, well thanks, Ian.'

'It's nothing.'

He then proceeded to give me a full sex summary of the three birds he had living with him, including Diana. Then he unlocked a desk drawer and produced a stack of polaroid pictures of them in various stages of undress. They became obscene. I felt sick to my stomach.

'I took them all,' he said proudly. 'Sometimes I have special parties. Next time I'll see you're invited.'

Here was a man after Fontaine's heart! Was I climbing from the frying pan into the fire? What about getting down to business?

I flicked quickly through the rest of the polaroids and said, 'Very nice, Ian. Now what about contracts and things?'

'Contracts?' he said. 'What's the matter, don't you trust me?'

'Of course I trust you, but if I'm going to start knocking myself out looking for locations, I want to be sure everything's cool—you know, have it down in black and white. Of course as soon as we find somewhere I'll leave "Hobo".'

148

One thing I was sure of. I wasn't going to be Tony Schmuck again. If I had to get involved with this slimy bastard it was all going to be legal, so that when he wanted me to attend any of his parties I could safely say no without getting chucked out. Fontaine unwittingly had taught me to be smart.

'All right,' Ian said, 'I'll have an agreement drawn up. Meanwhile start looking. What about Mrs Khaled?'

I looked at him in surprise. How did he know about me and Fontaine?

'What about her?' I said suspiciously.

'Shall I mention her in the agreement?'

'What for?' Now I was really surprised.

'She's your—er—partner, isn't she? She'll be in it with us, won't she?'

I was speechless.

Ian carried on. 'I'd like to meet her. When can I meet her?'

This was charming. When had I ever mentioned Fontaine?

'She's in New York,' I said vaguely.

'Now there's a beautiful woman,' Ian said admiringly, locking his polaroids away.

I stood up. 'O.K., Ian, I'll wait to hear from you.'

'Yes, I'll have my solicitor draw something up. Shouldn't take long.'

'Fine, I'll start looking.'

We shook hands. I didn't trust him, but as long as he thinks Fontaine is involved he'll probably come up with an agreement and the money. I don't know why he thinks she's my partner, but if it keeps him sweet, let him think it. Why disillusion the poor schmuck before the time came?

I couldn't wait for my little Alex to come home from her office. I wondered what she would want to do tonight. I wasn't going to take her on any wild outings, just a nice quiet dinner somewhere small, and a serious talk about us. Then she was going home to bed early. My darling must get some sleep. I figured I would drop by a few estate agents to pass the rest of the afternoon. May as well start the ball rolling.

27

ALEXANDRA

I don't think I've ever been so embarrassed in my life! Mr McLaughton himself summoned me into his office. I was half-an-hour late this morning, and I suppose this is it.

He was a huge man with bushy eyebrows from under which peered watery red eyes. I don't know why *he* has to fire me, I'd never even seen him before.

'Sit down, Alexandra,' he boomed. 'You don't mind me calling you Alexandra do you?' and he chuckled.

I sat nervously. Daddy was right. I should have taken a job with one of his friends.

'Well, well, well,' Mr McLaughton said, suddenly lapsing into a fit of coughing, 'so we have a celebrity in our midst.'

'A celebrity, sir?' I questioned dimly.

'You are Ben Khaled's daughter are you not?'

How on earth had they found out?

'Yes, sir.'

'You should have told us. Why so secretive?'

I blushed, 'I don't know, sir.'

Honestly, what was I expected to do? Come marching in for the job announcing to all and sundry that my father was Benjamin Khaled?

'I think we can give you a better position than you have,' Mr McLaughton said, beaming. 'I think we can bring you into my office as a junior personal assistant, at an extra five pounds a week. Not that the money matters to you, I'm sure.'

I didn't want to be brought into his office as a junior personal assistant at an extra five pounds a week just because he knew who Daddy was.

'Thank you, sir,' I muttered. I'm weak. I hate to cause scenes. I would have to phone up or get Maddy to phone and say I couldn't work there any more.

'My two daughters are great fans of Steve Scott, you'll have to get them his autograph.'

I looked at him in astonishment, 'Steve Scott . . .' I stammered.

He picked up a newspaper from his desk and waved it at me, 'Pretty girl he married,' he said. 'Is she a friend of yours too?'

I took the newspaper from him and read it quickly. The whole thing became clear. That's how they knew about me. What would Mummy say if she saw this, and Daddy? He would be furious.

'I haven't seen this,' I mumbled.

'Don't forget about the autographs. You can take the rest of the week off if you like, start your new job on Monday heh? Perhaps I can meet your father one night, have a little chat about his talented daughter.' He chuckled again.

'Yes, sir. Thank you.' I fled.

By three o'clock I was home. Madelaine was out. I phoned Mummy. Apparently she hadn't seen the newspapers because she didn't mention anything about the whole mess.

'You are bringing some friends this weekend, aren't you?' she said.

I hadn't even asked Michael yet, I hoped he *would* come. 'Yes, Mummy, just one.'

'All right, jolly good, darling. See you tomorrow.'

Madelaine came in shortly after, laden with packages. 'I've been shopping.' she announced, 'got myself some terrific gear. What on earth are you doing home?'

We talked while she unwrapped her parcels and tried everything on.

'You must get one of these crochet dresses,' she enthused, 'they're so terrif, and with your figure it will look fabulous! If you like you can borrow mine tonight.'

Maddy had discovered via Jonathan that Suki had been sleeping at their flat, and that even worse she had moved lots of her things in.

'Jonathan's absolutely livid!' Maddy said. 'It's only a tiny flat and her things are everywhere. He says Michael is dotty about her. Sorry, but I'm sure it won't last.'

'Why is he taking *me* out tonight?' I was confused.

She shrugged. 'Search me. I say, when are you seeing Tony again?'

151

'I don't know. Never I hope.'

'Oh, Alex, he's nice, awfully good-looking. He's your lover anyway, you'll have to see him.'

'I won't.'

We had discussed my losing my virginity from seven a.m. when Maddy finally woke, to eight-thirty, when I had dashed off to the office. Maddy had asked a thousand questions. Did it hurt? Did I love him? Was he enormous? Did I scream? I couldn't really remember any details. I suppose he did have a nice body. Of course I didn't love him, I loved Michael, Michael, Michael, that's all I could think of.

At six o'clock Tony phoned. 'Well, beautiful, how do you feel?'

'Fine, thank you.'

'What time shall I fetch you?'

'Fetch me?' I racked my brains to think if I had made any arrangement with him for tonight, and I was sure I hadn't.

'How about eight o'clock? We'll just have dinner and then I'll bring you straight home.'

'Look, Tony, I'm awfully sorry but I am already going out.'

There was a long pause and then he said, 'You're kidding?'

'No, I've had this arranged for ages.'

There was another long pause and then he said, 'Break it.'

'Break what?'

'Your date, idiot. I'll fetch you at eight.'

'Tony, I can't, it's—'

His voice was suddenly very angry. 'Who are you seeing that's so bloody important?'

I hated people being angry with me. 'I'm sorry, Tony, it's—it's family, I just can't get out of it.'

'Oh, Alex, Alex. What are you doing to me?'

'I'm not doing anything to you.'

'Are you angry with me about last night, is that it?'

'Honestly I'm not angry. I'd love to see you, but it's just not possible tonight.'

'All right, little girl. How about later?'

'I'm not sure, I don't know—'

152

'I'll phone you at eleven. If you're not tired I'll pop round for an hour before going to the club. How's that?'

'Terrific.' I breathed a sigh of relief to get him off the phone without a nasty scene.

I borrowed Maddy's crochet dress and Michael actually gave a whistle when he saw me. 'You *are* growing up,' he commented.

He took me to a little restaurant, very dark and cosy, then he lectured me solidly about how I was mixing with bad company, and if I didn't watch it I would get into trouble, and all these people I was always with smoked drugs and things. Well, I *knew* that.

'I feel responsible for you,' he said. 'You can't come straight out of school and turn into the town swinger. What did your parents say about the papers today?'

'Nothing,' I muttered, I was sulky and disappointed. I thought he had wanted to have dinner with me, but he just wanted to tell me what a silly little girl I was.

'Anyway, what about you and that awful model?' I finally said, unable to keep quiet any longer, 'What do *your* parents think of *you* living with her!'

'I'm not seventeen years old,' he said grimly. 'I'm only trying to help you, Alex, you're only a kid.'

I hated him!

I was home by ten-thirty, having bid a cold goodbye to Michael immediately we finished dinner. Tony phoned promptly at eleven.

I would show Michael. I invited Tony to spend the weekend in the country at Mummy's house. Michael had called Tony common and loud. Well, let's see what he thought about this! If this doesn't make him jealous I don't know what will!

28

TONY

You drift through life from day to day and everything's cool. Life is good, things swing along nicely, plenty of birds, friends, food, enough bread to gamble a little, eat out every night, hand Sadie a fiver occasionally. Beautiful!

Of course I always wanted to do a bit better, get my own joint. But I knew I didn't have to push, it would all happen. I could just relax and enjoy life. It was such a blast to have names I'd only ever read about treat me like their long lost brother, and fantastic birds available.

Then along come Miss Alexandra Khaled, auburn shining hair, big brown eyes, knockout body, young, innocent, classy, sweet, shy, kind. And I fall—POW!! In love.

It means an immediate change in my life. I need plenty more bread, not for gambling, or eating out, or handing more to Sadie. But I need to make a home. I have to have something to offer her.

She looks at me with those big trusting eyes and I melt. I never in my life felt this way before. I feel I must look after her, protect her from the world.

When she said she couldn't see me tonight I was destroyed. My whole day had hinged around seeing her in the evening. I was angry and jealous and sick to my stomach. But she explained so nicely, so sweetly.

Oh boy, I never thought I'd get caught like this. I've known a lot of women and I thought as far as they were concerned I had it licked. Screw 'em and leave 'em wanting more. Never failed. But now I was caught in that well-known trap.

When she said she couldn't see me, it was a physical feeling of pain.

Of course, I have to marry her. This is it. Put her in a little flat, give her a few kids. I wonder if she can cook?

I spent a miserable evening with Sammy and his whiney-voiced scrubber from the night before. We ate at a steak house and I'll

154

swear she was giving him a quick one under the table. She sucked her thumb between mouthfuls of food, and wiped her nose with the back of her hand. Charming!

Eventually she went to the loo and Sammy said, 'What's the matter with you—what are you dragging for?'

I shrugged, 'Nothing, I'm fine.' I wasn't about to tell *him* what the matter was.

'What do you think of my bird? Still at school, isn't she a little darlin'?'

'You won't be happy until you get caught, schmuck. She's under age.'

'Who's going to catch me, then? She says 'er parents never ask any questions. She can come and go when she wants.'

'Sammy,' I shook my head sadly, 'what do you want it for?'

'You're kidding, aren't you?'

She came back. She looked all of fifteen in her wisp of a dress and long stockinged legs.

Eleven o'clock came very slowly. I tried to stay cool and phoned Alex.

She was adorable. 'I'm in bed, Tony. I've been home ages.'

'I'll come round and read you a bedtime story.'

Oh God, I was coming out with lines *I* didn't even believe.

'I'm just going to sleep, but I'll tell you what, would you like to come to the country for the weekend?'

'When?' I asked stupidly.

'I thought tomorrow afternoon, and we could come back Sunday evening.'

'Yeah, that would be great.'

Screw the club, it would have to manage without me over the weekend. A whole three days with my Alex. Couldn't be better.

'Shall we take the train?' she said. 'Or do you want to drive? It's only an hour's journey.'

I didn't think Sammy would see fit to part with his E-type over the weekend so I said, 'We'll take the train.'

'There's a four o'clock from King's Cross. Mummy will meet us the other end.'

I had forgotten about dear old Mummy. That sort of put a

155

dampener on things. What if Mummy told Daddy and Daddy told Fontaine? Oh well, I'd soon be away from 'Hobo'.

'Yeah, that's perfect. I'll pick you up around three.'

'What happened to you?' Sammy asked. 'You look like you found gold.'

'Yeah,' I laughed, 'let's go to the club.'

It was going to be one of those nights, jamming up early, plenty of faces. Franco on his toes, Flowers playing Wilson Pickett. Hal, Franklin and Massey in already. Massey with a zoftic blonde, Franklin alone as usual, and Hal stoned, celebrating his last night of freedom before Rome and Mamie.

I socialised a bit. It was too soon to put out the word I would be opening on my own, but it was as well to spread my charm heavy. I must remember to pinch the members' list and get it copied.

'The Twang' came in with a film group, pouty lips, mane of tangled orange hair, she had got over her temper with me. She gave a hug and a kiss. Her tits were hanging out of a black velvet dress. She wasn't a bad kid, we had had quite a lot of fun. She was certainly well built.

'Guess what, Tonee baby?' she squeaked, 'I'm starring in *Mud* with Steve Scott. Isn't that fabulous?'

'Yeah, great.' I felt full of goodness towards the world.

'What did *she* have to say?' Franklin asked when I sat down.

'She says she's starring with Steve Scott in *Mud*.'

'Huh!' exclaimed Franklin. 'Candy Cook is the lead, she's probably got a bit part.' He still hadn't recovered from his encounter with 'The Twang'.

'Franklin,' I said seriously, 'what are we going to do about you?'

'What do you mean?'

'I mean getting you laid, that's what I mean. What are you saving it up for? Wow—if I was your age with your connections I'd be having a ball.'

'I just haven't met the right girl.'

'Shit, man, by this time *any* girl would be the right one. You can't jerk off all your life you know.'

156

Franklin lapsed into silence and I went and had a scotch with one of the 'Must' just back from a record-breaking concert in Paris.

There's something about a scotch and Coke I like. It's a good long drink with hidden punch. I must have had about six or seven when I went to take a piss and realised I was well and truly loaded. I usually just get a little buzz on when I'm working, but tonight— like POW! it had really hit me.

I was sweating hot, having been dancing with Molly Mandy, who's a wild dancer. She had wandered in on her own and sat at our table. I had this vague idea of fixing her up with Franklin, but God almighty, she'd eat him alive! Maybe that's what the kid needed.

Out of the blue I found myself dancing with 'The Twang'.

'Ooh! Tonee, this is fun,' she said. 'You never used to dance with me when we were together.'

'Funky Street.' Flowers freaking out at his stand. 'The Twang' shaking her boobies at me. Man, I was gone. Flowers grinning broadly. 'Jumpin' Jack Flash.' Sweat pouring off me. Hal having a screaming match with Franco. Everyone laughing. Everyone having a ball. Sammy doing it with his schoolgirl. 'Tramp.' Why did Otis Redding have to get it in a lousy plane crash? Flowers in mourning for weeks, more so than for Martin Luther King. 'You're Lookin' Good.' 'The Twang' falling out of her dress, giggling, tossing orange hair around. Suddenly she changed into Molly Mandy and I said, 'Do me a favour and ball Franklin.'

The music was getting slow, slower. Who was I dancing with? Carla Cassini, beautiful Italian movie star. She smelt fantastic, but ruined the whole thing with hairy armpits. 'You ees beeg man, yes?' 'I Left My Heart in San Francisco.' Was that Massey with Suki? And the zoftic blonde dancing with Hal? Hal never danced but he was swinging tonight. Who wasn't!

'My producer—he 'ave to return Roma for one day only, so I come see you tonight. Good idea, yes?' She was an armful of woman. What about Alex? Would one more time be wrong? 'Who Can I Turn To?' She moulded her body into mine, rubbing a leg between my thighs. Christ, she caught me in the balls and it

157

hurt. 'We must be careful,' she muttered, 'I am followed—'ee always has me followed.' Can't take my eyes off you. She churned her body into mine, keeping perfect time to the music.

'I stay at 102 Marlofield, a leetle 'ouse. You come in one 'alf hour to the back window—I arrange everything.'

Shit, man! Franco and the Italian waiters were hovering at the edge of the dance floor trying to get a better look.

'I go now,' she said abruptly, and left me standing there.

It never rains but it pours. I sat down.

Molly Mandy was hard at work whispering in Franklin's ear. He looked a bit stunned. Man, the room was turning. 'The Twang' appeared. 'How about tonight for old time's sake?' She whispered in my ear, wriggling her tongue about in there at the same time.

Molly Mandy gave me a wink across the table. Massey and Suki came and sat down. A short fat guy who I didn't know came over to 'The Twang' and clamped a chubby hand on her shoulder. He had a cigar clamped between his teeth. 'You gonna stay with this jerk all night?'

'Oh, Chucky, sorry, I'll be right back.'

'You'd better,' he said.

'Who's that?' I asked.

'That's Chuck Van Marless Junior,' she said, 'the producer. I'd better get back.'

'So who's keeping you?'

She gave me a sad look. 'You're such a bastard, Tonee.'

Her voice got on my nerves. She wriggled her way back to Chucky junior, and the group she was with.

I love Alexandra.

What number Marlofield square did Carla say? After all I wasn't married—yet.

Franklin and Molly Mandy suddenly got up. 'We're going,' she announced with a big smile, flashing her gold fillings. Franklin studied the ground in embarrassment. At last, at last!

'What about my sister?' Suki said.

'Where *is* your frigging sister?' I asked.

'She's here—somewhere. She saw some friends when we came in, but she'll be over soon and she thinks Franklin is her date.'

'Listen, baby,' Massey said, 'I do not believe she's too anxious. You've been here an hour already, and where is she?'

Suki shrugged. 'Let's dance.'

They went off, happy to be together again.

I couldn't remember the goddamn number—a hundred and something, a hundred and two, that was it. I was going. After all a movie star is a movie star, and what Alex didn't know wasn't going to hurt her. It certainly doesn't mean I don't love her. Anyway it's a well-known fact that fellows need it more than birds. So what about Fontaine?

I grabbed a taxi, and remembering Carla's warning, had him drop me off in the square, where I wandered around looking for a hundred and two. It was impossible work finding the numbers, and pissing with rain, but I went from house to house peering at doors with my trusty cigarette lighter. Oh God, what one wouldn't do for a star!

I found it. I hoped she had some scotch and coke. I needed it. I pushed my way past clumps of trees to the back and started trying the windows. I was soaking.

Suddenly a light shone in my eyes and a loud voice said, 'I'd stay just where you are if I were you.' And then a big nasty copper loomed into view. 'What do you think you're doing then?' he enquired politely. One thing about our policemen, they've got lovely manners.

So there I stood wet through and just approaching a hangover in West London Central Police Station. Charming! The bloody copper had never heard of Carla Cassini, and nor had the couple who lived in one hundred and two Marlofield Square. Too late I realised it should have been Marlofield Street, but the sweet arm of the law didn't want to know about checking my story.

I imagined Carla waiting for me in a clinging black slip, the sort of thing she wore in most of her movies.

I was in a right mess now. What a scene! After long arguments they finally sent someone round to check my story at a hundred and two Marlofield Street, and Carla, the bitch, denied she'd even heard of me!! So then more arguments until I finally got them to phone 'Hobo', and Franco and Sammy came rushing over and

159

identified me. Franco confirmed that Miss Carla Cassini had been in the club that night, and had been dancing with me. So they finally believed me and let me go.

Shit, man! Sammy was laughing so much that tears were rolling down his cheeks.

'I can just picture the scene,' he said, 'you trying to get in a window with an 'ard on, and the copper pouncing down on you!'

Oh very funny. Very funny indeed.

Franco was trying to look grave and concerned, wedged in the back of Sammy's E-type, but I knew as soon as we got back to the club the story was going to be all over.

'Now, I don't want this spread around,' I said grimly.

'Meester Blake!' Franco exclaimed in horror, 'I cut off my right arm eef I say anything.'

Lying sonofabitch!

29

FONTAINE

I sat and planned my revenge. It was about time Benjamin was taught a lesson. God almighty, he was treating me like a wife!

I dressed, went out and bought the sable coat anyhow. Benjamin's credit was good, and they knew who I was. 'Send the bill to my husband's office,' I said, 'he always likes me to pick my own Christmas presents.'

That would teach dear old Benjamin to say no. Doesn't the old fool realise how lucky he is to have a wife like me? I am beautiful, elegant, chic, famous. What more could anyone want from a woman?

Tonight, when he expects me to entertain his beastly son I shall make mincemeat of them both. Benjamin can't expect to treat *me* this way and get away with it. First of all I intend to return to London tomorrow, with or without Benjamin. I will show him who calls the tune in *our* marriage. My God, if he thinks he can push me around the way he used to treat his dreary first wife, he can think again.

I put on a white lace Courrèges cat suit. Roger came by and fixed my hair in a devastating style, then Adamo made me a champagne cocktail, and I awaited my darling husband's return.

He puffed in promptly at six, followed closely by Ben junior, who peered at me through owl-like glasses.

'Hello, Benjamin, darling,' I purred coldly, ignoring the son, '*so* sweet of you to call me back.'

'Did you see young Ben?' Benjamin said pointedly.

'Yes, I saw young Ben,' I replied in a sing-song voice.

'Fontaine, pull yourself together. We'll talk about it later.'

'There's nothing to talk about. Oh, by the way, I bought the coat—it's in the bedroom, it's absolutely divine. Thank you, darling.'

His face sagged, but he was loath to argue in front of his precious son. He turned brightly to Ben junior. 'Well now, what restaurant would you like to go to?'

'Anywhere, sir,' Ben junior replied, studying the floor in embarrassment at being caught in the middle of an argument.

'What about you?' Benjamin turned to me, desperately trying to keep the proceedings bright.

'I don't think I'll come.' I savoured his look of annoyance, 'I have a headache.'

There was a short delicious silence, then Benjamin said, 'Make yourself comfortable, Ben, have a drink, look at the magazines. I think there's a new "Playboy".' He winked at his son as only a decrepit old man can. 'Fontaine, why don't you come in the bedroom and show me your coat while I shower?'

Oh, I see. He was going to forgive me for buying the coat if I came out to din-din like a good girl and was nice to dreary boring son.

I was right.

'Fontaine, don't be a bitch!'

'A bitch?'

'You know what I mean.'

'What?'

'The boy is sensitive, don't hurt him, make him at ease.'

'And how about *me*? I'm sensitive too, especially when some goddamn little secretary won't even put me through to you on the goddamn phone.'

'You must understand—'

'So must you. I don't expect to be treated like this.'

'You have the coat now, at least you can be civil.'

'Yes—I have the coat *only* because I ignored you and got it anyway.'

'Please, Fontaine, for the boy.'

'He's not a boy, Benjamin, don't baby him. He's probably bored stiff at having dinner with us anyway, and so am I—very bored by the whole thing.'

'I'll see you get the rest of the money you want tomorrow morning.'

'Oh, all right, but just remember to *never* treat me in such a way again.'

'Very well, Fontaine, but please let us have a nice amicable evening.'

I hate Benjamin. I hate a man you can tread all over.

His punishment wasn't over yet, he would see. As soon as he comes pawing me, expecting to go to bed with me, he will just have to wait. Just as he had to wait before we were married. Oh God, I had him mad for it then, and that's just the way it's going to be again. He'll have to beg for it. On his knees. Poor old bastard.

30

TONY

Charming! Hauled down to the police station like a common criminal! Sadie would have a thousand fits if she knew. All over some bird that, if you want the truth, I didn't even fancy! Well, not much anyway. I mean if she hadn't've been who she was I certainly wouldn't have gone creeping down to Marlofield Square—Street—or wherever it was. Really I don't fancy anyone except Alex.

It is two o'clock in the afternoon, and I'm shaved and dressed (very casual—white sweater, black slacks, suede jacket). I am wondering what kind of jazz to take with me. A suit in case my darling wants to go out? Pyjamas? I don't even have any, on account of the fact that I always kip in the raw—lets the skin breathe, y'know.

In the end I bundled a couple more sweaters and my shaving gear in a bag. After all, a weekend in the country was bound to be slopping about.

I didn't feel too fantastic. Slight touch of your actual hangover. But I looked good, with some overnight tan I could have just got back from South of France.

Alex was waiting for me. Very pretty in a green trouser suit, with her hair tumbling around her lovely little face. She had a huge suitcase and, blushing, she said, 'I'm taking all my dirty washing home.'

Sweet!

'Do you want some coffee?' she asked.

'I've got a cab waiting.'

'Oh, O.K. Maddy won't be a sec.'

Maddy?!? Don't tell me she was coming with us. What a lumber!

She was. Maddy in a mauve trouser suit, with a big fat bottom, a John Lennon cap and plain face.

I had been looking forward to a nice quiet chat with my Alex,

163

but it was not to be. On the train Maddy kept up a non-stop stream of unintelligent conversation, all about clothes and some schmuck called Jonathan and wasn't Christmas going to be absolutely 'super'. I gathered from the conversation that Alex was going to spend Christmas at Madelaine's home. Charming! I would have to talk her out of *that*.

'Mummy always goes to St Moritz for Christmas,' Alex remarked to me—*finally* including me in the conversation, 'it's so lovely there with the ski-ing and everything. This will be the first Christmas I haven't gone with her.'

'Only another week and I haven't bought *one* present yet,' Madelaine exclaimed. 'What do *you* want, Alex?'

Alex laughed. 'Nothing actually. Where are you spending Christmas, Tony?'

Where *was* I spending Christmas? The Elephant and Asshole I supposed. 'Er, I haven't decided yet.'

As a matter of fact Sadie and Sam don't keep Christmas—I mean, nothing special. Usually on Christmas Day I get up late and wander over to the Hilton with whatever bird I happen to be with, and eat their special Christmas lunch. It's very nice. Then I wander home, get into kip and watch the telly.

I fell asleep to the sound of the girls' chatter. I would get Alex alone later, I could wait.

'Wake up, we're here!'

I staggered off the train behind the girls, carrying Alex's enormous suitcase, Madelaine's ton-weight overnight bag, and my carryall. Tony the porter

The girls raced up the platform and I followed. Alex threw her arms around a fair-haired woman, standing beside a station wagon. She smiled at me when I came lumbering up with all the gear.

Alex said, 'Mummy, I should like to introduce you to Tony Blake.'

'Mummy' gave me a friendly smile. I could see where Alex got her beautiful brown eyes from. Her mother was an attractive woman, a lot better than any of the old birds Hal ever appeared with.

'So glad to meet you, Mr Blake. You'll have to excuse my

daughter leaving you to carry everything, she has absolutely no manners.'

We all laughed. I liked 'Mummy'.

We reached the house, I was shown around, then left alone in a mahogany lined guest-room with an adjoining marble bathroom. What a house! Stables, swimming pool—the lot. Servants darting around everywhere, three cars in the drive. I had imagined poor abandoned 'Mummy' living in a cottage with a daily help. Really, I was a bit choked. How could Alex have a billionaire father, a mother that lived like this, and *still* work as a crummy secretary? I couldn't understand it.

A butler came in with my bag. 'Shall I unpack for you, sir?' He looked disdainfully down his long thin nose.

Oh shit, man—if Sammy could see me now!

'No, that's all right,' I said airily, thinking of my two crumpled sweaters and a clean pair of pants with a hole in.

'Are you sure, sir?'

'Yeah, I'm sure,' I glared at him, hoping he would go away.

'Can I fetch you a drink, sir?'

Now that was more like it. 'Yes, I'll have a scotch and coke, plenty of ice.'

'Scotch *with* Coca-Cola, sir?'

'Yeah—*with* Coca-Cola.'

'Very good, sir.'

Skinny old bastard, didn't know what it was all about, stuck down in the country.

I opened my only piece of luggage and wished to hell I'd brought a suit. Alex and Madelaine had deposited me in this room saying gaily, 'We're going to change for dinner—see you downstairs at seven.' I had nothing to change into except another sweater, and I was saving that for tomorrow. I had an awful feeling that I'd brought the wrong gear. I hadn't even been alone with my baby Alex yet. Where the hell was her bedroom, anyway? I'd have to know that for later.

Long Thin Nose came back with a tiny slug of scotch in a glass, a full ice bucket and a bottle of coke.

I downed the scotch in one fell swoop. Then I changed sweaters and went off in search of Alex.

It was a huge bloody house with massive oak doors everywhere—all closed. I went downstairs and in front of a roaring fire I found 'Mummy' in a blue chiffon cocktail gown, with a red faced giant of an old chap in a dinner jacket.

'Ah, Mr Blake,' 'Mummy' said. I wished she would cut out the Mr Blake jazz. 'I'd like to introduce you to Doctor Sutton.'

I shook hands. Well, at least they were going out somewhere the way they were all dolled up.

'Mr Blake is a friend of Alexandra's from London.'

'Oh yes,' said Doctor Sutton. 'how do you do—yes, London, I shall be going there in three weeks time. Friend of Alexandra's. Charming girl, just like her mother, y'know—charming. Yes—very nice, very nice.'

'Would you care for a drink, Mr Blake?' asked 'Mummy'.

'Yeah—I mean yes, thank you, lovely, er I wish you'd call me Tony.'

'Certainly.' She smiled. She had a smile like Alex, only it was a little worn round the edges.

She summoned Long Thin Nose who smirked knowingly at me and said, 'Scotch *with* Coca-Cola, sir.'

'Yeah.'

'Now that's a funny drink.' Doctor Sutton wasn't one to miss out on a bit of conversation. 'Very funny, you drown the taste of the alcohol with the carbonated drink. You may just as well drink plain Coca-Cola.'

I wished the old goat would get going, and where was my Alex? As if on cue she came giggling in with Maddy. Both of them wearing quite dressy outfits. It suddenly dawned on me that maybe dressing for dinner meant dressing up for dinner.

Maddy confirmed my suspicions, 'Haven't you changed yet, Tony?' she asked, just as Old Long Nose was bringing me my drink.

'Hush, Madelaine,' 'Mummy' said, 'Mr Blake doesn't have to change.'

'Oh gosh, Tony,' Alex interrupted, 'I forgot to tell you we always dress for dinner. I thought you would know . . .' she trailed off lamely. 'Oh golly, I'm so silly, please forgive me, why on earth should you?'

Yeah. Why on earth should I know? After all I'm only a lousy ex-waiter. I felt like a right berk.

'Don't worry about it, Mr Blake. You look quite respectable as you are,' said 'Mummy'.

So I stood there with egg on my face while they all inspected my black and white striped (at least it was Simpsons) sweater and tight black trousers.

Madelaine stifled a giggle. What she needed was a good stiff kick up her backside.

'Dinner is served, M'Lady.' Old Long Thin Nose was back. I thought scenes like this only existed in the movies.

We all trooped into the dining-room, Alex holding my arm and whispering, 'Sorry!'

The dining-room table was loaded with enough silver to sink a ship. It's a good job I was once a waiter—otherwise I'd never have known which knives and forks and jazz to use.

Dinner was a gas, Doctor Sutton entertaining us with a story about a patient of his with a terminal disease; 'Mummy' telling us about how she was coming up to town for the January sales and what she was going to buy; and Alex and Madelaine occasionally giggling together.

I was well and truly fed up. After dinner, which dragged on, there was coffee in the study, then everyone started yawning and 'Mummy' said, 'we'd better all have an early night if we're to go riding in the morning.'

I tried to catch Alex's eye, but she was in a huddle with her girl-friend as usual.

'You *do* ride, don't you, Mr Blake?' asked 'Mummy'.

I'd kill her if she didn't stop calling me Mr Blake.

I felt like saying—'Yeah, baby, I ride, but not the way you have in mind!' Instead I said, 'No.'

'What a pity. But you can have a nice lie-in and we shall be back by lunchtime.'

Oh, very jolly.

Everyone said goodnight to everyone else, and the girls and I started upstairs while Mummy saw the Doctor out.

'Where's your room?' I hissed at Alex.

'Oh!' she looked flustered. 'Maddy's in with me.'

Charming! 'Then you come to my room.'

'Tony I *can't*, not here.'

I took her sweet little hand and squeezed it, 'I just want to talk to you, only talk, I promise.'

My body was talking already, I was as hard as a rock.

'All right, I'll try.'

I gave her a kiss on the cheek as Madelaine stood and stared.

'Make it soon.'

She nodded, 'If I can.' And then she was off with her girl-friend.

What a lousy situation. I mean what a drag this whole thing is. I looked at my watch. Only nine-thirty. I haven't been to bed at nine-thirty since I was ten!

I went to my room. No television, no radio, no telephone. Someone had turned the bed down and unpacked my bag. Well what the hell—I didn't care what some thin-nosed butler thought of me.

I lay on the bed and smoked a cigarette—then another one, then another.

This was ridiculous, nearly half an hour and no Alex.

I couldn't bear the thought that she wasn't going to come. My body was in a nervous sweat already. I would give her another five minutes—ten minutes—fifteen minutes. Goddamn it! Nearly an hour and where was she?

I went into the passage. No sign of life, just a dim light burning. Like an idiot I had no idea where her room was. I peered through the keyhole of the door next to mine, the room was in darkness. Then the next keyhole—it was a john—then the next—a cupboard. I was making great progress.

The passage curved round a corner, and there was a door with light showing under it. I bent down to peer through the keyhole and jerked back with astonishment. Naughty old 'Mummy'. She was spread out on the bed, yards of blue chiffon round her waist, legs high in the air, and crouched above her was dear old Doctor Sutton. 'Mummy' was a right raver.

I couldn't help smiling. What a scene! Doctor Sutton still had most of his clothes on—couldn't be too comfortable!

Well, well, well. I dragged myself away from the keyhole—I was a doer not a watcher.

Now I felt horny. Where was Alex?

I went down the other end of the passage and started the keyhole routine again. Her room was in the same position as her mother's, but *she* wasn't. She was lying asleep in a divan bed with a small table separating her from Madelaine, also asleep.

I looked at her for a while. I felt like a thief. She was breathing softly with the covers pulled up to her neck and her hair spread out on the pillow. I had such a feeling of LOVE. Keeping a wary eye on Madelaine, who was giving out with a few snores, I gently pulled the covers off Alex. She was wearing a white frilly nightgown. She sighed and turned on her back.

I was eating her up with my eyes. My body was choking to hold her. I put my hand on her breast, so soft and still. Her eyelids fluttered and I quickly took my hand away.

She opened her eyes. 'Tony!'

'Sssh.' I didn't want the girl-friend awake. 'What happened to you?'

She looked a bit sheepish. 'I *meant* to come to talk to you but I fell asleep'.

Very flattering—I mean she really must have the hots for me.

'Well, come on,' I whispered.

'But it's so late, and what about Maddy?' she protested.

All the same she climbed out of bed and slipped on a pink quilted dressing-gown.

I took her hand. 'Maddy's fast asleep, and I'll have you back in bed in no time.' She didn't realise I meant my bed of course.

We crept off down the passage to my room, and she curled up in a chair and stared at me with those big brown eyes.

I paced about a bit and turned all the lights off except for a bedside lamp.

'What do you want to talk about?' she asked sweetly.

169

I stood behind her chair and stroked her hair. If I didn't have her soon I was going to explode.

'I'm sorry about dinner,' she said, 'I should have warned you we always dress. Mummy's a stickler for doing things properly.'

Yeah, baby!

'Alex,' I said, my voice strangled. I started to undo the buttons of her dressing-gown.

She pushed my hands away. 'It's a shame you can't ride,' she said in a high little voice.

Oh but I can—I can.

My hands reached her beautiful breasts and I squeezed her nipples. She wriggled around in the chair, trying to get away.

'Stay still—relax,' I said. I was shaking, I wanted her so badly. I was a fine one to tell *her* to relax.

'What about Mummy?' she asked desperately.

I ignored *that*, and managed to slip her nightie over her head. Her hands flew to cover herself and she started to shiver.

'Come on, into bed.' Then I played the strong man, carried her over and plopped her on the middle of the bed. She still had on a pair of white panties and she lay quickly on her stomach, so all I could see was her velvet smooth back, rounded bottom through the panties, and long knockout legs.

I ripped my clothes off. If I wasn't quick I was going to blow the whole set-up. I lay on top of her. Oh Man, I could have made it all over those sexy legs! But I gathered a little control and pushed myself between the back of her thighs.

She tried to throw me off.

'Please, please, stop it, Tony, I don't want to—*please*.'

Birds were always saying no when they meant yes. But when she started to cry, loud sobs, I suddenly felt like the world's worst heel. This wasn't some bird I was on the make for. This was the wonderful girl I wanted to marry.

'Hey,' I got off and cuddled her softly. 'Quiet, darling, if you don't want to, we won't—no problem.'

She stopped crying, 'I'm sorry, Tony.' Then she got up and put her things on. I took her to the door and kissed her. She smiled at me. She looked like a little girl. 'Goodnight, Tony. Thank you.' Then she was gone.

Man, this is love! If I can give up what I just gave up I really have it bad.

And now I have a problem, and not even a 'Playboy' magazine in sight!

31

ALEXANDRA

Maddy woke me in the morning by pummelling my back until I was forced to open my eyes. I yawned. 'What time is it?'

'It's seven, and where were *you* last night? I got up to go to the loo and you were gone. Did the devastating Tony drag you off to his room? I tried to stay awake, but you were ages.'

'I wasn't.'

'You were. Did he ravish your girlish body?'

'Maddy, shut up, you sound like some woman's magazine.'

'Did he screw you, then?'

'Maddy!'

I went off to the bathroom before she could bag it, and took a cold bath. Mummy say cold baths are better for you than hot ones.

I tried not to think about the previous evening with Tony.

Maddy was all huffy when I finished in the bathroom.

'You've become very secretive,' she remarked coldly.

We had a breakfast of scrambled eggs and bacon, then we set off riding. It was glorious fun. I had my own horse, Pinto.

I felt guilty about last night, guilty about upsetting Maddy, and guilty about everything in general.

We were riding through the woods and approaching a stream when suddenly Pinto reared up and I came tumbling off. 'Ouch!!'

Mummy and Maddy had already crossed the stream, but they stopped, and turned back.

I felt all right, nothing broken, but when I tried to stand my left leg gave way and I felt an awful pain.

'I think you've got a nasty sprain,' Mummy said.

'Oh, Alex!' Maddy lamented.

They piled me back on to Pinto who was now standing quietly, and back to the house we all went.

Mummy sent for Doctor Sutton, who came immediately. He is such a sweet old man. He brought me into the world and has looked after me ever since.

It was a sprain, and a nasty one.

'Off your feet for five or six days at least,' Doctor Sutton pronounced.

'Poor Alex,' Maddy wailed.

Mummy was very businesslike. 'Can't be helped. I think there's a two o'clock train to town that Mr Blake can take. What about you, Madelaine dear? Do you want to stay, or will you leave too?'

I groaned. I was beginning to feel sick. 'I think you had better go back, Maddy. I'm not going to be much fun to be around.'

'If you're sure, Alex. I'll stay if you like.'

'No.' I shook my head. Doctor Sutton had given me some pain killer and sleeping pills and I was feeling drowsy.

'Come along, Madelaine dear,' Mummy said, 'she'll feel better if she has some sleep.'

They went out of the room. My leg throbbed, my head ached and my eyes soon closed.

32

TONY

Too bloody much! Sitting on another train next to best friend Madelaine, without so much as a last glimpse of my adorable little Alex.

'Rotten luck, isn't it?' Madelaine questioned for the sixth time.

I think she gets some sort of perverted thrill seeing me so choked.

'Yeah,' I muttered, wishing she would shut up.

'What will you *do* tonight?'

'What I always do on a Saturday night, go to the club.'

'You're so lucky. I'm left in the lurch, my boyfriend's away and I hate staying in the flat alone.'

Tough!

We had five minutes of beautiful silence, then—

'I say, Tony, could I come to the club with you? I'd be ever so good, stay out of your way and everything.'

I frowned. Who needed her?

'Well no, Maddy, it would be a real drag for you, you'd get shoved around all over the joint, Saturday night's a mad-house.'

'*Please*, Tony, I don't mind. I'm sure Alex would want you to take me. In fact she did mention something about us sticking together.'

Sticking together? What was *that*?

Shit—why had my little darling gone and fallen off her god-damn horse?

'That's settled, then?'

Christ! Didn't she ever shut up? The poor guy that ever got lucky would probably have to gag her while he had it off.

'All right,' I said reluctantly. I didn't want her carrying tales to Alex about how I wouldn't take her to the club.

She prattled on about God knows what, I was bored by her. King's Cross at last!

'Can I share your taxi, Tony?'

Caught once more.

She talked all the way to Chelsea and left me with—'Can you pick me up about eight o'clock?'

Oh no, definitely no.

'Sorry, Mads, I've got to pop over and visit my mum and dad. If you want to come to the club I'll be there from about twelve.'

That should fix her. Her face dropped.

'What a shame. I thought we could have dinner first.'

'Sorry, darling, duty calls.'

'Oh, Alex will be disappointed when I tell her.'

Anyone would think it was Alex I was turning down!

'You know how it is. Maybe I'll see you later.'

I hopped back in the cab and muttered at the driver to get moving.

'See you later.' Madelaine shouted bravely.

She didn't intend to give up, but I doubted if she would come waltzing into the club alone at midnight.

I felt pretty blue. I'd been feeling like a king the night before on account of that whole scene with my darling, but now she was lying injured in bed and they hadn't even let me see her before I left. Dragtime. I had decided to talk to her about our plans, get everything settled over the rest of the weekend. I certainly wouldn't have minded staying at the house while she was in bed, but 'Mummy' had Madelaine and me out of there like a shot out of a gun.

My flat looked worse than ever. I could never expect Alex to move in here, even to start off with. Maybe if we got rid of Madelaine *I* could move in with Alex.

I was thinking of perhaps Caxton Hall for the wedding, do it quickly before anyone could object. I'd have to talk to her about it as soon as I saw her again, and when would that be? With randy old Doctor Sutton in charge, who knew?

Anyway—come Monday morning I am going to be out and looking for new club premises. As long as Alex is away I may as well get *something* settled.

33

FONTAINE

Benjamin and I flew back to London in silence.

Our whole relationship has been based on silence ever since that ghastly evening out with Ben Cretin junior.

When we were coming in to land, Benjamin suddenly gripped my arm and said, white-faced and shaking, 'I want a divorce, Fontaine.'

Well of course I was astounded! 'You want *what*?'

He cleared his throat and I studied the network of tiny aged lines all over his face.

'I want a divorce,' he repeated.

I gazed out of the window completely at a loss. The old fool asking *me* for a divorce! How ironic. How humiliating. How dare he!

I smiled coolly. 'Sorry, old boy, but I don't think I care for that idea.' Inwardly I was in a burning rage.

'You have no choice,' he said sourly, 'I've had you watched.' He produced a thick wad of papers from his briefcase. 'I know *all* about you and Allen Grant and Tony Blake. I even have photographs.'

He handed me a glossy ten by eight of me and Tony on the bed in the New York apartment.

Oh my God, I looked awful, and Tony so hairy, like a great ape—ugh!

'Where did you get this?' I asked pleasantly.

'Adamo.'

'Oh!' That little bastard! I couldn't think properly. I had to see my lawyer immediately.

'There will be two cars meeting us at the airport.' Benjamin said, 'I have a suite at Claridges, and you may stay at the house until it's sold.'

My head was spinning. What had I done to this old man that he could treat me like this?

'Of course I will make you a reasonable allowance, though I don't have to, and we'll call the sable coat a farewell gift.' He stored his evidence back in his briefcase, and the wheels of the plane touched gently down.

For some utterly stupid reason my eyes filled with tears and I said, 'But I thought you loved me.'

He looked at me seriously, 'And I thought you loved me.' He unclicked his seat belt and stood up, 'Goodbye, Fontaine. Good luck.'

34

TONY

I had a good kip. Didn't feel like seeing anybody, so went to a movie on my own and arrived down the club early. There was nobody in yet. I sat down and told Franco to have the chef fix me a steak and chips.

Flowers wandered in and sat down beside me. He looked moody and miserable.

'How's it going?' I asked.

He shrugged. 'Not good man!' He chewed on his fingernails.

'What's the problem?' I knew it was bound to be a touch, but I wanted to keep him sweet as I had plans for him and Tina in the new joint.

'I need a fast fifty for Tina, she's in trouble.'

Charming! A touch is a touch, but fifty?

He chewed on his fingernails some more while I did some quick thinking. I wanted them with me when I went, and what better way to guarantee that fact than by having him in my debt? Besides which, I liked Tina, she's a good, hard-working kid.

'O.K. I'll get it for you. Monday.'

Flowers beamed 'You're great, Tony. I knew we could count on you.' He rushed off to tell Tina the good news.

Fontaine will be definitely choked when I am gone. I don't give 'Hobo' ten days without me. The plan is to set the new place up, have it all ready to go, and then bye bye, Mrs Khaled.

Where is Mrs K. anyway? Still in New York, I hope, enjoying her strange scenes.

The money people started to arrive and were placed carefully out of the way. Flowers put on an early Antonio Carlos Jobim album. One of the 'Must' arrived alone and sat down with me. He was about the most intelligent of the group, but always high on acid. We discussed sounds and how the police were always raiding his joint, but he was too smart for them—he kept all his gear buried in the garden!

'Where's Lissy?' I asked. Lissy was his flaxen-haired sixteen-year-old-freaked-out wife.

'She's taking a health bath in Germany.'

'Oh.' I mean what else do you say to *that*?

Sammy bounced in alone. 'I've been workin' me bleedin' balls off!' He announced, 'I'll have a scotch and coke.'

I got up to greet some faces. A well known politician and his new wife. Who should they be with but mumsy old Vanessa and husband Leonard. She smiled nervously at me, huge tits escaping from purple tulle. Leonard shook my hand, good clean masculine stuff. I had a feeling he couldn't stand me. In this business you get a pretty reliable sixth sense about things like that.

Everybody started to arrive at once, and Franco got busy sorting them all out. There were certain places certain people would sit, and certain places they would not. Franco knew exactly, and he was great at arranging them all.

I stayed near the entrance, greeting, kissing, cuddling, flattering.

Vanessa came out to the Ladies room and whispered. 'Can I talk to you, Tony?'

'Yeah.' Why all the hush? We were well out of sight of hubby.

'Have you heard about Benjamin Khaled?'

'Heard what?'

'Apparently, and I know this from a very good source, my hairdresser actually.'

'Get on with it.' I was impatient.

'You must promise not to breathe a word of this to Fontaine. Do you promise?'

'Yeah, I promise.' She was impossible.

'Actually he's been seeing another woman, and not just any other woman—Delores! My dear, Fontaine will be beside herself with utter rage when she hears. She would never dream Benjamin could stray. Isn't it too, too frightful?'

Without tits I would never have looked at Vanessa in the first place, now, even with them, I couldn't fancy her. Gossip gives me a pain. Who cares? Good old Benjamin, getting one back on Fontaine. And with Delores yet! Sensational new model, on the cover of you name it she's on it. Yeah! Fontaine will be double choked!

I patted Vanessa on her fat bottom and winked. 'Don't believe it.'

'But it's true! Honestly Tony. Delores goes to the same hairdresser as me and I heard that—'

'Still don't believe it.'

She pouted. 'Nanny takes the children out every day between three and five as before. Why don't you pop in to see me?'

I shrugged. That scene was definitely over. 'Yeah, maybe.'

She laughed nervously. 'Don't say maybe, say yes.'

I was saved by Sammy appearing. ''Ere, any loose stock around?'

Vanessa gave him a look of distaste and disappeared into the loo.

Sammy chuckled. 'You've always got a bird 'anging around you. What you got that I 'aven't?'

One of the good things about Sammy is that you never have to bother to answer him.

The evening roared on. I stayed sober, rejected a few girls and felt pleased with myself. I wasn't going to be unfaithful to my darling Alex. I didn't want to be, and I wasn't going to. There's true love for you.

Just before one, Madelaine appeared. 'I've had a simply dreadful time getting in,' she complained. 'I came at twelve and that ghastly foreign girl said you weren't here yet, and she wouldn't even let me in to wait. Then I came back and she *still* said you weren't here, so I waited 'til she wasn't looking and just came right on in. Really, I do think you should fire her.'

She looked lumpy in some sort of crochet dress, and a bit red faced. Tina had *strict* instructions *never* to let any unaccompanied bird in, especially if they asked for me.

I sat her down next to Sammy who looked her over with disinterest. I ordered her a Coca-Cola, wasn't getting *her* loaded. Then I did a fast vanish and sat down with a couple of songwriters who had the current hot show in town. Idle chat. Then up to greet old time movie star, five feet tall. He looked like a giant on the screen. He was with 'The Twang', fast becoming everybody's date.

'Tonee babee,' she squealed, 'you're going to be so proud of me, I'm signed for two new movies. First *Mud* and then a picture with my gentleman friend here.' She squeezed old time movie star's arm and giggled. Her left tit reached his mouth!

I wondered if she'd still be available for me if I wanted her, or did she only put out for a part in a movie now?

'That's wonderful,' I said, phoney bastard that I am.

'Yes, isn't it though? I'm so thrilled, it's all so wonderful! Have you got a good table for us?'

All of a sudden she was talking to me like a waiter!

'Franco will see to you.'

I went out front, where Tina said shyly. 'Thank you, Mr Blake.' The poor kid looked washed out.

'Why don't you go home? One of the boys can come out here.'

'Mr Blake, I'm fine—really.'

I felt like taking off early myself.

'Tony!!' A shriek from a deep throaty voice. 'You old sexy bastard. How *are* you darling? Still the greatest fuck in town, I bet!'

It was Margo Castile, famous sex change . . . lady. I mean *he* was originally a fishmonger or something, but after many operations *she* was a well-known personality around town. Rather exotic, lovely looking, but with this deep butch voice and language like a fishwife. She was with two men, a small beaming Italian and an English actor.

'Tony darling. When are you going to show *me* what you keep in those sexy tight pants?' She shrieked with laughter. She was always drunk.

'Yes, Tony,' the English actor lisped excitedly.' When are you going to show Margo?'

I smiled weakly. I wasn't ready for *this* group tonight. We all went inside.

'I say, let's have an organised fuck!' Margo shouted. 'All those that want to join in, hands up!'

'Shut up, you are awful,' giggled the actor.

I got them seated at a table and warned them to behave. Margo laughed and patted a pretty blonde girl sitting at the next table. 'You're sweet,' she drawled, 'perfectly sweet! Do you fuck?'

The girl gasped and turned away. Margo roared.

'Look, if you can't behave,' I said, 'I'll just have to throw you out.' I was always threatening her with that, but it never did any good.

'I promise to be a good girl,' she smiled at me 'Promise promise!'

She was a nut, but you couldn't help liking her. Back at my table, Sammy was chatting Madelaine.

''Ere, who is she?' He whispered.

I told him all I knew.

'Not much to look at, but I bet she's a lunatic in bed!'

He was welcome.

I suddenly decided the hell with it. I was going home. The place gave me a goddamn pain. I briefed Franco and quietly left.

Who needed it?

35

FONTAINE

The old millionaire bastard can think again if he imagines he can treat *me* like this. Oh no, definitely not. I am not his ugly first wife, ready to be quietly discarded like a frightened white mouse.

Of course, the whole thing has come as such a surprise. Although I should have realised when he came to New York and wasn't ready to leap straight into bed with me that *some*thing was amiss.

There must be another woman. A scheming money grabbing *bitch*! I go hot and cold with sheer and utter anger. *How dare he.*

And as for that Adamo. I shall see he never works anywhere again. How revolting to think of him watching me in bed. Where on earth was he hiding? And Tony, Allen. Were they in on it?

I can't wait to phone my darling friend Vanessa. If there is gossip around, she will know of it.

As it was a Sunday I was forced to wait until at least ten to phone her, and then I got Leonard.

'She's still sleeping, Fontaine. We were at your club last night. When did you get back?'

'This morning. How was the club? Anyone interesting?' Leonard then started to tell me a boring story about how Margo Castile had done a striptease down to brief bikini panties.

'Fantastic bosom,' he added, 'all there, just like a real woman.'

'Injections, darling, you too could have one like that. Although what you're worrying about bosoms for with *your* wife's mammoth proportions I don't know.'

He laughed, slightly embarrassed. 'I'll get Vanessa to phone you when she wakes. I'm sure you two have a lot to catch up on.'

Did he know something?

I prowled around my house. My beautiful house that was up for sale. Oh, just wait until I get in touch with my solicitor tomorrow.

Vanessa didn't phone until twelve.

'Fontaine, sweetie, how are you? When did you arrive?'

181

'This morning.'

'You must be exhausted!'

'No, I feel wide awake actually. I thought I might come over and catch up on all the gossip. I'm sure there's lots of it.'

'I'm still in bed but I'd adore to see you. Come for lunch, Leonard's out golfing.'

'Divine.'

I was depending on Vanessa being able to tell me exactly what was going on.

I was right. She couldn't wait to tell me all about Benjamin and a ghastly scrubber model called Delores.

'Why on earth didn't you phone me in New York?' I demanded. My God, had I known I would have been in a much stronger position.

'I thought you knew,' replied my loyal friend, sloppy in a blue cashmere cardigan with a button missing. 'Apparently he's given her a huge emerald and diamond ring, a car, and several fur coats.'

'How nice.' My voice was acid.

'What are you going to do?' Vanessa gushed.

I shook my head slowly. 'Divorce the bastard, and take him for every penny he's got.'

36

TONY

I have phoned my lovely Alexandra every day. But each time I get old hawk nose the butler or 'Mummy'. Both tell me Alex is fine, making wonderful progress, but can't come to the phone yet. Charming! Today is the last straw. Phoned as usual and was told Miss Khaled had left to spend Christmas with the Newcombes.

It's Christmas Eve, pissing with rain, and miserable. I have spent a lousy week searching for a new place. Haven't come up with anything. The club has been a drag, everyone away for Christmas. Even old Sammy hasn't been in.

I miss Alex like mad, in *every* way. It is getting difficult not to take some bird home and bang her purely for physical reasons. Fontaine is back, but I haven't heard from her. On top of everything else I have a lousy cold.

I spent hours trying to find the Newcombes in the phone book. Why hadn't I been nicer to Madelaine? Now she was with my Alex somewhere, and I couldn't even phone. Choked! Mind you, Alex should have phoned me or something. But then I remembered she didn't have my number or address. Oh well, get Christmas over with and then she'd be back, everything was going to be fine.

After Christmas Eve the club shut down for five nights, opening again on the night before New Year's Eve. I got flu and collapsed in bed during that time. Ate out of cans and spent a really wonderful Christmas in a cold sweat and fever.

Sadie came over once with a jar of chicken soup and a lecture about how this was all due to too much sex. Too much sex yet!! Ha!!

'You live like a pig,' she said. 'When are you going to settle down, get yourself a decent job. You should see your cousin Leon now, living in a big house at Finchley, a lovely wife, baby on the way. When are you going to find yourself a nice girl that you're not ashamed to bring home to your mother?'

I was too sick to tell her about me and Alex, she'd know soon enough. I gave her a hug and kiss and told her not to worry. 'I'll have a surprise for you soon,' I said.

Dear old Sadie, her one ambition in life was to see me married so she could have a few grandchildren to cluck over.

A doctor friend of mine came by, gave me a shot and told a few dirty stories. The next day, I felt better and got up. I had wasted away five days. Hey—it got me through the holiday season.

I shaved, dressed and phoned Alex. *Still* no reply at her Chelsea flat.

I phoned Ian Thaine and he was out. I wanted to get hold of the contract. I was sure to find a property this week.

I went to the club and looked through the reservations for New Year's Eve. The place was going to be a mad-house—booked solid.

When the hell was Alex coming back?

37

ALEXANDRA

'Super to see you,' Maddy said, 'I have *so* much news.'

It was good to be out of bed and about again. My ankle felt fine, and I was looking forward to spending Christmas at Maddy's house.

'Is Michael here?' I asked anxiously.

'Coming down tonight, it's all over between him and that model girl, you'll be glad to know.'

'Oh,' My heart did a lurch. I couldn't *wait* to see him. 'What's it been like in London all alone? How's Jonathan?'

Maddy shrugged. 'All right. I say, Alex, I've met this awful man and I'm simply *mad* about him!'

'Who?'

'Well after I got back to London, Tony insisted I went to "Hobo" with him. I think I was next on his list. Then I met this friend of his, quite old, a raging cockney, but *so* funny and frightfully sexy. I just couldn't help myself. I did the most ghastly things with him!'

'Maddy! What about Jonathan? And what do you mean you were next on Tony's list?'

'I think he just goes to bed with as many girls as he can, and I was to be the next victim. That's what Sammy says anyway. I saw Jonathan one night, but he was so dull. Sammy makes hats and I went to his office one day and he gave me two. Alex, he's Jewish. My mother would have a fit!'

'Maddy, I can't believe it. Have you actually—well you know . . .'

'Not exactly—everything but, though. I think I shall after Christmas. I promised him I would. He's frightfully pleased I'm a virgin. Oh, and, Alex, I have the most juicy piece of news. Sammy said that Tony and your dearest stepmother are having a violent affair. What do you think of that?'

I felt sick. How could I ever have let him touch me? It was obscene. How awful. He had probably been laughing at me all along. Perhaps he had even told Fontaine about me. I shuddered.

'Maddy, you're kidding.'

'No, it quite true. Sammy told me all about it, said it's the only reason Tony is at "Hobo". Ghastly isn't it? I say, Alex, I thought we might pop down to the shops, get a few last-minute things.'

I shook my head numbly. 'You go, Mads, I've got a headache.'

38

FONTAINE

'Mrs Khaled?'

'Yes.'

'My name is Ian Thaine.'

'Yes?'

'Er—you do know who I am?'

'No, Mr Thaine, I do not.'

'About the new club, our new club. Tony Blake *has* told you it's me that's putting up the money?'

'What new club?'

'The new club, the place that's going to take over from "Hobo".

I thought perhaps you and I should meet since we're going to be partners.'

'Mr Thaine, I don't have the slightest idea what you are talking about, but it sounds interesting, perhaps we *should* meet. Tell me, are you anything to do with "Thaine" shops?'

'I am Thaine shops.'

'How nice. Perhaps you would care to come for tea today, about four. Oh, and Mr Thaine, don't mention anything to Tony Blake about our conversation, let's just sort it out between ourselves first.'

39

TONY

New Year's Eve is a drag. They should print little badges with that slogan on and have everyone who feels the same way as me wear one. A poor excuse for a giant booze up, wreck up and fuck up.

The club was festooned with balloons, paper balls, party hats, blowers, the lot.

I got there very early, choked because I had finally got an answer from Alex's Chelsea flat, and Madelaine had informed me that Alex was out and wouldn't be back until late. Out where? Madelaine Newcombe is an up-tight cow. I left the club's number and my home number and told her to have Alex phone me the minute she came in. I was going to get some things sorted out fast. In fact I didn't see any reason why we couldn't get married at once, nip into Caxton Hall and keep it a secret until the new club was all set. Great idea—maybe tomorrow—New Year's Day. It was the best way. Do it, then tell people. That way Fontaine couldn't try and stick her nose in.

Flowers appeared wearing yellow pants, black shirt, and embroidered sheepskin waistcoat.

'Very smart,' I said, thinking that some of my bread had ended up on his back.

He put on Sergio Mendes and went in the kitchen for food. Not a bad idea, there was at least another hour until people would start arriving. I hadn't phoned Sammy, Massey, or any of the boys. They were probably at Steve Scott's party. I wouldn't go near the little bastard, although his wife (Ha!) had phoned while I was sick and begged me to come.

I had a steak and a couple of scotches—had to get in some sort of festive mood. Then a sheepish Franklin arrived with Molly Mandy—dressed—though only just. She was beaming all over her face, and kept on throwing her arms round his neck and kissing him. He smiled politely. I guess he has finally blown his cherry!

Flowers launched into James Brown and the evening began.

On New Year's Eve it all starts much earlier and by eleven the place was pretty jammed. Franco and his boys were doing a great job serving chicken in the basket and champagne—standard fare for the special entrance tickets. Ian Thaine had a table booked for ten, even old Sammy had reserved. The thing was to make it before twelve, and by eleven-thirty a stream of faces appeared. 'The Twang', Suki with Massey, three of the 'Must', a couple of film stars, two Members of Parliament, and the whole group of models, photographers, actors, who made up the scene.

Then Fontaine, looking really fabulous in some kind of fantastic coat. I hoped Franco had somewhere for her to sit as I didn't remember her name being down as having booked. Trust her to try and screw up the table plans.

'Funky Broadway' was blasting out, and I laid a smile on my face and went to greet her.

She gave me an ice cold look and brushed past, followed closely by Ian Thaine, then Vanessa, Leonard, and a whole tacky group.

'Hi, Ian,' I put out my hand. He squeezed it limply. 'I've been trying to phone you, you're always out.'

Vanessa edged forward and I kissed her on the cheek. Her face was flushed and she looked uncomfortable.

187

Where the hell is Franco? Some schmucky waiter is sitting Fontaine down with Ian.

'Get me Franco quickly,' I hissed to another waiter.

Franco came running over, sweat streaming down his face.

'What's happening here?' I demanded. 'Get Mrs Khaled her own table.'

He rushed over to where they were all seated and spoke to Fontaine, then he rushed back to me and said, 'Is O.K., Mr Blake. Mrs Khaled is with Mr Thaine's party.'

'What?' I couldn't believe my ears. I stared over at the table and caught Fontaine's eye. She smiled coldly at me and then turned to Ian, beside himself with joy.

I had a funny feeling in the pit of my stomach that I had just blown a deal. Well, screw Ian Thaine and his millions. Who needed him anyway? I could find someone else, there must be lots of people who would be only too delighted to put up some loot for me. Yeah, but who?

Someone was throwing paper balls at me. It was the luscious Carla Cassini, squeezed into a black dress with lots of bosom popping out.

''Ello, Tonee darling,' she purred gaily, sitting safely with her 'Producer' and several other people ''appy New Year!!'

A whole group from Steve Scott's party came rolling in. I was getting loaded. What the hell. Then Sammy with Madelaine— what a daily double! Then Alexandra, my wonderful precious baby had come to see the New Year in with me after all.

I lifted her chin in my hand and smiled softly. 'Hello, my lovely.' She looked knockout in something pink and soft.

'Hello, Tony—you remember Michael Newcombe, don't you?'

Michael the schmuck. What the hell was *he* doing with her? 'Come on,' Maddy shrieked, 'let's sit down before midnight. I say, Tony, has Alex told you the super news, she and Michael are engaged! Can you imagine, we're going to be sisters-in-law!'

There comes a time in life when the bottom drops out. When everything just collapses and you don't care about anything. This was it for me. I stared at my Alex in disbelief, and she looked back at me with her big liquid brown eyes and I felt like I'd been kicked in the stomach by a thousand horses. I made it out to the kitchen and grabbed a bottle of scotch, drank from it until the fire burned through me.

I've never cried in my life. But the kitchen was so god-damned smoky and it gets underneath your eyelids.

Franco came in looking for me. 'Mr Blake, only five minutes to midnight.'

'Yeah, baby.' I was out of my skull. I weaved back inside and grabbed the nearest girl.

'Hey,' she protested as I dragged her up to the stand next to Flowers.

'O.K., everybody,' I yelled! 'Make the most of it. Five more glorious minutes—drink up.'

The girl pulled herself away from me. 'My boy-friend will be choked,' she said dashing off.

I got a waiter and told him to get Miss Cassini up here to announce the New Year. Smiling, escorted by two waiters, she was soon beside me, her 'Producer' beside her. Flowers was just finishing 'Land of 1000 dances' and the streamers were flying, balloons popping.

'Here, count down from ten.' I handed Carla the mike and she started to count—

'Nine, eight, seven.'

Why had Alex done this to me?

'Six, five, four.'

How *could* she do it?'

'Three, two, one—'appy New Year everyone!'

'Auld Lang Syne' blared out and everyone was kissing and laughing and shaking hands. I grabbed Carla and forced my mouth down hard on hers. She struggled, and I bit her tongue. Pay the bitch back for that night.

She pushed me away, and her 'Producer' gave her a stream of abuse in Italian.

I laughed and wandered into the crowd. Happy New Year. What was so bleedin' happy about it?

''Ere, Tony,' Sammy was calling me over, 'come and 'ave a drink with us.'

189

'Oh yes, do,' Madelaine urged.

Sure. Sit and watch Alex and Michael gazing into each other's eyes.

'The Twang' appeared and I clung on to her, kissing her fleshy lips and pressing my leg between hers.

'What about you and me later?' I mumbled.

'Oohee, Tony, I can't. I'm with such an important director, and he says there may be a part for me in his next film.'

'Yeah, but I've got a part for you now.' I leered.

She giggled.

'Come on, come down to the office a minute, I've got something for you.'

She hesitated, then thought better of it. 'Another night, Tony, I really can't leave this very important director.'

Screw her then. The room was spinning. Screw everyone.

I could give one to Fontaine now, I could really wham it to her the way she likes.

I went over to her table. 'Happy New Year everyone.'

'Thank you, Tony,' Fontaine replied, twirling her finger in the champagne glass. 'Oh by the way, masses of luck with your new club. Ian has decided to become partners with me here, so count him out, but lots and lots of luck, I'm sure you'll do very well. Oh, and in the circumstances I think it's best that you don't work here any more. I've arranged for you to get two weeks' money, so you really needn't bother turning up after tonight.'

Her face weaved in front of me. Mean cold eyes, thin lips. She ignored me and turned to speak to Ian. They made a good pair. He didn't even dare look anywhere near me. I caught Vanessa peering at me, looking concerned, so I laughed. Didn't they all realise that the place would fold without me anyway?

The noise, the screaming, the bursting of balloons. People tangled up in streamers of coloured paper. I want my baby, Alex. Where is my darling girl?

I staggered out on to the balcony and shut away the gang bang. The cold air hit me like a punch and my eyes were running. I wished I hadn't drunk so much. I wanted to think clearly, sort things out.

I sat on the ground. It was spitting with rain.

Nice. I'd lost my girl, I'd lost my club. What was I going to do? I sat there for a bit and then I thought. So what? There's other girls and there will be other clubs. Life is *great* baby. So I went back inside and drank, danced, shouted, burst balloons, and threw streamers, and drank drank drank.

Then Hal appeared with his old dreamboat, Mamie.

'Hey, Tony, sweetheart, Mamie and I got married, say congratulations.'

I looked at Hal. The last of the great promoters was finally caught. Mamie was smiling and clinging to his arm fondly. She could have been his mother.

'We flew in from Rome to sign some papers, I'm taking over the studio you know.'

What studio? 'Great!' I tried to smile.

Mamie beamed. 'Tony dear, this is my dear friend, Delphine Cohen from Miami. This is her first trip to Europe and Hally and I are going to show her the sights.'

Delphine Cohen was a dyed blonde, somewhere in her late fifties. I nodded at her. She showed me a lot of teeth back. She was wearing a pale mink coat and lots of what looked like real diamonds.

We all sat down and I ordered champagne. Sammy came hopping over to see what was up. Mamie and Delphine went off to the Ladies room and Hal immediately grabbed a hold of me.

'Listen, Tony, don't be schmuck! I know it's not your scene but Delphine Cohen's old man practically *owned* Miami, and he dropped off with a heart attack six months ago, so she's hot as a pistol, raring to go. What are you going to do, hang around this joint all your life? Smarten up, fellow, look at me, I'm a big man now.'

I looked at Hal. He was so stoned his eyes held a permanent glaze.

Mamie and Delphine came back and we drank more champagne. Franco kept rushing over to me with minor dramas but I told him to stuff 'em. 'Hobo' wasn't my bag any more, let someone else run their ass off.

Delphine had plump arms with freckles on. I suppose she wasn't too bad for an older bird. Oh boy, more champagne. Much much more.

Mamie was saying, 'Tony, why don't you come to Rome with us for a few days. Hally's so busy now and we need a man to protect us on the streets. It's true what they say about the Italian men, poor Delphine's black and blue!'

Poor Delphine laughed and jangled a heavy diamond bracelet in time to the music. She was wearing a black dress cut wide and low to reveal a load of fat. I wondered if I could make it? I wondered if I *should* make it?

She was very suntanned, very lined, very over made-up, and very old-fashioned in her dress.

Hal gave me a wink. 'Yeah, Come to Rome, baby, we'll have a great time. What do you say, Delphine?'

'Sure,' she smiled at me, 'wonderful idea. Will you come?' Her eyes lingered on my face asking their own personal question.

I stood up abruptly. 'Yeah, maybe. I'll have to see. Excuse me, got to see what's going on, I'll be back in a minute.'

I rushed out to the desk.

'Happy New Year, Mr Blake,' said Tina.

A group of people were coming in, girls dressed up like Christmas trees, an agent and a well-known American actor. Automatically I went into the whole greeting bit. One of the girls was fantastic, long dark hair with pearls, a white-fringed outfit, staring green eyes. Someone introduced us.

She smiled at me and licked full pink lips.

I felt a familiar stirring, which I knew I should be keeping for Delphine Cohen.

The girl's name was Miranda. I asked her to dance. The agent and the actor had three other girls with them, so nobody minded. Flowers was freaking out on Clarence Carter. I gave him the signal and he switched to Jose Feliciano's 'Light my Fire'.

Miranda was tall and soft in my arms. I held on to her tightly. To hell with Delphine Cohen and all her loot, I wasn't getting caught in one of those sick scenes again.

So I'll be busted out. So what? Something will come along,

something that I won't have to sell myself for. And if it doesn't? Well, that's life. I can always wash dishes.

The girl in my arms isn't Alex, but she is certainly a beautiful girl. Creamy skin, and bright eyes.

'I wasn't expecting to meet anyone like you tonight,' I whispered, pulling her a little closer.

'Me neither,' she said, laughing softly. 'I only flew in from New York yesterday. I thought Englishmen had this reputation for being all uptight and stuffy.'

'What do you think now?'

She just pushed her body hard against mine.

We danced and danced. Hal and his group eventually left. 'Schmuck!' he came up and muttered to me. 'You're blowing a great set-up for another ding-a-ling!'

Fontaine swept out after three with her entourage. Ian Thaine smirking at her heel.

I didn't see my Alex go. I didn't want to, I just wanted to forget her.

Miranda and I left at six in the morning. She was trailing a load of balloons and we walked through the deserted streets to my pad.

I loved her face. It was serious and sexy. She had a boy's firm body with lovely small breasts, and I had to push her long dark hair away to kiss them.

'I just got disengaged when I left,' she said as I explored her with my hands. 'My fiancé could only make it in group scenes. Ugh! I hated that. My daddy said I should fly off somewhere and forget about him. He certainly knew what he was talking about. Oh, I love *that*!'

'My fiancé just got engaged to someone else.'

'How awful. Oh, oh, oh—do *that* again! You should come to New York to forget.'

'Yeah.' I climbed on top of her. She was a gorgeous girl. 'With what?'

She wriggled around. 'Hey, Tony, you're *fantastic*! just *too* much!! Listen. I know. You can come and work for my daddy, he's got all sorts of businesses. Oh—wow! Happy New Year!

193

Baby, baby, baby! Do that again. We've got this insane disco in New York called "Picketts". It would be just right for you and, ooh, Tony, that's so beautiful, so *wild*. I love it! I love it! Like yes! Wowee, Tony—you're *such* a stud!'

The Bitch

1

Nico Constantine rose from the blackjack table, smiled all round, threw the pretty croupier a fifty-dollar tip, and pocketed twelve shiny gold five-hundred-dollar chips. A nice round six thousand dollars. Not bad for a fast half hour's work. Not good for someone who was already down two hundred thousand.

Nico surveyed the crowded Las Vegas Casino. His intense dark eyes flicked back and forth amongst the assembled company. Little old ladies in floral dresses exhibiting surprising strength as their skinny arms pulled firmly on the slot machines. Florid couples – weak with excitement and too much sun – picking up a fast eighty or ninety dollars at the roulette tables. Strolling hookers – blank eyes alert for the big spenders. The big spenders themselves, in polyester leisure suits, screeching away in middle-American accents at the crap tables.

Nico smiled. Las Vegas always amused him. The hustle and the bustle. The win and the lose. The total unreality.

A carousel town set in the middle of arid desert. A blazing set of neon signs housing all the vices known to man. And a few unknown ones. In Las Vegas – if you could pay for it – you could get it. Just name it.

He lit a long narrow Havana cigar with a wafer-thin gold Dunhill lighter, and smiled and nodded at the people who went out of their way to catch his eye. A pit boss here, a cigarette girl there, a security guard on his rounds. Nico Constantine was a well known man in Vegas. More important – Nico Constantine was a gentleman – and how many of those were there left in the world?

He looked good. For forty-nine years of age he looked exceptionally good. Black hair – thick, curly, with slight traces of grey that only enhanced the jet. Black eyes – unfairly surrounded with thick black lashes. A strong

197

nose. Dark olive skin beautifully tanned. A wide-shouldered, thin-hipped body that would make many a younger man envious.

However, the most attractive thing about Nico was his style – his aura – his charisma.

Hand-finished, tailor-made three-piece suits in the very finest cloth. Silk shirts of exquisite quality. Italian-made shoes in glove-soft leather. Nothing but the best for Nico Constantine. It had been his motto since he was twenty years of age.

'Can I get you a drink, Mr Constantine?' A cocktail waitress was at his side, long legs in black cobweb stockings, a wide mouth smiling and full of Las Vegas promise.

He grinned. Naturally he had wonderful teeth, and all his own, with just one vagabond gypsy cap. 'Why not? I think vodka, on the rocks, be sure its 90° proof.' His black eyes flirted with her outrageously, and she loved every minute of it. Women always did. Women positively adored Nico Constantine – and he, in his turn, was certainly not averse to them. From a cocktail waitress, to a Princess, he treated them all the same. Flowers (always red roses); Champagne (always Krug); presents (small gold charms from Tiffany in New York, or, if they lasted more than a few weeks, little diamond trinkets from Cartier).

The cocktail waitress went off to get his drink.

Nico consulted his Patek Phillipe digital gold watch. It was eight o'clock. The evening was ahead of him. He would sip his drink, watch the action, and then he would step once again into the fray, and fate would decide his future.

Nico Constantine was born in 1930 in a poor suburb of Athens. He was the first brother to three sisters, and his childhood had been that of a small boy caught up in a sea of femininity. His sisters fussed, bullied, and smothered him. His mother spoiled him, and various female relatives kissed, cuddled and catered to him at all times.

His father was away a lot, being a crewman on one of the fabulous Onassis yachts – so Nico became the little man of the family. He was a beautiful baby, a cute little toddler, a devastating young boy and by the time he left school at 14, every female in the vicinity loved him madly.

His three sisters, not to forget his mother, guarded him ferociously. To them he was a prince.

When his father decided to take him away on a trip as a cabin boy, the entire family rebelled. No way was Nico to be allowed out of their sight. Absolutely no way.

His poor father argued, but to no avail, and Nico was given a job in a nearby fishing port, on the small dock, not a hundred yards from where one of his sisters worked scraping fish. She watched him like a hawk. If he so much as even talked to a member of the female sex she would appear, bossy and predatory.

The Constantine family desired to keep young Nico as innocent and untouched as possible. They worked on it as a team.

Nico meanwhile was growing up. His body was developing, his balls were dropping, his penis was growing, and most of the time he felt as horny as hell. Well who wouldn't, living in close proximity to four women? His sexual senses were assailed on every level. Naked breasts. Body hair. Creamy female smells. Under-clothes hanging up to dry every way he turned.

By the time he was sixteen he was desperate. To jerk off was his only relief, but even that had to be planned like a military operation. Female eyes watched him constantly.

He realised he must run away, although it was a difficult decision to make. After all, leaving behind all that love and adoration . . . It had to be done though. He was being smothered, and it was the only answer. The only way he could become a real man.

He left on a Sunday night in December 1947, and arrived in the City of Athens two days later, cold, tired, hungry, certain he had made a wrong move, and already anxious that his family would come chasing after him.

He had no idea what to do, how to get a job, or even what kind of job to look for.

He wandered around the city, freezing in his thin cotton trousers and shirt, and only an oilskin to keep out the biting ice and sleet.

Finally he took shelter in the entrance of a large apartment building, and stayed there until a chaffeured car pulled up, and two women in furs got out, chattering and laughing together.

Instinct told him to attract their attention. He coughed loudly, caught the eye of one of the women, smiled appealingly, winked, projected unthreatening vulnerability.

'Yes?' the woman asked. 'Do you want my autograph?'

He was always quick, and without hesitation said, 'I have travelled three days to get your autograph.'

He had no idea who she was, only that she was mysteriously beautiful, with soft pale curls, a slender figure beneath the open fur, and a sympathetic smile.

She walked over to him and he inhaled sweet perfume. It reminded him of the womanly smells of home.

'You look exhausted,' she said. Her voice was magical, vibrant, and comforting.

Nico didn't answer. He just looked at her with his black eyes until she took him by the arm and said, 'Come, you shall have a hot drink and some warm clothes.'

Her name was Lise Maria Androtti. She was a very famous opera singer, thirty-three years old, divorced, extremely rich, and the most wonderful person Nico had ever met.

Within days they were lovers. The seventeen-year-old boy, and the thirty-three-year-old woman. She taught him to love her exactly as she had always wanted. And he was a willing learner. Listening, practising, achieving.

'God, Nico!' she would exclaim in the throes of ecstacy. 'You are the cleverest lover I have ever had.' And of

200

course, after her expert tuition – he was.

Her friends were scandalized, and warnings abounded. 'He's hardly more than a child.' 'There'll be an outcry!' 'Your public will never stand for it!'

Lise Maria smiled in the face of their objections. 'He makes me happy,' she explained. 'He's the best thing that ever happened to me.'

Nico wrote a short formal note to his family. He was fine. He had a job. He would write again soon. He enclosed some of Lise Maria's money. She had insisted; and every month she made sure he did the same again. She understood how painful losing Nico must have been to them. He was truly a wonderful boy.

On Nico's twentieth birthday they were married. A ceremony Lise Maria tried to keep private, but every photographer in Greece turned up, and the small ceremony became a mad circus. The result was that Nico's family finally found out where their precious boy was, and they rushed to Athens, and added to the scandal Lise Maria had tried so calmly to ignore.

Of course there was nothing they could do. It was too late. Besides which, Nico and Lise Maria seemed so unbelievably happy together.

For nineteen years they remained locked in a state of bliss. The age difference seeming to bother neither of them. Only the world press made much of it.

Nico grew from a gauche young male, into a sophisticated man of the world. He developed a taste for the very best in everything, and Lise Maria was well able to afford the millionaire life style they adopted together.

Nico never bothered to work, Lise Maria didn't want him to. He travelled everywhere with her, and taught himself fluent English, French, German, and Italian.

He dabbled on the world stock market, and occasionally did well.

He learned to snow ski, water ski, drive a racing car, ride horses, play polo.

He became expert at bridge, backgammon, and poker.

He acquired an expert knowledge of wine and cuisine.

He was a faithful and ever expanding lover to his beautiful, famous wife. He treated her like a Queen right up until the day she died of cancer in 1969 aged fifty-five.

Then he was lost. Set adrift in a world he did not wish to live in without his beloved Lise Maria.

He was thirty-nine years old and alone for the first time in his life. He had everything – Lise Maria had bequeathed him her fortune. But he had nothing.

He could no longer stand their Athens penthouse, their island retreat, their smart Paris house.

He sold everything. The four cars. The fabulous jewellery. The homes.

He said goodbye to his family, now ensconced in a house in the very centre of Athens, and he set off for America – the one place Lise Maria had never been accepted as the superstar she was all over Europe.

America. A place to forget. New beginnings.

'Here's your vodka Mr Constantine,' the cocktail waitress twinkled at him, '90° proof – not our regular cra . . . er stuff.' She met his eyes with a bold glance, then reluctantly retreated at a signal from a surly blackjack player.

Las Vegas. A truly unique place. Twenty-four-hour non-stop gambling. Lavish hotels and entertainments. Beautiful showgirls. Blazing sunshine.

Nico remembered with a smile his very first sight of the place. Driving from Los Angeles in the dead of night, and after hours of blackness suddenly hitting this neon-lit fantasy in the middle of nowhere. It was a memory that would always linger.

Was it only ten years ago? It seemed like for ever . . .

Nico had arrived in Los Angeles with twenty-five pieces of impeccable Gucci luggage in the summer of 1969.

He had rented a white Mercedes, taken up residence in

a bungalow attached to the famed Beverly Hills Hotel, and sat back to see if he liked it.

He liked it. Who wouldn't in his position?

He was rich, handsome, available.

He was jumped on within two minutes of settling himself in a private *cabaña* beside the pool.

The jumpee was Dorothy Dainty, a sometime-in-work starlet with a mass of red hair, thirty-eight-inch silicone tits, and an unfortunate habit of talking out of the corner of her mouth like a refugee from a George Raft movie. 'You a producer?' she asked conspiratorily.

Nico looked her over, treated her with respect, and allowed her to show him the town.

To her annoyance he didn't try to fuck her. Dorothy Dainty was amazed. *Everyone* tried to fuck her. Everyone succeeded. What was with this strange foreign creep?

She took him around. The Bistro. La Scala. The Daisy. The Factory. One visit and Nico and the *maître d'* were the best of friends.

After two weeks he didn't need Dorothy. He sent her a gold charm inscribed with a few kind words, a dozen red roses, and he never called her again.

'The guy has to be a fag!' Dorothy told all her friends, 'Has to be!'

The thought of a man who didn't actually want to fuck her threw her into a decline for weeks!

Nico had no intention of screwing the Dorothy Daintys of this world. His wife had been dead three months, and he certainly felt the physical need of a woman, but nothing would make him lower his standards. He had had the best, and while he accepted the fact that he would never find another Lise Maria – he certainly was looking for something better than Dorothy Dainty.

He decided young girls would be best for him. Fresh-faced beauties with no track record.

He had never been to bed with a woman other than his wife. During the next ten years he made up for lost time

203

and made love to one hundred and twenty fresh-faced beauties. They lasted on an average four weeks each, and not one of them ever regretted having been made love to by Nico Constantine. He was an ace lover. The very best.

He bought himself a mansion in the Hollywood hills, and settled down to having a good time.

The bachelors of the Beverly Hills community flocked around to be his friend. He had everything they all wanted. Class. Style. Panache. The money wasn't so impressive, they all had money, but he had that indefinable quality – a charm that was inborn.

For ten idyllic years Nico lived the good life. He played tennis, swam, messed around on the stock market, gambled with his friends, invested in the occasional deal, made love to beautiful girls, sunbathed, saunaed, hot bathed, went to the best parties, movies, restaurants.

It was a grave shock to him when his money finally ran out.

Nico Constantine broke. Ridiculous. But true. His late wife's lawyers in Athens had been warning him for two years that the estate was running dry. They had wanted him to invest, diversify his capital. Nico had taken no notice – and gradually he had spent everything there was.

The thought of having no money appalled him. He decided something must be done immediately. He was a brilliant gambler, always had been – and the lure of Las Vegas was so very close.

He thought about his situation carefully. How much money did he need to maintain his present life style? He supported his entire family in Athens, but apart from them there was only himself to think about. If he sold his mansion, and rented instead, he would have a substantial lump sum of money, *and* cut his weekly expenditure immediately. It seemed like a wonderful idea. He could take the money from the sale of his house, and in Vegas – with his luck and skill – he would double it – treble it –

certainly build it into a substantial stake that he could invest and then live off the income.

Nico had been in Las Vegas exactly twenty-three hours. Already he was down one-hundred-and-ninety-four thousand dollars.

2

Fontaine Khaled woke alone in her New York apartment. She removed her black lace sleep-mask, and reached for the orange juice in her bedside fridge.

Gulping the deliciously cold liquid she groaned aloud. A mammoth hangover was threatening to engulf her entirely. Christ! Studio 54. Two fags. One black. One white. What an entertainment!

She attempted to step out of bed, but felt too weak, and collapsed back amongst her Porthault pillows.

She reached over to her bedside table and picked up a bottle of vitamin pills. E was washed down with the orange juice, then C, then a multi-vitamin, and lastly two massive yeast tablets.

Fontaine sighed, and stretched for a silver hand-mirror. She sat up in bed and studied her face. Yes. She still looked incredible – in spite of the terrible year she had suffered through.

Mrs Fontaine Khaled. Ex-wife of *the* Benjamin Al Khaled – multi billionaire Arab businessman. Actually Fontaine could describe him very accurately as an Arab Shit. I mean what kind of man got away with saying to his wife 'I divorce thee' three times, and then walked away totally and utterly free?

An Arab Shit, that's what kind of man.

Fontaine conveniently blanked out on the more gory details of why Benjamin had divorced her. He had compromised her with sneak photographs of her and a variety of young men making love. It just hadn't been fair. She was entitled to lovers. Benjamin – in his sixties – was hardly likely to satisfy her most demanding needs.

The divorce still upset Fontaine – one of the reasons she had spent the better part of the year in New York, rather than London, where everyone knew. It wasn't Benjamin she missed so much, it was the world-wide respect and security of being Mrs Benjamin Al Khaled.

Of course she still *was* Mrs Khaled, but she made up a neat set of two with his other ex-wife – the one he had left to marry *her*.

Now there was a new Mrs Khaled Mark One. A disgustingly young model by the name of Delores. A very tacky looking girl, Fontaine thought, who was making a complete fool of Benjamin and spending all his money even faster than she had!

To Fontaine's way of thinking the divorce settlement was not equitable to her needs. Her standard of living had taken a sharp dive. She was even reduced to wearing last year's Sable coat. Last year's! *Quelle* horror!

She climbed out of bed, naked as usual. A fine body, full of muscle tone and skin lotion. Firm skin, small breasts as high as a sixteen-year-old.

Fontaine had always looked after herself. Massage. Steam baths. Facials. Exercises. Head-to-toe conditioning.

The work she had put in paid off. Soon she would be forty years old, and she didn't look a day over twenty-nine. No face lifts either. Just classical English beauty and good bones.

She put on a silk housecoat and rang for her maid, a fat Puerto Rican girl she was thinking of firing if only help wasn't so difficult to find these days . . .

The girl walked into the room without knocking. 'I wish you'd knock, Ria,' Fontaine said irritably. 'I've told you a million and one times.'

Ria smirked at her reflection in the mirrored bedroom. Oh Jeeze – would she like to fuck her boyfriend, Martino, in *these* surroundings!

'Sure Mrs K.,' she said. 'You want I should run you a bath?'

'Yes,' replied Fontaine shortly. She really couldn't stand the girl.

Sarah Grant, Fontaine's closest friend in New York, waited patiently at the Four Seasons for Fontaine to turn up for lunch. She consulted her neat Cartier Tank watch and sighed with annoyance. Fontaine was *always* late, one of her less endearing little habits.

Sarah signalled to the waiter to bring her another martini. She was an extremely striking looking woman, with intense slavic features, and jet black hair starkly rolled into a bun. She was rich in her own right, having been through two millionaire husbands, and now she was married to a writer called Allan who joined in her tastes for rather bizarre sex. At the moment they were both enjoying an affair with a New England transvestite who wanted to become a folk singer.

Fontaine made her entrance. Heads still turned.

The two women kissed, mouths barely brushing each other's cheeks.

'How was Beverly Hills?' Fontaine demanded. 'Did you have a divine time?'

Sarah shrugged, 'You know how I feel about Los Angeles. Boring and hot. Allan enjoyed it though, someone has finally been fool enough to option his screenplay. They paid him twenty thousand dollars. You would think he had personally discovered gold!'

'How sweet.'

'Adorable. My man has money at last. It will just about cover one quarter's payment on my jewellery insurance!'

Fontaine laughed, 'Sarah, you're so mean . . . The poor man has balls, you know.'

'Oh yes? *Do* tell me where he keeps them. I'd simply *love* to know.'

Lunch passed by in a flurry of the latest gossip – both women were experts. By the time coffee arrived they had carved up everyone and anyone, and loved every minute of it.

Sarah sipped her Grand Marnier, 'I saw an old friend of yours on the Coast,' she said casually. 'Remember Tony?'

'Tony?' Fontaine feigned ignorance, but she knew immediately who Sarah was talking about. Tony Blake. Tony the stud.

'*He* remembers *you*,' Sarah mocked. 'And with a quite violent lack of affection. What *did* you do to him?'

Fontaine frowned, 'I took him from being a nothing little waiter, and built him into the best manager of the best discothèque in London.'

'Oh yes. Then you threw him out, didn't you?'

'I dispensed with *his services* before *he* dispensed with mine. The cocky little bastard was only trying to open up on his own, knock me out of business.'

Sarah laughed, 'So what happened?'

'I thought I told you all about it. *I* went partners with his money man before *he* could. Poetic justice. I haven't heard from him since. What *is* he doing in LA?'

'Sniffing, snorting, what everyone does in LA. By the way, whatever happened to your club, "Hobo" wasn't it?'

Fontaine extracted an art deco compact from her Vuitton purse and minutely studied her face. 'My club is still going strong, still *the* place.' She selected a small tube of lip gloss and smoothed it over her lips with her finger. 'As a matter of fact I had a letter from my lawyer this morning. He seems to feel I should be getting back, sort out my affairs.'

'And *what* affairs are those?' Sarah teased.

Fontaine snapped the compact shut. 'The monetary kind darling. They're the only kind that matter aren't they?'

After the lunch they parted and went their separate ways. Fontaine felt that she had to keep up a certain front, even with a close friend like Sarah. As she strolled along Fifth Avenue she thought about the letter from her lawyer and what it had *really* said. Financial difficulties . . . Unpaid bills . . . Spending too much money . . . 'Hobo' in trouble . . .

Yes, the time had certainly come to return to London and sort things out.

But how could 'Hobo' possibly be in trouble? From the moment Benjamin had bought the place for her it had made money. Tony – her manager – lover – and stud – had become the most wanted man in London when she had put him in charge. And when she had got rid of him – Ian Thaine, her new partner – had redecorated the place, put in a new manager, and then got pissed off because she was not prepared to extend the partnership on to a personal level. So she had bought him out, and when she had left London 'Hobo' had been flourishing. And it was all hers, and should be a substantial asset; not a goddamn drain on her finances.

It was starting to rain, and Fontaine looked around in vain for a cab. God! It was about time she found herself another millionaire – who needed this searching for cabs garbage – she should have a chauffeur-driven Rolls, as she had always had when she was Mrs Benjamin Khaled. As it was she could only afford to hire a limousine and chauffeur for the evenings. She needed it desperately then, as the escorts she chose barely owned more than a motorbike – if that. Fontaine liked the men in her life to keep their assets on show.– right up front – in their trousers.

She had never really pursued money, because of her devastating beauty it had always managed to pursue her. Benjamin Al Khaled for instance had spotted her when she was modelling in a St Moritz fashion show and dumped his first wife quicker than a hooker gives head.

After life with Benjamin, money was a necessity. Fontaine had a taste for the best that was very hard to quench. But she had wanted a pause before searching out another billionaire husband. Billionaire equalled old (unless you counted the freaked-out rock stars who always seemed to tie themselves up with young blonde starlets anyway). And old was not what Fontaine needed. She needed youth – she enjoyed youth – she revelled in the male body

210

beautiful and an eight- or nine-inch solid cock.

A drunk weaved across Fifth Avenue and planted himself swaying and dribbling in front of her, blocking her path. 'Ya wanna get laid?' he demanded, displaying a mouthful of leer.

Fontaine ignored him, attempted to pass.

'Hey,' he managed to obstruct her way. 'Wassamatter? You don' wanna fuck?'

Fontaine gave him a hard shove, saw a cab, ran for it, collapsed in the back and sighed.

It really was time to get out of New York.

The very moment Fontaine departed for her lunch date, Ria, her Puerto Rican maid, rushed for the phone. Ten minutes later her boyfriend arrived. Martino. The best looking black guy in the whole of fuckin' New York City.

'Whatcha say, babe?' He greeted her with a kiss and a goose, while his stoned eyes checked out every inch of the luxurious apartment.

'We got two hours,' Ria said quickly. 'The bitch won't be back before that.'

'Let's go then, babe, let's go.'

'Sure, hon. Only thing is . . . Well I got me a fantasy. Martino, can we waste five whole minutes? Can I show you her bedroom? Can we make it all over her crazy fuckin' bedroom?'

Martino grinned. He was already unzipping his shiny leather pants.

Fontaine spent the afternoon at the beauty parlour listening to more gossip. Some of it was a repeat of what Sarah had already told her, but it was interesting to have it confirmed.

'I'm going back to London,' Fontaine confided to Leslie, her hairdresser.

'Yeah?' Leslie grinned, he had nice teeth, a good face, a nice body, but he was minus where he should be plus – a

211

fact that Fontaine had personally checked.

'It's about time I had a change of scenery,' Fontaine continued. 'I feel as though I'm getting too static here.'

'I know what you mean,' Leslie replied sympathetically. Christ! Fontaine Khaled getting static! That was a laugh. The old bitch must have balled everything under twenty-five that walked in New York City!

Leslie himself was twenty-six, and not pleased that the notorious Mrs Khaled had taken him to bed only once, and then abandoned him like a bad smell. Oh, he was still all right to do her hair – and why not – he was the best goddamn hairdresser in town. The most fashionable too.

'Will you miss me, Leslie?' Fontaine fixed him with her lethal kaleidoscope eyes.

She was flirting and Leslie knew it. *What's the matter Mrs Khaled? Got a few hours to fill?*

'Of course I'll miss you, every time I set a wig I'll remember you!'

Game set and match to Leslie. For a change.

Fontaine was not in a good humour when she returned to her apartment. The horrible man in the street. Leslie getting smart ass. And then a foul-smelling cab driver who insisted on discussing President Carter's piles – as though they were a serious part of political history. Cretin! Ass hole! And she had a headache too.

Going up in the elevator she didn't bother to search for her key. She rang the doorbell, and cursed when it took Ria forever to answer.

It finally occurred to her that the stupid girl wasn't going to come to the door at all. She was probably asleep, slouched over a soap opera on television.

Furious, Fontaine rifled through her bag for her Gucci keyring, found it, and let herself into the apartment with an angry commanding shout of – 'Ria! Where the *hell* are you!'

The sight that greeted her eyes was not a pretty one.

Her apartment had been stripped, and from what she could see at first glance, what had been left was wrecked.

Shocked, she took two steps inside, and then realizing that Ria might be lying mutilated and murdered amongst the debris, or even that the robbers might still be on the premises, she backed quickly out.

The police were very good. It only took them an hour and a half to arrive, and they discovered no murdered Ria, just 'Fockin' Beetch!' scrawled in lipstick all over the mirrored bedroom.

Fontaine recognized the scrawl as being Ria's illiterate scribble.

Everything that could be moved was gone. Her clothes, luggage, toiletries, sheets, towels, small items of furniture – even light fitments and all electrical gadgets including the vacuum that Ria had pushed so disdainfully around the apartment.

The bed, stripped of everything except the mattress, bore its own personal message – a congealing mess of sperm.

'God Almighty!' Fontaine was fuming. She glared at the two patrolmen. 'Where the hell's the detective that is going to investigate this case? I have *very* important friends you know, and I want some action – fast!'

The two cops exchanged glances. Let's hope to Christ they don't put Slamish on this case they both thought at the same time. But they both knew it was inevitable. Slamish and Fontaine were destined to meet.

Chief Detective Marvin H. Slamish had three unfortunate things going for him. One – an uncontrollable defect in his left eye that caused him to wink at the most inopportune moments. Two – a tendency to store wind, and never to be quite sure when it would emerge. Three – a strong body odour that no amount of deodorants could smother.

Chief Detective Marvin H. Slamish was not a happy man.

He used mouthwash, underarm roll-ons, powders and sprays, and female vaginal deodorants sprayed liberally over his private parts.

He still smelled lousy.

Fontaine sniffed the moment he entered her apartment, 'My God! What's that terrible smell?'

Chief Detective Marvin H. Slamish winked, farted and removed his raincoat.

Fontaine was unamused. She gestured around her looted apartment, 'What are you going to do about this?' Her voice zinged with English authority. She glared at Chief Detective Slamish as though it was his own personal fault. 'Well?' her kaleidoscope eyes regarded him with disdain. 'Have you found my maid yet?'

Chief Detective Slamish slumped into a remaining chair, the stuffing bulging from where it had been ripped open. He had not had a good day. In fact his day had been pure shit. A drug bust that hadn't stuck. A row with his one-armed Vietnam-war-veteran brother-in-law who was the biggest con artist in Manhattan. And now this stiff-assed English society broad. Wasn't it enough that his balls ached? Wasn't it enough that his strong odour was beginning to pervade even his insensitive nostrils?

'Everything's under control ma'am,' he mumbled unconvincingly.

'Under control?' Fontaine arched incredulous eyebrows. 'Have you recovered my property? Have you arrested my maid?'

The two cops exchanged glances.

Slamish tried to summon an air of confidence and authority. 'Just give us time, ma'am, just give us time. An investigation is getting under way right now. In fact there are a few questions I'd like to ask you.'

'Questions? Me? You have to be kidding. *I'm* not the criminal in the case.'

'Of course you're not, ma'am. But then again it hasn't been unheard of for people to er . . . arrange things. Insurance . . . You know what I mean?'

Fontaine's eyes blazed. 'Are you implying that I might have set this up myself?'

It was an unfortunate moment for Slamish to wink.

'You *horrible* little man!' Fontaine screamed. 'I'll have your badge for your . . . your impertinence!'

Wearily Slamish rose, farted, and attempted to apologise.

'Get out of here,' Fontaine stormed. 'I don't want you on my case. My husband is Benjamin Al Khaled and when I tell him of your accusations . . .'

Chief Detective Slamish headed for the door. Some days it just wasn't worth getting out of bed.

Five long hours later Fontaine was comfortably installed in a suite at the Pierre Hotel. Thank God the bastards hadn't taken her jewellery. It had been safely locked up at the bank – a precaution Benjamin had always insisted on, and one that she had followed through with.

As for the apartment – well it had needed decorating. And her clothes . . . A new wardrobe was never a problem, and fortunately she was adequately insured.

Yes. A couple of days at the Pierre while she got herself together and did some shopping.

Then home . . . London . . . 'Hobo' . . . And a sorting-out of her life.

3

Bernie Darrell had been divorced four months, two days and twelve hours exactly. He knew, because his ex-wife, Susanna, never tired of telephoning to let him know. Of course there were other reasons she telephoned. The pool was malfunctioning. Her Ferrari had broken down. Their child missed him. Was he really tasteless enough to be seen at 'Pips' – a Beverly Hills discothèque – with another woman? So soon? How did he think she felt?

God! He would never really understand women. Susanna and he had spent a miserable five years as a married couple – in spite of how the gossip columns and fan magazines built them up as love's young dream.

Susanna Brent, beautiful young actress daughter of Carlos Brent, the famed singer/movie star/rumoured mafioso. And Bernie Darrell – hot shot record company mogul.

Mogul! Him! That was a laugh! He had managed to keep Susanna in the style to which she was accustomed. Just. Only just. And she had never tired of throwing daddy in his face, and how much better he could do it.

One morning Bernie had packed a suitcase, stacked it in the back of his silver Porsche, and fled. Susanna had been begging him to come back ever since.

Bernie didn't have much sense, but with the counsel of his friends, he had realised that to go back was to present Susanna with his *balls* – on a plate – nicely garnished. The longer he stayed away, the more he knew this to be the truth.

He was lucky to have a friend like Nico Constantine. Nico had allowed him to move into his house with an invitation to stay as long as he wanted. So far he had stayed seven months, and enjoyed Nico's company so much that he had no desire to find a place of his own.

Nico was his idol. He was everything that Bernie aspired to be. Bernie copied him religiously, but the result was not yet perfect.

At twenty-nine years of age Bernie had youth on his side. He was slim and athletic, and did all the good things such as tennis, jogging, working out at a gym. He also smoked grass profusely, sniffed coke constantly, and drank like a new generation Dean Martin.

Nico didn't touch drugs, and Bernie vowed he would give them up. But it was always tomorrow as far as he was concerned . . . and he never seemed to get around to tomorrow. Anyway he *needed* drugs, it was a social politeness. I mean as boss of a West Coast record company, how could he sit around at a meeting with one of his groups and not indulge? Professional murder. They would move on faster than a fag at an Anita Bryant coffee clutch.

Bernie attempted to imitate Nico's style of dress, but the suits were never that immaculate fit that Nico so effortlessly achieved, the shirts never laid correctly around the collar – even the hand-made ones. He looked good, but only until he stood next to Nico.

Bernie had a handsome bland face, capped teeth, bad breath, permed hair, a scar on his stomach, a perfect permanent suntan, and a small penis.

One of the great things about Susanna was that in all their mud-slinging arguments she had *never* mentioned his little dick. Never. He loved her for that.

Now Bernie sat on a Las Vegas bound plane, staring out of the window, wondering how the *hell* he was going to explain Cherry to Nico.

Cherry sat beside him, elegant hands crossed primly on her lap. Beautiful face in repose. Long straight blonde hair hanging luxuriously down.

She was a knockout. Nico's knockout to be precise. He had dumped her a week ago with the roses, and the diamond trinket, and the usual speech about how he was

217

only leaving her for her own good – and how much happier she would be without him.

What a bullshit artist Nico was. The absolute best. The original fuck-and-run merchant. He always left the girl thinking *she* had left him! Clever.

In seven months Bernie had seen him do it to six of them. All staggeringly beautiful in that newly-scrubbed, wholesome young way. They all left without a whimper. Nico was right, they *would* be better off without him, (quite why they never seemed to figure out) but they parted the best of friends, and wore his diamond trinket from Cartier (usually a mouse or a butterfly) and spoke about him in only the most glowing of terms.

Bernie had never had that kind of luck with women. Whenever he tried to dump a girl they had hysterics, called him a motherfucking son-of-a-bitch bastard, and badmouthed him all over town.

What was he doing wrong?

'How long before we land?' Cherry asked sweetly.

Oh Christ! Cherry. She had turned up at the house looking for Nico. And she had been there when Nico had phoned from Las Vegas telling Bernie to grab some money and get on the next plane out. Then, firmly, but of course with bags of innocent girlishness, she had insisted on coming too. 'I have to talk with Nico,' she explained. 'My life is at a crossroads, and only he can help me.'

'Can't you wait a coupla days?' Bernie had grumbled, 'He'll be back in LA before that.'

'No. I have to see him immediately.'

So he had been unable to shake Cherry. And what *really* bugged him was she had let *him* pay for her ticket. The nerve! Not one move towards her purse, just a sweet smile, a soft hand on his arm and a 'Thank you, Bernie.'

Of course everyone thought he was loaded. If he didn't know better he would think so himself.

The newspapers described him as Bernie Darrell, millionaire record boss. Well the company did OK. But millionaire? Forget it. He could barely scrape enough together to make Susanna's ludicrous alimony payments. And of course, being Carlos Brent's son-in-law – even though he was *ex*-son-in-law – meant always having to pick up the check.

He wondered what Nico had meant by 'grab some money'. It seemed like such a strange request coming from Nico. Nico was always very flush, always the big spender. And in Vegas surely he could get as much credit as he could use? Anyway, Bernie had stopped by his office and extracted six thousand cash from his safe. It occured to him that ever since moving in with Nico he had never made an attempt to pay one household account. Even the liquor he ordered at the corner store and had them bill it to the house. He felt a bit guilty now, but Nico was truly the perfect host, and never expected a guest to put his hand in his pocket – even a seven-month guest.

Somewhere in the back of his mind Bernie knew that maybe something was amiss financially for Nico. An occurrence of events pointed to this. Firstly, why had Nico suddenly sold his house two months previously? He had got a good price, but everyone knew that if you had Beverly Hills real estate the name of the game was to sit on it. Prices were escalating at an exciting rate.

Bernie had joked at the time, 'Trying to get rid of a difficult house guest, huh?'

Nico had smiled that enigmatic smile of his, and made all arrangements to move them over to the new house he had rented. No discomfort for anyone.

Then another thing Bernie had noticed, stacks of unpaid bills were starting to accumulate on Nico's desk, and Nico had always been meticulous at settling his accounts immediately.

Just little things, but enough to make Bernie wonder somewhere in the back of his mind – a place he didn't visit too often.

Cherry said, 'Ooops! I'm not too fond of landings.

She looked a little green. Bernie handed her the paper bag to throw up in, and sat back to enjoy the descent.

Nico had no sense of time. He had been sitting at the baccarat table how long? Two, three, four hours? He just didn't know. He only knew that the losing streak he was on had no intention of quitting.

A thin film of sweat skirted his brow, but otherwise he was unaffected – his usual smiling charming self.

His plan had gone disastrously horribly wrong. What had started out as a fool-proof scheme to make a big killing – had turned into a joke. He had lost every single dollar he had made on his house – worse – he had gone beyond that – and was now into the Casino for five hundred thousand dollars.

So much for skill and talent and luck. If the cards and dice were against you there was simply nothing you could do. Except stop playing. And he hadn't done that. He had kept right on going like some schmuck from the sticks.

He was now in a far more difficult situation than merely being broke. He was in debt to people who were hardly likely to be thrilled when they found out he couldn't pay up.

It was like a bad dream. It seemed to have happened before he knew it.

Two days. That's all it had taken.

The woman sitting beside him was pushing the baccarat shoe towards him. She was winning, quite heavily, and flirting with Nico, although she must have been well on her way towards being sixty. Her chubby arms and fingers were garnished liberally with jewellery, quite incredible jewellery – tasteless but effective. On her left hand she wore a gigantic diamond. Nico was fascinated by the size of it. It had to be worth at the very least five hundred thousand dollars.

As the cab took him and Cherry from the airport, Bernie

was disgusted to see that Carlos Brent himself was head-lining at 'The Forum Hotel'. Why the hell had Nico picked there?

'I've never been here before,' Cherry remarked, smoothing down her skirt with delicate pale hands.

'Don't get too comfortable,' Bernie muttered, 'you may be on the next plane back.'

'I don't think so,' replied Cherry, primly.

Oh yeah? One thing Bernie knew about Nico was that once a broad was out she was out. No going back, how-ever golden the muff.

Bernie was greeted regally at the reception desk. As Carlos Brent's ex-son-in-law he was a well-known figure at the Forum. He and Susanna had spent part of their honeymoon there – they had had to, Carlos was appearing at the time and he had insisted that the whole goddamn wedding party flew back to Vegas with him to celebrate.

Shit! Making love to his new bride with her famous daddy in the adjoining penthouse suite had not been the greatest of experiences.

'I'd like to freshen up before I see Nico,' Cherry was saying.

'Yeah,' Bernie agreed. 'Give me the key to Nico Con-stantine's suite,' he told the girl behind the desk. 'It'll be fine, he's expecting us.'

'Certainly Mr Darrell,' she said, giving Cherry a quick once-over from head to toe. News would have filtered over to Carlos that Bernie had arrived in Vegas with a nineteen-year-old blonde within the hour.

'This is Miss Cherry Lotte,' Bernie said quickly. 'Mr Constantine's fiancée.' Fiancée! Sweet! What a lovely old-fashioned word! Nico would kill him. But it was better than having Carlos Brent pissed off.

The baccarat shoe was emptied of cards by the bejewelled woman. Pass after pass she won, until the shoe was finished. She sorted out her stacks and stacks of chips with

221

fat hands, and Nico was once again mesmerized by the size of her diamond ring.

He stood up. The pit boss said, 'Staying for another shoe Mr Constantine?'

Nico forced a smile as he left the enclosure, 'I'll be back later.'

He felt sick to his stomach, and then he saw Bernie hurrying towards him, and his spirits lifted. Bernie would have a way to bail him out. Bernie was a sharp kid, and anyway – after seven months of free everything he owed him a favour.

On the very top floor of the Forum Hotel, Joseph Fonicetti kept his eye on the proceedings. He owned the Forum, and with the help of his two sons, Dino and David, he ran a tight ship. Not too much happened within the confines of the Forum that Joseph Fonicetti didn't know about.

For instance – the fourth girl on the right – back chorus line – had obtained an abortion the previous afternoon. She would be back at work tonight.

For instance – two waitresses in the Orgy Room were stealing – nickel-and-dime stuff. Joseph would keep them on, good waitresses were hard to find.

For instance – one of his pit bosses was planning to screw the Casino manager's wife. That would have to be stopped – immediately.

'What about Nico Constantine?' David asked his father.

'How much is he in to us for now?' Joseph replied, his eyes flicking across his four closed-circuit TV screens that showed him plenty of action.

David picked up a phone to get up-to-the-minute information.

'He's given us six hundred thousand of his money – and he's into us for five hundred and ten thousand. He just left the baccarat table and is meeting with Bernie Darrell.'

'I like Nico,' Joseph said softly. 'But no more than

222

another fifty thousand credit, and see that he pays us before he leaves Vegas. You take care of it, Dino.'

'Do we take a cheque?' Dino asked.

Joseph closed his eyes, 'From Nico? Sure. Nico has plenty of money. Besides, he's too smart to ever try to shaft us. Besides, Nico Constantine without his balls — what kind of a ladies' man would that be?'

4

Fontaine zipped through the New York stores at an alarming pace. When it came to shopping for clothes there was nobody better at spending money than she was – except perhaps Jackie Onassis.

She used her credit cards liberally, unworried by the fact that her lawyer in England had warned her to run up absolutely no more bills.

She had been robbed. Surely she was entitled to clothe herself for her imminent return to London?

Armani, Cerrutti, Chloe – name-designer clothes had always looked well on her.

She had lunch with Allan Grant, Sarah's husband. He amused her, wanted to take her to bed for the afternoon. She demurred. She had so much more shopping to do. And she was to depart for London the very next day. She really didn't want to hurt Allan's feelings, she had been to bed with him before, but he was simply not her style. At thirty-six he was too old for her. Why settle for an old model when you could have the very latest twenty-two-year-old actor with a body like a young Marlon Brando?

Fontaine had always been a puller supreme. Men could never resist the lure of her perfumed thighs. Besides which, she had that very rare commodity – good old-fashioned glamour – and men – especially young men – loved it.

She left Allan, and went shopping in Henri Bendels, where she bought two pairs of boots at a hundred and eighty five dollars apiece. A simple black crocodile shoulder bag – four hundred dollars. An art deco necklace and earrings – one hundred and fifty dollars. And three hundred dollars' worth of make-up and perfume.

She charged everything, and ordered it sent special delivery to her hotel. Then she decided that she really must get some rest before the evening's activities, and she took a taxi to the Pierre, where she had a long luxurious bubble bath, carefully applied a special cucumber face mask, and went to sleep for three and a half hours.

Jump Jennings checked out his appearance one more nervous time before leaving his seedy village apartment. He looked good, he knew *that*. But the question was – did he look good enough? Tonight was the night to find out.

Jump had been christened Arthur George Jennings, but he had been nicknamed Jump in high school because of his athletic prowess, and it had just sort of stuck. Jump wasn't a bad name to be stuck with either. Jump Jennings. It sounded pretty good. It would *look* pretty good one day – stuck up on a marquee in lights next to Streisand or Redford. Rock, Tab, Rip . . . The world would be ready for Jump. His time would come. He hoped desperately that his time would come that very night.

He hitched up his black leather trousers, and adjusted the collar of his black leather bomber jacket. Sylvester Stallone was the look. Yeah – and it suited him too.

Confident at last, he left the apartment.

Fontaine awoke an hour before her date was due to pick her up. There was an exciting evening ahead. An art gallery opening, two parties, then the inevitable Studio 54 – a wild huge discothèque where anything could happen, and usually did.

She dressed with care after applying an impeccable makeup. She wore a deeply V-necked brown satin wrap dress, tightly belted over narrow crêpe de chine trousers. Strappy high-heeled pewter sandals by Halston completed the look.

One of Leslie's juniors arrived to comb out her hair.

225

and by the time he was finished teasing and crimping, she looked a knockout.

Of course her diamonds and emeralds helped. They always did.

Jump Jennings turned up on time. Fontaine shuddered at his choice of outfit. He looked like a refugee from the Hells Angels. Would her friends laugh? After all there was such a thing as going too far.

'Don't you have a suit?' she asked rather testily.

'Wassamatter with the leather?' Jump questioned aggressively.

'It's very . . . macho. But a suit might be more . . . well *right*. Something Italian, double breasted . . .'

Jump narrowed his eyes, 'Lady – you wanted a suit you should've bought me one. I'm an actor, man, not a fuckin' fashion plate.'

And so their evening started. Jump, broody and discontented. Fontaine, ever so slightly embarrassed by her escort.

Several glasses of champagne later she couldn't have cared less. So what if he wore leather? He was six feet tall and had muscles in places other men didn't even have places. He would do very nicely to round off the evening with.

Jump was doing his best early Brando, and it was knocking everyone sideways. Boy, he could've laid every woman in the place – they all looked like they could do with a good seeing to. But he concentrated all of his energies on Fontaine. She was some lady.

They had met the previous week at a loft party in the village, and she had whisked him back to her apartment in a chauffeur-driven limo real quick. There, they had indulged in a four-hour sex marathon that had taxed even Jump's giant strength. Wow – some wild woman! And rich. And classy. And stylish. And he was sick of dumb twenty-year-olds anyway. And he wanted her to take him to London with her. He ached to go to Europe.

'Having fun?' Fontaine sneaked up behind him.

226

'Beats jackin' off.'

She smile, 'Oh my, you're *so* crude.'

'You like it.'

'Sometimes.'

'Always.' His hand slid around her backside.

She pushed it away, 'Not here.'

'You'd like it anywhere.'

'I knew there was something about you that I found irresistible – it's your perception and intelligence.'

He moved very close to her and grinned. 'Naw – it's my cock!'

They made love for hours. It seemed like hours. It probably was hours.

Fontaine lay in bed, her head propped against the pillows, a cigarette in her hand. She was covered by a sheet in the semi-dark hotel room. Outside she could hear the occasional bleat of police sirens, and the usual New York street noises.

Jump was curled around in the foetal position at the foot of the bed. He was asleep, his muscled body twitching with occasional nervous spasms. He snored lightly.

Fontaine wished he had gone home. She wasn't too sure that she liked them staying the night. Why couldn't they just get dressed and go? In all honesty the only man she had ever enjoyed spending the night with was her ex-husband Benjamin, and that was strictly a non-sexual thing. Oh yes – they had made love on occasion – but Benjamin's stamina was low. To put it crudely, a two-minute erection was about all he could manage. So she had looked elsewhere for sex. And who could blame her? But Benjamin had been a friendly all-night companion – in spite of the fact that business calls came through from all over the world all night and every night – and *that* hadn't been too much fun. But still, she missed the basic companionship. The fact that at one time Benjamin had *cared* about her.

227

What did this muscled lump lying at the bottom of her bed care about? Certainly not her, that was for sure.

Oh maybe he liked her, was in awe of her, thought she could do him some good. But care? Forget it.

Most of the sexual athletes of this world were users. They bargained with their bodies. She should know – she had done it herself.

With a sigh Fontaine got up and went into the bathroom. She gazed at her reflection in the mirror. Her hair was a mess, and her make-up smudged. Good. Maybe Jump – what a positively *ridiculous* name – would take one look at her and leave. I must be getting old, she thought, with a wry smile, if all I have in mind is getting rid of him.

She ran the shower, and stood beneath the icy needles of water.

Jump stirred and woke. He reached up for Fontaine's leg, groped around, and realized that she wasn't there. He was annoyed with himself for falling asleep. After the sex should have come the talk. He was all ready to hurry back to his apartment, throw some clothes in a bag, and jet off to London with Fontaine. What would an extra ticket matter to her? Anyway he would give her plenty of value for money.

He could hear the sound of the shower. He leapt off the bed and padded into the bathroom.

Fontaine's body was silhouetted through the shower curtain. Jump didn't hesitate, he climbed right in with her. His entrance was spoiled by the fact that he hadn't realized it was a *cold* shower, and it took exactly two seconds for his powerful erection to become a shrivelled inch and a half!

Fontaine couldn't help laughing, but Jump was mortified.

By the time he recovered, Fontaine was briskly towelling herself dry, and brushed him away with a curt, 'Not now, I have to pack.'

Whiningly Jump seized his last chance. 'Hows about taking me with you?' he suggested. 'We could have ourselves a real good time.'

Fontaine had a fleeting vision of returning to London with a twenty-year-old, leather clad, dumb actor. *Not* exactly the image she wished to project.

'Jump,' she said kindly, 'one of the first things an actor should learn how to do is to make a good exit. You played your part beautifully, but darling, this is the end of the New York run, and London is not exactly beckoning.'

Jump scowled. He didn't know what the hell she was talking about – but he recognized a no when he heard one.

5

'Cherry?' Nico's black eyes glared at Bernie, 'Why the *hell* did you bring her?'

They sat in the bar lounge together, and Bernie had never seen Nico so angry.

'I had no choice,' he explained weakly. 'She was there when you called, and she just sort of insisted.'

'There is always a choice in life,' Nico said bleakly, and he gazed off into space sipping his vodka.

Bernie coughed nervously. 'So?' he ventured, 'What's happening? Are we having fun?'

'We're having shit. How much money did you bring?'

Bernie patted his jacket pocket. 'Six thousand dollars – cash. Are we going to play it?'

Nico laughed mirthlessly. 'I have already played it my friend. I am indebted to this very fine Casino to the tune of five hundred and fifty thousand dollars. And that is not to mention the six hundred thousand of my own that I lost upfront.'

Bernie sniggered. 'What is this? Some kind of a joke . . .'

'No joke,' Nico snapped. 'The truth. Feel free to call me any kind of schmuck you like.'

They sat in uneasy silence for a few minutes, then Bernie said, 'Hey listen, Nico, since when did *you* become the last of the great gamblers? I mean I've seen you play enough times and you've never been into heavy stakes.'

Nico nodded. 'What can I tell you? I got greedy, and I guess when you get greedy your luck flies out of the window. Right, my friend?'

Bernie nodded. He had seen it happen before. When gambling fever hit, sometimes there was nothing you could do about it. It carried you along with a force that was breathtaking. Win or lose you couldn't stop.

'How are you going to pay them?' he asked.

'I can't,' Nico replied calmly.

'Jesus! Don't even kid around on the subject.'

'Who's kidding? I can't pay, it's as simple as that.'

'The Fonicettis would never have given you that kind of credit if they didn't know you were good for it.'

Nico nodded. 'I realize that now. But at the time I wasn't thinking straight, and nobody put a limit on my markers. I suppose they figured if I could lose six hundred grand of my own, then I didn't exactly have a cash flow problem. The six hundred was my house. My final stake. I'm broke, kid, busted out.'

The full enormity of Nico's dilemma was only just occurring to Bernie. To lose was bad enough. But not to be able to pay . . . Suicide . . . Pure undiluted suicide. Everybody knew what happened to bad debtors . . . Bernie personally knew a guy in LA who had owed the bookies seven thousand dollars. *Seven thousand measly dollars for crissakes*. He had been washed up on Malibu beach one morning, and the word had gone around that he was 'an example'. A lot of outstanding debts had got settled that week.

'You're in trouble,' Bernie said.

'An understatement,' Nico agreed.

'We'll figure something out,' Bernie replied, and as he spoke his mind was already checking out the limited possibilities.

Cherry explored Nico's suite with childish delight. She even jumped up and down on the huge bed, and blushed when she thought of the fun they could have on *that* later.

Cherry had been in Los Angeles a little over a year, but already she had decided that the hustle and grind of being an actress was not for her. She had been a successful model in Texas when the call of Hollywood had brought her to a modest apartment on Fountain Avenue. Twenty-five auditions, two bit parts, and a commercial later, she

231

had met Nico. Love had entered Cherry's life for the first time.

Sex had already entered it. First in high school with the football pro. Secondly with a blue jeans manufacturer. Thirdly with a Hollywood agent who promised her big things. She saw big things, but they weren't exactly what she had had in mind.

Nico was something else. He was everything she had always imagined a man should be. He was Nicky Ornstein, from *Funny Girl*. Rhett Butler, from *Gone With the Wind*, and Gatsby from *The Great Gatsby*.

Cherry always looked at life through the movies, things seemed more real that way.

Nico had swept her off her feet, from the moment they met at a party, to the moment he gave her his famous farewell speech.

At first she had cried and realized how right he was. Then she had thought, 'Why is he right? Why will I be happier without him?'

Then the thought had occured that without him she was miserable – so it stood to reason why they should be together.

Immediately she had rushed over to his house to tell him this exciting news, but he was not there, and Bernie had been kind enough to invite her to Las Vegas to find him.

She washed her hands, brushed her long golden hair, and sat and waited patiently. But after two hours she wondered if maybe she should go and look for them.

She checked her perfect appearance one final time, and set off to the elevator.

Dino Fonicetti had often been told he was the absolute image of a young Tony Curtis. It was true. He was the best-looking goddamn guinea in the whole of goddamn Las Vegas, and as such he had the pick of the girls.

Not that appearance had that much to do with sexual success. His brother David had the misfortune to look like a mack truck, and he also scored with monotonous regularity.

Dino entered the elevator, and was stopped in his tracks by just about the most exquisite-looking female he had ever seen.

Of course it was the delectable and innocent-looking Cherry.

Dino said, 'Hello there.'

Cherry looked demurely at the floor.

Dino, master of the fast line racked his brains for something to say. He came up with, 'Are you staying at the hotel?'

Not a bad opening. Not particularly good.

Cherry looked at him with wide blue eyes, 'I'm just visiting,' she said primly.

Some answer. Everyone was just visiting in Las Vegas.

The elevator reached lobby level and stopped. They both stepped out. Cherry hesitated.

'Where are you going?' Dino asked.

'I'm meeting a friend.'

He decided that he couldn't just let this exquisite girl walk out of his life. He extended his hand, 'I'm Dino Fonicetti. My family owns this hotel and if there is anything at all I can do for you . . . anything . . .'

Her hand, as she gripped his, felt soft and small. He was in love. Pow! Just like that, he was getting a hard-on!

'I'm trying to locate Mr Nico Constantine. Do you know him?' Her voice was soft and small, almost as good as her hand!

Did he know Nico. Why, he was the very man he was looking for himself.

Did *she* know Nico? Shit!

Nico and Bernie were still in a huddle discussing the possibilities, when Bernie said, 'I don't believe what I'm seeing. Dino Fonicetti is heading our way hand in hand with Cherry.'

233

Nico glanced around, and then stood as they approached the table.

Dino was indeed leading Cherry by the hand, determined not to let go. She went with him meekly, heads turning as she passed.

She looked at Nico, her eyes brimming over with the emotion of the moment. 'I had to come,' she murmured softly.

Nico's eyes flicked quickly between her and Dino.

'I met Mr Fonicetti in the elevator. He was kind enough to help me look for you,' Cherry said quickly.

'Nico!' Dino exclaimed warmly.

'Dino!' Nico's greeting was equally warm.

'And Bernie,' Dino added, 'why didn't you let me know you were coming?'

Bernie grinned, 'I didn't know I *was* until today.'

'Are you comfortable? Is everything all right?' Dino asked.

Nico grinned easily, 'Perfect.'

'Let me know if there's anything you need at all,' Dino said. 'By the way – how long will you be staying?'

The question was casual enough, but Nico felt he knew why it was asked. 'Long enough to recover some of my money,' he joked.

'Sure, sure,' Dino flashed his best Tony Curtis smile. 'We like everyone to leave here winners. Now tonight I want you all to be my guests for dinner.' He looked at Cherry. 'We'll catch Carlos Brent's late supper show. You'd like that, wouldn't you?'

She glanced at Nico. He nodded.

As a parting shot Dino turned to Bernie, 'Susanna's here,' he said. 'She looks great.' Then he strolled off.

'Who gives a shit,' Bernie muttered angrily.

Cherry asked, 'Who is Susanna?'

'Nobody important. Just my ex-wife.'

Nico was busily counting out some money. He handed Cherry two hundred dollars, 'Be a good girl, run along

234

and play something. Bernie and I have things to discuss.'

'But, Nico. I want to talk to you. I have some very important things to say to you. I came all this way just to . . .'

'I didn't ask you to come,' he interrupted mildly.

Her eyes filled with tears. 'I thought you'd be pleased.'

'I am pleased, but right now I'm busy.'

Cherry pouted, 'I don't know how to gamble.'

Nico pointed out Dino talking to one of the pit bosses. 'You friend will teach you. I have a feeling he'll be only too delighted to show you how it's done.'

Cherry departed reluctantly, and Bernie and Nico exchanged glances.

'I think little Cherry is going to work in our favour,' Bernie said. 'I haven't seen Dino so excited since he got laid by the whole of the Forum chorus line on two consecutive nights!'

'Right,' Nico agreed. 'Now let's go over the plan one more time.'

Solicitously Dino offered Cherry more wine. She declined, holding a delicate hand over her glass to prevent him filling it. 'I never drink more than one glass,' she said solemnly.

'Never?' Dino chided.

'Never,' Cherry replied. 'Unless of course it's a wedding or a big event.'

'This *is* a big event,' Dino insisted, moving her hand and filling her glass to the brim. He felt extremely elated at the way things were turning out. Nico had practically handed over Cherry on a plate. The four of them had eaten together – then Nico had taken Dino to one side and explained that he had a late date, and that Cherry arriving in Vegas had been an embarrassment that he didn't need. Dino had assured him not to worry. He would be more than happy to take personal care of Cherry.

'She's a wonderful girl,' Nico had enthused. 'But no more

235

than a sister to me now, and yet . . . well, I wouldn't want to hurt her feelings. I'll probably spend the night with my date . . .'

'I'll make sure Cherry never even finds out,' Dino said. If she spent the night with him how could she find out?

So after dinner Nico had made an excuse and left, and then Bernie had been set upon by his ex-wife Susanna, and gone off in a huddle with her, and now it was just Cherry and Dino.

Cherry was confused, but determined to help Nico out. He had asked her to keep Dino busy . . . 'Do anything, but be sure he is totally absorbed by you until at least noon tomorrow.' Nico had kissed her softly, 'It's important to me, and one day I'll explain it to you.'

Cherry sipped her wine slowly, 'Dino?' she questioned softly. 'Do you actually *live* in the hotel, or do you have a house?'

'I live right here, babe,' Dino said proudly. 'There are five penthouses, and one of them is all mine. Best view of the strip you're ever likely to see – that's if you want to see it.'

'Ooh, I'd simply *love* to see it. Can I?'

Could she? Goddamn. Things were working out better than he had hoped.

Dino's full concentration was on Cherry. He forgot about everything else. Going to bed with this exquisite little doll was his prime concern. He quite forgot about the fact that he was supposed to quiz Nico about his markers and get his personal cheque to cover them. Five hundred thousand big ones was quite a debt by anyone's standards. But still . . . Getting to Cherry was enough to take anyone's mind off anything. And it wasn't like Nico was taking off anywhere . . . He was around. Dino would talk to him about it the following day.

As soon as he made his excuses at the dinner and was able to get away, Nico headed straight for the Casino. His

236

black eyes scanned the room searching for the lady who was to be his date.

Mrs Dean Costello scooped in another stack of hundred-dollar chips. God it was fun! It's a shame Mr Dean Costello hadn't dropped off a few years earlier. He had been so stingy with his massive fortune. Hadn't he realized that money was to have fun with?

Whoops – here came another number. Thirty-five. She had five chips on the centre and a cheval all round it.

'You're very lucky tonight, madame,' Nico said.

She turned to see who was speaking, and there, right behind her, stood that handsome sonofabitch from the baccarat table. She *knew* he had been after her.

'Yeah, I'm lucky,' she giggled, raking in her chips.

Nico watched her giant diamond ring catch the lights and sparkle invitingly. It had to be worth enough to get him out of trouble.

He wondered vaguely how much she weighed. Two hundred or three hundred pounds? Somewhere between the two.

He wondered how old she was. Fifty, maybe even sixty.

'You're a beautiful woman,' he muttered in her ear, 'and beautiful women shouldn't waste a night like tonight at the gaming tables.'

'Are you foreign?' she asked, flattered by his compliment but not surprised. Mrs Dean Costello thought that she was indeed beautiful. A few pounds overweight perhaps, and a little old for some tastes. But this guy was no chicken, and he knew a good-looking, *mature, sexual* woman when he saw one. He was no fool.

Busily she began to cash in her chips. Opportunities like this did not happen every day.

A half hour later they were in her room. When Nico wanted something he did not waste time.

'I don't usually invite strange men up to my room,' Mrs Costello giggled.

'I'm not strange,' Nico replied, opening up champagne

237

and surreptitiously slipping two strong sleeping draughts into hers. 'What is so strange about wanting to be alone with a beautiful woman?'

Mrs Costello cackled with delight. This was the best one to come her way since the twenty-year-old black waiter in Detroit.

Susanna had not been part of the plan – but what could Bernie do? She grabbed a hold of him, bossy as ever, and now she lectured him in an increasingly whiney voice about what a sonofabitch his lawyer was.

Bernie sat and nodded, hardly able to get a word in. He watched Dino and Cherry at a nearby table, and *that* all seemed to be going well.

Susanna tapped him sharply on the arm. 'I said, what are you doing here? Aren't you listening to me?'

'Sure,' he snapped back to attention and focused on Susanna. She had her mother's sharp features softened by a very good nose job.

'Well?' she glared at him.

'I didn't think I needed your permission.'

Susanna sneered, 'That's right, give me one of your smart-ass answers – that's all you know.'

Bernie stood up. He didn't need this crap. 'You'll have to excuse me, Susanna. I have a hot date with a black jack dealer. The cards are calling, and *that's* why I came here.'

'Gambling!' Susanna spat. 'And I have to fight you for every stinking cent of my alimony.'

He threw her a cold look. He was paying her fifteen hundred dollars a month, and she was insisting on more. It really was a joke. Carlos Brent was worth millions, and Susanna was his only child. Out of the corner of his eye he saw Cherry and Dino rise from their table.

'Got to go,' he said quickly.

'Bernie,' Susanna restrained him with a hand on his arm, her voice softening. 'Why don't we get together for a drink later? I really am sick of all the arguments.'

Oh, Christ! More complications! Susanna had that 'I wanna get laid' look about her.

Bernie managed an encouraging look. 'I'd like that. Where will you be?'

'I'm spending some time with daddy after the show, then I'll be in my room. Come for a drink.'

'Right. I'll see you later.' He made his escape just in time to check Cherry and Dino getting into the elevator. The kid had really come up trumps – one word from Nico and she was prepared to do anything to help.

Bernie hurried outside. He had his part to do as well.

They all wanted to help Nico.

6

New York's Kennedy airport was as busy as ever. The weather hadn't been too good, and a lot of people were sitting around and complaining, waiting for their flights to take off.

Fontaine Khaled arrived at the airport in her usual style. She swept in, followed by two porters organizing her luggage.

An airport official rushed over immediately.

Jump hovered in the background thinking about the day *he* would get treated in such a fashion.

'Mrs Khaled. So good to see you again,' said the official.

'Will you check me in?'

'Of course, of course. Would you like to wait in the lounge?'

Fontaine was irritated. 'There's not a delay is there?'

'Only slight.'

'Oh, Christ!'

The airport official signalled to a ground hostess. 'Escort Mrs Khaled to the lounge, please.'

'Lets go,' Fontaine beckoned Jump imperiously.

Nico's flight from Los Angeles had arrived one hour previously. He was not delighted to discover that his ongoing flight to London was delayed. He sat in the VIP lounge sipping vodka and musing on the events that had led him to where he was. He felt strangely elated when he really should be scared shitless. Christ! Maybe he had been stagnating for the last ten years. What had seemed like a good time had certainly not sent the adrenaline coursing through his veins like it was now.

Bernie had been very helpful. It had been *his* suggestion that if Nico couldn't pay his markers he split.

240

'Don't stay around to explain,' Bernie had urged. 'Get the hell out – get the money – and don't let them find you 'til you have it.'

Good thinking. But Nico had no idea at all how he was going to get the money. Then it had come to him. An idea so out of character – and yet so obvious. He would steal the fat lady's ring – it must be worth at least as much as he had lost.

At first Bernie thought he was kidding. Then he saw that Nico was indeed serious, and his mind had started to work. Steal the ring. Get the hell out of Vegas without the Fonicettis knowing. Sell the ring. Pay off the markers – and then worry about compensating the fat lady – for Nico insisted that she must be paid back.

It was a bizarre plan, but they both decided it would work.

Dino's crush on Cherry took care of him watching Nico too closely, and she had entered into the spirit of the whole caper with great enthusiasm. Bernie hired a car – and once Nico had the ring, he took the car – drove back to Los Angeles – picked up some clothes – and headed straight for the airport.

Bernie had a friend – Hal – in London, who had connections, and would be able to get the right deal on the ring. London was far enough away for Nico to have time to operate. By the time the Fonicettis had even realized he had left Vegas, he would be back with the money.

Of course the plan had holes. The fat lady would start hollering the moment she woke from her drug-induced sleep. But Nico had given her a false name – and who would suspect him anyway? He had taken care to make sure that they had left the Casino separately, and their only connection was sitting next to each other at the baccarat table.

Bernie and Cherry would stay in Vegas, and make believe Nico was still there too.

Now Nico waited for his connecting flight, and fingered

241

the ring lying loosely in his pocket. He was worried about customs. What if they stopped him and found it? Not a good thought.

A woman swept into the room. She was sophisticated, assured, and beautiful. Late thirties, very expensive, totally in control. Almost a female version of himself. He couldn't help smiling at the thought.

She was accompanied by a muscle-bound young man, who hung on to her every word. And her every word was very audible, as she spoke in a piercing voice that didn't give a damn about who might be listening.

'God! This is all so boring!' she said loudly. 'Why can't the bloody plane take off when it's supposed to?' She threw herself dramatically into a chair, shrugged off her sable coat, and crossed silken legs. 'Do order some champagne, darling.'

'Who *is* that?' Nico asked the girl serving drinks.

She shrugged. 'Mrs Khaled. Some Arab millionaire's wife. We have orders to look after her. She's been through here before and she's an absolute bitch.'

Fontaine wanted Jump to leave. He was annoying her. He was so obvious it was pathetic. All those little hints about how he longed to go to Europe. How he would miss her desperately. How she was bound to miss him. And of course – hadn't their love-making been the most erotic and sensual experience ever.

'I don't think you should hang around here any longer,' Fontaine said abruptly, 'I think I might just try and have a sleep.'

'I can't leave you,' Jump replied anxiously. 'The flight might be cancelled. I don't mind staying.'

Of course he didn't mind staying. He was hoping she would change her mind and take him with her.

'No, darling, I insist. You're been here quite long enough.'

Jump stood his ground. 'I'll stay, Fontaine. You never know what might happen.'

Before she could reply a hostess appeared and announced that the flight was ready to board.

'About time,' Fontaine complained, standing up and allowing Jump to adjust her sable coat around her shoulders.

He moved as if to hold her in a passionate embrace. She responded deftly, offering him an informal cheek to kiss. 'Not in public,' she murmured. 'I do have a certain reputation.'

'When will you call me?' he inquired anxiously, more concerned about a trip to London than her reputation.

'Soon enough,' she replied succinctly.

Nico secured the seat next to Mrs Khaled for two reasons. One – who better than to unwittingly carry his diamond through British customs than an English woman who it would seem unlikely they would stop. Two – the flight ahead was long and boring, and while Mrs Khaled was slightly long in the tooth for his admittedly juvenile tastes, she at least looked like she could amuse him, and if his luck was in – perhaps play a passable game of backgammon.

He allowed Fontaine to settle into her window seat before taking his place.

She glanced at him, amazing kaleidoscope eyes summing him up.

He smiled, full Nico charm. 'Allow me to introduce myself, Nico Constantine.'

She raised a cynical eyebrow, he was attractive, much too old for her, and conversations she didn't need.

Nico was not to be brushed off, 'And you are . . .?'

'Mrs Khaled,' she replied shortly. 'And I may as well warn you, that even though we are travelling companions for the next few hours, I am totally exhausted, and certainly not in the mood for polite conversations. You do understand, Mr er . . .'

'Constantine. And of course I understand. But perhaps I can offer you some champagne?'

'You can offer away. But let us not forget that they serve it free in first class.'

'I meant when we arrive in London. Perhaps dinner at Annabels?'

Fontaine frowned. How crass to have to cope with a man on the make when all she wanted to do was sleep. She glanced across the aisle at a thirtyish blonde in a striped mink coat, 'Try her,' she said coldly. 'I think you'll have more success.'

Nico followed her glance. 'Dyed hair, too much make-up, please credit me with some taste.'

Oh, God! What had she done to be stuck next to a man on the make. She turned and stared out of the window. Perhaps she should have brought Jump if only to protect her from bores on planes.

'Your seat belt.'

'What?'

'The sign is on.'

She fiddled for the seat belt, couldn't find one half of it. Nico realized it, and attempted to help her buckle up.

'I can manage, thank you,' she snapped.

Nico was perplexed. A woman who did not respond to his charm? Impossible. Unheard of. For ten years he had taken his pick of the best that Hollywood had to offer. Ripe juicy young beauties – at his beck and call day and night. Never a turn down. Always adoration. And now this . . . this English woman. So full of herself, waspish, and frankly a pain in the ass.

But still . . . If he wanted to plant the diamond on her he had to develop *some* line of communication.

The jumbo-jet was taxiing down the runway preparing for take-off.

'Are you nervous?' Nico asked.

Fontaine shot him a scornful look. 'Hardly. I have been flying since I was sixteen years old. God knows how many flights I have taken.' She shut her eyes. How many flights *had* she taken? Plenty. The first year of her marriage to Benjamin she had accompanied him everywhere. The perfect wife. Trips all over the world, boring business trips that had driven her mad, until at last she had begged off and only taken the interesting ones. Paris. Rome. Rio. New York. Acapulco. Marvellous shopping. Exciting friends. And then the lovers . . . Well, Benjamin had driven her to the lovers . . .

She felt the thrust as the big plane became airborne, but she kept her eyes tightly shut, didn't want to encourage her travelling companion to indulge in any more inane conversation. He *was* an attractive man. Not her type of course, much too ancient. Probably appeal to her friend Vanessa, who liked them a little worn.

'You've been asleep for two hours,' Nico announced.

Fontaine opened her eyes slowly. She felt hot and creased, and the taste in her mouth was truly vile.

Nico handed her a glass of champagne. She sipped it gratefully.

'Do you play backgammon?' he asked.

'Oh God! So that's what you are.' She couldn't help smiling. 'A backgammon hustler! I should have known.'

Nico grinned. 'A backgammon player – yes. A backgammon hustler – no. Sorry to disappoint you.'

'But you look the part – my God, you're almost better dressed than I am!'

'That would be impossible.'

Suddenly they were talking and laughing. The stewardess served food and more champagne.

He wasn't so bad, Fontaine decided. Rather nice actually. And what a refreshing change to have a conversation with a man who was neither a fag nor a young stud. Idly she wondered if he had money. He was certainly dressed well enough – and the jewellery was expensive and in perfect taste.

'What business are you in?' she asked casually.

Nico smiled. 'Commodities.'

'That sounds like it could be anything.'

'It usually is, I don't like to be pinned down.'

245

'Hmm . . .' She fixed him with a quizzical look.

'And you? Where is Mr Khaled?'

'Benjamin Al Khaled no longer has the pleasure of being my husband. Ex is the word – but keep it to yourself – I get better service when the world doesn't know.'

Nico looked her over admiringly. 'I'm sure *you* would always get good service.'

'Thank you.'

Their eyes met and locked. There was that moment when nothing is said but everything is known.

Fointaine broke the look. God! Maybe it was the plane trip, maybe she was overtired, but suddenly she felt incredibly horny.

'Excuse me,' she got up and moved past him to visit the toilet. She wanted to check out her appearance. She probably looked a mess.

Nico watched her go, and sniffed at the cloud of 'Opium' perfume she left behind. Lise Maria had always worn 'Jolie Madame'. It was the first time he had thought of his late wife in a long time. Lise Maria belonged in the past, wrapped in a beautiful memory he did not care to disturb. Why was he thinking of her now?

'Will you be watching the movie, Mr Constantine?' the stewardess inquired.

'What is it?'

'*The Fury*. Starring Kirk Douglas.'

'Sure – leave the earphones.'

'And Mrs Khaled?'

'Yes. Mrs Khaled will watch it too.'

Making decisions for her already! And thinking about how it would be in bed with a woman like that . . . It had been so long since he had had a woman. Plenty of girls – gorgeous sweet creatures who enjoyed his expert tuition . . . But to have a real woman again . . . A sophisticated sensual female . . .

Idly he wondered if she had money, what a plus *that* would be.

7

Polly Brand stirred in her sleep and reached out. Her arm encountered flesh, and she woke with a start. Then she remembered, grinned, and reached for her glasses. 'All the better to see you with my dear!' she giggled, as she trailed her fingers down her companion's back.

'Get off . . .' he mumbled, still half asleep.

'Oh come on,' Polly responded, full of enthusiasm. 'We've just got time to do it before we go to the airport.'

'Do what?'

'*It*, of course.' Her hand reached for his slumbering penis.

He moved away. 'I gotta sleep. Ten more minutes . . .'

'Ricky. I've got you a very good job, and I do expect you to be grateful – *very* grateful.'

'I'll be fucking grateful tonight. Right now I need sleep.'

Polly squirmed all over him. 'You'll be working tonight, Ricky Tick. Our Mrs Khaled will have you hard at it ferrying her around 'til all hours. The bitch never sleeps. She has to be seen – constantly – and your chauffeur duties will not be over 'til dawn. And that's when *I* like to sleep. So come on – let's fuck!'

Reluctantly Ricky allowed the energetic Polly to go to work on him until he was in a ready state to do her bidding.

A six-minute thrash and it was over.

'Thanks a *lot*!' complained Polly.

'Morning is not my best time,' Ricky grumbled, reaching for his watch. '*Especially* not five-a-bleedin'-clock.'

'We have to be at the airport by seven. Mrs Khaled cannot be kept waiting, she'll throw a right mood if she is. Your new employer is *very* temperamental.'

'Can't wait. Are you sure this job isn't just one big drag?'

Polly giggled, 'You'll love it. You'll have a great time. If I know dear old Fontaine . . .'

247

'Yeah?'

Polly climbed out of bed still giggling. 'Just wait and see, you're in for a big surprise . . . If she likes you that is . . . And oh boy . . . I've got a feeling she'll like you.'

Fontaine Khaled and Ricky the chauffeur. The thought sent Polly off into gales of laughter.

Ricky followed her out of bed. 'Come on, share the joke.'

'You'll know soon enough.' Polly clicked a cassette into her tape deck and the sound of Rod Stewart filled the room. She proceeded to exercise to the sound of his voice – unconcernedly naked.

Ricky watched her for a minute, then he went into the bathroom. Funny little thing that one. She had chatted him up in his mini-cab two weeks earlier – and before he knew it he had quit his job to accept the position as Mrs Khaled's chauffeur. Well, driving a mini-cab was not for him. Too many bleedin' headaches. Now chauffeuring was another thing . . . If you had to drive around London day and night you may as well do it in a Roller.

Polly stretched to the ceiling, back to touch the floor. Twenty-four . . . twenty-five . . . Finished.

She couldn't be bothered to wash, a bad habit but no one had ever complained. She pulled on a fluffy angora sweater and tight jeans, knee-length boots, and pulled a comb through her short spiky hair. Make-up was lipgloss only. Her tinted glasses did the rest. Polly was not pretty – more unusual and certainly attractive. She was twenty-nine years old, and head of her own Public Relations outfit. Not bad for a girl who started out as a secretary at seventeen. Her firm represented Fontaine Khaled's discothèque 'Hobo', and Mrs Khaled called on her whenever she needed anything. Polly didn't mind. For each service she performed she added a little extra on the bill. Finding Ricky would be worth at least a couple of hundred.

He emerged from the bathroom clad in a pair of

jockey shorts decorated with a garish picture of a rhinoceros and a slogan saying – 'I feel horny.'

'Christmas! Where did you get *those*?' Polly fell about laughing.

'My kid sister.' Ricky walked over to the mirror to admire himself. 'They look all right, don't they?'

'All right? They're a fucking scream!'

Ricky frowned. 'It's only a joke, no need to wet your panties.'

Polly tried to stop laughing. 'I didn't know guys actually *wore* things like that.'

Ricky's dignity was affronted. He pulled on his trousers quickly.

Polly leaned back and studied him through narrowed eyes. Great body. Thin, wiry, rock-hard thighs and stomach, and a nice tight ass. Sexy, sexy face, dirty blond hair, and when he was in the mood – a natural enthusiasm for screwing. Nice and normal. Not into grass or coke or tying you to the bed. Probably didn't even know what bondage was.

Fontaine Khaled . . . if she wanted to . . . would absolutely adore him.

The interior of the plane was dark as the big jet winged its way towards England. The movie had finished, and now most of the passengers were asleep.

Fontaine wasn't.

Nico wasn't.

They were indulging in a necking session – teenage in its intensity.

Who could ever forget the excitement of one's first furtive gropings. The hands under the sweater, up the skirt. The lips, tongues, teeth. The eroticism of investigating a strange ear. The exquisite thrill of a clandestinely fondled nipple.

Fontaine felt as flushed as any fifteen-year-old. It was an amazing sensation. Nico, too, was filled with an unremembered excitement.

249

To touch but not to be really able to. To feel – but not properly.

Whoever said making love on a plane was easy was a fool. It was goddamn difficult. Especially when a stewardess flitted up and down the aisle every ten minutes.

So they contented themselves with the sticky fondlings of first experience. And it was erotic to say the least. It was also fun. And it was a long time since either of them could remember sex being fun.

'When I get you in London, Mrs Khaled, I want time, space, and the luxury of a bed,' Nico whispered. His fingers were on her thigh, travelling up, sneaking round the leg of her panties.

Fontaine's hand fiddled with the zipper on his trousers. She could feel his maleness through the silk of his undershorts, and it was turning her on with a vengeance. 'Oh, yes, Mr Constantine, I think that could be arranged.'

The stewardess passed by, brisk and efficient. Could she see what was going on? They both remained stock still.

'I want to see your body,' Nico whispered. 'I know you have a very beautiful body.'

Fontaine traced the line of his mouth with her tongue, 'None of your bullshit lines please, Nico. None of your stock phrases. You don't have to play the perfect gentleman with me.'

She had him figured out pretty quickly. He liked that. 'So I want to fuck you,' he muttered. 'I want to fuck your beautiful body.' Christ! He hadn't felt free enough to talk to a woman like that since Lise Maria. Fontaine was right – he did open his mouth and out poured the perfect gentleman bullshit.

'That's better,' Fontaine sighed. 'I want to feel you're talking to me, not doing your number.'

Their tongues played sensuous games. Then dawn and lightness started to filter through the windows, and it was time to stop playing and brush out clothes and adjust things.

The stewardess served them breakfast with a thin smile. She had seen what was going on – and frankly she was jealous. It wasn't like she hadn't seen it all before. But a man like Nico Constantine . . . Well – if he hadn't been stuck next to that Khaled bitch there might have been a chance for her.

Fontaine nibbled on some toast, sipped the awful coffee, and smiled at Nico. 'That was —'

He put a finger on her lips. 'Don't give me any of *your* bullshit lines.'

'But it was.'

'It was.'

They grinned at each other stupidly.

'I'd better go and get myself together,' Fontaine said at last. 'A little makeup job, and my hair needs mouth to mouth resuscitation!'

It wasn't until she had gone that Nico suddenly remembered the reason he had struck up an acquaintance in the first place. It didn't seem so important now. But he had the ring, and it was burning a hole in his pocket. If he asked Fontaine he was sure that she wouldn't mind taking it through customs for him. But why involve her? The best thing was to have her do it for him unknowingly.

She had taken her makeup case and left her purse. Easy. He glanced across the aisle. The dyed blonde in the striped mink coat was engrossed in conversation with a drunken writer who was en route to London to get married for the fifth time.

Nico opened the purse. Easy. A double zipped compartment into which he dropped the ring. Easy.

Fontaine returned, her hair pulled sleekly back, a subtle makeup emphasizing her perfect bones. She smiled at him. 'Have I got time for a cigarette before we come down to earth?'

Ricky drove the large silver Rolls-Royce much too fast.

Polly, enjoying an early morning joint, admonished

him. 'Mrs K. sets the speed when you're driving her. Don't you forget it.'

'What's she like?' Ricky asked for the sixth time.

'Oh, you'll either like her or you'll hate her. She's a difficult lady. No in-betweens. Typical Gemini – only ever does what she wants to do – hears what she wants to hear.'

'Has she still got a lot of money?'

Polly shrugged. 'Who knows? "Hobo" ain't making it any more, but her old man was so loaded . . . Look out Ricky – you nearly hit that car. You're supposed to be a chauffeur, not a racing car driver. And don't forget – call me Miss Brand in front of her. Wouldn't do to let her know I'm screwing the hired help.'

'Mrs Khaled. Welcome back to London.' Fontaine was greeted by an airport lackey paid to smooth the way for VIPs. He took her makeup case. 'This way, Mrs Khaled. Everything's taken care of. If we can just have your passport . . .'

She glanced around, looking for Nico. He stood at the back of a long line for foreign passports.

She waved, blew him a kiss, and swept right through British passport control.

Nico was impressed. Still married to her Arab billionaire or not she knew how to do things in style. What a stroke of genius planting the ring on her. No way would customs dare to stop her.

He thought about where he would take her for dinner. It was many years since he had been in London. But Annabels was always safe, then maybe a little gambling at the Clermont, and then bed. He anticipated a stimulating evening in every way.

Fontaine feigned surprise at seeing Polly. 'So early, darling? You shouldn't have bothered.'

Polly knew that if she hadn't bothered, Fontaine would never have let her forget it.

They kissed, the usual insincere brushing of cheeks.

'You look gorgeous!' Polly exclaimed. 'Have you had a wonderful time?'

'Terrible actually. Didn't you hear about my robbery?'

They walked to the car where Ricky respectfully held the Rolls door open.

'No! How awful! What happened?'

'I was wiped out. They took everything, absolutely everything!'

'Your jewellery?'

'Not my jewellery. That – thank God – was in the bank.'

Ricky shut the door on them. So this was the famous Mrs Khaled. Really something. She made Polly look like a bit of old rope.

Nico stood in line patiently for twenty five minutes. It was annoying, but a fact of life when entering a foreign country.

Naturally he was detained at customs. 'You have the look of an expensive smuggler!' Lise Maria had once told him. 'Don't ever change, I love that look!'

The customs official was polite but insistent. Every one of his Vuitton suitcases was opened up and searched. For one horrible moment Nico thought they might also search him, but luck was on his side, and he did not have to suffer the indignity of a body search.

At last he was free. He hoped that Fontaine had waited for him – she had mentioned something about her car and chauffeur meeting her. But she was nowhere to be seen. Long gone. He should have known she was not the sort of woman who would wait around.

Damn. It was annoying. He wanted to recover the ring as soon as possible. What if she discovered it? The idea of that was not a welcome one, but he would just bluff it out – tell her the truth – not about actually stealing the ring – just about her helping him through customs with it. And a good job too, considering he had been stopped.

Fontaine would probably be amused by the whole incident.

Still . . . it would be better if she didn't find the ring . . . which meant he had to see her as soon as possible.

He signalled a cab and directed the driver to the Lamont Hotel. He had been warned that no one of any note stayed at the Dorchester since it had been bought by the Arabs. The Lamont was *the* place – quiet, very English, with an excellent restaurant comparable to the Connaught.

'Cor blimey, mate,' sneered the cabbie. 'Sure you got enough bleedin' suitcases?'

8

Cherry's first night with Dino was a mechanical affair. He took her to his penthouse apartment atop the Forum, showed her the view – which she admired. Fixed her an exotic liqueur – which she drank. Played her some sensual Barry White sounds – which she enjoyed. Then moved in for the kill.

'I don't make love on a first date,' Cherry said demurely, long brownish black eyelashes fluttering over huge blue eyes.

'What?' snapped Dino. He had a hard-on that was threatening to burst the zipper on his pants.

'I like you a lot,' Cherry continued in her sweet baby girl voice, 'and I admire you. But I can't make love to you, it's against my principles.'

'Principles!' exclaimed Dino. 'Forget your goddamn principles.'

'Don't get mad,' Cherry replied firmly. 'You have no right to expect me to do anything I don't want to.'

He looked her over, every gorgeous inch of her, and for the first time in his life realized he was getting a turn-down. He couldn't offer her a better part in the show. She didn't want to be a cocktail waitress. If he proffered money she would throw it back in his face. But his father had taught him well – every woman has her price – and every smart man should be able to find out what that price is.

'What do you want?' Dino asked thickly.

Cherry shook her long blonde curls. 'Nothing,' she replied. 'But I like being with you, and if you want I'll stay the night with you – but I won't do anything, and you must promise not to force me.'

In all his many experiences with women this was a first. Dino was perplexed. He was also fascinated. He was also in love.

They spent the night together. They kissed. They caressed. She stripped down to a skimpy lace chemise that would give any red-blooded male a heart attack. He put on a bathrobe over a pair of restrictive jockey shorts.

He just did not believe what was going on. He fe'l asleep with a wrecking gut-ache, and woke at seven in the morning with the same nagging pain.

Cherry lay asleep beside him, yellow hair fanned out around her face, legs slightly apart, the chemise revealing just a wisp of lacy panties.

Enough was enough. Dino rolled on top of her, ripping her panties with one hand, and freeing himself with the other. He was inside her before she even awoke.

'Dino! You promised!' She was not as outraged as she might have been.

'That was last night,' he husked. 'Our first date. Now it's our second date and it's my turn to call the shots.'

Cherry didn't argue. She wrapped her long and beautiful legs around him and gave a little sigh. Nico was a marvellous man – but as he had pointed out – what kind of a future did she have with him?

Now Dino was a different matter . . .

So far so good. Everything was going according to plan.

Bernie placed a stack of chips on red and watched black come up. Roulette. What a game. Why was he even bothering?

He glanced at his watch. Two o'clock in the morning. Nico should be well on his way.

He eyed one of the cocktail waitresses. It wasn't his imagination that she had been coming on to him all night.

He gestured for another scotch, and wondered if he should hit on her for a fast fuck. He decided against it. He had too much on his mind, and anyway sex drained his vital energies.

At that precise moment his name was paged, and he thought – Christ! The shit has hit.

He rushed to the phone. It was Susanna. She was

drunk. Just what he needed in his life, a drunken ex-wife.

'I thought you were coming up for a drinkie,' giggle giggle, 'or something . . .?'

'Hey,' How should he play *this* one? He was in enough trouble with Susanna as it was. 'I called you earlier, guess you weren't back,' he explained.

'Daddy had a party,' she hiccoughed. 'Fifteen gofers, twenty hookers, and half the mob.'

The only time she put daddy down was when she was drunk. Then she saw him for the egotistical mean sonofabitch he really was.

Bernie played for time. 'Sounds like fun.'

'It wasn't. It was awful,' she paused, then in a sexy whine. 'Come on up Bernie, for old times' sake. We can just – talk.'

Oh shit! What did he have to lose?

Besides which, Susanna gave the best head in Holly-wood. Or if there was anyone better *he'd* never found them.

Cherry and Dino spent the morning in bed.

They talked. They investigated the possibilities of get-ting further involved. They would have stayed there all day if Dino's father hadn't called and demanded his presence.

'What I want you to do is go back to Nico's suite, collect your things, and tell him bye bye,' Dino told her.

At the mention of Nico's name Cherry felt a twinge of guilt. Surely if she was planning to stay with Dino her loyalties lay with him? Maybe she should tell him that Nico had already left . . . But then again she had promised Nico she would help . . . And of course she wouldn't want him to come to any harm.

Dino was dressing. White slacks, a black shirt, white sports jacket. Las Vegas casual.

Cherry sat up in bed, blonde hair tumbling around her shoulders. 'Dino,' she ventured shyly, 'have you ever been married?'

257

Dino grinned at himself admiringly in the mirror.

'Me? No, of course not.'

'Why of course not?'

'Well . . . gee . . . I don't know . . .' Why *hadn't* he ever got married? Never met anyone he would want to marry. He looked at Cherry lying in his bed. She was so . . . delectable . . . He wanted to eat her up. His grin widened, he would later.

She climbed out of bed innocently unaware of his scrutiny – or so he thought.

Now that was what he called a body. Streamlined and golden. Soft and firm.

She walked to the bathroom door, turned, and smiled sweetly. 'I'd *like* to get married,' she said softly. 'Wouldn't you?'

Bernie did not escape Susanna's clutches until six in the morning. He staggered from her room bleary-eyed and exhausted. They had run through the whole book of emotions – plus some very wild sex.

He hurried back to Nico's suite, and collapsed on the bed.

He had blown checking with Nico on the phone, but hopefully, by this time, he was on a plane to Europe.

Now if the pretence of Nico still being in Vegas could only be kept up . . .

Bernie fell into a fully clothed sleep.

As Bernie fell asleep Mrs Dean Costello woke up. She felt as if someone had hit her over the head with a hammer, and she was surprised to note that she was still fully dressed.

She struggled to recollect the events of the previous evening . . . But she just couldn't, her brain seemed to be all fogged up.

She vaguely remembered an extremely charming gentleman . . . Champagne . . . And hadn't she won a fair amount of money . . .?

Her winnings! She struggled to sit up, and switched on a light.

Her winnings were neatly stacked on the bedside table. Eighteen thousand dollars if her memory served her correctly. Propped beside them was a note—

'Madame. You are a charming and gracious lady – and I am sure you would help a gentleman out of trouble. I have borrowed your diamond ring – but the loan is temporary and you shall be repaid in full . . . I would appreciate your co-operation of not going to the police . . .'

Mrs Dean Costello started to laugh. Why that cocky son-of-a-bitch. The nerve. The goddamn bare-assed nerve.

9

The Chelsea house was looking a little tacky, Fontaine decided. It was part of the divorce settlement – Benjamin had kept their Belgravia mansion and she had been bought what she considered to be a rather unimpressive abode.

It was certainly not unimpressive. It was a five-bedroomed, three-receptioned-room elegant house with a large garden. However, it was not the Belgravia mansion with the indoor swimming-pool, sauna, private cinema, internal elevator, and landscaped roof-garden.

Fontaine had furnished her new house in a hurry before she had left for New York, and it did have style. The trouble was that nobody had been living there except Mrs Walters, her ancient and faithful housekeeper, and the rooms smelt musty and unused, and there was even the faint aroma of cat pee.

'Christ!' Fontaine exclaimed. 'Why the hell didn't someone air this place out? And why aren't there any fresh flowers?'

Polly shrugged. Fontaine's domestic arrangements really were not her affair.

'Mrs Walters!' Fontaine yelled.

The old woman came running out from the kitchen. 'Welcome home, Mrs Khaled—' she started to say.

Fontaine cut her short with a barrage of complaints.

Ricky came through the front door carrying some of the luggage.

Polly winked at him. He frowned.

'I never said she was easy to work for . . .' Polly murmured as he passed by.

Nico checked into the Lamont Hotel and requested a suite.

He was shown to a smallish suite overlooking the back.

He handed the porter a five-pound note, and said, 'Stay

here a minute.' Then he picked up the phone and asked to see the Manager immediately.

The Manager, Mr Graheme, was with him ten minutes later, a thin harassed man whose main concern at that moment in time was whether he could prevent the entire kitchen staff from walking out. Earlier in the day he had fired an assistant chef who had been caught stealing fillet steaks – handing them to an accomplice as he took out the garbage. This had resulted in a flat statement from the rest of the kitchen workers that either the thief stayed or they walked. What to do? Mr Graheme had still not decided.

'Yes, sir, what can I do for you?' he snapped at Nico, a little too harshly but he *was* under a strain.

Nico gestured at his surroundings, 'Nice,' he said warmly. 'Very comfortable.' Then he moved over to Mr Graheme and offered him a cigar, then he put his arm conspiratorially around his shoulders, 'Mr Graheme. I stay at your hotel for the first time. The place has been highly recommended to me by many of my friends in Beverly Hills. But really . . . a suite like this for a man like me . . . Perhaps I should try the Connaught . . .'

Fifteen minutes later Nico was ensconced in the best suite in the hotel.

Mr Graheme knew a big spender when he saw one.

Once rid of Polly, Fontaine couldn't wait to get on the phone to Vanessa Grant, her very best friend in London.

'I'm back,' she announced dramatically. 'Exhausted and destroyed. I can't wait to see you. How about dinner tonight?'

Vanessa hesitated, she and her husband Leonard already had dinner plans, but once Fontaine wanted something it really didn't do to argue.

'I think that will be fine,' she said.

'Fine!' Fontaine snorted. 'Bloody enthusiastic welcome that is!'

'We weren't expecting you until next week . . .'

'I know, I know. I had to change my plans because of my *robbery*.'

'What robbery?'

'Darling – haven't you heard? It's all over the papers in New York.'

They chatted some more, arranging where and when to meet, then casually Fontaine asked, 'By the way, do you and Leonard know a man called Nico Constantine? An Americanized Greek. Lives in Beverly Hills, I think.'

'No, I don't think that name rings any bells. Who is he? Another of your juvenile delinquents?'

'Hardly juvenile, rather more mature.'

Vanessa laughed. 'Doesn't sound like you at all. Is he rich?'

'I don't really know . . . Maybe.'

'Are you bringing him tonight?'

'Certainly not. I have a rather divine Italian Count who is flying in especially to see me.'

Vanessa sighed, she had been married for too many years and had too many children. 'Sometimes I envy you . . .'

'I know,' replied Fontaine crisply. 'If you're a good girl I'll throw him your way when I'm finished with him. He's twenty-six years old and horny as a rutting dog!'

It occured to Nico that he had no idea how to get in touch with Fontaine. He had been so sure that she would wait for him at the airport that he had not even bothered to find out her phone number. Stupid really. But usually women waited . . . And after their undeniably erotic encounter on the plane he had felt sure that Fontaine would not go rushing off. Well, hardly rushing . . . Between passport control and customs it had taken him an hour to emerge. But still . . . She could at least have left a message.

He called the reception desk, told the porter her name, and asked him to find out her phone number and address immediately.

Half an hour later the porter gave him Benjamin Al Khaled's London office number, and a frosty secretary there said she could not possibly reveal the previous Mrs Khaled's phone number or address, and if he wished to contact her he should write in and his communication would be forwarded on.

Nico turned on his telephone charm – not as potent as the real thing – but effective enough to get him the number with a little gentle persuasion.

He phoned Fontaine immediately. A housekeeper answered his call and said that Mrs Khaled was resting and could not be disturbed.

He left his name and number and a message for her to call him back. Then he contacted the hotel florist and sent her three dozen red roses with a card saying – 'The flight was memorable – when do come in for landing? Nico.'

Next he phoned Hal – Bernie's London friend, whom he had never met – but who apparently knew everyone and everything – and who would be able to take excellent care of the ring situation – once he had it back of course.

They arranged to meet in the bar later.

Nico then called for the valet. Time to get his personal grooming in order. It would never do to look anything but perfect.

Fontaine slept all day. At seven o'clock Mrs Walters woke her, and she got up and started her numerous preparations for the evening's activities.

'A Mr Constantine phoned,' Mrs Walters informed her. 'Also Count Paulo Rispollo. They would both like you to phone them back.' Mrs Walters busied herself with running Fontaine's bath. She had worked for her for over ten years and felt she understood her – although Fontaine was extremely difficult to work for, what with her sudden screaming fits and unreasonable demands.

'Call the Count back, tell him to collect me at nine o'clock.' Fontaine handed Mrs Walters a number. 'And if

Mr Constantine phones again you can say I'm out.'

'They both sent flowers,' Mrs Walters continued. 'Three dozen roses from Mr Constantine. A bowl of orchids from Count Rispollo. I told the new chauffeur to be back at eight sharp, shall I send him to pick the Count up?'

'I suppose so,' Fontaine stripped off her thin silk dressing gown and stretched. 'I don't think for one moment he has his own.'

Mrs Walters scurried off, and Fontaine climbed into a deliciously hot bath.

Count Paulo Rispollo. Young. Good-looking. Unfortunately didn't have a pot to piss in. But he adored her. Had met her in New York and declared undying love. Probably bi-sexual, but very passable in bed – and that's where it all mattered – wasn't it? Besides, it was so good for her image . . . A young good-looking escort . . . especially a titled one.

She thought briefly of Nico Constantine, then put him quickly from her mind. Trouble. She sensed it. And anyway – since when did she date men older than herself? What a positively boring idea. Who needed real conversations? All she needed was a fine young body – no complications – just sex. And if sometimes she had to pick up the bills . . . well, that was life, wasn't it?

Nico was irritated when Fontaine failed to return his call by the time he met with Hal. He was more than irritated, he needed to recover the ring urgently.

Hal turned out to be an amiable fortyish American promoter operating out of London. Attractive, if you liked the Dean Martin gone-to-seed type. Constantly stoned, and well dressed. His speciality was hustling elderly widow ladies.

He greeted Nico warmly, asked after Bernie, and mumbled, 'Where's the item? I have a good set up waiting to accept. I'm working on a split percentage – five per cent from you – five from them – does that suit you?'

'Sure, but I have a problem,' Nico explained. 'I met a woman on the plane. I thought it would be safer for her to bring it in. I don't have it back yet.'

Hal made a face, 'I was given to understand time was of the essence.'

'It is, it is. The woman . . . I'm trying to reach her. Her name is Fontaine Khaled.'

Hal let out a whistle. 'The ice queen herself! Is she back?'

'Do you know her?'

Hal laughed. 'Sure I know her. She owns "Hobo". My good friend Tony Blake used to run it for her – along with a few more personal services. He's living in LA now trying to recover from the experience! What the hell was she doing with *you*? You're a little over her age limit.'

'What the hell was *I* doing with *her*?' Nico retorted quickly. 'She's a little over mine.'

'Does she know about the ring?' Hal asked.

'No. I hid it in her purse. I've been trying to contact her.'

'Don't worry. We'll see her tonight. The first place Mrs Khaled will go is "Hobo". We'll be there to greet her.'

'What you need is another Tony,' Vanessa whispered. 'Franco just doesn't have it where it counts.'

Fontaine glanced around the half-empty restaurant at 'Hobo'. She didn't even know any of the people who were there – a dreary-looking bunch of bores.

'Do *you* know who any of these people are?' she asked Vanessa.

'Absolutely not,' Vanessa replied. 'It seems anyone can get in nowadays. Now when Tony was here . . .'

'For Christ's sake do shut up about Tony. I know you had the hots for him, but he's long gone. He got a little too big for his . . .boots.'

'Or something!' giggled Vanessa.

265

'Quite,' agreed Fontaine. She glanced around the restaurant again. It was a bore – but it was quite obviously true. 'Hobo' was no longer *the* place to be seen. Franco had let things run to rack and ruin.

Count Paulo seemed to be enjoying every minute. His boyish face glowed with the thrill of being out with the glorious Fontaine Khaled. He watched her admiringly. Leonard, Vanessa's husband, tried to indulge him in a business dialogue, but Paulo was more interested in gazing at his date.

Fontaine tapped impatient scarlet fingernails on the table. 'Why don't we move on,' she suggested. 'Where *is* everyone going now?'

'There's a divine new club called "Dickies",' Vanessa enthused. 'Gay, of course – well, more mixed really. The waiters wear satin shorts and roller skates and they serve the most decadent drinks, they make you drunk for a week!'

'Let's go,' said Fontaine. 'I think I should see where the real action is.'

She rose from the table and swept out of the restaurant.

Franco snapped to attention. 'Mrs Khaled, you 'ees leaving so early. Something the matter?'

'Yes, Franco,' her voice was cold. 'You, as it happens. You're fired.'

Hal produced two beautiful girls. A black croupier on a two-week vacation, and a streaked blonde who was into meditation. Nico got the blonde, although he insisted to Hal he didn't want a date.

'It'll look better,' Hal explained. 'Trust me, I know Fontaine. Besides, tonight is my night off. Once a week I treat myself to a broad under sixty.'

'So have two,' Nico suggested. 'I don't want one.'

They arrived at 'Hobo' ten minutes after Fontaine had left.

'Mrs Khaled around?' Hal asked Franco.

'She come, she go,' Franco replied, then he burst into a stream of Italian abuse about his soon-to-be-former employer.

'Nobody ever called Fontaine a pussycat,' Hal agreed.

'A beetch!' Franco shrieked. 'I work my ass to the bone – and like that – poof – she throw me out.'

'Yeah,' said Hal. 'Like Tony. Remember Tony? You took his job.'

Franco glared.

'Come on,' Hal said to Nico. 'Knowing our Fontaine, she's checking out the competition.'

Fontaine was indeed checking out the competition, and she could see immediately why 'Dickies' had taken over. The disco music was great, the waiters outrageous, and the whole ambience reminded her of 'Hobo' when it had first opened.

Her kaleidoscope eyes surveyed the scene. Yes – All the same old faces. Every *one* of the 'Hobo' regulars.

'Fun, isn't it?' Vanessa enthused.

'Hmmm . . . Not bad.' Fontaine turned to Count Paulo, 'Let's dance.'

The floor was crowded – unlike the barren expanse at 'Hobo'. As Fontaine moved her body expertly in time to the Bee Gees, her mind was racing. What 'Hobo' needed was a revamp. New lighting. A change of menu. Definitely a different disc jockey. And a manager with the charisma Tony had possessed.

The music changed to a horny Isaac Hayes singing 'Just the way you are.'

Count Paulo pulled her close. Funny, but she didn't fancy him one little bit. He just seemed . . . boring.

'Fontaine, gorgeous! When did you get back?' Suddenly she was the centre of attention – so-called friends greeting her on all sides.

She smiled and nodded and enjoyed the scrutiny. She was no fool. She knew what they were all thinking – Poor

267

old Fontaine – no more millionaire husband – no more successful discothèque. What was she going to do?

Well, she bloody well wasn't going to do what they all wanted – fade away defeated. She was back with a vengeance, and they'd better all believe it.

'Hello darlin', what you doin' here? "Hobo" not the same since you threw Tony out?'

She turned to confront the owner of the raucous cockney accent. It was Sammy, a small wiry-haired dress manufacturer who only went out with girls under the age of sixteen.

Fontaine smiled coldly. 'I'll find another Tony. He was never an original.'

'Oh, yeah?' Sammy winked knowingly. 'What you need is a guy like me to run the place for you. I'd soon get it all back together – 'ave 'em raving in the aisles in no time. Want to give me a try?'

Fontaine looked him over with a mixture of amusement and contempt. 'You?' the one word said it all.

'All right, all right, I know when I'm not appreciated,' Sammy backed off.

Count Paulo rubbed thighs. 'Who was that?' he asked possessively.

'Do you have to hold me so tight?' Her voice was ice. 'You're creasing my dress.'

Nico noticed Fontaine immediately. Well, she could hardly be missed. She certainly was striking.

He watched her on the dance floor clutched in the arms of some young stud. She obviously had a prediliction for young studs – just as he had for fresh-faced young beauties.

'Told you she'd be here,' Hal announced triumphantly.

'Can we dance, Nico?' The black croupier was pulling on his jacket sleeve. 'Hal won't mind – he doesn't dance.'

Nico gently removed her tugging hand and adjusted his sleeve. 'Not right now, dear.'

Hal spotted his friend Sammy, and moved over to join him and his teenage companion.

After introductions Hal explained to Sammy that Nico wanted to get together with Fontaine.

Sammy laughed. 'Are you kidding? No chance, her highness wouldn't sniff in your direction!'

'Oh, yes?' Nico headed confidently towards the dance floor. 'Just watch her sniff!'

10

In Las Vegas, Bernie Darrell began to realize that protecting Nico was not exactly going to do him any good. Okay – so he was on fairly friendly terms with Dino Fonicetti – and he knew the father and the brother to nod to. But they were hard people . . . They had their reputation to consider . . . And when the fact that Nico had skipped town owing five hundred and fifty thousand grand was revealed . . . And then it came out that he, Bernie, had helped in the deception . . . Well . . .

By Tuesday evening he was apprehensive. And when Cherry baby came knocking at the door to pick up her things he was even more so.

'I shall have to tell Dino that Nico has left,' Cherry announced. 'I refuse to lie.'

Bernie was startled. 'What the hell are you talking about?' he snapped. *'We're* helping Nico – remember?'

'I have a certain loyalty to Dino,' Cherry replied primly.

'Loyalty? To Dino?' Bernie was amazed. 'What the *fuck* are you talking about?'

Cherry was oblivious to his anger as she packed up the few things she had brought with her. 'Of course, I won't mention that Nico left last night, I'll just say he's gone—'

Bernie grabbed her wrist roughly. 'You'll do no such fucking thing!'

'You're hurting me,' Cherry's blue eyes filled with tears. 'I'll tell Dino.'

Bernie released her. 'I don't believe this! I just don't believe it!' He mimicked her voice – ' "I'll tell Dino . . ." What is this – love's young dream all of a sudden? A one-night screw and the blonde and the hood see stars?'

Cherry raised her voice for the first time since Bernie had known her. 'It is possible, you know, for two people to fall in love. Dino is a warm and kind human being . . .'

'Holy shit!'

'We're going to get married if you must know.'

'I need a drink,' Bernie fixed himself a large scotch. His mind was racing. This was a beautiful situation. It could only happen to him. One moment the dumb cunt was trailing Nico to Las Vegas determined to sort out their future together. The next – true love with a mafioso one-night stand. Unbelievable!

He tried to soften his voice. 'Hey, Cherry – I'm really pleased for you and Dino, really I am. But if you tell him Nico has split, we're all in trouble – you included.'

'Not me,' Cherry protested indignantly.

'Yes – you, baby. How do you think your future bridegroom is going to feel when I tell him last night was a set-up?'

'What do you mean?'

'You spent the night with Dino so that Nico could get out of town. Right?'

'I suppose so . . .'

'Don't suppose. It's a fact of life. Now if Dino finds that out he is not going to be exactly thrilled.' Bernie took a deep breath. 'So listen carefully. You know nothing. Nico was here today when you picked up your things. You told him goodbye – that's all you know. And as far as you're concerned he's still here.'

'But I still think—'

'Will you listen to me sweetheart. Listen and learn. If your future plans include being Mrs Fonicetti, play it my way. You tell Dino the truth, and who knows how he'll react. Personally I wouldn't want to risk it.'

Cherry frowned. Bernie did have a point. 'Well, all right,' she said hesitantly. 'But when will Dino find out that Nico has gone?'

Bernie poured himself another scotch. 'By the time he finds out, Nico will be back – so don't you worry your pretty little head about it.'

Cherry nodded. 'OK Bernie, if you say so.'

So far so good. But could she be trusted? She was such a fucking idiot. Bernie sighed. How the hell had he ever got involved in this whole caper? Here he was – stuck in Las Vegas. What about his business? He had meetings to attend, and it would be at least a couple of days before Nico returned. That was if all went according to plan.

Cherry was packed up and ready to go. She smiled sweetly at him and stuck out a small delicate hand.

'Goodbye Bernie, and thank you for everything.'

Christ! She sounded like she'd taken a course in good manners!

'Yeah . . . well . . . I won't be leaving yet, so I guess we'll be seeing each other around. Now don't forget what I told you. Be a smart girl and you'll go far.'

She departed.

Bernie made a few mental calculations. Nico should be arriving in London about now. Hal was alerted to the situation. If all went smoothly the ring would be sold and the money in Nico's pocket within twenty-four hours. He would get on a plane immediately and be back in the suite before anyone realized he was gone. Pay off his markers. Back to LA. Mission accomplished. No broken bones.

It sounded easy.

Bernie wished the whole goddamn caper was over and done with.

'Mrs Khaled,' Nico cut in on the dance floor, subtly elbowing Count Paulo aside. 'What a pleasure to see you again so soon.'

'What do you think you are doing!' Count Paulo exploded. 'You cannot—'

'It's all right, Paulo,' Fontaine waved him aside. 'Run along and sit down, I'll join you in a minute.'

The Count glared, then reluctantly departed.

Nico took her in his arms, even though the beat was strident disco.

'Nice-looking boy,' Nico remarked. 'Similar to the one with you at Kennedy airport.'

'Yes. I like them full of energy.'

Nico raised an eyebrow.

Fontaine laughed.

'Did you get my flowers?' he asked.

'Very nice. How did you find my address?'

'If I want something I usually manage to get it.'

'Oh, really? We're so alike.'

'Thank you for waiting at the airport.'

'I'm hardly a taxi service.'

'I thought we had a date.'

'A date? How delightfully old world of you.'

'Has anybody ever told you that you're a bitch?'

'Frequently.'

Nico pulled her in very close indeed. Count Paulo, skulking at the edge of the dance floor, glared.

'Well, Mrs Khaled,' Nico said softly, 'are we going to finish what we started on the aeroplane?'

Fontaine responded to his maleness. 'Why not, Mr Constantine. Why not indeed?'

'Bleedin' hell!' Sammy exclaimed, as they all watched

Nico and Fontaine exit. ' 'E's only done it! What's 'e got? Mink-lined balls!'

'Oh, Sammy, you are awful!' his teenage girlfriend squealed.

'The guy has a lot of charm,' Hal stated. 'Not to mention the best tailor I've ever seen.'

'Charm schmarm – all Fontaine wants to know about is the size of the bank balance or the cock!'

'Honestly Sammy!'

'It's all right darlin' – you'll be OK on both counts!'

'I do believe she's leaving,' Vanessa whispered to Leonard.

'I think you're right,' he replied.

'Absolutely charming – you'd think she'd have the manners to say goodnight.'

'Nobody ever accused Fontaine of having any manners. Who is that man anyway?'

Vanessa peered at the couple swiftly leaving the dance floor.

'I don't know, he doesn't look her style at all – slightly too mature . . . but rather attractive.'

'Rich, I suppose,' said Leonard brusquely.

'Yes, I suppose,' Vanessa agreed.

'Oh, God!' Leonard exclaimed, 'Don't tell me we're stuck with her Italian juvenile.'

'Looks like we are.' Vanessa watched a surly Count Paulo approach. Oh yes. There was certainly something to be said for the young ones . . .

Maybe if Fontaine had finished with him . . .

Vanessa wasn't proud. She had accepted seconds from her friend before.

Ricky tried to concentrate on his driving, but it wasn't easy. God Almighty – you would think he had a couple of teenage ravers in the back.

He attempted to keep his eye on what was happening in

the rear-view mirror. Naturally Mrs Khaled had pressed the button which sent the glass partition up cutting him off from their sounds.

He drove the Rolls-Royce slower than usual, until Fontaine lowered the glass partition an inch and snapped, 'Do hurry up, Ricky.'

Bitch!

He wondered if he was free after he dropped her at her house. He was feeling extremely randy, and wondered if Polly would be up . . . Better than sleeping the night in that pisshole of a room he had rented.

The Rolls glided up to Fontaine's house. Ricky jumped out and opened the car door for them. He gazed disinterestedly off into space.

'Will you be needing me again tonight, Mrs Khaled?' he ventured.

'No, Ricky,' her voice was light and full of excitement. 'Tonight I will not be needing you.'

'What time tomorrow, Mrs Khaled?'

'Ten o'clock – I'd like you here every morning at ten o'clock.'

'Yes, Mrs Khaled.'

He waited until they turned to walk in the house, then he glanced at his watch. It was already two in the morning. Some job. It was a good thing the wages were right.

He wondered what had happened to the Italian ice cream. Must have got himself dumped . . .

Ricky couldn't help smiling. He liked a woman who behaved like a man.

It was an erotic experience.

It was clothes off on the stairs.

It was hot tongues and warm bodies.

It was touch – feel – smell.

Fontaine felt herself out of control for once. Here was a man she didn't have to tell what she wanted. He knew everything. He was very . . . accomplished.

'You're like a dancer,' he breathed in her ear. 'You make love like a dancer who has been in training.'

'Hmmm . . . And you . . . you're like a stallion . . .'

He laughed. 'The Greek Stallion. It sounds like a bad movie! When I was twenty I was a stallion – now I *know* what I'm doing.'

'You certainly do!'

They made love endlessly – or so it seemed to both of them. And they were comfortable together – there was none of the awkwardness that sometimes happens the first time two people are in bed together.

The added bonus was that they could talk, not about anything special, just conversation.

Fontaine never had conversations with her transient studs – sometimes verbal skirmishes, but never conversations.

The same applied to Nico and his fresh-faced beauties. How boring and bland they all seemed once the initial thrill of a new body was over.

The thing that turned him on about Fontaine more than anything was her mind. She might be one tough lady – but she had wit and perception, and he wanted to dig deeper and find out more about the woman beneath the sophisticated veneer.

'I want to know all about you,' he said softly, 'who – why – how. From the beginning.'

Fontaine rolled over in bed. She felt delightfully satisfied. '*You're* the man of mystery. I meet you on a plane – the next minute we're in bed. But all I know about you is your name. You could be—'

'What?' He pinned her arms to the bed playfully. 'A mass murderer? A maniac?' He kissed her hard and released her. 'And don't tell me Mrs Khaled hasn't gone to bed with a man she met on a plane before.'

'Well . . . once or twice.'

'Oh, yes, once or twice I bet.' He smiled. 'How many men *have* you had?'

276

Fontaine stretched and got out of bed, 'Let's put it this way, Nico – a meal a day means you never go hungry.'

'Come back here, I want my dessert!'

'I'm going to take a shower, I need reviving. Why don't you go downstairs and bring up some Grand Marnier, I'll show you a delicious new way to drink it.' She went in the bathroom and closed the door.

Nico lay back still smiling. He felt fantastically relaxed. Then he remembered the ring. Wasn't that the reason he was here? Well, originally . . .

He could hear water running in the bathroom. He got off the bed and looked around the room for the purse Fontaine had carried on the plane. He couldn't see it around, but the mirrored door of a large walk-in closet stood invitingly open. He peered inside. Racks and racks of shoes stacked in neat rows. Shelves for sweaters, shirts, T-shirts, scarves, gloves. Belts and beads hanging in rows. Underclothes in perspex drawers. And handbags. All on a bottom shelf. About twenty-five of them.

He looked through them quickly, searching for the Gucci stripe. There were five with Gucci stripes, but none were the right one.

He swore softly under his breath, then suddenly saw the one he was looking for. It was hanging on the back of the door.

He grabbed it quickly, unzipped the side compartment, and there, nestled at the bottom, was his ring.

Fontaine appeared at the wrong moment, a pink towel wrapped around her sarong style. Her voice was icy, 'What exactly do you think you are doing?'

Nico jumped. He felt like a schoolboy caught with his hand inside the cookie jar. He wished he had put his pants on at least. There is nothing more daunting for a man than to be caught in an awkward situation with a limp dick hanging down.

'Well?' Fontaine could make one word a meal.

Nico smiled. Charm. His smile had got him through

277

many tricky situations. 'You're never going to believe this.'

'Try me.' Her glacial expression did not crack.

'Well . . .' he tried to edge past her back into the bedroom.

She blocked his way.

'It's a long story,' he said quickly. 'I'm sure it will amuse you. Let me put some clothes on . . .'

Patiently, calmly, Fontaine interrupted him. 'Just tell me what you were doing in my bag – and just show me what you have in your hand. Now, Nico, right now. I don't want to hear any amusing stories, I'm not really in the mood for a good laugh.'

Nico shrugged, 'I can assure you I'm not taking anything of yours.'

'I can assure you of that too.'

'I had this ring . . . I thought maybe I would have problems with customs . . .'

He opened his hand and showed her the diamond.

She looked at it briefly, then at him.

'I was going to ask you if you would mind bringing it through for me . . . but I didn't know you that well . . . Of course, I was going to tell you—'

'You bastard. You son-of-a-bitch nasty little hustler,' her words struck icily through his. 'You *used* me – on the plane, this evening. How *dare* you!'

'I only—'

She held up an imperious hand. 'I don't want to hear. I just want you out – of my house, my life.'

'But Fontaine . . .'

She wasn't listening. She was in the bedroom gathering his clothes together, and when he emerged from the closet she threw them at him. 'Out!' she snapped. 'Before I have you thrown out.'

'I think we should talk about it.'

'Why? What more do you want from me? You've fucked me every way you can – and I might add that the screwing I got in bed wasn't half as good as the screwing I *really* got from you.'

She walked into her bathroom and slammed the door.

Quickly Nico got dressed. There was no point in staying around to argue. After all – he had what he had come for.

12

'What?' Joseph Fonicetti regarded his youngest son through narrowed eyes. 'What the fuck did I just hear you say?'

Dino shuffled his feet uneasily. How come everywhere he was a king – and in front of his father – zero – nothing – a goddamned kid again.

'I . . . I . . . er . . . well . . . I'm gonna get married.'

Joseph threw him a long unnerving stare. 'Just like that. Out of the blue you've found yourself a girl fit to be your wife. In *Las Vegas* you've found a girl to take the Fonicetti name. What is this beauty? A showgirl? A cocktail waitress? A *hooker*?' Joseph spat with disgust into a handy ashtray.

'She's a very lovely girl,' Dino said quickly. 'Not from Las Vegas.'

'None of them are *from* here – they only come here to develop their cunts and their bankrolls!'

'She's a nice girl,' Dino said defensively. 'You'll love her.'

Joseph shut his eyes and mulled over the fact that Dino was a good-looking boy, but when it came to women he was dense. Now David, his elder son, was smart. He had a wife, a plain Italian girl who would never give him a moment's trouble, and he fucked around with Las Vegas gash on his terms only.

'When did you meet this girl?' Joseph asked. 'A month? Two months ago? How come I've never heard you mention her before?'

'Well, Cherry only got here this week . . . You know how it is . . . this is the girl I want to marry. It happened just like that.'

Yes. Joseph knew how it was. Some smart broad had hooked her little finger round Dino's cock and thought she was going to get lucky. Well, she could think again. When Joseph was ready for Dino to get married – *he personally* would arrange it. A selection of Italian virgins would be shipped in – just as they had been for David – and Dino could take his choice.

'So . . . this Cherry. Who did she come here with?'

Dino answered quickly. He wanted to lie, but his father would find out the truth anyway. 'She came here with Bernie Darrell, they're just friends.'

'Sure. Bernie Darrell brought a girl all the way to Vegas and they're just friends. I believe that. Who wouldn't?'

'She came to see Nico Constantine, then she met me. Neither of us expected this . . . it just happened.'

'And what did Nico do? Kiss you both and wish you luck?'

'She and Nico . . . It was over anyway.'

Joseph nodded. 'Of course, she wasn't influenced by the fact that Nico was losing his ass at the tables. By the way – have you made arrangements with him about paying?'

'I will, I will.'

'Sure – leave it go while you make wedding arrangements. Who cares about five hundred and fifty thousand dollars.'

'Nico's good for the money.'

'He'd better be.'

'He is. I'll deal with it today.' Dino coughed nervously. 'Now, about Cherry, when can I bring her to meet you?'

Jospeh nodded thoughtfully, he had an idea. 'Tonight,' he said, 'we'll have dinner. The whole family. We'll discuss your wedding plans.'

Dino was relieved. It seemed his father was accepting Cherry without too much of a fight. Well – he must have known it was no use fighting – after all – he, Dino, was not exactly David who could be forced into a dull marriage with a placid Italian lump.

Dino smiled. They would all love Cherry. From the moment Joseph met her it would be smooth sailing.

'We have an invitation,' Susanna said, sitting down and joining Bernie in the coffee shop.

'We do?' He was halfway through a prune danish – wondering if it would solve his bowel problem.

'Yup.' Susanna studied the menu. 'Daddy wants us to have dinner with him and the Fonicettis tonight. I accepted on our behalf.'

'You did?' Bernie wondered how they had become a pair again. Two nights of torrid love-making and was the divorce supposed to be a past memory?

'He's invited Nico Constantine too, will you tell him please – there's no answer from his suite.'

Bernie nearly choked on his danish. 'Why Nico?'

'Why not? Daddy likes Nico.'

Yes, and hates me, Bernie thought. The last time they had met had been just before the divorce. Carlos Brent had confronted him at the Beverly Hills Hotel in the Polo lounge.

'You kike bastard – all I need is the word from Susanna, and my boys' club will be playing catch with your balls. You're lucky she's not vindictive.'

Charming! They had not spoken nor met since.

'I don't know if Nico will want to make it,' Bernie hedged. 'He's gotten very involved with a girl here.'

'Who?' Susanna demanded.

'Some chick, I don't even know her name.'

'Well he can bring her, a date will be OK.'

'I'll try to reach him.'

Susanna yawned and giggled. 'Can you believe what's happened to us? Can you believe it, Bernie? My analyst will have a blue fit!'

To be truthful Bernie was finding it very hard to believe himself. One moment he and Susanna were the worst of enemies – the next – making love like randy soldiers on

282

twenty-four-hour leave! He had to admit that for him she was the absolute greatest in bed, but a pain in the ass to live with. Carlos had spoiled the pants off her, that was why.

A chubby waitress came rushing over. 'Miss Brent,' she gushed. 'And what can I get for you today?'

Miss Brent. It had always been Miss Brent, never ever Mrs Darrell. And on a couple of memorable occasions – memorable because of the blazing fight that followed – he had even been addressed as Mr Brent.

'I dunno, Maggi,' she knew all of the elderly waitresses by name – she had been coming to the hotel her entire life. 'I think maybe a cheese danish, and a black coffee.'

Maggi beamed. 'Certainly, dear.'

'I was thinking,' Susanna said, turning to Bernie. 'Why don't you and Nico fly back to LA with me? I can use daddy's plane whenever I want. I thought maybe tomorrow . . . You could stay at the house, Starr would like that.'

Starr was their very beautiful four-year-old daughter. She was also Carlos Brent's only grandchild, and as such she was spoiled rotten, just like her mother.

'I don't know,' Bernie answered, his mind racing. 'I promised Nico I'd stay with him . . .'

Susanna shot him a dirty look. 'Whose hand would you sooner hold? Mine or Nico's?'

'Yours, of course.'

'Anyway, his new girlfriend seems to be doing a pretty good job of holding his. I haven't even seen him yet.'

'You know how it is.'

'I certainly do.' She pushed her tinted shades up into her hair and sighed, 'We must have been mad to have gotten divorced. Why did we do it?'

Did she really expect an answer?

Because you nagged the shit out of me, Susanna.

Because you required my balls to be your balls.

Because daddy daddy daddy is enough to drive anyone to divorce.

Bernie shrugged, 'I don't know.'

Susanna giggled, that 'I wanna get laid' look came into her eyes. 'Why don't we forget about lunch?' she suggested. 'Why don't we just toddle on upstairs and smoke a little tiny bit of grass.'

'Yeah, why not.'

He certainly had nothing else to do with his time while he waited for Nico to surface.

13

'Who *was* he?' asked Vanessa.

'Some boring little con artist,' snapped Fontaine.

'He didn't look little to me, rather Omar Sharif actually.'

'A poor imitation.'

'You certainly left in a hurry, Paulo was furious.'

'Look, darling, I have to go, got a million things to do. I'll call you later.'

'Don't forget the fashion lunch tomorrow.'

'I've written it in my book.' Fontaine put the phone down, and checked out her appearance in the mirror. Chic, but understated. Silk shirt, pleated skirt, checked blazer. Just the outfit to interview aspiring managers for 'Hobo'. She had phoned Polly first thing and given her a blast. 'Get me some young, attractive, would-be front men. Franco's the reason "Hobo" is down the drain. Find me another Tony. I'll be over to see what you have at four o'clock.'

Polly hung up the phone and snuggled up to Ricky. 'You'd better move it,' she said. 'Mrs K. is up early and raring to go.'

'She told me ten o'clock,' Ricky replied.

'In that case . . . we might just have time . . . Oh shit! I forgot. I'm the one with the early appointment.' She bounced out of bed. 'Any ideas on how I go about finding a tall sexy man with a big dick?'

Ricky laughed crudely. 'Don't I fit that bill?'

'Yes, you do. But you got the chauffeur's job, and Mrs K. would never understand a change of image mid-stream.'

'Why not? She seems like a pretty smart lady to me.'

'Oh, really?' Polly winked. 'Fancy her already, do you?'

He laughed. 'I wouldn't mind dipping my toe in.'

'She'd want more than your toe, sonny. Much more . . .'

'Why don't you come here and shut up.' Every time he thought about his employer he got quite randy.

With the ring back in his possession Nico felt more secure. The delay had not been planned, and he imagined that Bernie must be worried by his silence. They had arranged that they would not make contact until he had actually fenced the ring and was on his way back.

But still, maybe he should call. Put Bernie's mind at rest. And then again, maybe not. Didn't want to alarm him unnecessarily. If all went well, and Hal came across, he could be on a plane within hours.

He delivered the ring personally to Hal the morning after his scene with Fontaine.

Hal wasn't pleased as he groped his way to the front door of his Park Lane service flat clad in a pair of black silk pyjamas. 'Jesus Christ!' he exclaimed, 'what the frig's the time?'

Nico glanced at his watch. 'Nine forty-five. Too early for you?'

'Too right it is. I never get up before two or three.'

'This is an emergency.'

'Yeah. I understand.' He led the way into an unused kitchen, and set about making some coffee. 'What happened? Fontaine throw you out early? Or didn't you get to stay?'

'I didn't stay.'

'Very wise. She's a balls-breaker.'

'Do you know her well?'

'Well enough.'

'Did you ever . . .'

'Me? Are you kidding?' Hal began to laugh. 'Fontaine wouldn't glance in my direction – not that I would ever want her to. She likes 'em young. When she was married to the Arab, she used his money to set them up in business.'

Nico produced the ring from his pocket and showed it to Hal.

Hal let out a long whistle. 'That's really something, absolutely bee-u-tiful.'

'When can I hear from you?' Nico asked. 'I have to be on my way as soon as possible.'

Hal poured water over instant coffee, already thinking of how he would spend his commission. 'A cash transaction like this . . . I should think some time tomorrow.'

'Christ!' Nico exclaimed, 'It has to be sooner than that.'

'I'll do my best, but there's a lot of money involved here. Just be patient and relax. Why don't you do some gambling? The London clubs are the best.'

Nico gave a hollow laugh. 'Why do you think I'm in trouble today?'

'Hmmm . . . Not bad,' Fontaine yawned. 'What did you think, Polly?'

'I think that the cockney accent was just a little passé.'

Fontaine picked a nut from the glass dish on the table and tossed it into her mouth. 'Yes. I suppose you're right. Cockney was in last year – now it seems to be chinless or gay, but I *still* say what we need is a macho front man.'

'I know, I know, just like the fabulous Tony.'

Fontaine smiled dreamily. 'You never met him, did you?'

'I wish I had. But I was in America the year of "Hobo's" ascent.'

'Tony – at the beginning – was the best. In every way I might add.'

'So why did you get rid of him?'

'His ambitions screwed up his head.'

Polly and Fontaine sat together in the empty discothèque at 'Hobo' interviewing would-be managers. So far they had seen six, none of them suitable.

287

Fontaine was irritated, and getting more so by the minute. Why was it so goddamn difficult to find an attractive, ambitious, sexy, ballsy, young man?

She thought briefly of Jump Jennings. Thought even more briefly of importing him. Changed her mind, and peered at the next young man in line for the job.

He was better than the others. Curly black hair, tight faded jeans, a certain confidence.

Polly consulted a businesslike clipboard. 'And you are . . .?'

'Steve Valentine.'

Fontaine and Polly exchanged quick amused looks.

'You're running a disco in Ealing?' Polly asked. 'Is that right?'

'I've been the manager there for eighteen months.'

'Do you enjoy it?' Fontaine husked, her kaleidoscope eyes inspecting every inch of him.

Steve stared at her. 'Yeah, well it's all right. But I want to get into the West End.'

'I'm sure you do.' Fontaine picked up a cigarette, and waited for him to light it.

He fumbled for a cheap lighter and did the honours.

'Hmmm . . .' said Fontaine, still inspecting him. 'Do you have a girlfriend?'

Steve's stare became bold. 'One wouldn't be enough for me, Mrs Khaled.'

'I bet it wouldn't.' She turned to Polly, 'I think we should give Mr Valentine a try, don't you, Polly?'

When Nico left Hal's apartment he decided to make the most of his last day in London. He had in his possession the six thousand dollars that Bernie had withdrawn from his office safe – and apart from his hotel bill he would have no other expenses in London. By the time Hal disposed of the ring he would have more than enough cash to pay his debts in Vegas, repay Bernie, and still have a few thousand dollars over.

288

Of course, then he would have to start thinking of his future. But he would worry about that when the time came. Also Mrs Dean Costello must be compensated, and that would be his responsibility if her insurance company had not already taken care of it. He had every intention of repaying her if she was not insured. How, he didn't quite know. But Nico had the quality of supreme confidence in his ability to deal with any situation. Plus the fact that no way would a ring like that be uninsured.

He thought about Fontaine Khaled. Flowers of course. Red roses naturally. Six dozen with a discreet note of apology. And a gift. Not the usual token trinket. But something nice and substantial. Something beautiful that she would love.

Even though he would be leaving London he had every intention of seeing her again. It was not inconceivable that he might return as soon as everything was settled.

Fontaine interested him like no other woman had since Lise Maria. He knew her, and yet he also knew that he had barely scratched the surface. She was a woman – arrogant, assured, tough. And underneath the veneer was the woman he really wanted to know. Vulnerable, soft, lovable. Searching for the right man – just as he – unknowingly – had been searching for the right woman.

He hailed a taxi and directed the driver to Boucheron, the Bond Street jewellery shop.

Ricky watched Fontaine in the rear-view mirror as the Rolls glided through heavy traffic. Her eyes were closed, legs crossed, skirt riding up to reveal stocking tops. She wore suspenders! Christmas! Bloody suspenders! The only place he had ever seen those were in girly magazines!

He immediately felt randy – in spite of fifteen hot sticky minutes with Polly in the morning.

'Ricky.'

He shifted his eyes quickly to her face. She had woken up.

289

'Yes, Mrs Khaled?'

'Did you collect my things from the cleaners?'

'Yes, Mrs Khaled.'

'And pick up my prescription?'

'Yes, Mrs Khaled.'

'Good. When we get home you can take some time off. I won't be needing you until ten o'clock tonight.'

'Thank you, Mrs Khaled.' He glanced at the clock on the dashboard. It was nearly five. He was rather bushed himself. He sneaked another look in the mirror. She had pulled her skirt down. Spoilsport.

'Oh, and Ricky.'

'Yes, Mrs Khaled?'

'Be a good boy and keep your eyes on the road.'

'Yes, Mrs Khaled.'

Bitch!

Nico enjoyed himself. He had always had a knack for spending money. Three thousand dollars went on a diamond-studded heart for Fontaine. Another thousand on a Cartier watch for Bernie. And twelve hundred on clothes for himself – cashmere sweaters and silk shirts from Turnbull & Asser.

Well pleased, he returned to his hotel.

Hal waited in the lobby. Things were progressing even faster than Nico had hoped.

'Good news?' he questioned.

'Let's go upstairs,' Hal replied.

They travelled up to Nico's suite in silence.

Once inside Hal produced the diamond ring and flung it down on the bed. 'Glass – fuckin' glass!' He spat in disgust. 'What the hell kind of game are you playin', Nico?'

14

Bernie was stoned. Nicely so. Just enough to be able to face Carlos Brent and the Fonicettis with a smile.

He prepared to leave Susanna at six o'clock with the promise to collect her at seven.

She lay in bed, also stoned, and suggested for the sixth time that they should get married again.

'Why?' Bernie asked. 'We're having such a good time together *not* being married.'

'I know,' agreed Susanna. 'But for Starr's sake it would be nice.'

Not to mention Carlos, Bernie thought. Big daddy would be furious if he knew what was going on.

'Don't forget to invite Nico,' Susanna called out after him.

'If he's around,' Bernie replied.

'He must be back by now. Who is the new girlfriend anyway?'

'I told you, I don't know. See you later.'

Bernie made his escape and returned to the suite.

Wouldn't it be nice if Nico was waiting to greet him.

He wasn't.

Bernie wondered if a phone call was in order. He certainly wanted to know what was happening. How much longer could he keep up the pretence that Nico was around? Of course he couldn't risk phoning from the Forum. He would have to stroll over to Caesars or Circus Circus and use an anonymous phone booth. He hoped to Christ that Nico had checked into the Lamont in London as he had told him to.

He took a shower and changed his clothes. Then he sprayed his mouth with a fresh breath spray, and set off to make the phone call.

*

Cherry twirled in front of the full-length mirror. 'Do you like it?' she asked Dino breathily.

'Pretty,' he replied, more concerned with how the evening would go, than Cherry's new dress.

'You don't like it,' she pouted.

'Honey, I do,' he caught her up in his arms and hugged her reassuringly. 'You look like a great big beautiful doll.'

'I'm your wife,' she said proudly. 'Mrs Dino Foncetti!'

His stomach turned over with fear. In the entire thirty-one years he had been alive he had never made one important decision without consulting his father. Now he had really done it. He had sneaked off that very afternoon and married Cherry before Joseph thought of some smart way of getting rid of her.

'Your father's going to like me,' Cherry said, as if reading his mind. 'You'll see, he really will. I can promise you that.'

'I know, I know. Just keep your pretty mouth closed about us being married. I'll tell him in my own way.'

'Tonight?'

'Yeah, sure, tonight.'

She smiled. 'What a surprise it'll be! Me and your father meeting for the first time to talk about you and me getting married – and then boom – you'll tell him!'

'Yeah – boom.' Dino tried to smile. It was a struggle.

Joseph Fonicetti arrived in the Magna Carter restaurant precisely at six forty-five. He inspected the dinner table, pronounced it suitable, and the head waiter sighed with relief.

Working for Joseph Fonicetti you learned to be meticulous.

'Bring me some Perrier water,' Joseph requested. 'And some of those little white cards.'

The waiter responded immediately, then stood at a respectful distance while Joseph scrawled in his atrocious handwriting on the placement cards.

At exactly two minutes to seven, David, the eldest son, arrived with his wife, Mia. They both embraced Joseph, and took their places at the table. They both ordered Perrier water to drink.

At exactly two minutes past seven Dino arrived with Cherry. He was holding her hand, but his palm was sweating so badly that her hand threatened to slip away.

'Cherry, I want you to meet my father, Joseph Fonicetti,' he said nervously.

Cherry stepped forward, wide-eyed. 'Mr Fonicetti, I have been *so* looking forward to this moment.'

Joseph beamed, 'So have I, my dear, so have I.' The girl was prettier than he had expected. Dino had always gone for the sour-faced big-boobed kind before. 'Sit right here, next to me. What'll you have to drink?'

Cherry's eyes didn't waver, but she had already noticed the Perrier bottles. 'Oh, Perrier water if I may – you don't mind, do you?'

'Mind? Of course not.' Smarter than he had expected.

Dino went to sit beside her.

Joseph waved him away. 'Down there, next to your sister-in-law.'

Dino moved obediently to the other end of the table and ordered a double scotch.

Susanna and Bernie arrived next. He did a double take when he saw Cherry. A part of the family? So soon?

Susanna rushed to kiss Joseph. 'Uncle Joe, you look younger every time I see you.' She blew kisses at David and Dino. They had been friends since childhood.

Then Carlos Brent made his entrance. A typical Carlos Brent entrance with noise and excitement and an entourage of six.

The dinner party was almost complete.

'Where's Nico Constantine?' asked Joseph. 'It's nearly a quarter after seven.'

Anyone who knew Joseph at all knew he was a stickler for punctuality.

293

Susanna looked at Bernie. 'Where *is* Nico?'

Bernie shrugged and tried to look suitably casual. 'He sent his apologies, hopes to make it later for coffee.'

'He's got a new girlfriend,' Susanna announced, 'I don't think she ever lets him out of bed!'

Joseph turned to Cherry. 'You're a friend of Nico's, aren't you?'

She smoothed down the front of her new pink dress. 'Nico's been like a father to me,' she said demurely.

I bet, thought Joseph. He was on to Cherry. Miss sweetness and light. She had dazzled Dino with the first clean pussy he had seen in years.

He wondered what it would take to get rid if her. Maybe Nico would know – after all he had brought her into Dino's life, and he could take her right on out again.

She was amazingly pretty. Bad wife material. She'd be screwing around before the ink was dry on the marriage licence.

Joseph glanced down the table at Mia. Now *that* was wife material.

'Mr Fonicetti,' Cherry gushed, 'You don't know how exciting this all is for me . . . Meeting Dino . . . you . . .'

'Where are you from, dear?' Joseph asked. May as well find out her version of her background before he put a private detective on to her.

As far as Bernie was concerned the dinner dragged on for ever.

He needed it like he needed piles.

Susanna playing girl wife again. Carlos throwing him fishy dago false smiles. Mia and David both as dull as each other. Dino a nervous wreck. And Cherry – little Miss Blue Eyes – all innocence and golden curls and not fooling crafty old Joseph Fonicetti one bit.

Bernie had been unable to contact Nico in London. No answer in his hotel room. So he had left a message relaying the fact that everything was fine – so far. But how long before it was noticed that Nico's handsome face was no longer in evidence? And how long could Bernie fool them with a mystery girlfriend who didn't even exist?

As if on cue, Joseph said, 'Hey, Bernie, where's Nico? I thought you said he'd be here for coffee.'

'I guess he got hung up . . .'

'I invite people for dinner, they usually come. I want to talk to Nico . . . Business . . . Have him come up to my suite later.'

Oh, sure. Just like that. Bernie was beginning to seriously consider the possibility of jetting back to LA the next day with Susanna. Get out while he was clean.

'If I see him,' he said lamely. 'Like he's taken off with this girl . . .'

'Taken off?' Joseph snapped. 'Dino, did you hear that?'

'What?' Dino jumped. His mind had been exploring the possibility of a honeymoon in Europe, far far away from his father.

'Nico Constantine has taken off,' Joseph said grimly.

'Not taken off,' Bernie attempted a weak laugh. 'I mean he's around, but this girl . . . Well, you know how it can be . . .'

'What girl?' Joseph inquired, his eyes suddenly steely.

'I don't know her name . . .'

'Does she work here?'

'No, I don't think so.'

'So who is she? What does she do?'

Susanna joined in, 'Yes, who is this woman of mystery?'

Bernie could have belted her. He didn't like the look in Joseph's eyes. He was one smart old man.

'I told you, I don't know. Some broad who's dragged him away from the tables all the way into her bed.'

'Everyone!' Cherry clapped her hands excitedly, 'I can't keep it to myself any longer! Today, this very afternoon! Dino and I got married!'

Bernie could have kissed her. It was one heck of a good way to take everyone's mind off of Nico.

15

'What?' Nico could not believe what Hal was telling him.

'Glass,' Hal stated flatly, 'one helluva chunk of beautifully cut glass – set in real platinum of course. A copy – a beaut – but the real thing it ain't.'

'I don't believe it!' Nico felt an insane desire to laugh. 'I just don't believe it!'

'Start believing, kid. It's not worth more than a few hundred.'

Nico shook his head in amazement. So – Mrs Dean Costello had fooled him. Or had she? The old dear had never claimed that her ring was real. She had never handed him papers to prove its authenticity. She probably had the real thing locked up in a bank vault. Of course. It was obvious. A diamond that size – all the rich women had copies made of their gems. And excellent copies too. Good enough to fool everyone except the experts.

Nico was embarrassed. 'Hal, what can I say? I had no idea . . .'

Hal was friendly. 'Of course you didn't. Even I thought it was the real thing, and I have an eye – I can spot the real stuff a mile off. Listen, it was nice nearly doing business with you.' He prepared to leave. 'Give my best to Bernie. Will you be leaving today?'

Nico shrugged, 'I don't know what I'm going to do.'

'You know what you really need? A rich, old broad.' Hal laughed, 'Rich, old, and grateful.' He warmed to his subject. 'Now I have a couple of hot ones flying in from Texas tomorrow. You want a million dollars – no problem. But you'll have to work for it . . .'

'How old?'

'Not spring chickens . . .'

'How old?'

'In their sixties, maybe creeping up to seventy . . . But

296

you'd never know, what with silicone tits and face jobs and . . .'

'Forget it.'

'Suit yourself, but it's a winning game.'

Yeah. A winning game. That's what he really needed.

Hal left, and Nico paced his hotel room wondering what his next move should be. Alert Bernie. That had to be first. Tell him to get out of Vegas and stop covering up for him.

Then what? How was he ever going to get half a million dollars?

How had he ever lost half a million dollars?

Gambling.

His bankroll was almost non-existent, but that didn't phase him. He picked up the phone and requested the Manager.

Full Nico charm. 'Mr Graheme, I have a slight problem, my bank in Switzerland is transferring funds – by tomorrow no problem. In the meantime if you could let me have – say – five hundred pounds cash – and charge it to my bill I would be most grateful . . .'

The six dozen red roses arrived late afternoon. They were waiting for Fontaine when she returned to her house after the auditions. Mrs Walters had set them out in matching cut glass vases.

'Christ!' Fontaine exclaimed irritably. 'The place is beginning to look like a funeral parlour! I know I asked for fresh flowers Mrs Walters, but this is ridiculous.'

Mrs Walters clucked her agreement, and handed her employer the card which had accompanied the roses.

Fontaine read it. The message was brief – just – 'Thank you. Nico.'

Thank you for what? For a great screw? For throwing him out? For what?

Fontaine tore the card into tiny pieces and let it flutter over the carpet.

Mrs Walters pursed her lips. Who would have to clear *that* up later.

297

'I don't want to be disturbed,' Fontaine sighed. 'I simply have to rest.'

'Your lawyer has telephoned three times, Mrs Khaled, he says it's urgent that he arrange an appointment with you immediately.'

'How boring.'

'And Count Rispollo telephoned.'

'Even more boring.'

'What shall I say if they phone again, Mrs Khaled?'

'Tell them I am resting, and to telephone tomorrow.'

'Oh, and this arrived.' Mrs Walters produced a small package.

Fontaine took it from her and balanced it in her hand. Boucheron. Was it a token of Count Paulo's esteem?

'Wake me at eight o'clock.' She walked upstairs.

The thought occurred that maybe she should have brought Steve Valentine home with her. Personally seen to it that he had what it takes in all the right places.

Once that would have been exciting. But somehow the thrill of just another horny body was beginning to pall.

Now Nico . . .

Screw Nico . . . She didn't even want to think about him. Lousy hustler. Using her to smuggle his stuff through customs. Sharing her bed only to recover his ring.

She ripped open the packet from Boucheron, and read the card that fell out.

Same card. Same message. 'Thank you. Nico.'

Thoughtfully she stared at the diamond-encrusted heart. It was very lovely. She took it out of the box and held it in her hand.

Nico . . . He *had* been a very special lover . . .

So far so good. Nico was winning. Nothing sensational – but a beginning.

He had started the evening with a stake of a thousand pounds – this he had managed to work up to twenty-five thousand pounds. A nice beginning.

For a change everything seemed to be going his way.

And if his luck kept right on . . . Who knew what could happen?

He was enjoying the ambience of a British gaming club. So different from the brashness of Vegas.

Delightful female croupiers in low-cut dresses. Discreet pit bosses. Respectful girls serving unobtrusive drinks.

The atmosphere was that of a rather elegant club.

Nico lit up a long thin cigar, and moved from a black-jack table to roulette. The limit was not as high as he would have wished, and he was unable to bet more than five hundred on black. It came up. Good. But certainly not good enough. He needed to get into a high stake poker game, and he looked around for someone who might be able to arrange it.

The manager seemed a likely prospect, and sure enough he was. He recommended another club which would be happy to accommodate Nico as far as poker, backgammon, whatever he wished.

Nico took a taxi there.

He had tried to telephone Bernie earlier, but had been unable to reach him. Now he just wanted to concentrate on making some sort of big score.

'Hmmm . . .' Fontaine stood in the doorway and surveyed the disco at 'Hobo'. 'Well I suppose I mustn't expect miracles. It *is* his first night.'

Polly nodded. 'He looks good though, don't you think?'

Fontaine watched Steve through narrowed kaleidoscope eyes. 'He doesn't have the walk.'

'What walk?'

'The John Travolta cock thrust. You know what I mean, Polly.'

Polly couldn't help giggling. Cock thrust. It sounded like something you did in an aeroplane!

Steve came towards them. He was clad in a rather cheap black pinstripe suit, shirt, and tie.

'Mrs Khaled. A table for how many?'

'The look is wrong, Steve,' she snapped. 'You're running a disco – not your uncle's wedding!'

'Sorry.'

'Don't worry, I should have told you. Obviously they're a touch more formal in Ealing. Now, let me see . . .'

She reached for his tie, undid and removed it. Then she unbuttoned his shirt three buttons. 'That's better. Tomorrow I'll take you out shopping.'

Oh God! Shades of Tony! How well she remembered their first meeting. A disaster. He had possessed an animal charm, a sexy walk, but that was about all. And in bed – nothing but raw ability.

She had seen his potential, and trained him to make full use of it in every way.

He had learned quickly. And then he had got far too big for his newly acquired Gucci loafers.

Now Steve stood before her. Raw material. Was it worth building him into a monster too?

Count Paulo, who was lucky enough to be escorting Polly and Fontaine, gave Steve a dirty look. 'Mrs Khaled's table?'

'Of course,' Steve jumped to attention.

Count Paulo ordered the obligatory champagne, and asked Fontaine to dance.

'You dance with him Polly,' Fontaine commanded. 'At least try and make the place look busy.'

Nico's run of luck continued to the tune of fifty thousand pounds. He was smart enough to quit as soon as the cards began to turn.

He felt elated . . . so elated that he risked a phone call to Fontaine.

A disgruntled housekeeper – obviously woken from a deep sleep – informed him that madam was out.

Then he spotted the girl again. A very tall blonde in a very stark dress. He had noticed her earlier in the evening at the other gaming club. She was certainly striking. Not a fresh-faced beauty nor a sophisticated Fontaine. But very very striking . . .

She smiled at him across the room, and he smiled back.

He thought no more about her.

He collected his coat from reception, tipped the man at the desk handsomely, and signalled the doorman for a cab.

She appeared just as he was climbing in. 'Can you give me a lift?' Her voice was soothingly husky. 'I am escaping from an over-amorous Arab, and if I don't vanish immediately I'm in trouble.'

Nico raised a quizzical eyebrow. 'You are?'

'Please?'

'Hop in. I always help beautiful women in trouble.'

She smiled. 'I knew you'd say that.'

'You did?'

'You look like Omar Sharif – so why shouldn't you sound like him.'

'I'm not an Arab, I'm Greek.'

'I know that. There's no way I would've shared a taxi with an Arab, thank you.'

'How did you know I was Greek?'

She opened her purse, took out a compact, and inspected her face. 'I didn't know *what* you were . . . I just knew you weren't an Arab.' She clicked the compact shut. 'Hi – I'm Lynn.' Formally she extended her hand. 'And you?'

'Nico Constantine.'

'Greek name, but you sound American.'

'Yes, I've lived in LA for the last ten years. Now – where can I drop you?'

Lynn mock pouted, 'Trying to get rid of me so soon . . .'

Nico laughed, 'Not at all.'

'Did I hear you tell the cab driver the Lamont?'

'That's where I'm staying.'

'They only do the best scrambled eggs in town, don't they.'

'They do?'

'If you don't know you must try.'

'The restaurant will be closed . . .'

'And room service will be open . . .'

❖

301

Vanessa, Leonard, and a whole group of people arrived at 'Hobo' as Fontaine's guests.

She watched the women's reactions to Steve. Nothing special.

'Do you fancy him?' she whispered to Vanessa.

'He's not Tony.'

'*Fuck* Tony. I'm sick to death of hearing about Tony. He's not the only stud in the world you know.' Fontaine drained her champagne glass, and gestured for more.

'He *is* quite cute . . .' Vanessa ventured.

'Cute! Christ! That's hardly what I'm looking for.'

The evening sped by in a haze of champagne. Fontaine allowed herself to get delightfully, pleasantly bombed.

Count Paulo clutched her in his arms on the dance floor and declared undying love and lust. 'We must be in bed together soon,' he panted, 'my whole body screams for you.'

He rubbed embarrassingly against her, and she wished he'd take his juvenile Italian horniness back to Italy with him.

She danced with Leonard.

'How about a cosy lunch one day, just the two of us?' He suggested.

God save her from the middle-aged husbands who considered her fair game.

Goodbyes were said in the early hours of the morning on the pavement outside 'Hobo'.

Ricky stood obediently holding the door of the Rolls open while Fontaine, Polly, and Count Paulo piled in.

'Drop Miss Brand first,' Fontaine ordered. 'Then Count Rispollo.'

'Yes, Mrs Khaled.'

Polly managed a surreptitious wink as she was dropped off. 'Later?' she whispered.

'You bet,' Ricky replied, *sotto voce*.

Count Paulo was complaining loudly about being driven to his hotel. 'Tonight I thought we would be together,' he said bitterly. 'I come all the way to see you – and you treat me like . . . like dirt.'

'I'm tired,' Fontaine replied coolly. 'Maybe tomorrow. Call me.'

A disappointed Count Paulo was deposited outside his hotel.

'Home, Ricky,' instructed Fontaine.

He glanced at the clock. Four o'clock in the bleedin' morning. He hoped she wasn't expecting him bright and early at ten a.m. By the time he made it back to Polly's and gave her a good seeing to . . . Well, he'd need some sleep, wouldn't he?

They arrived at Fontaine's Pelham Crescent house. Ricky jumped out of the Rolls and held the door open for her.

She yawned openly and sighed. Dawn was beginning to break. Her kaleidoscope eyes swept over him. 'Coming in for an early morning cup of tea, Ricky?'

Nico and Lynn made love in his hotel suite. A room service trolley bearing two plates of congealed scrambled eggs stood forlornly in the centre of the living room.

Lynn was accomplished, striking, pleasant.

The sex was enjoyable.

Nico wished he hadn't.

She was just another female. A beautiful body – yes. But a stranger. And somehow sex with strangers was not the way he wanted to lead his life anymore. He was too old for one-night stands. And too smart. And he wished he was with Fontaine beneath her black silk sheets exchanging lives.

'That was good,' Lynn said, getting up from the bed.

'Very good,' Nico agreed, hoping she would dress and go.

She stretched, naked and cat-like. 'Are you into bondage?'

'What?'

'Bondage. You know, being tied up and beaten. The Arabs love it.'

303

'I told you, I'm not an Arab.'

'I know.' She arched her back, then touched her toes. Her body was somewhat sinewy. 'You're a Greek who talks American.' She picked up her dress from the floor and started to pull it on. 'And you're also a dumb son-of-a-bitch who had better pay back the money you owe the Fonicettis or you're going to find yourself an unrecognizable son-of-a-bitch. Am I making myself clear?'

'What did you say?' Nico sat up in bed, shocked.

Lynn fiddled with the zipper on her dress. Her smoky voice was very sensuous. 'You heard me. I'm a messenger, so you had better listen very very carefully.' She searched for her spike-heeled shoes and put them on. 'You have a week, seven days, no credit. Understand?' She picked up her purse and moved towards the door. She paused and smiled. 'Every cent, Nico, or . . . well . . . they're going to cut your balls off, and wouldn't that be a shame?'

She exited, closing the door quietly behind her.

'Isn't this fun?' Fontaine watched Ricky through slitted eyes as he poured the tea.

He wasn't sure whether to answer or not. In fact he didn't know how to act at all.

'You know,' Fontaine murmured thoughtfully, 'you're really rather sexy. Why didn't I think of using *you* for the club?'

'Sugar, Mrs Khaled?'

'No, thank you,' she turned her back on him. 'Bring the tea up to the bedroom, Ricky, yours as well.'

He stood in the kitchen and watched her go. Then quick as a flash he whipped out a tray and put the two cups of tea on it. 'Ricky m'boy,' he muttered to himself, 'I think you just got lucky.'

'Ricky,' her slightly drunken voice called from the top of the stairs, 'are you coming?'

Of course he was. Polly would just have to wait.

16

Bernie, Susanna, and Cherry sat in silence aboard Carlos Brent's private plane. Each one of them in deep thought.

Susanna smiled slightly. The shit had hit – Bernie's charming expression – but it hadn't flown in her direction.

Cherry sobbed quietly, occasionally dabbing at her baby-blue eyes with a silk monogrammed handkerchief taken from one of Dino's drawers.

Bernie sat stoically. Mr Fall Guy. Mr Schmuck. It was just good luck he was connected to Carlos Brent, even if it was only a fragile connection. If he hadn't been . . .

If Susanna had not intervened on his behalf . . .

Well, he didn't like to think what would have happened.

Bernie reflected on the previous evening's happenings. It all seemed like a bad fucking dream.

First it was pure shit-luck that Joseph Fonicetti had decided to throw a dinner party. Second, the fact that Nico was an invited guest. And third, that Cherry and Dino had sneaked off and gotten married.

What a joke *that* was.

The whole mix was disaster time.

Joseph Fonicetti was far too canny an old animal to let anything slide past him. And the fact that Nico owed – and owed big – was reason enough for him to be suspicious when Nico failed to show.

Of course, when Cherry announced the fact that she and Dino were married the party really took off.

Joseph Fonicetti did not like surprises – especially of that kind. And he had risen from the table, small mean eyes burning in his nut brown face. 'Is this fuckin' true?' he had screamed at Dino, down the table. 'Are you gonna tell me you've *married* the dumb cunt?'

Cherry had joined in then, blue eyes tearful but determined. 'How dare you call me that – *how dare you!*'

Appealingly she had looked to Dino for support.

Dino had slunk down in his chair. How could he argue with his father? The unfortunate truth was that she *was* a dumb cunt for opening up her mouth.

'Get me Nico Constantine, cut out the bullshit and find him,' Joseph demanded.

Bernie had visibly blanched. He did not know what to say.

Joseph sensed this immediately. 'He *is* still here, isn't he, Bernie?' The voice was menacing.

Susanna cut in quickly with – 'Of course he is, Uncle Joe.'

Joseph ignored her. 'Check it out, David. I want that son-of-a-bitch, Nico, and I want him now.' He indicated a by now sobbing Cherry. 'She's his – this . . . this Barbie doll! He can take her right on out of our lives.'

'Mr Fonicetti!' Cherry had gulped. 'Dino and I are *married*.'

'Find out where the stupid fuck did it, and take care of that too, David,' Joseph snapped. 'And get me Nico – pronto. There's also the matter of the money he owes us. Dino was supposed to take care of that – but he's been too busy taking care of his cock.' At this point Joseph had burst into a stream of angry Italian – a language that had stayed with him since childhood.

Carlos Brent had risen from the table, gone to Joseph, and put his arm around him.

The dinner party was over.

So was Cherry and Dino's marriage.

So was Nico when they found out he had split.

And so was Bernie when they found out he had aided and abetted.

Quickly he had put his arm around Susanna, 'Let's get married again,' he suggested. 'We've had such a great time this last couple of days.'

'Anything to save your ass, huh Bernie?' But she grinned when she said it.

Naturally it did not take them long to find out that Nico was gone.

Bernie had been hauled up to the Fonicetti penthouse for questioning. Susanna had insisted on accompanying him.

To save his own ass he was forced to tell them where Nico was.

'We'll take care of it,' Joseph had muttered ominously.

'He only went so he could raise the money to pay you,' Bernie insisted. 'He's probably on his way back now.'

'Sure, sure.' Joseph stared him down with his mean little eyes. 'Remember one thing in your life, Bernie. Loyalty. But don't fuck it up. Loyalty to the *right* people. When you knew Nico couldn't pay you should have come to me immediately. No hesitation. You understand?'

Bernie nodded vigorously.

'But . . . you're young . . . you have a lot to learn. And I myself have loyalty to Carlos Brent. So you are lucky. You understand?'

'He understands, Uncle Joe,' Susanna kissed the old man on the cheek. 'It won't happen again. And thank you.'

So Bernie's balls were intact. Only thing was, they now belonged to Susanna again.

Cherry shared an apartment in Hollywood with two other girls. They were both away. One on a fishing trip with a porno-movie star. The other on location in Oregon.

Cherry wandered around the empty apartment in a daze. It had all happened so quickly. One moment she was Mrs Dino Fonicetti. The next – just plain Cherry, unsuccessful actress.

It wasn't fair. What was wrong with her? What made her unsuitable material to be Dino's wife? Why did his father automatically hate her?

She stared at her exquisite reflection in the mirror. Blonde hair. Blue eyes. Perfect features. With Dino's dark good looks, what beautiful babies they would have made together.

Dino. His behaviour had not been very nice. Allowing his father to call her horrible names.

She gave a long drawn-out sigh, walked in the tiny bathroom, removed a line of drying underclothes from across the bath, selected her favourite bubbles, and started to run the water.

Then she stripped off her clothes and stepped into the bath.

'Operator, try that number again please.' Bernie bounced his daughter Starr on his knee, and tried to locate Nico for the fifth time.

Susanna was busy unpacking his clothes. On the way from the airport she had insisted on picking up all his things from Nico's rented house.

'We can do it tomorrow,' Bernie had complained.

'Now. I want to feel you're really back. Not just sharing my bed for a night.'

As she unpacked she complained, 'Look at these shirts! My God what kind of a laundry did you send these to!'

'Bernie, these socks should have been thrown away, they're full of holes.'

'Oh no! This is my favourite sweater and you've got a cigarette burn in it. How could you?'

Bernie tuned out, and concentrated on reaching Nico. The least he could do was warn him.

'I think we should have a small wedding, nothing flashy, something tasteful, with Starr as a bridesmaid. What do you think, Bernie?'

'Good idea.'

'Daddy suggested his house in Palm Springs. We could fly everyone up. That would be fun, wouldn't it?'

'Sure.' Goddamn daddy again.

'And I'll wear blue – and how about you in a blue suit

so that we match? And Starr in blue frills. Oh Bernie, it's all so exciting!'

There was nothing Susanna liked better than planning a party – or a wedding for that matter. Bernie remembered with a feeling of dread their famous Saturday night intimate dinner parties for fifty or sixty. Shit. This time he would have to put his foot down.

'We're ringing Mr Constantine's suite,' the hotel operator's voice said.

Three rings and Nico answered.

'I've been trying to reach you for days,' Bernie exclaimed. 'The shit has —

'Hit. I know.' Nico replied.

'How do you know? What's happened?' Bernie stuttered.

'They have given me a very generous seven days to come up with the money.'

'And the ring?'

'Glass, my friend.'

'What'll you do?'

'I'll think of something.'

'Listen, Nico. It wasn't my fault they found out. I tried. I kept it going for days. What happened is a long story.'

'Save it. I'll be back to hear it personally. In one piece, I hope.'

'I'm glad you can take it so calmly.'

'What other way is there?'

'If you need me I'm at Susanna's.'

'Reconciliation?'

'I'll explain.'

'Keep hold of your balls.'

'You too.'

Nico hung up the phone. He *was* calm. His energies could not be wasted on panicking. He had sat and thought from the moment of Lynn's departure.

There were two moves that he could make. One – take his fifty thousand pounds winnings and escape. South America, Athens . . . Change his name, start a new life. The snag was he had no particular desire to change his name and life.

Two – pay them the money he owed. If he could somehow raise it that was.

Two was the only answer of course. But how?

He fell asleep still trying to work it out.

Fontaine awoke to the smell and a taste of a hangover,

and a hammering on her locked bedroom door.

Oh God! She felt positively dreadful.

'Mrs Khaled,' the voice assaulted her, 'it's past twelve, I have your breakfast tray.'

'Leave it outside, Mrs Walters.'

Oh God! Her headache was lethal. She tried to remember fragments of the previous evening – and did.

Oh God! Ricky. He was still asleep in her bed. She sat up and surveyed the room. It looked like a party had taken place.

Oh God! It had. Just the two of them. Talk about shades of Lady Chatterley's lover!

She slid from the bed into a silk kimono, and thought about how to get rid of him.

Mrs Walters wouldn't be shocked that she had had a man spend the night, she was used to that. But the fact that it was her chauffeur! Oh God!

'Ricky,' she gave him a short sharp shove. 'Kindly get up and piss off.'

'What? What?' He opened his eyes. 'Where am I?' Then he remembered. 'Oh – yes, 'course. C'm here darlin', I'll give you a bit more of what you enjoyed last night.'

She withered him with a look. 'Forget about last night, Ricky. And I am not darling, I am Mrs Khaled, and don't you forget it. Now kindly dress and get the hell out of here.'

He sat up in bed. 'Are you giving me the old elbow?'

'If you mean am I firing you, the answer is no. But just remember, last night was a figment of your imagination.'

Bloody hell! Some figment. He had a very good recollection of Mrs Khaled sitting astride him in nothing but a mink coat and his chauffeur's cap yelling, 'First one to the gate is the winner!' Bloody hell!

Fontaine retired into the bathroom, and Ricky dressed quickly. He let himself out of the locked bedroom, nearly tripped over the breakfast tray, and sneaked downstairs.

Mrs Walters was busy dusting. She gave him a look of disdain and a disgusted sniff.

'Morning Mrs Walters.'

She turned her back on him.

Backgammon had always been a game Nico excelled at. He presented himself at a London club and exercised his skills. London had no lack of backgammon hustlers, but Nico was more than a match for them.

He spent the afternoon at play, and emerged in the early evening a few thousand pounds richer.

Not bad, but not nearly enough to even begin to help.

He needed advice. He called Hal.

They met in 'Trader Vics' for a drink, Hal resplendent in a new white suit.

Nico fingered the lapel. 'Looks good.'

'Gotta be my best for the ladies. They're here. If I play it right I could well own half of Detroit by tomorrow morning! Sure you wouldn't like to join us for dinner?'

'If they have five hundred thousand dollars to hand my way . . .'

Hal laughed. 'Five years solid fucking could probably get you that.'

Nico grimaced. 'I need it a little sooner.' His black eyes fixed on to Hal, almost hypnotic in their intensity. 'I am deadly serious about needing the money, Hal. I blew out of Vegas owing. Thought the ring would cover it. Now' – he made a gesture of hopelessness – 'they've found me. They sent a woman messenger. I thought she was a beautiful girl looking to get laid. She got laid all right – and then she delivered the message. Seven days. They mean business – you know it and I know it. Do you have any suggestions?'

Hal summoned the pretty Chinese waitress and ordered another Navy Grog. He was sympathetic. But not *that* sympathetic. He liked Nico very much. But if trouble was coming he wanted to be long gone.

'Let me get some details here,' he said, stalling for time while he thought of a fast excuse to be on his way. 'Who do you owe? And how much?'

'I wasn't kidding you. I owe the Fonicettis five hundred and fifty grand.'

Hal let out a long low whistle, 'Jeez! I know old Joe Fonicetti. Are you gonna tell me they let you run up markers for that much? It's impossible.'

'Not when you lose six hundred thou of your own money up front.'

Hal whistled again. 'You are in trouble, my friend. Big big trouble.'

The Chinese girl brought his drink, and smiled inscrutably at both of them.

'I've never fucked a Chinese,' Hal said absently as she walked away. 'Now tell me, Nico. Who was your lady messenger? Did they send somebody over?'

Nico shook his head. 'She was English. Said her name was Lynn.'

'Very tall? Good body?'

Nico nodded. 'You know her?'

'She used to be a dancer on TV. Never made it out of the back line until she met the man himself.'

'What man?'

'Feathers. Lynn's his right-hand woman. One tough lady – expert judo – the martial arts – you were lucky you only got fucked!'

'Thanks a lot.'

'I wish I could talk to Feathers,' Hal mused aloud. 'Maybe we could figure out something . . .'

'Why can't you?' Nico asked.

'We're not on the best of terms right now. A debt. It's dragged on.'

'How much?'

'Five thousand pounds. I keep him happy with a payment here a payment there. But he'd be a lot happier to see a lump sum.'

313

'Pay him the lump sum. I have it. Call it a fee for your help.'

'Hey, Nico. You don't have to do that.'

'I know I don't. But if you can work out some deal with Feathers – that *he* can work out with Fonicetti. Maybe an instalment plan like you had . . . What do you think?'

Hal nodded slowly. 'Whatever I can do, I'll do.'

Nico patted him on the shoulder. 'Thanks. I'll appreciate anything you can manage.'

Wild looking model girls in exotic underclothes undulated frantically down the catwalk.

Fontaine, at a ringside table, openly yawned.

'Aren't you enjoying it?' Vanessa asked anxiously. The fashion show was raising money for one of her charities and she desperately wanted it to be a success.

'I never did get turned on gaping at other women's bodies,' Fontaine replied. 'Aren't there any *male* models? You know – horny little nineteen-year-olds in nothing but their jockeys and a smile?'

'Oh Fontaine! Really! It's the clothes you're supposed to be looking at.'

'Hmmm . . .' Fontaine allowed her gaze to wander around the restaurant where the fashion show was taking place. Tables and tables of boring women, all dressed in the latest most expensive clothes. Just as she was.

God! Was this what her life was all about? Fashion and Getting Fucked. Both were beginning to pall.

'I have to leave soon,' she whispered to Vanessa. 'Got to meet with my lawyer. Boring old Arnold is threatening me with the workhouse if I don't come up with some money soon. That pittance Benjamin pays me hardly covers my weekly expenses. I simply *have* to get "Hobo" back in action.'

'You will,' Vanessa replied. 'When you put your mind to it nothing can stop you.'

'I know, I know. I always get what I want. But don't you see, Vanessa, that's just an impression I create.'

Vanessa looked at her friend disbelievingly. She envied Fontaine her life, and could never imagine her being dissatisfied. All the women envied Fontaine's life style – even if they pretended not to. She had beauty, freedom, and certainly no visible lack of money.

Vanessa had a rich husband, four children, an overweight figure, and not a moment to call her own.

Fontaine had a seemingly never-ending supply of fanciable young men.

Vanessa had only managed two affairs in twelve long years of marriage.

'I'm so bored!' Fontaine stated. 'Shall I tell you a secret, Vanessa? Just between you and me. Don't you *dare* tell anyone.'

Vanessa nodded, her eyes shining. 'Tell me! Tell me!' she pleaded.

'Last night, I was so bored that I screwed my chauffeur.'

'You didn't?!'

'I certainly did. And let me tell you it was even more boring than being bored!'

'What?' Vanessa frowned. 'Wasn't he any good?'

'All the attributes, my darling. Big cock, firm balls, and lovely thighs. But BORING!'

Vanessa blinked. Fontaine was the most outrageous outspoken person she had ever met.

'The thing is,' Fontaine continued, 'when I was married to Benjamin, all these little adventures seemed so much more exciting. Now . . . well . . . It's all so bloody predictable.'

'I've met someone —' Vanessa began.

Fontaine ignored her, and continued speaking. 'Now that man on the plane – Nico. Not my usual scene at all, darling. But I must say, with him, it was just . . . different. He was so . . . I don't know – it seems a silly word for me to use, but he was so worldly, *and* amusing. Maybe I made a mistake throwing him out.'

'I never did get to meet him —' Vanessa started to say.

They were interrupted by the arrival of Sammy at their table.

'Mornin' gels! Havin' a wonderful time?'

He sat himself down.

'Do have a seat,' Fontaine murmured.

'Ah, her highness is in form today.' He poured himself some wine. 'Listen darlin's, want you to take a look at my new collection.' He indicated the models, now in sports clothes. 'Anything you want – it's yours.'

'You're very generous today,' Fontaine said. 'Why?'

''Cos you're gorgeous, darlin'. Bit long in the tooth for me . . . but . . .'

'Piss off, Sammy,' Fontaine said mildly.

'No offence, my darlin'. I like 'em twenty. Everyone to their own. Know what I mean?'

Fontaine couldn't help smiling. Sammy was a genuine character, and a likeable one.

'Your clothes aren't my usual style,' she said.

'So – wear 'em at the beach. Big deal. Pick out what you want – it'll be good for me if you have 'em.'

Fontaine ticked off a halter jump suit on her programme, and a white track suit. Actually his designs were quite fun.

'So – ready for me to take over "Hobo" yet?' Sammy asked.

'I'll tell you what, Sammy, I *am* giving it serious thought.'

He laughed, 'Really?'

'Why not? You *are* Mr Personality.'

'Oh, yeah?'

'I think you could be quite an attraction. Not in the same way as Tony of course.'

'Oh, of course.'

'But in your own way . . .'

'Hey – hang on. I was only joking you know. I've got a business to run.'

Fontaine fixed him with her kaleidoscope eyes. 'Sammy?' she said briskly. 'How does the idea of becoming a *partner* in "Hobo" appeal to you?'

316

18

Bernie settled back into married life like a mouse into a trap.

Susanna gaily made second wedding plans, nagged him continually about this and that, and phoned dear old Carlos for a loving conversation at least twice a day.

'Find out what they're doing about Nico,' Bernie instructed.

'How can I?' Susanna replied innocently.

'Don't give me that shit,' Bernie snapped. 'You know, and *I* know, and so does all of Hollywood, that Carlos Brent – superstar supreme – has connections that make Watergate look like a kiddies' tea party. He probably owns the fucking Forum hotel for all we know.'

'Don't be ridiculous. Daddy's so called "connections" are in your head.'

'Bullfuckingshit. I want you to find Nico. He's a good friend of mine, and I don't want anything to happen to him.'

Shrilly, Susanna sniped, 'He didn't seem to care so much about what happened to *you*, did he? Left you holding the can, and if you and I hadn't gotten back together . . . Well, you *know* how daddy felt about your treatment of me.'

'Yes, I know. He'd have been only too pleased to have me pushing up cacti in the fucking desert.'

Susanna made a face. 'You're such a smart ass, you really are. What a stupid thing to say.'

Two hours later she casually relayed the information that Nico had been allowed a week to pay.

'You see, Uncle Joseph is a kind and generous man.'

'Uncle Joseph! Only *you* would call one of the biggest mobsters in Vegas, Uncle.'

Susanna pursed her lips. 'The trouble with you, Bernie,

317

is that you think everyone even remotely associated with Las Vegas is a gangster. Uncle Joseph is a perfectly respectable *hotel* owner.'

'Yeah, and the Pope's Jewish!'

Bernie waited until Susanna and Starr went out to order their wedding outfits, then he went up to the bedroom, and checked in Susanna's clothes closet to see if her safe was still there.

It was. Concealed behind a shoe rack.

It occurred to him that she might have had the combination changed. But as he twiddled the knob he realized it was the same.

The door swung open, and facing him was her myriad collection of jewellery boxes, each one containing a diamond encrusted gift from her father.

Also there were the one hundred thousand dollars in cash that Carlos had handed them as a wedding present.

One hundred neat, crisp, thousand-dollar bills. Untouched. Intact. And half his – although Susanna had never allowed him near it.

What kind of a schmuck hung onto *cash* when the money could have been sitting in a bank accumulating interest?

His ex-soon-to-be-present-wife – dear Susanna.

'We'll keep it as emergency money,' she had stated five years before. And that was the last he had seen of it.

Susanna didn't even realize that he knew the safe's combination, but he had watched her fetch a necklace from it one night, and the numerals had stuck.

Well . . . half was his. He was entitled.

He extracted fifty one-thousand-dollar bills, and replaced them with singles at the bottom of the stack.

If he could help Nico with the money – he would.

19

Sammy said yes. Just like that.

He surprised everyone, including himself. But what was money for if not to spend it? And he had always had a hankering to front a club. It was the extrovert in him.

'I'm not another Ian Thaine tryin' to creep into your bed,' he warned Fontaine.

'God forbid!'

So they set a deal, shook hands, and then they were in business together.

For Fontaine it was a lifesaver. Her finances really were in a frightening state. She needed Hobo to be a success again.

Once involved, Sammy did not hang about. He hired incredible black sixteen-year-old twin disc jockeys – a girl and a boy. New waiters, all young, ambitious, and highly paid. He liked Steve Valentine, and decided to keep him on as a backup. He sent him to Leonard for a perm, and Bruno for an all-white wardrobe. The difference was startling.

'It's amazing, you've given him style,' Fontaine exclaimed.

''Course I have,' agreed Sammy. 'Now let's concentrate on changing the menu, and getting a new light system going.'

Fontaine and Sammy were the odd couple. Working together until all hours. Planning, laughing, joking. To their mutual surprise they actually liked each other. Nothing sexual – purely platonic. Sammy was amazed at Fontaine's sense of humour. When she wasn't busy doing her bullshit sexy Mrs Khaled number, she was witty, down to earth, and a lot of fun to be with.

Fontaine found that she adored Sammy. He was warm and humorous and natural.

She was so busy that she even forgot about sex. At night she was happy to collapse into bed – alone – after a hard day at the club.

Sammy had decided they should close 'Hobo' down for a few days while they made their changes. Then reopen with a huge party. 'Expensive, but worth it my darlin',' he assured her.

She agreed. She didn't want to tell him that her lawyer was now suggesting she should sell her house and car to meet all the mounting debts. Her lawyer was an idiot. She would prove to him how wrong he was.

She forgot about her problems and launched into planning a really lavish party.

Champagne and caviar for two hundred of London's most fun people. What did a few more bills matter? In for a penny, in for the whole bloody lot.

It took Hal almost a week to arrange a meeting between Nico and Feathers.

'He is not an easy man to get to see,' Hal explained. 'And a meet with one of his minions would do you no good at all. But don't worry, I've explained your situation, and he'll see you tonight.'

'Christ!' Nico exclaimed. 'Tomorrow my seven days are up. This is cutting it rather too fine for my nerves.'

'Feathers has connections in all the right places. I'm sure it'll be worked out. Don't forget, he's in direct contact with the Fonicettis – your debt is his concern now.'

Nico had spent an uneasy few days. His luck at the gaming tables had held, and his original stake was up to ninety thousand pounds. He planned to hand that to Feathers as a sign of good intent. But where did he come up with the rest?

The thought of getting out of town had occurred to him daily. But to return to Los Angeles seemed even more dangerous. He felt safer where he was.

He had telephoned Fontaine Khaled on three occasions

and, even though he left messages, she never returned his calls. Not so much as a note to thank him for the diamond heart or the six dozen roses. Perhaps she was the bitch everyone said she was.

He had put her out of his mind, and concentrated on the tables.

Hal picked him up outside the Lamont at eight-thirty precisely.

'Nine o'clock meeting. We can't be late or early. Feathers is funny like that, so we'll play it safe and ride round the block when we get there.'

'Where does he live?' Nico asked.

'He never sees anyone at his home,' Hal explained. 'One of his Casinos is where we're meeting.'

Fontaine surveyed herself in the full-length mirror one final time before leaving.

How could you beat perfection?

The long tube of black silk jersey, the blood red embroidered Chinese kimono, the Madam Butterfly hairdo. Startling, true, but very effective.

If she was in America now she would certainly appear on the front page of *Womens Wear Daily*.

She swept downstairs, and Mrs Walters was duly impressed. 'Oh, you do look lovely Mrs Khaled.'

Fontaine accepted the compliment as her due, and nodded regally. 'Is Ricky outside?'

'Yes, madam, and the Count is waiting in the living room.'

Oh God! The Count. She had forgotten about him. But then it certainly wouldn't have looked right if she had arrived at her own party without an escort.

Count Paulo waited impatiently. He leapt up when Fontaine entered the room.

'*Bellissimo*! *Bellissimo*!' he exclaimed.

'Calm down, sweetheart. Don't get yourself all excited.' Who would have thought that she'd ever be bored by a twenty-five-year-old horny Italian Count? But she was. Indeed she was.

Lynn met them at the reception desk. She acted like she had never set eyes on Nico before.

'Please follow me, gentlemen,' she said formally, 'Mr Feathers is expecting you.'

She led them through a door marked 'Private' which in turn led them through a narrow corridor.

'Great ass,' Hal managed to mutter as they followed Lynn.

She stopped at another door marked 'Private' and knocked three times.

A male voice called for them to come in.

They entered a luxurious office. Feathers sat behind an ornate desk. He was a big man with a taste for flashy suits and coloured shirts. His face was nightclub white and pasty, and his greased-down hair very obviously dyed black. In spite of the cheapness of his look he managed to throw out an aura of sinister and powerful menace.

He studied Nico through surprisingly small bloodshot eyes. Then he extended an even more surprising beautifully manicured hand, gave a dead fish kind of handshake and said, 'Take a seat, Nico. Hal, why don't you let Lynn take you for a walk?'

Hal quickly nodded, 'Sure, sure.'

Lynn directed a cold smile his way. 'Come along fat ass.' Her voice was as sensuous as ever. 'The big boys want to talk.'

She led Hal out of the room.

'Drink?' Feathers barked.

'Vodka, please.'

Feathers snapped his fingers, and a previously unnoticed hood stepped from the background and opened up a rather garish 1940s cocktail cabinet.

'Vodka,' snapped Feathers, 'and order me up a weak tea and some biscuits.'

The hood nodded obligingly. He looked like he belonged in the 1940s too.

'So,' Feathers sighed, 'you're Nico Constantine. I was interested to meet with a man who can play such a dangerous game with his life.'

Nico shrugged, 'I always intended to pay the Fonicettis back.'

'That's what they all say. Some of them even say it when their balls are decorating their ears, and their kneecaps are hanging by a thread.'

'You don't have to threaten me. I came here to try and work things out.'

'Good, Nico. Good. I'm glad.' Feathers leaned back in his chair. 'I understand that your luck at the tables has been remarkable since you've been in London.'

'Not that remarkable, but I can make a substantial deposit towards my debt.' He accepted a giant tumbler of neat vodka from the 1940s hood.

'Excellent. Of course, while you are in England your debt with the Fonicettis is my concern. We have a mutual agreement.'

Nico nodded. 'I understand that.'

'The Fonicettis were not thrilled by your sudden secretive departure. If only you had discussed things with them . . .'

Nico could feel himself getting irritated. He didn't like Feathers. He didn't like being lectured.

'Can you help me postpone the rest of the debt?' he asked abruptly.

'I can get you an extension,' Feathers said blandly. 'If you co-operate on a minor hustle.'

'What sort of hustle?'

'Nothing illegal . . . just slightly bent.' Then Feathers laughed, a particularly nasty laugh, 'Do you really feel you have a choice?' he asked.

'There is always a choice in life.' Nico replied shortly.

Feathers' small mean eyes darkened. 'Not for you. Not

323

if you want to remain in good health.'

The tea arrived on a neat tray, with a selection of sweet biscuits.

Nico gulped a great slug of vodka. He had an insane desire to get out of there. 'What's the hustle?' he asked again.

'A certain horse is running in a big race next Saturday. This horse is the favourite, an out and out winner. What we want is the horse to lose. What we want is for you to arrange it.'

Nico frowned. 'How can I do that?'

'The horse is called "Garbo". It belongs to Vanessa and Leonard Grant. The jockey, Sandy Roots, is giving a regular screwing to Mrs Grant – and while her husband might not mind – Sandy's wife would be more than put out. She's a lovely girl, daughter of top trainer, Charley Watson.' Feathers paused to dunk a biscuit in his tea. 'Now, if Charley got a whiff of what was going on . . . then Sandy may as well pack up and leave the business.'

'I don't understand,' Nico was puzzled. 'What does this all have to do with me?'

'Easy. Vanessa and Leonard Grant. Best friends of Fontaine Khaled.'

'So?'

'So we know all about you and Mrs Khaled. The plane. The night together.'

'We are no longer in touch.'

Feathers coughed. 'You'd better arrange to be. The Grants are having a house party this weekend. Mrs Khaled is already invited. So are the Roots, and Charley Watson. It will be easy for you to get an invite – you could fit right in with that lot.'

Nico hesitated, 'I don't know,' he said uncertainly. There was no way he wanted to use Fontaine Khaled again. Once was enough.

Feathers' tone was sharp. 'You join the weekend party, you persuade 'Sandy Roots to throw the race, and if you succeed . . . Well I am sure we can give you more time. Of course, if you don't succeed . . .' The menace was thick in Feathers' tone.

Nico had no choice but to agree.

'Hobo' was packed when Fontaine made her entrance. Just like old times.

Steve Valentine rushed forward to greet her. He did look very effective all in white with his new hairstyle.

Sammy was doing a wonderful job of circulating, his natural warmth and friendliness appealing to everyone.

The new disc jockeys were wild, looning about in outrageous white satin outfits, and playing amazing sounds.

Even the waiters looked good in their new black and white uniforms.

'I love it!' Vanessa was already there. 'Sweetie, the atmosphere! It all makes "Dickies" seem rather old hat.'

'Do me a favour and dance with Paulo,' Fontaine hissed. 'He's boring the pants off me.'

'Is that a bad thing?'

'Oh, didn't I tell you? I've given up sex.'

'*You*?'

'Yes, me darling. Don't look so surprised.'

'How did it go?' Hal asked.

Nico shrugged, 'Complicated. I don't want to involve you.'

Hal nodded, 'Suits me.'

'I have to see Fontaine,' Nico said.

'Business or pleasure?'

'Both.'

'You're in luck. It's the "Hobo" party tonight.'

'Let's go.'

They took a cab over. Nico wondered what the hell he was going to say to her. If it was any other female he

325

would have had a whole line of stock phrases. But Fontaine . . . Well, she was different.

Life could be very unfair at times.

Fontaine was in her element. All the hard work of the previous days had been worth it. Everything was going right. She danced with various admirers, and thoroughly revelled in all the attention she was receiving.

Sammy was having as good a time as she was. Two sixteen-year-old groupies and a rock star were his personal guests.

Count Paulo hovered attentively wherever Fontaine went. 'Do take care of him,' she hissed in Vanessa's direction. But Vanessa was busying herself with a really boring, frighteningly short jockey, and his equally boring, rather tall wife.

Leonard invited Fontaine to dance. 'You are coming this weekend?' he asked anxiously as he jigged about in an embarrassing way.

'Of course. I could do with just lying about and relaxing.'

Leonard grinned. 'I can hardly imagine *you* relaxing.'

'Oh, I do, you'd be surprised.'

The frantic Wilson Pickett disco sound changed to a slow throbbing Donna Summer. Leonard seized his chance and grabbed her. His hands were hot and sweaty through her dress.

'A little looser, Leonard, I can't breathe.'

'What about lunch one day?'

'What about Vanessa?'

She managed to edge away. Horny husbands. She wished they would leave her alone.

Hal had a date with a geriatric widow. He insisted on collecting her and bringing her to the 'Hobo' party.

Nico decided to fill him in on his conversation with Feathers, and Hal whistled and commented, 'Guess it's better than having your legs chopped off at the knees!'

Hal really knew how to make a person feel good.

They walked into 'Hobo', and it was all happening. The place was alive again. Excitement hung heavy in the air.

Sammy greeted them effusively, then insisted that they join his table in the discothèque.

Nico spotted Fontaine immediately. Other women paled beside her. She was an original. On the crowded dance floor she stood out.

Sammy was busy making introductions. Nico caught the name Sandy Roots, and he realized that he was practically sitting beside the jockey and his wife.

Hal pointedly tapped Nico on the arm. 'Have you met Vanessa Grant?' he asked.

Nico turned to the plumpish blonde woman and generated full wattage charm. 'My pleasure, madam.'

Vanessa sparkled. What more could she ask for? A magnetic stare from a very attractive stranger on one side. And her famous but rather short lover on the other.

Fontaine, returning from the dance floor, saw Nico, ignored him, and squeezed between Sandy Roots and the rock star.

Nico leaned across Vanessa. 'Good evening, Mrs Khaled.'

She pretended to notice him for the first time. 'Oh, Nico. How are you?' Her voice was cold, but suddenly her heart was racing like some stupid little teenager.

Count Paulo, sitting opposite her, said, 'Fontaine, we dance now?'

She dismissed him impatiently. 'In a minute, Paulo.'

'How have you been?' Nico inquired.

'Busy,' she replied.

At this point Vanessa got up to dance with Sandy Roots, and just as Count Paulo attempted to sit next to Fontaine, Nico moved up beside her, blocking him.

'You didn't return my calls,' Nico said softly.

'I told you, I've been busy.'

327

'You had no intention of returning my calls.'

'True.'

He reached out and touched the heart he had sent her, 'But you wear my heart.'

'It's pretty.'

'No – thank you?'

'Oh, I'm so sorry. Did I forget to say thank you like a good little girl?'

'You're still a bitch.'

'And you're still so fucking sure of yourself.'

'Why don't we get out of here? I want to talk to you properly.'

'There is nothing to talk about.'

'So, we'll make love. We both want to. Then, if you feel like it, we'll talk.'

He stood up, grabbed her firmly by the arm, and propelled her to the door.

She didn't protest. She didn't want to.

Count Paulo came running after them. 'Fontaine . . . Bellissimo – what is happening?'

'Go back inside, order a drink, and find someone of your own age to play with, sonny,' Nico said.

'But . . .' Paulo's mouth dropped open while he thought of something to say.

'Goodnight,' said Nico. And he and Fontaine exited up the stairs.

20

Dino bided his time for a week. He behaved as he always behaved. He dated a couple of showgirls, he wandered around the Casino with his usual Tony Curtis smile, he reported to his father every day.

As far as everyone connected to him could see, Cherry was just a distant memory, a slight brain storm. What had happened was in the past. Dino had been a naughty boy, and Joseph had rapped his knuckles. Now it was all over.

Or was it?

Beneath the Tony Curtis smile lurked an angry bitter man.

What his father had done to him was unforgivable. He had made a public fool of him. He had annulled his marriage as if he was some crazy teenager.

Dino would never forgive him for that.

Joseph Fonicetti felt good. Everything taken care of. No loose ends. Even that bastard Nico had been found and warned.

Dino was a good son. A sensible boy. He had realized the error of his ways. Dumb cunts were not for marrying. They were for humping out of your system.

No way could Bernie marry Susanna again.

There were several reasons – the main one being that she would drive him fuckin' nuts!

She had a bossy streak that was to be believed. And nag nag constantly. And Daddy. And Starr, his own kid, a real little spoilt pain in the ass.

But how could he leave with the matter of Nico still unresolved?

It was impossible. He knew Susanna, she would go

running straight to Carlos and blame the whole thing on him.

He sat in his office and pondered on what to do. The fifty thousand dollars was locked securely in his office safe, but he had not yet been able to contact Nico to offer his help.

His secretary walked into the office. She was a long-legged California blonde with lethal teeth.

She sat herself on the edge of his desk exhibiting an exciting length of leg. 'Your wife called,' she announced, 'while you were in the john. Wants you to call back right away.'

'She's not my wife, Tina.'

'Ex-wife. So what?'

That was the trouble with secretaries today. No fuckin' respect.

'I'm flying to LA tomorrow morning,' Dino casually told Joseph.

'What for?' Joseph asked.

'The usual. Collect personally on a few of the outstanding markers.'

'Oh, yeah – yeah. Good.'

It was only acceptable to some of the Forum's more famous patrons to have their debts picked up by either Dino or David.

'I thought it was David's turn,' Joseph remarked.

'I'm doing him a favour. Mia's not feeling so good – only another six weeks and you'll be a grandpop again.'

Joseph chuckled. David and Mia were doing well for him. A suitable few weeks gap and he would ship in a prospective bride or two for Dino.

'Will you be staying over?' he asked.

'I don't know. Maybe, I'll let you know.'

Bright and early the next morning Dino was on a plane.

A car waited for him at LA airport. He knew exactly what he was going to do.

330

He wasn't nervous any more. He was suitably calm.

He was thirty-one years old and perfectly capable of making his own decisions.

Fuck Joseph Fonicetti and all he stood for. He, Dino, was going to be his own man. He wanted Cherry, and goddamnit he was going to have her.

'Let's go upstairs,' Susanna suggested after dinner.

'I want to play some tapes over,' Bernie replied.

'You're becoming a real workaholic. Put the tapes on, switch the speakers through to the bedroom, and we'll listen to them together. OK?'

Her 'I wanna get laid' look was coming across loud and clear. 'They're long,' Bernie said desperately.

'That's fine. We've got all night, haven't we?'

'Sure.' Suddenly he was a sex object. *Her* sex object. Something was wrong somewhere.

'So, come on, Bernie. Do it, what are you waiting for?' She winked, and walked ahead of him up the stairs.

Dino parked outside Cherry's apartment building. He hadn't wanted to phone her, after all, her first reaction might not be exactly friendly. He hadn't dared to call her from Vegas – he wouldn't put it past Joseph to have a tap on his phone.

The apartment house was slightly on the seedy side. Peeling paintwork and garbage cans right out front where you could see them.

The communal pool had rotten tiles, and dilapidated lounging chairs around it.

Dino was used to luxurious surroundings, always had been. He turned up his nose in distaste at the various cooking smells. It was a shame that delectable Cherry had to live in such a sordid place. It stunk of failure and survival on the lowest level.

Oh well, he would soon be taking her away from all this.

331

He found her apartment number and pressed the buzzer. No answer. So he tried again.

A faded redhead with enormous tits and a sackful of cat droppings emerged from the next-door apartment.

'Hi,' she said, looking Dino over appreciatively.

'Do you know if anybody's home?' he asked.

'Shouldn't think so. Those little ladies keep themselves *veree* busy. Know what I mean, buster?' She smiled broadly, forgetting the fact that she had not put her two front false teeth in.

Dino was surprised that Cherry lived with room-mates. She certainly had never mentioned them.

'Wanna come in for a coffee, honey?' the redhead leered.

Dino threw her a cold stare.

'Only trying to be neighbourly, dear. Hey,' she peered at him closely, 'anyone ever tell you that you look like Tony Curtis?'

A commotion heralded the arrival of one of Cherry's room-mates. She was a very tall girl, accompanied by two large alsatian dogs, a lot of fishing tackle, suitcases, and her porno movie star boyfriend who looked like Mr Universe.

The redhead sniffed and vanished quickly inside her apartment, cat droppings and all.

'Lookin' for someone?' the girl demanded, while the two alsatians sniffed around his crotch.

Dino tried to shove them away.

'Watch it,' Mr Universe porno movie star said in a falsetto voice.

'Jesus Christ!' the girl exclaimed for no particular reason.

'Is Cherry around?' Dino asked.

'I dunno. I've been away. For crissakes open up the door.'

Mr Universe struggled with the key, and the three of them entered the apartment.

332

'What the fuck's that Godawful smell?' The girl exclaimed. 'Cherry? You around? There's some guy here for you.'

Dino backed towards the door. He didn't like the apartment. He didn't like the occupants. He didn't like the whole set up.

'Shit!' the girl said.

She was certainly no Cherry. More like a tough little hooker.

'You wanna hang around?' she asked unenthusiastically.

'Gotta take a piss,' Mr Universe announced.

A really lovely couple.

'No,' said Dino, 'I think I'll come back later.'

'Suit yourself,' the girl shrugged. 'You leavin' a message?'

'Sheeiit! Jeez!' Mr Universe's falsetto tones screamed out. 'Get in here, get in here quick.'

The girl and Dino and the two alsatians rushed into the bathroom.

Cherry lay in the bath – quite quite dead.

Susanna woke early, fixed a big pitcher of orange juice, and went into her study to work on the design for the wedding invitations.

She hummed softly to herself. It was quite nice having Bernie around the house again. Only quite.

He was as neurotic as ever. He picked his nose all over her special lavender sheets. He sulked a lot. And he was still jealous of daddy.

However . . . he *was* pretty nifty in bed. He could do more with his tongue than a whole legion of upstanding pricks.

Susanna giggled to herself.

The phone rang and she picked it up.

An incoherent babbling voice was screaming at the other end.

'Who is this?' she demanded.

It was Dino.

By the time Bernie got up, Dino was already at the house.

Susanna had him comparatively calmed down and coherent.

It must have been shock enough for him to find Cherry's body, but the fact that the girl had lain in a bath filled with her own blood for a week . . .

She had slit her wrists.

Dino had run from the apartment at once. But not before he had been forced to take a good look. 'Christ, Susy, it was the most horrible sight of my whole life,' he babbled.

Susanna comforted him. She fed him brandy, held him, and stroked his forehead. She and Dino had known each other all their lives. When she was thirteen she had developed a big crush on him that had lasted all of six months. They had made love once, and ever since that time remained close friends.

'I thought of you immediately,' Dino said. 'I mean you and Bernie knew Cherry . . .' He broke off into sobs.

Bernie couldn't believe the news. Cherry. Killed herself. Why? It was such a waste.

He thought of Nico. Knew he would blame himself, and decided not to tell him.

'Dino, I want you to stay here,' Susanna insisted. 'You need the rest, I'll call Uncle Joseph.'

Gratefully Dino accepted her hospitality. He had a nagging gut ache and he knew why. Something was bothering him.

Had Cherry taken her own life?

Or – had his father arranged it?

It was something he would never know. But it would certainly be a long time before he went back to the family business.

21

Ricky drove the Rolls. Eyes straight ahead. Face impassive.

He had a feeling that his days were numbered as Mrs Khaled's chauffeur. Ever since their one drunken evening together she had become frostier and frostier. Never once had she mentioned it. He was beginning to think that maybe it had never even happened!

Of course he had told Polly all about it, thinking that she would enjoy the juicy details. Wrong. Polly had listened, asked questions, pursed her lips, and never allowed him into her bed again.

Women were funny creatures.

They were approaching the driveway of the Grants' country estate. Very impressive. Parked casually outside the front entrance of the mansion were two Ferraris, a Bentley, and a Lamborghini.

'We're here, Nico,' Fontaine exclaimed. 'You're going to love the house.'

He held her hand and squeezed it tightly. 'I'm sure I will.'

Fontaine was positively glowing. She even looked different – softer and more relaxed, her biting edginess in abeyance.

Leonard came out to greet them.

He kissed Fontaine and gave Nico a quizzical once-over. 'A little old for you, isn't he?' he murmured discreetly to Fontaine.

'Leonard, I think I'm finally growing up.'

'Really, How boring. I hope he's rich at least.'

'Naturally. But that's *not* the reason I'm with him.'

Leonard nodded knowingly.

Nico, meanwhile, was organizing the suitcases from the trunk of the car.

'Good God!' Leonard exclaimed, noticing all their luggage. 'You're only here for the weekend!'

Fontaine smiled. 'You should know me by now, I just can't stand to look tacky, and Nico's exactly the same. We're soulmates.' She gave Nico a very long and intimate look. 'Aren't we darling?'

'You could put it like that.' His eyes locked with hers.

'I will put it like that.'

Their eyes carried on a secret conversation.

Leonard stamped his feet impatiently. 'Shall we go inside?' he suggested.

Fontaine broke the look. 'Wonderful. Who is here?'

'Susan and Sandy Roots, my trainer – Charley Watson. Pearson Crichton-Stuart, and a most delightful little Chinese piece.'

'Got your eye on her already, Leonard?' Fontaine mocked.

'Not at all.'

Fontaine suddenly turned her stare to Ricky. 'You can leave the car,' she said brusquely. 'Take the train back to town. I won't be needing you again this weekend.'

Ricky nodded. He had made a decision. The randy Mrs Khaled could stuff her chauffeur's job. He was quitting.

'Yes, Mrs Khaled.' Bitch!

The weekend got off to a good start. Everyone seemed to get along well.

Nico watched Sandy Roots carefully. He seemed a nice enough lad, but Nico did not miss the secret glances passing like fire between him and Vanessa at lunch.

After lunch Fontaine wanted to go riding. 'Can we?' she asked Nico.

'I don't feel like it,' he replied. 'But you go.'

'Come on, old girl,' Leonard said. '*I'll* take you. Anyone else want to come?'

'I wish you wouldn't call me "old girl",' Fontaine snapped. 'Nico, are you sure you won't come?'

'I feel like a game or two of backgammon, if I can interest anyone.'

Pearson Crichton-Stuart piped up with, 'Me, I'm rather good at the game actually.'

Nico winked at Fontaine. 'Then we shall play for stakes, don't you think? Makes the game more interesting.'

Fontaine kissed him on the forehead. 'I'm going to change. I'll see you later.' She bent, and whispered in his ear, 'Hustler!'

'You bet!' he replied.

While she was changing she thought about their relationship. Nico was the most exciting, interesting, attractive man she had ever met. After all the boys – here was a real man. And yet he was also mysterious, and she liked that too. She had a horrible feeling that for the first time in her life she was in love. God forbid!

Downstairs Leonard waited for her, and they set off for the stables in a Land-Rover.

'I hope you've bet your all on our horse tomorrow,' Leonard commented. 'In all my years involved with racing I've never seen form like it.'

'Yes, Vanessa told me. I've placed a few very substantial bets.'

'Good girl.'

She didn't want to elaborate and tell him that she had her house and car riding on it. She needed a big win.

Nico trounced Pearson at backgammon twice, but still he came back for more.

His tiny Chinese girlfriend – Mai-Ling – watched attentively.

Charley Watson snored, asleep in front of the roaring log fire. Susan Roots had gone out shopping.

Nico was the only one that noticed Vanessa and Sandy slip quietly away.

Riding through the wooded grounds was very exhilar-

337

ating. Fontaine threw her head back and enjoyed the wind tearing through her hair. Terrible for the complexion of course. But so what . . .

'Let's take a rest,' Leonard shouted.

They dismounted in a clearing, and before Fontaine even had time to think, Leonard was all over her.

She tried to push him off. 'What *do* you think you're doing?' she asked sharply.

Leonard pulled at her clothes. 'You want it . . . You can't fool me . . . this is your scene . . .'

Fontaine found herself struggling with him in earnest. 'Leonard. For crissakes stop it.'

'You like it . . . you want it . . . I've always fancied you, Fontaine, and don't you deny it. You've always fancied me, too.'

He was tearing viciously at her clothes now.

She couldn't believe what was happening. With a violent kick she managed to throw him off her, but it was too late to stop him having an orgasm.

He rolled on the ground groaning in ectasy and pain.

Fontaine got up quickly. 'You filthy bastard!' she hissed.

She mounted her horse and rode back to the house, seething with fury.

Nico was still playing backgammon and taking a bundle off the rather chinless Pearson Crichton-Stuart.

'I want to leave,' Fontaine stormed.

Nico didn't take his eyes from the board. 'Why?'

Fontaine couldn't think of a reason. The truth was too humiliating.

'I just feel like going home.'

'No,' said Nico firmly. 'We'll stay for the big race tomorrow, *then* we'll go home.'

Fontaine had to admit that one of the things she loved about Nico was that he did what he wanted to – not what she told him to.

It made a very acceptable change.

*

Dinner that evening was a formal affair. Vanessa had decided it would be fun to dress up.

Nico was in high spirits. He had managed to take over two thousand pounds off Pearson Crichton-Stuart.

'It's just not done,' Fontaine chided him gently in the privacy of their room before dinner. 'Let the poor fellow win some of it back later.'

Nico laughed. 'You're so English! He wanted to gamble. He lost. That's all there is to it.' For a moment he was tempted to tell her of his gambling debts and everything else. But he curbed the temptation. She would probably be horrified. And worse – she would probably offer to bail him out. And he didn't want her money. Although a couple of her diamond rings would no doubt raise enough to solve all of his problems. One lady who would *never* be caught dead in fake gems was Mrs Khaled.

The opportunity to talk to Sandy Roots in private was not easy to obtain. Nico finally cornered him after dinner. He hated what he had to do, but then again, he had no choice.

He engaged the young jockey in a this and that conversation about racing. Then he sprung the surprise. At first Sandy pretended not to know what Nico was talking about. Then, at last, he realized that Nico meant business. And of course, in the end, he had to agree. He was just about smart enough to know that his racing career could well be over if Charley Watson wanted it that way. And if Charley Watson found out that he was screwing Vanessa Grant . . . He would definitely want it that way. No doubt on *that* score.

'I'll do it,' he finally agreed. 'But I don't know how a lousy bastard like you can sleep at nights.'

Nico felt like a lousy bastard. Sandy was right.

Pearson Crichton-Stuart was bugging him for another game of backgammon.

Fontaine gave him a warning look.

He blew her a kiss.

339

'Don't forget to lose,' she mouthed.

'Never!' Nico mouthed back.

'What do you think of Sandy?' Vanessa whispered to Fontaine.

'Sandy?' Fontaine questioned vaguely. 'Oh, you mean the little jockey chap.'

Vanessa rolled her eyes meaningfully. 'Not so little!'

Fontaine didn't catch the drift of what she was trying to tell her at all. She was too busy directing icy stares at Leonard, across the room.

'Leonard's getting fat,' she snapped. 'Why don't you send him away to a health farm?'

'Do you think so?'

'Yes, I do. He's at a dangerous age. True heart attack material.'

'Oh, no!' Vanessa was anxious.

'Oh, yes,' Fontaine replied coldly, 'He's looking positively *old*.'

'I like Nico,' Vanessa changed the subject. 'I've never seen you so . . .'

'Hooked?'

Vanessa giggled. 'It does seem that way.'

Fontaine smiled. 'Yes. And to tell you the truth, I'm loving every minute of it.'

The day of the big race everyone got up early. It was crisp and cold, but the sun was shining.

Vanessa served a buffet breakfast with the help of three servants.

'This is *delicious*!' Fontaine exclaimed. 'I haven't had kippers for simply years!'

Nico picked up a copy of *Sporting Life* and started studying the form. Since 'Garbo' would definitely not be winning the big race he may as well check out the other runners.

He found a real outsider. A French horse called 'Kanga'. Twenty-five to one. The odds were right, so he decided to phone Hal and find out the form.

Hal was encouraging. He knew of the horse. It had come second in a race earlier in the season. Since then – nothing. But the early form was promising, and if the weather conditions were right . . .

'I want to place my bankroll on it,' Nico said.

'What bankroll?' Hal laughed.

'I held ten thou back when I paid Feathers. I want you to get on to two or three bookies and place it for me. But not until just before the race. I want to keep those odds.'

'It's a gamble,' Hal warned.

'Ah,' replied Nico. 'But isn't that what life is all about?'

22

Bernie was the last to realize what was going on. And when he found out he was the most grateful.

It all started very innocently. Dino moving in with them. Susanna consoling him day and night – sometimes very late into the night. And Susanna suddenly Miss Sweetness and Light. No nagging. No mention of wedding plans. And certainly no sex.

When Bernie thought about it after, he realized what a dumb schmuck he must have seemed to both of them. He almost laughed out loud when he thought of the Dear John scene. It went as follows.

They had dined, the three of them. Then Bernie had gone into his study to play some tapes, and Susanna and Dino had stayed in the dining room chatting intently.

An hour later, they had presented themselves to him, hand in hand.

He hadn't even thought twice about *that*.

'Bernie, we have to talk to you,' Susanna said. 'Make yourself a stiff drink and sit down.'

Christ! Nico! The sons-of-bitches had done something to Nico.

'I don't need to sit down and have a drink. What the fuck is going on?'

Susanna had come to him then. Comforting hand on the arm, maternal cluck-clucking sounds coming from the lips.

'I knew you'd be upset, Bernie. But *please*, *please*, for all of us, try to understand.'

'Understand *what* for crissakes?' He was roaring with anger.

'Dino and I want to get married,' Susanna said simply.

'What?' He couldn't believe his ears. Or his luck.

'I know it must be hard for you, but we fought it, we

really did, and then . . .' She shrugged helplessly. 'We knew we had to tell you.'

Bernie wanted to laugh out loud.

Susanna and Dino. What a pair! And Joseph and Carlos would be celebrating for weeks – months even.

Bernie forced his face into a suitably miserable expression.

Dino said smoothly, 'I know it's tough, but Jeez – it's hit us both like a ton of bricks.'

A ton of shit more like.

'I'm confused . . .' Bernie managed to mumble.

'Yes. You must be,' said Susanna, her voice becoming more businesslike. 'The thing is, Bernie, I think you should move back into that house you were sharing with Nico.'

Oh, sure. Get rid of him immediately.

'We've discussed everything,' Susanna said. 'And we all know how close you and Nico are.'

She made them sound like a couple of closet queens!

'So,' Dino continued, 'we've decided to allow Nico more time to pay. I've spoken to my father about it and he's agreed. Three months. But that's the limit.'

It was a swop. Bernie move out of Susanna's life with no fuss and bother, and Nico would get more time.

'How about six months?' Bernie ventured.

'Forget it,' Dino snapped.

'They're being very fair,' Susanna said, in her new Florence Nightingale voice.

So Bernie had moved out. What an escape!

He phoned Nico in London immediately with the good news, but the hotel operator at the Lamont said that Mr Constantine was away for the weekend and would be returning on Monday.

Oh, well, the good news would just have to wait.

343

23

The racetrack was packed.

Fontaine, wrapped up warmly in an Yves Saint Laurent pant suit, and a three-quarter length red fox jacket, squeezed Nico's arm tightly. 'Isn't this exciting!' she cooed. 'Have you backed "Garbo" yet?'

He shook his head. He had just placed the three thousand pounds he had ended up winning from Pearson Crichton-Stuart with various bookies around the track. And all of it was riding on 'Kanga' to win. Plus the ten thousand Hal would have placed for him.

'Oh, but you must,' Fontaine insisted. 'It's a sure thing. Cannot lose. And it better not lose either, I have my house and car riding on it.'

'What?' he stared at her in disbelief.

'I didn't want to mention it before, darling. But I am slightly what they call – busted out. So I have risked everything except my jewellery today. I told you it was exciting!'

Nico could not believe what he had just heard. Fontaine broke. Ridiculous!

'Excuse me, my darling,' he said quickly. 'Little business I have to attend to.'

'Don't forget to back "Garbo",' she called after him.

Nico rushed through the crowds. He had to find Sandy – pronto. For once in his life – well the first time since Lise-Maria actually – he was putting someone else before himself.

'Don't be a fool,' a voice screamed in his head.

He ignored it.

Finding Sandy was no joke. But he managed it, and the jockey was duly relieved and grateful to be let off the hook.

Ruefully Nico went through his pockets to see if he had

anything left to place on 'Garbo'. Nothing. Every cent he had was riding on a long chance – now a no-chance with the favourite once more in the race.

On his way back to Fontaine he passed Lynn and Feathers. She ignored him. Feathers signalled, an imperceptible knowing nod.

Nico nodded back. There was only one thing for it. After the race – stick with the house party until he could make a very fast exit out of town.

By the time Nico got back to Fontaine the big race was preparing to start.

She was as excited as any schoolgirl.

Nico watched her with affection. He would be sorry to leave her . . . more than sorry . . .

'Garbo' shot right into the first three horses surprising no one.

Where was 'Kanga'? Who knew? With all those runners it was difficult to tell.

'Garbo' was holding steady. Running beautifully. Taking the jumps in her stride. A magnificent horse totally at one with her jockey.

At the fifteenth jump the crowds went mad – 'Garbo' fell.

'Oh, my God!' Fontaine looked ready to faint.

Nico put his arms around her. 'It's only a race,' he comforted.

'Only a race! Nico, I had *everything* on that horse – bloody everything!'

He hugged her. No need for him to skip town now. 'So we'll be broke together.'

'You . . . broke?'

'I'm afraid so.'

They both started to laugh at the same time. Hugging, kissing, laughing.

'What shall we do?' Fontaine asked.

'We'll be together, we'll think of something.'

They stared at each other as if for the first time, totally

oblivious to the noise and chaos around them.

'You'll backgammon hustle, and I'll sell my jewellery,' Fontaine joked.

'Never your jewellery. Never. I forbid it!'

'You're so macho.'

'And you're still a bitch.'

'But you like it.'

'I love it . . . and you.'

'. . . and you.'

'Give me those lips . . . those luscious beautiful lips.'

They kissed, and Nico didn't even hear them announce 'Kanga' as the winner of the race.

'I will look after you,' he said. 'No more flirting. No more Italian studs.'

Fontaine smiled. 'And you. No more oozing charm over any woman that passes your way.'

They looked at each other warmly and embraced.

Over Fontaine's shoulder Nico spotted a stunning-looking girl. He eyed her appreciatively.

Over Nico's shoulder Fontaine saw an extremely good-looking young man. She looked him up and down with interest.

They drew back, looked at each other, and laughed.

The Love Killers

CHAPTER 1

'I don't care if you can't do anything else. I don't care if you lose your income, your home, your possessions. Fuck all of it, baby. Just gather up your self-respect and walk right out. To be a prostitute is to be nothing, a mere tool of man. Take no notice of your pimps, your bosses. *We* will help you. *We* will give you all the help we can. *We* will get you so together that your old life will seem like a bad dream.'

Margaret Lawrence Brown had been speaking for fifteen minutes, and she paused to sip from a glass of water handed to her on the makeshift podium. The crowd gathered to hear her talk was gratifyingly large. They occupied a vast area of Central Park, mostly women, a few men scattered among them. It was a warm August day in 1974, and her followers had turned out in force.

Margaret's tone was strong and outright. Her voice didn't falter. Her message came across loud and clear.

She was a tall woman in her early thirties. No make-up decorated her strong radiant face. Her hair was long and black, and she wore denims, boots and love beads.

Margaret Lawrence Brown was a cult figure in America. A ceaseless campaigner for women's rights, she had won many a victory. She had written three books, appeared on television regularly, and made a great deal of money, all of which she used for her organization – FWN – FREE WOMEN NOW.

Everyone had laughed when she'd first taken up the cause of the prostitutes. But they weren't laughing now, not after three months, not after thousands of women appeared to be giving up their chosen profession and following her.

'You've got to get it together NOW!' Margaret yelled, a determined thrust to her chin.

'YEAH!' the women yelled back.

'You're going to live again. You're going to come alive!'

'Yeah! Yeah!' The reaction from the crowd was gospel in its intensity.

'You're going to be FREE!' she promised them.

'YEAH!'

Margaret slumped to the ground while the crowd continued to stamp and shout its approval. Blood spurted from a small, neat hole in the middle of her forehead.

It was minutes before the crowd realized what had happened, before hysteria and panic set in.

Margaret Lawrence Brown had been shot.

The house in Miami could only be approached by passing through electric gates, and then undergoing the scrutiny of two uniformed guards with pistols stuck casually in their belts.

Alio Marcusi passed this scrutiny easily. He was a fat old man, with liquid booze-filled eyes and the walk of a pregnant cat.

As he approached the big house he began humming

softly to himself, uncomfortable in his too-tight grey check suit, sweating from the heat of a cloudless day.

A maid answered his ring at the door. A surly, big-limbed Italian girl, she spoke little English, but she nodded at Alio and told him that Padrone Bassalino was out by the pool.

He patted her on the ass, making his way through the house to the patio which led out to a kidney-shaped swimming pool.

Mary Ann August greeted him. Mary Ann was an exceptionally pretty young woman, with old-fashioned, teased blonde hair, and a curvaceous body exhibited in a skimpy polka-dot bikini.

'Hi, there, Alio,' she said with a giggle, rising from her lounger. 'I was just gonna make myself a little drinkie. Want one?' Posing provocatively in front of him, she toyed with a golden chain hanging between her generous breasts.

Alio contemplated the young vision, licking his lips in anticipation of the day – not far off, surely – when Enzio would grow tired of Mary Ann, and pass her on like all the others.

'Yeah, I'll have a Bacardi, plenty of ice. And some potato chips, mixed nuts, an' a few black olives.' He rubbed his extended stomach sorrowfully. 'I had no time for lunch. Such a busy day. Where's Enzio?'

Mary Ann gestured out towards the never-ending gardens. 'He's around somewhere – pruning his roses I think,' she said sweetly.

'Ah, yes, his roses.' Instinctively Alio glanced back at the house, and sure enough there she was, Rose Bassalino herself, peering out through a narrow chink in her curtains.

Rose, Enzio's wife. She hadn't left her room for years, and the only people she would talk to were her three sons. Rose kept an endless vigil at her window just waiting and watching. It gave Alio the creeps. He didn't know how Enzio endured it.

Mary Ann swayed over to the bar and began preparing drinks. She was nineteen years old and had lived with Enzio Bassalino for almost six months – something of a record, for Enzio never kept them around long.

Settling into a chair Alio slowly closed his eyes. Such a busy day . . .

'Hey, *ciao*, Alio, my friend, my boy. How you feeling?'

Alio awoke with a start, and guiltily jumped up.

Enzio loomed over him. Sixty-nine years old, but with the hard, bronzed body of a man half his age, all his own teeth, a craggy, lined face, topped by a mass of thick steel-grey hair.

'I feel good, Enzio, I feel fine,' Alio said quickly. They clasped hands, patted each other on the back. They were cousins, Alio owed everything he had to Enzio.

'Can I fix you a drinkie, sweetie-pie?' Mary Ann asked, gazing at Enzio adoringly.

'No.' He dismissed her with a look. 'Go in the house. I'll ring if I need you.'

Mary Ann didn't argue, she obeyed him at once. Perhaps that was why she had lasted longer than the others.

As soon as she was gone Enzio turned to his cousin. 'Well?' he asked impatiently.

'It is done,' Alio replied in a low voice. 'I saw it myself. A masterful job. One of Tony's boys, he vanished before anyone knew what happened. I flew straight here.'

Enzio nodded thoughtfully. 'There is no greater satisfaction than a perfect hit. This Tony's boy, pay him an extra thousand an' watch him. A man like that could get himself promoted. A public execution is never easy.'

'No, it's not,' Alio agreed, sucking on a black olive.

*

'She must be thirty,' the woman hissed spitefully.

'Or older,' her friend agreed.

Lined, and over made-up, the two middle-aged women watched Lara Crichton climb out of the Marbella Club pool. Lara was a perfectly beautiful woman of twenty-six. Thin, sun-tanned, with rounded sensual breasts, a mane of sun-streaked hair that only the very rich seem to be able to cultivate, and wide crystal-clear green eyes.

Lara dropped down on the mat next to Prince Alfredo Masserini and sighed loudly. 'I'm getting bored with this place,' she said restlessly. 'Can't we go somewhere else?'

Prince Alfredo sat up. 'Why are you bored?' he demanded. 'Am *I* boring you? Why should you be bored when you are with me?'

Lara sighed again. Yes, the truth of the matter was the Prince could be very boring indeed. But who else was there? She'd made it a rule never to let go of anyone until there was someone else firmly ensconced in his place. She had been through most of the available princes and counts, a few movie stars, and a lord or two. It really was tiresome she had set herself such high standards.

'I don't understand you,' Prince Alfredo complained. 'No woman has ever told me she was bored with me. I am *not* a boring man. I am vibrant, lively. I am – how you say – the life and brains of the party.'

Lara noticed with an even heavier sigh that as he spoke he was getting an erection in his nifty Cerrutti shorts.

'Oh, God, do shut up,' she muttered under her breath. Sex was becoming the biggest bore of all. So predictable, worked out, and mechanical.

Prince Alfredo did not hear her. 'Come, my darling.' Aware of his erection, and proud, he pulled her to her feet. 'First we take a rest,' he winked slyly. 'And then we drive the Ferrari into the mountains. What do you think, my lovely?'

'Whatever you say.' Reluctantly she allowed herself to be led inside. All eyes followed them as they left. They certainly made a beautiful and exciting couple.

They had separate suites, but by unspoken agreement all sexual activity took place in Lara's. She stopped him from entering at the door.

'What's the matter?' he asked indignantly. 'I have a good hard-on – a *very* good one.'

'Save it for later,' she said firmly, closing the door on his protests. 'I'll call you when I wake up.'

Lara felt restless and hemmed in. A feeling she had often felt when married to Jamie P. Crichton. A divorce had solved the feeling then, but what now?

The phone rang and she picked it up, ready to tell Alfredo no – definitely no. But it was not the Prince. The operator informed her it was an urgent call from New York.

'Yes?' She cradled the receiver, wondering who knew she was in Spain.

'Lara? Lara, is that you? Oh God! This is such a terrible connection.' It was a woman's voice, her tone bordering on hysterical.

'Who is this?' Lara asked sharply.

'God! Can't you hear me? Goddamn it – this is Cass.' A pause, then, 'Lara, something terrible has happened. Margaret's been shot. They've shot Margaret.'

CHAPTER 2

Margaret Lawrence Brown was rushed to the nearest hospital. She was still alive, but only barely.

Her loyal followers gathered in tight, silent groups. Only the closest to her were allowed inside the hospital where they waited with as much hope as they could muster. There were no tears, Margaret would have hated that.

Cass Long and Rio Java stood together near the door of the emergency room. A doctor had just announced they were doing a blood transfusion.

Cass was Margaret's personal assistant and confidante. They had met in college and been best friends ever since. Cass was a short, untidy-looking woman, with cropped brown hair and a cheerful disposition. Right now her regular features were frozen in shock.

Rio Java – Margaret's most famous supporter, one of her closest friends, and also a staunch and founder member of FWN – was a far more glamorous figure. Undisputed queen of the underground movies, she was a notorious public personality, fashion freak, mother of four children of various colours, and quite outrageous. Over six feet tall, she was starvation thin, with a long dramatic face, shaved eyebrows and exotic make-up. Part Cherokee Indian and part Louisiana hillbilly, she lived her life exactly as she pleased.

'Where's Dukey?' she asked, groping for a cigarette in her oversize purse.

'He's on his way,' Cass replied. 'And I reached Lara. She's flying in.'

They watched silently as more doctors appeared and

hurried into the emergency room.

'Can I at least *see* her?' Cass pleaded, catching one doctor as he emerged.

'Are you a relative?' he asked sympathetically, noting her blood-soaked dress. She had cradled Margaret's head on her lap until the ambulance arrived, and then travelled to the hospital with her.

'Yes,' Cass lied.

The doctor drew her aside. 'It's not a pretty sight,' he warned.

She bit her lip. 'I know,' she whispered. 'I brought her in.'

The doctor felt sorry for her. 'Well, I suppose if you're a relative,' he said. 'It's against regulations but— all right, come with me.'

Rio nodded at Cass to go ahead, and she followed the doctor into the emergency room.

A team of professionals were doing everything they could. Two catheters were allowing the first pint of blood to be transfused. A tube was at Margaret's nose. A doctor worked at massaging her heart.

Cass felt sick. 'There's not much hope, is there?' she asked, choking back tears.

Grimly the doctor shook his head and led her quietly out.

Rio looked at her. They didn't need words, they both knew.

'Who did it?' Cass demanded, rubbing her eyes. She had been asking the same question ever since the fateful moment in the park when Margaret fell. Margaret had so many enemies, a lot of people hated her because of the causes she fought for. *And* because she led her life exactly as she pleased, and didn't give a damn about criticism or gossip. The man she was currently living with was Dukey K. Williams, a black soul singer

356

with a dubious past. Cass didn't like him. She felt he was using Margaret to get publicity for his sagging career.

Rio dragged deeply on her cigarette. 'Listen – it's no secret Margaret made enemies. It comes with the territory. She knew it.'

'I kept on warning her,' Cass replied mournfully. 'She never listened. Margaret never thought anything through, she just went for it.'

'Ah, yes,' Rio replied. 'But that's what makes her so special, isn't it?'

'I guess,' Cass said, thinking about all the hate mail Margaret received. *'Nigger Lover', 'Commie Bitch'*, and the suchlike. There were also threats to kill her. *'Lawrence Brown. I saw you on the Tonight Show. I hate you. I hope you drop dead. I might kill you myself.'*

These letters were almost a daily occurrence, so mundane as to be casually deposited in the lunatic file and forgotten.

The ones that always worried Cass were the telephone threats. Muffled voices warning Margaret to leave certain causes alone. Recently it had been the matter of the prostitutes. So many had been following Margaret that suddenly the pimps, the madames, and the hoods that controlled it all were getting worried. A dearth of prostitutes, it was becoming an impossible situation, and each time Margaret held one of her open-air rallies, hundreds more vanished overnight, spurred on by the fact that FWN offered them more than words, it offered them a chance of starting afresh. The organization arranged jobs, living accommodation, even money if the need was urgent.

There had been many threats for Margaret to drop the 'Great Hooker Revolution' as *New Month* magazine called it. They had recently featured her on their cover with a six-page story inside. But Margaret had no intention of dropping anything. Margaret Lawrence Brown was fearless when it came to her causes.

Dukey K. Williams rushed to the hospital from a recording session. There was a struggle to get inside, the place was swarming with police, press and television crews.

Dukey, accompanied by his manager and PR, refused any comment as he pushed his way through the mob. At the elevator he was stopped by a security guard who refused to allow him to board.

'Jesus Christ!' Dukey screamed his frustration. 'Get this lowlife outta my way before I fuckin' cream him.'

The guard glared, his hand twitching nervously near his gun.

'Calm down, Dukey.' His manager tried to defuse the situation. 'They're only protecting Margaret. Cass must be up there.'

Cass was sent for, and the guard allowed Dukey and his entourage through.

'Jesus Christ! How did it happen?' Dukey demanded. 'Have they caught the sonofabitch who did it? Will she make it? What the *fuck* is goin' on?'

Sadly Cass shook her head. 'They don't seem to know,' she replied quietly. 'It doesn't look good.'

Rio was at the elevator to meet them. 'Forget it,' she said in a flat, toneless voice. 'Margaret just died.'

CHAPTER 3

Enzio Bassalino was a big and powerful man with huge shoulders and a wide girth. It always amused Mary Ann August when the mood took him to cook dinner. He would clear the kitchen of all the help, tie an apron around his waist, and then go to work cooking spaghetti, his special meat sauce *à la Enzio,* and hearty chunks of garlic bread.

'Honey – you look so *funny* in that apron,' Mary Ann trilled. She was allowed in the kitchen only as long as she promised not to interfere. 'Don't you want little Mama to help you?'

Little Mama was the nickname Enzio called her. She was unaware of the fact it had also been the pet name of every girl before her.

'No.' He shook his head. 'What you can do, little Mama, is you can bring me some more *vino. Pronto!*'

Mary Ann obliged, and then perched on the edge of the kitchen table swinging her long legs back and forth. She was wearing an extremely tight dress cut very low in front. Enzio chose her clothes, and they were always of the same style. She was not allowed to wear pants, shirts or anything casual. Enzio liked her to look sexy.

Mary Ann didn't mind. Life was certainly a lot better with Enzio than it had been before, and she catered to his every need. After all, Enzio Bassalino was a very important man, and she was thrilled and honoured to be with him.

'Taste this.' Proudly he offered her a spoonful of the steaming, rich meat sauce.

Dutifully she opened her mouth. 'Ouch, noonzi, it's hot!' She pouted, 'You've burnt your little Mama . . .'

Enzio roared with laughter. He was celebrating. Tonight he would laugh at anything.

'Sometimes you're really nasty.' Mary Ann lapsed into baby talk. 'Why you so mean to your rickle lickle girlie?'

'Ha!' he said with a snort. 'You don't even know what mean is.' He dipped his finger in the bubbling sauce, licked it approvingly, and added more wine. 'You're a cute girl,' he said condescendingly. 'Stay that way and you'll be all right. OK, little Mama?'

She giggled happily, 'OK, big daddy.'

In his own peculiar way he was quite fond of Mary Ann. She was dumber than most broads, and never asked any questions. She was also stacked just the way he liked, and obliging. Nothing was ever too much trouble.

Enzio hated the usual routine. They moved in, and within weeks they thought they owned you. Broads! They asked questions, got nosy, and sometimes had the nerve to plead a headache when he wanted to make love. Enzio was very proud of the fact that even now, aged sixty-nine, he could still get it up once or twice a week. Often he thought about the times when it was once, twice, or even three or four times a night. What a stud he had been! What a magnificent stallion!

Now it was up to his sons to carry on the Bassalino tradition with women. And he had three of them, three fine young men of whom he was more than proud. They were his life. Through them the name of Bassalino would remain a force to be reckoned with. And when he became old, really old, they would be there to protect him as he had protected them.

It was a good job they had not taken after their mother. Rose was crazy as far as Enzio was concerned, locked up in her room, spying, only speaking to her sons when they visited. She had been there for seventeen years. Ah . . . seventeen years of trying to break his balls, trying to make him feel the guilt.

But her little game hadn't worked with him. He refused to feel guilty about anything. Let *her* be the one to suffer. It was all her fault anyway. What he did was his business, and she had no right ever to interfere.

In his heyday Enzio Bassalino had acquired the nickname of The Bull. This was on account of his habit of mounting every agreeable female who crossed his path. One day, while dallying with the wife of a friend of his known as Vincent the Hog, he'd received his one and only bullet wound. 'Right up the ass,' the story went. 'Vincent the Hog caught them at it and shot him up the ass.'

Fortunately for Enzio that story wasn't strictly true. Vincent the Hog had shot him all right, but the bullet had landed in a fleshy part of his posterior and not caused any real damage. All the same, Enzio was hardly pleased. After the incident Vincent the Hog had suffered a series of mishaps beginning with his house burning down, and ending with him being fished out of the river on the other end of a concrete block.

Enzio did not take kindly to ridicule, and the story of him being shot had caused many an unwelcome snigger.

Shortly after that, he met and married Rose Vacco Morano, the daughter of a friend. She was slim and proud faced, with the fragile Madonna quality of a young Italian virgin. Enzio was smitten the first time he saw her, and wasted no time in asking her to marry him. It didn't take him long to plan an elaborate wedding. Rose wore white lace, and Enzio a shiny black morning suit, white shoes, gloves and a red carnation. He figured he looked pretty dapper.

On their wedding day Rose was just eighteen and Enzio thirty-three.

They became a popular couple, Rose soon shrugging off her quiet upbringing and joining in the more flamboyant life-style of her husband. She had no desire to become a housewife, stay at home and involve herself in cooking, children and church activities. When she dutifully gave birth to their first son, Frank, the baby was left at home with a nanny while Rose continued to spend all her time out and about with Enzio. Rose Bassalino was a woman born before her time.

Enzio didn't mind, in fact he was delighted. His wife was turning into a beautiful, smart woman, and Enzio knew he was much envied. While other men left their wives at home and took their girlfriends to the racetracks, bars and clubs, Enzio brought Rose. She became one of the boys, their friend and confidante, and everyone loved her.

Enzio often marvelled at his luck in finding such a gem. Rose satisfied him in every way, and even found time to present him with a second son, Nick, three years after the birth of Frank.

What a woman! Enzio kept no secrets from her. She knew all about his business activities, and as each year he grew more successful, took over more territory, knocked out more rivals, she was right there helping him. On more than one occasion she was at his side when he dealt out his particular form of justice to people who had double-dealt him. 'My Rose has more balls than most men,' he proudly boasted. 'She's one fine woman.'

Nobody argued.

Rose had many admirers and Enzio knew it. It puffed him up with pride. She was *his* wife, and nothing could change that.

When Angelo, their third son, was born, Rose finally

decided she should spend more time at home. Frank was twelve and Nick nine, and they needed attention. Enzio agreed. There was no point in her accompanying him on the short trips to Chicago and the Coast. Now they had a beautiful mansion on Long Island, and it was only right that Rose should spend more time with the children and enjoy it.

She persuaded him that maybe they should enlarge their circle of friends, as after all, most of the people they saw were involved in the rackets, and Rose thought it might be a good idea to have a different group around for a change. There was an actor and his wife who owned an estate close by, and soon Rose started inviting them over. A banking family came next, and then Charles Cardwell, a cash-poor snob who lingered at the bottom of high society. Gradually Rose surrounded them with new people, until eventually all the old faces were squeezed out.

By the time Enzio decided he didn't like it, it was too late. His business trips became longer, he acquired a small apartment in New York, plus a stream of whorish girlfriends. 'Dumb Heads' he called them. He still adored Rose, but she had changed, and he couldn't understand why.

One night he returned home hours before she expected him. He wanted to surprise her, it was the week of their twenty-first wedding anniversary and he thought they might talk, try to work things out. He wanted to explain how he wasn't happy. Maybe make an attempt to recapture the closeness they'd once shared.

At thirty-nine Rose was still a fiercely attractive woman. Her hair was a thick swirl of bluish black, her dark complexion unlined, and her figure the same girlish shape he had married.

She greeted him coldly. 'I want a divorce,' she said. 'I'm going to marry Charles Cardwell. I know about your apartment, your street whores, and I want to be free of you.'

Enzio listened in amazement. Charles Cardwell was twenty-six years old, his parents had money, but he had a long wait before he inherited a dime.

Enzio was calm. 'Have you slept with him?' he asked. 'Yes,' Rose replied defiantly. She never lied. The woman didn't know what fear was.

Enzio nodded thoughtfully and agreed to her requests. Satisfied, she went to bed.

For a while he sat in his favourite armchair and gazed into space. Eventually he made some phone calls, and later that night Charles Cardwell was brought to the house.

He was a pale young man, obviously shaken and frightened of his escort – four of Enzio's most trusted lieutenants. He smiled weakly at Enzio. 'Now listen—'he began. 'Let me explain—'

Enzio ordered his mouth taped, his arms and legs tied.

They carried him up to Rose's bedroom like a side of beef.

She awoke with a start and stared at the helpless figure of her lover. Then her eyes shifted to Enzio. Despairingly she shook her head, well aware of her husband's brand of justice.

He took her from the bed and held her so she couldn't move, only watch. And then the knives came out.

Charles Cardwell was sliced to death in front of her.

CHAPTER 4

It was not easy for Lara to extract herself from the Prince. They had been together constantly for six months and he was possessive, suspicious, and most of all – hotly jealous.

When she told him she had to leave immediately for New York, he jumped to the only conclusion possible for his mind to reach. 'Who is he? What has he got to offer you that I cannot give you? I *demand* you to tell me his name.'

'It's not a man,' Lara explained patiently. 'It's a family situation.'

'But you have no family, Lara, you always told me that,' he stated petulantly.

She nodded. 'I know, but I do have these distant relatives in America.' A pause. 'I have a half-sister called Beth, and she needs me.'

'A half-sister,' Prince Alfredo shouted. 'You can't just *acquire* a half-sister.' He stamped around angrily. 'I know it's a man, Lara. I know. You cannot lie to me.'

Her mind was on more important things. 'Oh please!' she exclaimed impatiently. 'Think what you like. I have to leave and that's that.'

'Then I will come with you.'

'I don't want you to.'

'I must insist.'

'*No*, Alfredo.'

'*Yes*, Lara.'

They argued some more until at last he left and she was able to finish packing. It was a relief to be rid of him, the man was impossible. Why was she wasting her time?

365

Lara Crichton always got first-class service wherever she went. Young, gorgeous, the ex-wife of one of the richest men in London, she was truly one of what the press referred to as 'the beautiful people'. Constantly featured in the glossy fashion magazines as a shining example of jet-set glamour, she epitomized all that Margaret Lawrence Brown was against.

It would have been a journalistic scoop for someone to discover that they were in fact half-sisters, sharing the same father but having different mothers.

For individual reasons, as each reached personal fame, they felt no need to reveal the fact to anyone. They had been raised in different countries, their whole lives were completely alien to each other. Occasionally they met, and there was a true warmth between them, a love that crossed their very obvious differences. They understood each other and never criticized the other's way of life.

Their father, Jim Lawrence Brown, had never married either of their mothers. Margaret was five when her mother died, and Jim had moved on, taking the child with him to California. There he met a married woman separated from her husband. Jim and Margaret moved in with her, and eventually the woman gave birth to Lara. A year later, when she and her husband decided to get back together, they gave Jim the child and six thousand dollars to move on again. The money tempted him. He didn't argue.

With the cash he bought an old car and trailer, which served as a sort of home. At seven years of age, Margaret was in complete charge of one-year-old Lara.

Jim was a natural drifter, he was always in a dream, playing his guitar, chasing pretty women or sleeping. He drove them to Arizona where they stayed on a farm owned by a widow called Mary Chaucer. She took care of Lara, and insisted Margaret start school. 'The girl is very bright,' she told Jim. 'Advanced for her years. She must have an education.'

After a while Jim began to get restless. He had been far too long in the same place, only now he was tied by two children, and it was a responsibility he wasn't up to. Lara often thought that was why he must have decided to marry Mary Chaucer. She was older than him, a plump, smiling lady, who never complained.

Exactly one month after their marriage, Jim took off, leaving nothing more than a scrawled note telling Mary to look after his kids.

Margaret was nine. She was the one who found his note. It was a coward's note, full of apologies, and five hundred dollars.

Eight months after his departure, Mary gave birth to Jim's third daughter, Beth, a child he never even knew existed.

After that things were different. With no man around, work at the farm became slapdash and unorganized. Mary was always tired and sick. The baby wore her out. Money started to run short, as did the once smiling Mary's temper. Margaret was packed off to boarding school, while Lara was sent to relatives of Mary's in England. They did not see each other again for ten years, by which time Margaret was attending college on a scholarship, and Lara was doing well as a teen model in London.

Beth, now ten, lived with Mary in a small apartment. She went to school while Mary worked.

Margaret wanted to help them, but it was hard enough managing to pay for her own education – an education she was determined to have.

At sixteen Lara was quite beautiful, natural, with none of the polish she later acquired. She was happy living in England, in fact to Margaret she seemed almost completely English – accent and all. They spent a weekend together in New York, and the closeness of their early years was still there.

Time passed and they went their separate, highly individual ways. Occasionally they wrote or phoned. But the need for contact was not there, there was a deeper bond of love and security.

Mary Chaucer died of cancer when Beth was fifteen, and although both her sisters invited her to come and live with them, she preferred a more independent life, and went off to a hippie commune with her boyfriend, Max.

Margaret didn't object. She was already launched on an equality for women project. Her first book *Women – the Unequal Sex* was about to be published. Her star was beginning to shine.

In London Lara met and married Jamie P. Crichton – whose father happened to be one of the richest men in England, and Jamie his only heir. Unfortunately their marriage did not last more than a year, but it was long enough to establish Lara as a personality in her own right. The gossip columns hardly went to press without carrying her picture or some anecdote about what she was wearing, doing, or who she had been seen with. Lara became the darling of life in the fast lane.

The shooting of Margaret Lawrence Brown was headlines, but the photographers still turned out at Kennedy Airport to welcome Lara Crichton.

She posed briefly in her Yves Saint Laurent suit and big hat, her cool green eyes hidden behind fashionably

368

large sun-glasses, Gucci bracelets jangling alongside her black-faced Cartier watch.

'What are you here for, Miss Crichton?' asked an inquisitive reporter.

'Business,' she replied, unsmiling. 'Personal business.'

There was a limousine waiting for her, and with a deep sigh she sat back and tried to relax.

Margaret was dead.

Margaret had been murdered.

Oh, God! Why?

In excruciating detail she remembered her last meeting with her sister. Visiting New York for two days of concentrated shopping, she'd almost skipped phoning her. But then she'd called, and as usual Margaret invited her over. She'd fitted the visit in between lunch at '21' and a hair-streaking session at Vidal's.

Margaret had greeted her clad in her usual outfit of faded jeans and worn shirt. The perennial blue-tinted shades she wore to help her eyesight covered her eyes, and her long hair was unkempt. Naturally she had no make-up on her striking face.

Lara tut-tutted. 'If you bothered,' she said, 'you could look really ravishing.'

Margaret laughed. 'Do you realize how much time you waste plastering yourself with stupid crap?' she asked good-naturedly.

'Don't knock it. I'm getting a directorship of a big make-up company,' Lara said firmly. 'I'll send you a crate of perfumes, lipsticks, glosses, all sorts of things. You'll love it.'

'No way, kid!' Margaret replied. 'You might think *you* need it. But honey-pie – *I* don't give a damn.'

'Well, you should,' Lara said primly.

'Says who?'

'Says me.'

Margaret smiled. She had a wonderful smile, it lit up a room. 'What's happening in your life, baby sister?' she asked, full of warm concern.

Without further prompting Lara launched into a full discussion of what was going on. Margaret fixed her a drink, and they sat down in the cluttered apartment, and she let it all come out. She always did with her sister, it was better than going to an analyst.

Without pause she'd talked about her problems for over an hour. Was Prince Alfredo the one? Should she sell some of her stocks? What did Margaret think of her new emerald ring?

Boring small chat. Looking back, Lara shuddered. She'd never asked Margaret about herself. She'd never even bothered to discuss any of her sister's causes, even though she knew how important they were to her.

How narrow she must have seemed. How selfish and completely involved with herself. And yet Margaret listened patiently as if she had all the time in the world. She always did.

Why was it, Lara thought, that you always found out how much you needed someone just when it was too late?

She stared out of the window as the limousine headed towards the city. Margaret was dead and she intended to find out why.

Somebody was going to pay for her sister's death. She would make sure of that.

370

CHAPTER 5

Beth Lawrence Brown came to New York by train. It was
the first time she had been there. In fact, the first time
she had been anywhere outside the commune which had
been her home since she was fifteen. Now twenty, she
was clear skinned and fair haired, with hair that hung
straight and thick, reaching below her waist. She was a
very pretty girl. Her face had a childlike innocence, with
large blue eyes and a wide soft mouth.

Beth wore her usual outfit, a long dress of Indian
fabric, patched in places, thonged sandals on bare feet,
and many necklaces of thin leather with hand-painted
beads and signs hanging from them. Close to her neck,
almost a choker, there was a thin gold chain with a gold
cross. On the cross were engraved the words LOVE—
PEACE—MARGARET.

The two sisters had been very close – not in terms of
distance, but in the same way that Lara and Margaret
were close, there was a true feeling of unity.

Beth carried with her a large suede, pouchy purse.
In it were her things – a hairbrush, a pair of jeans, a
flimsy blouse, and many books. She didn't believe in
possessions, only books – her passion was reading.

'Wanna buy me a drink, cutie?' A drunk sidled up to
her. 'I'll give ya a lil' action in exchange.'

She ignored him, her expression pensive and thoughtful. Margaret would have told him to fuck off. Lara
would have said what a dreadful little man. How different her two sisters were.

Cass had promised there would be someone to meet
her. She was supposed to wait at the information booth,

but the train was early, and she didn't want to hang around, so she decided to walk to Cass's apartment.

She couldn't believe what had happened. it was inconceivable that Margaret was dead. She was such a good person, so clever and bright and caring. So she was tough, everyone knew that, but how else could she have survived?

She hasn't survived, Beth thought sadly. *My sister is dead.*

Beth had last seen her six months previously. Margaret had arrived to stay for a weekend. Everyone at the commune liked her, in fact they welcomed her visits. She brought all the new books, record albums, and toys for the children – clever toys, not commercial junk. There were ten children living on the farm, and the responsibility of raising them was shared among the five women and eight men who also lived there. One of the children was Beth's, a little girl of four. Max was her father.

Margaret had greeted her niece, Chyna, with special hugs and kisses. 'She's going to grow up to be President one day,' she joked. 'She's so smart, I love it!'

Beth smiled serenely. 'With you to guide her I'm sure anything is possible.'

'Bet on it, kid. When she's ten she's coming to live with me in New York. We'll take it from there.'

Margaret shared in the work over the long weekend. She didn't mind what she did, washing floors, helping with the cooking, gardening. She said it helped her relax. She also found time to sit and talk to Beth, listen to her problems and give advice.

They had a party the night before she left. Great sounds and great hash Max had smuggled in from California. Margaret had gone off with Clasher because he was short and ugly and the least likely to be her choice. Sex was a very free thing at the commune. There were no hang-ups or jealousies. None of the pressures of life in the real world.

When Margaret left the next morning she had given Beth the gold chain, kissed her and whispered softly, 'You're really lucky, you're doing what you want to do, *and* you're happy. You can't ask for anything more, kid.'

And Beth had smiled, a wide, childish smile, and made Margaret promise to come back soon.

'After the summer,' Margaret had said. 'Maybe for Christmas.'

Now the summer was almost ending, and Beth was in New York. She didn't know for how long, but she knew it was where she had to be.

Enzio took the call in his study. He smiled and nodded. Of course things were back to normal. He had been right. His decision was the only way. Semi-retired he might be, but any major problem that had to be taken care of, and he was the one they all turned to.

Frank, his eldest son, had suggested other ways of dealing with the trouble. But what did Frank know? Thirty-six years old, a good businessman, but when it came to decisions his ideas were all soft. What good were threats if you didn't plan to carry them through?

Definite action like the old days was the only way.

Margaret Lawrence Brown had been dead two weeks, and the trouble had stopped. With no one to guide them, no leader to turn to, the hookers were quiet. It was almost as if the killing of Margaret had killed their fighting spirit. Fuck 'em. Goddamn whores.

Slowly, girls who had disappeared, taken other jobs, came drifting back. They seemed oblivious to the beatings and humiliations they faced. They seemed once more defeated.

Enzio was in a buoyant mood. He called up a furrier friend and ordered a full-length chinchilla coat for Mary Ann. It arrived within hours and they celebrated on it. Mary Ann was not quite sure what they were celebrating, but she was a willing partner in anything Enzio wished to do.

'You are my great big Italian lover,' she purred, knowing that he loved praise. 'My big, *big* man.'

'And you are one hot, juicy little broad,' he replied laughingly. 'My favourite tasty slice of lasagne!'

He liked to look at her, the curvy body, big breasts, silky skin and pouty mouth. It would be quite a while before he grew tired of this one.

Oh yeah, Enzio Bassalino knew a good piece when it came his way.

CHAPTER 6

Lola was not the girl's real name. She was thin and scruffy, with city-smoke eyes, and clothes that announced her as the hooker she was. She bit her nails all the time, hungry, addictive little nibbles. Her arms told the story of a heavy drug habit. She was nineteen years old.

Lola had been beaten up. Not badly, a few bruises around her body, cigarette burns on her legs and arms. Just enough to make her aware there was more to come.

She knew all about it. She had known about it before it happened. Lola lived with Charlie Mailer, and Charlie was one of Tony's boys. Charlie had pulled the hit on Margaret Lawrence Brown.

Lola scurried down the street. It was the first time she'd been out since it happened, the first time she'd dared.

She wore a short skirt, summer lace-up boots and a tight sweater. Her hair was untidily long, and her eyes were decorated with spiky eyelashes.

Charlie had kicked her out of bed – 'Get out and earn something, then maybe we'll catch a movie. An' listen, bitch – don't you come back with less than a coupla hundred or I'll fuckin' burn your dumb ass.'

She'd been huddled in bed for two weeks, and Charlie hadn't minded. Flushed with his own success, he was out celebrating. Tony was pleased with him. Tony wanted him around. And Tony was one of the big guys.

Lola knew Charlie was ready to dump her. He was moving up and he didn't want her hanging on.

She didn't care. She knew what she had to do.

A man stopped her, pulling her roughly by the arm. She jerked herself free. 'Not tonight,' she muttered feverishly. 'This girl ain't workin' tonight.'

She hurried on, occasionally glancing behind her, making sure she wasn't followed.

There was a torn piece of newspaper clutched in her hand, with an address circled in red. Stopping for a moment, she peered at it.

'Where ya goin', girlie?' A passing drunk rolled towards her.

'Piss off,' she snapped sharply, hurrying on her way.

When at last she found the circled address, she hesitated before going inside. For a while she hovered on the sidewalk, gazing up at the apartment building, thinking about Susie, her little sister. And then, suddenly she spat angrily on the pavement, and without further ado marched right in.

'I'm here to see uh ... Cass Long,' she told the doorman.

He looked her over, pursed his lips, and indicated the reception desk.

Behind the desk sat a grizzled old man with a sour expression.

'Cass Long,' she said.

'She expectin' ya?'

Lola shook her head. 'No. You'd better tell her it's urgent.'

Leaning forward, his watery eyes stayed fixed to her legs while he buzzed Cass's apartment.

Cass told him to send the girl right up. So many women had been to see her since Margaret's death, she was used to it. She gave them coffee and a chat, and a picture of Margaret inscribed 'Peace – Love'. In a way it was a solace to know how deeply so many people had cared.

Putting down the house phone she said, 'There's another one on the way up. Will you let her in?'

Beth nodded. She'd been there a few days and Cass didn't know how she could have managed without her – Margaret's baby sister had turned out to be strong and loving – a great comfort.

Beth opened the door for Lola, and led her into the kitchen to offer refreshments. She knew by the girl's eyes she was a junkie. Life on the commune had not sheltered her from the harder facts of life.

'I don't want anything,' Lola said restlessly. 'Are you Cass?'

'No,' Beth replied quietly.

'Well like I gotta see Cass. Get her.'

Cass came in then. She looked tired. There were deep purple shadows under her eyes, she was having trouble sleeping.

'I got somethin' t'tell you,' Lola said hastily. 'I don't want no reward, money, pity, nothin' like that. You can see what I am, it's no big secret.' She paused to nibble on a hangnail, realized what she was doing, and stopped. 'Margaret Lawrence Brown gave people hope, she wouldn't have gotten *me* together – I'm nothin' but a loser. Only I had a sister – just a baby. Aw *shit* – I can't even tell you what they did to her.' She paused again, wiping her nose on the back of her hand. 'Anyway – about Margaret. One of Tony's boys made the hit. It don't matter who – he was working on orders – Tony was working on orders too. The big guy who ordered it done was Enzio Bassalino – *he* arranged it – the hit was *all* his.'

'Who's Enzio Bassalino?' Beth asked.

'This big guy prick. He lives in some fancy mansion in Miami. They say he's retired, but believe me – he controls it all. The words to waste her came outta *his* mouth – not out of no gun.'

Cass didn't say anything. Intuition told her the girl was speaking the truth.

'Now I told you, I gotta get outta here.' Lola stood up and scurried towards the door.

'Wait a minute,' Cass said quickly. 'If what you're saying is true, let's get the police in on it.'

Lola laughed harshly. 'Cops. Are you shittin' me? Half of them are in Bassalino's pocket. *Everyone*'s on the take. If you want him you're gonna havta get him yourself.'

'I don't understand,' Beth said.

'Yeah, well think about it. You can do it. You're both clever. You got connections.' Lola shivered, she had more to do. '*I'm* gonna take care of the guy who made the hit. Yeah, I'm *really* gonna look after that motherfucker. He's called Charlie Mailer. Remember

377

his name an' watch the papers, you'll be readin' about him.' She stopped by the door, a forlorn figure. 'Just don't forget who the real murderer is. *Enzio Bassalino*. I admired Margaret Lawrence Brown, an' I wanna be sure you're gonna get that Bassalino bastard.'

'Can't you wait?' Cass pleaded. She wanted to call Dukey or Rio, someone who would understand this whole thing better than she and Beth did.

Lola shook her head. 'I gotta split. I've told you enough.'

Outside it was dark, and Lola headed for Times Square. She didn't have to pull a trick or make a score, but somehow it seemed right that she did.

Stationing herself in the foyer of a movie house she approached the first man going in on his own.

He was middle aged, with a throaty cough. They bargained and then walked briskly to his nearby hotel. He insisted on entering first, alone, and she followed a few minutes later.

His room was small and poky, the bed unmade. Lola began to undress, and the man told her to keep her boots on. He took nothing off, merely unzipped his trousers and shook himself free.

They started to have sex. Lola stared unseeingly at the ceiling. She was calm and detached, she knew exactly what she was going to do.

He finished quickly and Lola took her money and left. She walked slowly home.

Charlie was asleep. She went into the kitchen, stared into the fridge, took out a can of coke, opened it and drank straight from the can. The cold bubbles hurt her throat. Then she reached on top of the fridge groping towards the back where she knew Charlie kept his revolver. Reaching the gun she checked it carefully. It was loaded.

Lola fitted on the silencer. Living with Charlie had taught her a lot about guns.

Walking to the door of the bedroom she called out his name.

Charlie awoke slowly. He sat up rubbing his eyes, and the first thing he saw was Lola pointing a gun at him. 'What the fuck—' he began, leaping from the bed.

She shot him in the leg. The bullet made a satisfying soft thud.

His face was a mask of seething fury mixed with surprise. 'You dumb cunt—' he yelled.

She shot him between the legs, aiming at his crotch.

He screamed out in agonizing pain.

She didn't hesitate. She shot him in the chest, and he fell to the floor with a heavy thud and was finally silent.

Placing the gun down beside him she walked out of the apartment, took the elevator to the forty-seventh floor, and let herself out of the fire exit door to the roof.

Determinedly she walked to the edge, and without stopping hurled herself over.

Lola was impaled on some spiked railings and died in the ambulance on the way to the hospital.

CHAPTER 7

The revenge was Rio's idea. They couldn't kill, they weren't murderers, and anyway the man who pulled the trigger – Charlie Mailer – had been dispatched by Lola with a bullet through the balls. As she'd promised they read about it in the newspapers, *and* about her own sad death.

Rio hired a detective to get them a dossier on Enzio

Bassalino. It turned out he was a bad boy – a Mister Big bad boy. He didn't seem to care about anything or anyone. And yet he had three weaknesses – his three sons, Frank, Nick and Angelo.

If one wanted to hurt Enzio Bassalino, there were three logical ways to go about it.

'It's settled then?' Rio asked. She stared around at the small gathering in Cass's living room. "Cos I don't want *nobody* backing out once we agree. You got it?' She levelled her gaze at Lara. 'No getting bored and hightailing off to some hot-shit jet-set paradise.'

Lara spoke vehemently, her face flushed. 'Listen, Rio, this is no game to me. Margaret was my sister, and different though we may have been, I loved her as much as any one of you.' Her green eyes challenged Rio. 'I know what I have to do, and believe me I'll do it very well.'

'Rio didn't mean anything,' Cass interjected, always one to keep the peace. 'We're all uptight. Who wouldn't be after the last few weeks? Now that it's settled and we've decided what we're going to do, I think we'll all feel easier. I know *I* certainly will.'

Dukey K. Williams stood up, his powerful frame menacing the room. 'Nobody's goddamn listenin' to me,' he complained, 'but believe me – *my* way is the right way.'

'Your way!' Rio scoffed. 'Your way is shit. What do you think? That we can just go up to the dude and say – Oh – good morning Mr Big Boss Man Bassalino, I understand it was you who gave the order to shoot Margaret. Well come on over here Mister Bad Man, for I am going to beat you to a pulp with my big strong hands.' She snorted her disgust. 'Dukey, you're full of it. This guy Bassalino is a big-time capo. If you

380

got anywhere near him you'd get your ass burned good. And even if you *can* get to him – what then? Kill him? Hey man, what's dead? Dead is nothing. Dead is an easy scene. The way we've thought of is the *only* way to really get to the fucker – *the only way.*'

Dukey glared at her. 'Rio, baby, your problem is you live your life between your legs. A little bit of screwin' here, a little bit of ass there. So fuckin' what? These guys have had it all before. Your pussy got a fur lining or somethin'?'

'Fuck you, Dukey. I can make it work,' she said confidently.

'Yeah, *you* probably can. A sex freak like you. Maybe Lara too, I'm not into her whole scene. But Beth? You've gotta be kidding. A baby like her will get mashed up and eaten by the dudes *you're* talkin' about.'

Beth spoke up for herself. 'I can do it,' she said hotly. 'I haven't led such a sheltered life. Besides,' she widened her soft, blue eyes. 'I want to do it. For Margaret.'

'It's settled,' Rio announced. 'Fucking settled. And we start as soon as possible.'

Dukey K. Williams left the meeting shortly after, muttering under his breath. 'Dumb broads. What do they know? Nothin'. Like *nothin.'*'

He climbed into his white Rolls-Royce parked illegally outside Cass's building, angrily shoving a tape into the tape deck. It happened to be *Dukey K. Williams Sings Dukey K. Williams.* The first track was 'Soul, Grit and Margaret'. He had written it for her.

Jesus Christ, what a stubborn woman she'd been. One hell of a wild lady – in bed *and* out. If only she'd listened to him . . .

'Drop it,' he'd warned her time and time again. 'Don't fuck with the big boys. So you save a few hookers, it ain't gonna help. Save a few, lose a few, it's all shit.'

'What's the matter, Dukey? Don't you think hookers deserve saving?' Margaret had asked.

'Hell, honey – if you do get 'em off the streets – before you can say big bucks they'll be back out again.'

'Cynical.'

'Cynical – shit – I'm a realist. Give up, babe, it's a losin' proposition.'

'That's what everyone told me about you.'

'Yeah?'

'Absolutely.'

'So why are you with me?'

'Because I looked beyond the image and I found a man I could relate to. A man who's had his share of tough knocks.'

Margaret understood him better than anyone. She had taken the time to find out why he'd been in trouble in the past, and when he'd told her everything about himself, she'd stayed with him anyway. And it wasn't just sex. The sex was something else, but what really mattered was not so much the physical action – more a clash of two opposite and very strong personalities bound irrevocably together.

'Do me a favour, babe. Forget about saving any more hookers. Trust me – it's too dangerous,' he'd told her.

She had just smiled at him, that warm sexy Margaret smile, and ignored his advice.

He didn't know how it happened, but suddenly he was in the middle. Right in the fuckin' middle. There was money he owed, not a lot by his standards, a couple of hundred thousand. No big deal, he could pick that up on an album, or a couple of weeks doing a gig in some Las Vegas shithouse. But he owed it, and the way things were he just didn't have it on hand to pay back. He'd recently had to pay a giant sum to ex-wife number two, and his other expenses were big and immediate. Dukey K. Williams lived like a real duke would have liked to.

So anyway he owed money to some big boys in Vegas. Of course they knew he was good for it. Lots of stars lost at the tables before their salaries even hit their pockets, there was nothing unusual about that. The situation was under control.

It was no secret when he started going with Margaret Lawrence Brown. In her own way she was as famous as he was. The newspapers and magazines began discussing their relationship as if they were two slabs of prime steak, not human beings with thoughts and feelings.

At first it was tough, but it didn't seem to bother Margaret, and if it didn't bother her, who was he to complain?

Then she got on her kick about saving the hookers. It wasn't enough she had every little housewife across America up in arms and ready for a revolution. No. She wanted the whores. And when Margaret wanted something, she made sure she got it.

Her campaign was slow and clever, and at first people laughed. Save the hookers! For what?

Dukey was also sceptical. He couldn't help admiring her, but even he didn't believe she was *that* powerful.

But that powerful she was. And suddenly people were not laughing any more, and suddenly Dukey began getting a few calls, and suddenly, there he was, right in the fuckin' middle.

'Stop your girlfriend's action and we'll forget about your debt,' was the way the calls started. And as they got heavier and heavier, Dukey tried, *really* tried, to persuade Margaret to stop.

As usual she didn't want to know. Margaret did things her way.

Eventually he paid off his two hundred thousand debt just to get them off his back. He had to borrow the money from a friend out of his past, a narcotics boss named Bosco Sam.

Immediately the threatening calls stopped.

A week later Margaret was shot.

Dukey wanted revenge. He wanted it just as much as Rio and Cass and the two sisters he had known nothing about until after Margaret's murder.

Their plan was not going to work. Their plan was to grab Enzio Bassalino's three sons by the balls sexually and mentally, destroying their lives, and by doing so reduce the old man to a wreck.

Bullshit.

No chance.

Still, Dukey decided he would let them play around until he was ready to put his own plan into action.

Things were getting involved, but he knew it was going to be *his* way in the end.

Rio paced around the apartment. 'Dukey's going to be trouble,' she warned.

'He always has been,' Cass said dryly. 'Why should now be any different?'

'I can't imagine him and Margaret together,' Lara joined in.

'Oh, they were something together,' Rio said. 'Pure electricity. You know Margaret and her men. If they were easy – they bored her.'

No, Lara wanted to say. *I didn't know Margaret and her men. I wish I had*. The truth was, she hadn't really known anything about Margaret's personal life, because she was always too busy talking about herself.

She glanced over at Beth, the other sister she didn't know at all. Silently she vowed to make up for the past. She wanted to get to know Beth properly.

'Well.' Rio stood up. 'I gotta make tracks. Four starving kids are waitin' for mama's presence.'

'How old are your children?' Beth asked.

'Old enough to drive me *crazeee*!'

Cass stood up too. The meeting was over. The decision was made.

Soon revenge would be theirs.

CHAPTER 8

Tall and good looking, Nick Bassalino was the perfect Italian-American boy. Fine white teeth, often exposed in a ready smile, warm brown eyes, and longish black hair, slightly curling. He was thirty-three and favoured black Italian suits, silk shirts, handmade shoes. Nothing but the best for Nick Bassalino.

He lived in style in a large house high above the lights of Hollywood. Not an actor, he'd had many offers because of his almost unbelievable good looks. It was only on close scrutiny that you might suspect his nose was fixed – it wasn't. His teeth capped – they weren't. And his jet-black hair slightly helped along by a bottle of dye – it wasn't.

Nick headed an import/export company called Warehousing Incorporated. It was the biggest outfit of its kind on the West Coast and Nick was the boss.

When your father was Enzio Bassalino you certainly didn't start at the bottom.

Nick's current lady-friend was April Crawford, an

ageing movie star with four husbands behind her. The starlets and ding-a-lings were not for Nick. He liked to command a little respect when he went out, and in Hollywood the surest way of doing that was to be seen with a movie star.

They had been together a year. The arrangement suited both their public images. It pleased April that Nick had his own money and didn't free-load off her. He looked good, wasn't too young – not a baby – nothing to make a laughing stock of her. He got along with her friends – and of course – most important as far as April was concerned – he was sensational in bed. Pure stud all the way.

As for Nick, he enjoyed the respectability of being with April, mixing with the movie colony, and seeing his picture in the fan magazines. April brought a little class into his life.

The one thing he didn't understand was why Enzio objected to the relationship so strongly. His father was always phoning him and complaining. 'What's with you and the old bag? What's goin' on, Nick? You're making the name Bassalino a joke.'

'Better I should be with a piece of beautiful, dumb eighteen-year-old cooze, I suppose,' Nick would reply dourly.

'Yeah. Why not? Is it so terrible to have a pretty face, firm tits, a piece other men want – but you've got? Huh?'

'You just don't know . . .' Nick would say, tired of the same old argument.

'So I don't know, big fuckin' deal. Only I haven't done too bad for an old man who don't know. An' *you* haven't done too bad by being my son.'

'All right, all right. Forget it. I'll send you a greetings cable when we break up. You can go out an' celebrate.'

386

'Schmuck!' Enzio would mutter, and they both ended up laughing. It was a weekly conversation.

The two of them had a relationship based on love, the fierce, proud love that binds an Italian family.

Whatever Enzio had done in his life, and he'd done plenty, he knew he had always been a good father to his boys. In spite of their mother's ill health (he always referred to Rose's madness as ill health), he'd brought them up to be fine men. Nick was doing a good job of running Warehousing Incorporated. He was tough, people thought twice about messing with him. Yes, Nick was a true son of Enzio Bassalino.

'Are you ready yet, darling?' April Crawford approached Nick in his dressing-room. They had separate houses, but on weekends April liked him to stay with her.

April Crawford was a well-preserved blonde in her early fifties. She was petite, slim, perfectly groomed and made up. From a distance she looked late thirties, but up close tired little lines and a faint puffiness gave her secrets away.

'I'm always ready for you, sugar,' Nick said cheerfully, grabbing her, making her squeal with pleasure.

He had been eight years old when he'd seen her on the screen for the first time and fallen in love.

'I think we should arrive early tonight,' April said. After four husbands and numerous lovers she had never experienced such delights as Nick Bassalino had to offer.

'You're the boss.'

'I wish we didn't have to go at all. Perhaps if I phoned Janine she'd understand . . .'

'She will *not* understand,' he said firmly. 'We're gonna go. We're both dressed and you look great – like a little doll.' He had no intention of missing Janine Jameson's party. She was a contemporary of April's, and equally famous.

They rode to the party in Nick's black Mercedes. April wore a pale blue sequin dress. Some of the sequins came off and stuck to his clothes. He picked them off impatiently.

'Don't lean on me in that dress,' he warned. He always liked to look immaculate.

'You're so fussy,' she laughed gaily. 'But I love you all the same.'

At the party there were plenty of familiar faces, stars, directors, producers. Nick basked in the company. He loved show business.

A busty starlet approached him at the bar as he was ordering April a drink. They had made out once or twice, long before he met April.

'How's it going, Nicky Ticky?' the girl asked, thrusting her well-developed bosom towards him. 'Getting fed up with grandma yet? 'Cos you know any time you do, I'll be glad to hear from you.'

'Hey babe, what you gonna do when your tits drop?' he asked with a not-so-cavalier wink. 'Better stop hustling an' take yourself a typing course, 'cos it don't look to me like it's gonna be too long.'

'Cocksucker!' the girl muttered, furious.

'Excuse me, I have a *lady* waiting,' Nick said amiably.

April didn't carry her liquor well. After two Scotches her speech started to slur, and shortly after that her walk became lopsided and her face went slack. In short, she fell to pieces.

It irritated Nick. He didn't drink much himself, in his business it paid to be alert, so he usually stuck to plain club soda. He was always warning April to cut her intake. That's why he tried to mix her drinks himself, carefully watering them down. But she was on to him, and usually grabbed a fresh drink from every passing waiter.

Janine Jameson's party was no exception and April was soon rolling in the aisles. Nick knew from past experience to keep his distance. Drunk, April became belligerent and insulting. A real pain in the ass.

He was talking to a lady gossip-writer when he first saw the girl. She was standing by the bar with a group of people. She was of medium height with golden tanned skin, and a mane of auburn sun-streaked hair. She had an exquisite body clad in a clinging long white dress, slit high. She was about the most spectacular looking woman he'd ever seen – and in his time he'd seen a few.

'Who is *that*?' he couldn't help asking.

The lady gossip-writer smiled. A crisp, bitchy smile. 'Better not let April hear the hard-on in your voice,' she warned. 'The lady is Lara Crichton, one of those poor little rich girls whose picture is always in the fashion magazines.'

He quickly changed the subject.

Lara spotted him immediately. After all she had pictures of him, a short dossier on his life, and she knew all about his relationship with April Crawford.

After observing him across the room she angled herself at the bar, so that when he glanced up, she was directly in his line of vision.

When he first spotted her he did a classic double-take.

First part – easy – but then the initial impact had always been easy for Lara. Ever since she could remember men had noticed her. Even when she was a small girl of seven and been sent to London she had attracted attention. Very pretty, she'd had no trouble charming the childless couple she was staying with. They worshipped her, and although they didn't have much money, they lavished everything they could on her.

Lara soon grew used to attention, and as she developed and grew, she certainly received more than her fair share.

At fourteen she left school to study dancing, diction and movement. She entered a charm competition in a magazine and won. The prize was a free modelling course at a reputable school, where she was discovered by the best model agent in London, and shortly after became a successful teen model.

Photographers loved her, she had a chameleon quality essential for a good model. With no trouble at all she could look girlish, sophisticated, sexy, even plain. It was a matter of expression, and Lara mastered the art.

Her work was the most important part of her life. She dieted, exercised, ate health foods and slept at least eight hours every night. Dates were unimportant, work was all consuming.

Soon her incredible beauty deepened and bloomed, and she began to add polish to the diamond. She started to go out with specially selected men. One who could teach her about wine, another about racing, and yet another about baccarat, *chemin de fer* and *21*.

She refused to sleep with any of them, although they all tried. She hadn't found the man to teach her about sex.

A week after her twentieth birthday she met Jamie P. Crichton, and knew at once that this was the man she was destined to marry. Jamie had already inherited a trust fund worth several million pounds, and there was plenty more to come. He was young, good looking and arrogant. He was also surrounded by girls, and although his initial reaction to her was predictable, she knew that if she wasn't very careful she could sink without a trace into the sea of females around him.

So she played it very smart, refusing to go out with him at all. Instead she cultivated his friends. Everywhere Jamie went, she was bound to be.

His best friend, Eddie Stephen Keys, fell madly in love with her and proposed. Lara wasn't prepared to settle for anything less than her original choice.

It took several months for her to get through to Jamie. And then suddenly one day he knew, and that was that. He chartered a jet, they got married in Tahiti, and the world press embraced them as the latest Beautiful Couple.

Their marriage lasted exactly one year. A year during which Lara became a celebrity.

Then just as suddenly it was over, they both wanted a divorce. They were equally bored by the restrictions of marriage, and the drudgery of being with each other all the time.

It was a friendly parting of the ways. Jamie agreed to pay her a generous settlement, and she took off for Mexico where she got a quick divorce, and then on to Acapulco where she met her first Italian prince.

Since that time Lara had moved around. All the best places at the best times with the best men. It was only when Margaret was shot that she finally stopped to think. What was she doing with her life? Why was it so important to be in the right place at the right time with the right man? Why did she constantly seek out hedonistic boring escorts who could offer her nothing but money? Was it *that* exciting to be photographed at every airport? Quoted in every empty fashion magazine?

And why did she need to travel down the Nile? Safari in Africa? Ski in Gstaad? And summer in Sardinia?

On reflection it all seemed such an empty life. The death of Margaret, travelling to New York and spending time with Margaret's friends and her sister Beth, had finally made her realize this.

Now her mind was made up. She was determined to help avenge Margaret's death.

Nick Bassalino was the perfect opportunity. And soon he would be all hers.

Lara had been brought to the party by Jeanette and Leslie Larson, a young couple whose only claim to fame was that Les's mother was one of the richest women in the world. Lara had arrived in LA several days before. She was staying with the Larsons as their house guest, and they were thrilled to have her. Within a week she knew she'd get to meet Nick Bassalino, for April Crawford was known to be an avid party-goer. Running into him so soon was pure luck.

She pointed him out to Jeanette. 'Who's that man?' she asked casually.

'I guess you mean Nick,' Jeanette replied with a knowing laugh. 'He's April Crawford's boyfriend, and he's *strictly* not up for grabs. The guy is crazy about her, follows her around like a nanny. Why? Do you think he's attractive?'

'Is he an actor?' Lara asked, countering the question.

'No, he's some sort of hustler, wheeler-dealer. Les says he's a hood.' Jeanette giggled. 'You *do* find him attractive, don't you?'

'Not really.' She faked a yawn. 'A bit too obvious. All tight trousers and teeth.'

Jeanette nodded. 'Anyway, as I said, he's well taken care of, and let's face it, darling, hardly your style.'

Lara wondered exactly what Jeanette thought her style was.

The party was a bore, but Lara knew that somehow she had to meet Nick. Sammy Albert, an actor with the reputation of super stud, was busily trying to persuade her to split and go to a club called The Discotheque. She'd told him no three times, but he was enamoured, and continued to follow her around trying to get her to change her mind.

'Do you know April Crawford?' she asked at last. 'I'd love to meet her.'

'Do I know April! I've had her!' Sammy joked, taking her over and introducing her.

April's eyes were bloodshot, her lipstick smeared. 'Hello, dear,' she said icily. Competition was not her favourite thing.

Lara turned on the charm and flattered the movie star as she steered the conversation to a mutual friend who lived in Rome.

Suddenly Nick appeared. Deftly removing the too-full glass from April's hand, which was slopping on her dress, he replaced it with a half-full one.

'Do you know Nick Bassalino?' April asked, patting him fondly. 'This is Lara – Lara . . .'

'Crichton,' Lara said, gazing directly at him as she accepted his firm handshake with an equally warm pressure of her own. The man was too handsome for his own good.

He had brown eyes, friendly and open. 'Glad to meet you,' he said.

Want to bet? she thought.

'Why don't we go to The Discotheque?' Sammy asked yet again. 'April? Nick? Maybe one of you can persuade Lara to come too.'

'Wonderful idea,' April said gaily. 'I feel like dancing, and Janine's parties – dear girl that she is – do get rather stuffy.'

'Will you come?' Sammy asked Lara.

She nodded. 'I'd better tell Les and Jeanette.'

'How about that?' Sammy said, watching her walk away. 'Is she something or *what*?'

April laughed. 'Sammy darling, every time you meet a new girl it's always a grand love affair for about a minute and a half.'

'Just give me a minute and a half with this one and I'll be happy for ever!'

When Lara returned, they left. She went with Sammy in his Maserati, while April and Nick followed in the Mercedes.

'I could easily lose them,' Sammy said, placing an amorous hand on her knee. 'We could go by my place and pick up some outasight grass. Huh? What do you say?'

Lara removed his hot hand. 'I gave it up,' she replied coolly.

Sammy was speechless. He received thousands of fan letters a week from girls merely wanting to touch him, and this one didn't even care to go with him to his house. It had been a long time between turn-downs.

The Discotheque was crowded as usual, but a table was soon cleared for Sammy Albert and April Crawford. Movie stars always got premium treatment, it was one of the fringe benefits of being famous.

April ordered a double Scotch, and immediately dragged Sammy on to the tightly packed dance floor.

'They're old friends,' Nick said, feeling the need to explain. 'Sammy got his first break in one of April's films.'

Lara smiled. 'It doesn't bother me if it doesn't bother you.'

'Hell, I don't care. I like April to enjoy herself, it does her good. She's a great little gal, got a lot of energy, a real tiger!'

Lara looked at him intently to see if he was putting her on, but he didn't appear to be. He was watching April on the dance floor, a proud smile on his face.

'You and Sammy must be about the same age,' she remarked.

He knew what she was getting at. 'I don't know.' He shrugged. 'Who cares about age? You know something? April's got more energy in her little finger than I have in my whole body.'

April this, and April that. Nick Bassalino was not going to be quite as easy to crack as she'd imagined. She was used to men falling about – married, single, it made no difference. One of Lara's famous quotes – printed all over the world – was 'most men are easy lays'. She had always found that if there was a man she wanted, he was to be had.

Not that there had been that many. There was the count, he had lasted two years. Then the film star, only a few short months. After him the German prince, a year. And then the English lord, a mere eighteen months. The Greek shipowner had lasted nearly a year. And finally Prince Alfredo Masserini. She had thought that perhaps Alfredo was the right one. He had the film star's looks, the Greek shipowner's money, the English lord's youth, and the count's charm. But in spite of it all he'd turned out to be a self-centred egoist. *Like me*, she thought, with a short brittle laugh.

'What are you laughing at?' Nick asked curiously, trying to keep his eyes off her cleavage.

'Nothing that would amuse you.' She shook her head in a languid, sexual fashion, so that her long, thick hair swirled forward.

He glanced at her quickly. This woman was incredibly beautiful. But what was beauty in a town like Hollywood? So many girls, so many different shades of sexy, pretty and gorgeous. So many different shapes and sizes. Something to appeal to everyone. In Hollywood beauty was a commodity, a close relation of the hard sell.

April Crawford was something else. April was class, and distinction and acceptance. April was a ticket to ride up there among all the movie idols he'd worshipped since he was a little kid.

Oh no, he wasn't going to blow April out for a quick dip in this one's honey pot. April was a jealous lady, sharp, and full of pride. If she ever caught him straying the shit would really hit in no uncertain fashion.

'I hope you're coming to the party Jeanette and Les are throwing for me tomorrow night,' Lara said casually.

'April makes all our social arrangements. If she knows about it we'll be there. My lady hates missing a party.'

Lara smiled and widened her eyes. 'Great,' she murmured.

What a schmuck this guy was – he was going to be easy.

CHAPTER 9

Frank Bassalino was Enzio's eldest son, and Enzio depended on him more than the others, for when he had opted for semi-retirement, it was Frank who took over some of his more important business enterprises.

'One day,' Enzio was proud of saying, 'Frank is going to be the Man. One day not so far off.'

Frank got along well with Enzio's older business associates. They were difficult men, quick to criticize, but he was managing to create a connection.

In some ways Frank was stronger than Enzio. Born in one of the tougher districts of New York, he'd always had to fight for what he wanted, in spite of his father's position.

Frank was not a man to cross. Thirty-six years old, he had worked for Enzio since he was sixteen and seen all aspects of his business. He had been involved in protection, prostitutes, dope, the numbers racket, hoisting. Once he had enjoyed being the hit man, but Enzio didn't approve. It was too risky and dangerous.

In his time Frank had been a womanizer in the true Bassalino tradition, going through an incredible amount of females – used and thrown away like so many old Kleenex. Until, at the age of twenty-nine, he had seen a picture of Anna Maria, his cousin in Sicily, and immediately sent for her. She was fourteen years old and spoke no English. Enzio paid her family a dowry and arranged everything. When she arrived in America, Frank married her.

Like father like son. Both men had opted for a partner from the old country. Although unlike Rose, Anna Maria was timid and quiet. At twenty-one she still didn't speak much English.

Frank and Anna Maria lived in an old brownstone house in Queens with their four children, and she was expecting another.

Frank didn't stray much now. The occasional hooker he could beat up was about his only weakness.

When the time came to put the revenge plan in action, Rio said she wanted a shot at Frank Bassalino. She was outvoted. According to the extensive dossier they'd managed to get on him, she wasn't his scene, not his style at all. No, they all decided, the only chance with a man like Frank Bassalino was someone fresh and innocent. A girl who would remind him of his wife when he'd first brought her to America. Beth was the obvious choice.

It turned out there was the perfect opportunity. Frank was looking for a nanny to teach his children English. He had registered with three employment agencies, and turned down all the applicants who were mostly black or Mexican. It was decided Beth should apply for the job.

She changed her hippie clothes and put on a plain blouse and skirt. Then, with her pale hair tied back, simple outfit and false references, she showed up at his house for an interview.

A maid showed her into an old-fashioned living room. The furniture was worn, and there were many religious pictures on the walls. Beth glanced around, her heart racing with anticipation.

She waited for over half an hour, and then Frank Bassalino strode into the room with Anna Maria hovering behind him.

He was a powerful looking man with black hair, hooded dark eyes, a moody mouth and beaky nose. He was attractive in a brutal way.

Beth loathed him on sight. She knew men like him, big violent men who resented any change. Men whose physical strength was their prime weapon.

With an involuntary shudder she remembered the time at the commune when men like Frank Bassalino had come calling in the middle of the night. There were eight or nine of them, and they were drunk.

The band of drunken louts had roared up in two cars, laughing and swigging from bottles of booze. The farm was situated well off the main road. There were no neighbours, no one to whom they could run for help.

The front door wasn't locked, and the men had burst drunkenly in, kicking the old sheepdog, Shep, until he was a beaten pulp. Then they had dragged the girls out of bed and raped them one by one, while the boys were roughed up, laughingly, methodically. The men had jeered, and called them names, told them to get a haircut and a job and stop piss-assing around.

It was no match. The men were big and strong and filled with the righteous power of do-gooders.

'If you were my daughter,' one of them had hissed in Beth's ear as he'd pumped away inside her, 'I'd tan your hide until you couldn't walk for a week.'

Before leaving they'd cut the boys' hair – crudely hacking away with a rusty pair of kitchen scissors. Max had needed seventeen stitches in his scalp.

This outrage had taken place two years before, yet Beth still slept unsoundly, still felt revulsion when faced with a man like Frank.

'Hmmm.' He looked her over. 'You're kinda young, huh?'

'I'm twenty,' she replied. 'I've been working with children for the last three years. Did you read my references?'

He was surprised to see such a young and pretty girl. It was almost too good to be true after some of the garbage the agency had sent him. His kids would love this one, she looked so clean and nice.

There was no point in playing games. 'Listen, you want the job—it's yours. You get your own room, decent food, and a coupla nights off a week. OK?'

She nodded. Was it all going to be as easy as this? 'Can I meet the children?' she asked.

'Sure. Hey – Anna Maria.' He pulled his wife forward, a shy, dark girl with puffy features and a huge belly. 'You take – uh – what's your name again?'

'Beth.'

'Yeah, yeah. Beth, meet Mrs Bassalino – my wife. She don't talk much English – maybe you can teach her too. She'll take you to see the kids, show you around. Any problems you come to me. Just remember, I'm a busy man, so make sure there ain't too many problems. Got it? When can you start?'

Her heart was pounding. 'Tomorrow,' she said, hiding her excitement.

'Good girl. Anna Maria's about to pop any time now. Some help around here is just what we need.'

He gave Anna Maria a shove in her direction, looked Beth over one more time, and left.

CHAPTER 10

Angelo Bassalino had been sent to London after the trouble. It was only a temporary move, a discreet way of getting rid of him until the Camparo family calmed down. Gina Camparo was to be married soon, and after the ceremony – a few months perhaps – then the whole incident would be forgotten and Angelo could be brought safely home.

Enzio had been somewhat amused by the whole affair. Angelo was his true son, a boy who let nothing stand in the way of his fine upstanding Bassalino prick.

But it had been a touchy situation, and if Angelo had not been Enzio's son he might have found himself lodging inside a block of cement at the bottom of the East River. To screw a girl was one thing, but not at her engagement party to another man, and not where her brother and fiancé could discover you. And not when the girl was the daughter of a powerful rival – albeit a friendly one.

So Angelo was dispatched to London. There were gambling interests he could take care of there, and without too much effort Enzio arranged everything.

Angelo was not up to his expectations businesswise. The boy had none of the Bassalino drive or ambition. He had no hard core of toughness to call upon when dealing with people.

Enzio reasoned that Angelo was only twenty-four, a baby, he had plenty of time to wise up. But he also remembered himself at twenty-four, a veteran of six successful hits, already Crazy Marco's right-hand man, a man with a big future ahead of him.

In New York, Angelo had worked for Frank.

'He's a lazy little punk,' Frank constantly complained. 'You send him to a joint to shake loose some tight cash, and you havta send another guy chasing *him* 'cos he's shacked up with some broad. Cooze, that's all he's got on his mind.'

Enzio tried sending him out to the Coast to work for Nick, but that was even worse. Angelo fell for a sexy starlet, and ended up getting his ass beaten off by her 'producer'.

'You'd better get yourself together in London,' Enzio warned him. 'A Bassalino should command respect. Screw around all you want, but you gotta remember – *work* is the important thing – an' *money*. There's solid opportunities for setting up over there, an' one of these days I wanna see you control our end of it. To begin with, you work with the Stevesto organization – they'll show you around.'

Angelo had shrugged. He didn't care about making money – as long as there was plenty in the family, why did he have to work his butt off scoring more? It didn't make sense. Let Frank and Nick keep the Bassalino respect going – the, enjoyed it, he didn't.

But he didn't argue with his father. Nobody argued with Enzio. There had been a time when he had expressed a wish not to go into the family 'business'. He'd wanted to be an actor, or maybe a musician. At sixteen those were his ambitions. When Enzio found out about it he'd beaten him with a leather strap and locked him in his room for a week. Angelo never mentioned it again.

London was a fine town, as Angelo soon discovered. Lots of pretty girls, and friendly people. A person could walk the streets without fear of getting beaten up and robbed.

An apartment had been arranged for him, and he went to work for the Stevesto set-up. It was easy potatoes, all he had to do was keep his eye on a couple of casinos, and begin getting the hang of things.

Angelo was happy. He could have a different girl every week if he felt like it, and he did feel like it. He had to have sex every day, it was a habit – like morning coffee or doing push-ups – a habit he enjoyed excelling at.

Angelo was not tall and muscular like his brothers. He was slighter in build, almost skinny. And his face was more angular, with high cheekbones. He liked to wear his hair thick and long – a minor freak-out – and sometimes he featured a Che moustache and stubbly beard.

'You look like a fuckin' Commie,' Enzio was always screaming at him. 'Jesus! Whyn't you cut off that hair, buy some decent clothes – a suit maybe. You look like shit. Why can't you be like your brothers?'

Fuck his brothers. Angelo kept his personal appearance exactly as he wanted. It was about the only way

402

he could spit in his father's eye without doing too much damage.

The full contingent of English press turned out at Heathrow Airport to meet Rio Java. Her reputation always preceded her.

She stepped off the plane in an outlandish pink catsuit, trailing a full-length leopard-skin coat over one arm.

'Hi boys,' she greeted the army of photographers. 'What do you want me to do?'

What *didn't* they want her to do. Rio Java was always good for a front page picture.

She had been making headlines for years. A heroin addict at eighteen, Rio had first been discovered in a re-hab centre by the very famous avant-garde film maker – Billy Express, who was making a movie about drugs called *Turn On/Turn Off*. His intrusive camera followed her every move as she was given the treatment – the cure. He didn't miss a thing, and the result was instant stardom. It wasn't long before she moved into his life permanently, gave birth to his baby (an event he filmed in loving if somewhat lurid detail) and starred in all his future projects. Billy Express was extremely successful and very very rich. The more pornographic of his movies had made him a fortune.

Rio lived with Billy and his entourage in an elegant New York brownstone he shared with his mother. It was not the ideal arrangement, but his mother – a former Ziegfeld girl – came with the package.

Rio felt she owed Billy a lot. He was responsible for making her a celebrity, and she loved every minute of her notoriety. Off heroin, she had no objections to joining Billy, his friends *and* his mother on their constant LSD trips. One memorable night she found herself sharing Billy's bed with his Chinese boyfriend, Lei. It amused Billy to have them make it together while he filmed their love-making. The result was Rio became pregnant again, and Billy was delighted. He loved children, and lost no time in having the top floor of his house redecorated as a nursery, just in time for the birth of Rio's twins – two tiny Chinese boys.

They were all happy. Billy, his bizarre mother, Lei, the children, the entourage. They made their movies, threw outrageous parties and existed in a sort of delicious, stoned vacuum.

Until one day Rio met Larry Bolding. He was a very straight married senator in his mid-forties. He came to one of Billy's parties, and Rio took one look at the sun-tanned face, the suit, the honest eyes and flipped out. There was something about Larry Bolding that attracted her with a passion.

'I *have* to have him,' she whispered to Billy.

'No problem,' he replied easily – jealousy was an unknown emotion to Billy. He selected a pill from his pocket. 'Slip this in his drink and he's all yours.'

In a rare moment of clarity Rio decided against spiking the Senator's drink. She wanted him without having to resort to drugs. She wanted *him* to want *her*.

Larry Bolding had a politician's smile and a very direct gaze. Rio went to work. She was no slouch when it came to seduction.

It took some time to get him to a bedroom. More time to get him undressed. He was so sweet! He actually wore patterned jockey shorts and an undershirt.

Rio launched into her specialities. He was more interested in straight screwing.

It was the start of a six-month affair. An affair that had to be kept secret, due to the fact he was a married man.

Rio understood. He gave the age-old story about how he and his wife just stayed together for appearances, and worldly as she was, she believed him.

After a few week she told Billy she couldn't sleep with him any more. In fact, because Larry didn't approve of her set-up, she moved out, and took an apartment in the Village. It was more convenient for Larry, more private.

Billy gave her a generous allowance, and kept the children with him, because they both agreed it was for the best. She visited them every other day.

Eventually Billy decided he wanted her to do a new movie he'd written. After all – she was his superstar.

Larry Bolding said he didn't want her to do it. He preferred to keep her always available as he never knew when he could see her.

'The guy is an asshole,' Billy warned. 'He's going to ruin you.'

But Rio was in love and didn't listen. Instead she turned very straight for Larry, doing everything he told her to. She gave up drugs, drinking, parties, no screwing (except for him), no outlandish make-up, and no weird clothes.

Larry's visits grew fewer and fewer. Eventually they stopped altogether.

Rio was destroyed. In vain she tried to contact him, but the barriers were up. There was no way of getting past the many secretaries and aides. Absolutely no way of letting him know she was pregnant with his child.

When she finally realized she'd been used, it hurt more than she ever thought possible. One gloomy Saturday night she slashed her wrists and fortunately was found by a neighbour. The neighbour turned out to be Margaret Lawrence Brown.

It took Rio a long time to get over the way Larry Bolding had treated her. She developed a deep resentment for the way women allowed themselves to be used by men. Especially married men.

She listened to Margaret, and her words made sense. Why waste time brooding about the past when the future was all that really mattered?

Without him ever knowing she gave birth to Larry Bolding's baby – a little girl. Billy Express suggested she move back in with him and her other children. It wasn't the way she wanted to live any more, and she told him. She also told him she wanted her children to come and live with her. Billy said no, they would stay with him.

This clash of wills resulted in a long-drawn-out court battle which Rio finally won. She got her children back in spite of the abuse Billy Express publicly hurled at her. He was enraged.

They all stood up in the witness box and testified about what a bad mother she was, every one of her so-called friends, the entourage, and Billy's mother.

Margaret Lawrence Brown testified on her behalf, and in the end she got her children.

It was a juicy court case. The newspapers and gossips loved every minute of it.

Afterwards, Rio was inundated with film scripts. Everyone had a project she would be perfect for.

Soon she started to work again and never looked back.

Now she was in London and she was there for one purpose only.

Angelo Bassalino and the revenge.

She would destroy him as only she knew how.

CHAPTER 11

Old friends though they were, Bosco Sam wanted his money back, with interest, and Dukey K. Williams just didn't have it.

Dukey was hanging around in New York, still living in the apartment he had shared with Margaret, brooding about her murder.

'Come on, man, you gotta get back in action,' his manager pleaded daily.

'Cancel everything,' Dukey told him. 'I'm gonna sit still a while, an' get my head straight.' The shooting of Margaret had left a deep void in his life. He couldn't come to terms with her death.

He cancelled all his work dates, a European tour, and a recording session for a new album.

Several promoters threatened law suits.

Dukey didn't care. 'Fuck 'em,' was his only comment. He was not making any money, and the royalties coming in from record sales were going straight into the pocket of ex-wife number one and two 'ex-children'. He called them ex-children because his wife – the redheaded bitch – had obtained a court order forbidding him to see them.

Bosco Sam was not prepared to give up. 'I want my money,' he said, his tone becoming more threatening as each day passed. 'If it was anyone but you, Dukey . . .'

They had struggled through school together, known each other a long time.

'Let's meet,' Dukey suggested, thinking fast. 'Maybe we can cut a deal.'

'Yeah, let's do that.' An ominous pause. 'While you're still alive.'

They met at the zoo. Bosco Sam had a thing about privacy, he made sure that all his important meetings took place in public venues.

'I'll probably get mobbed,' Dukey complained. But it was a crisp October morning, and the Central Park zoo was almost deserted.

They were hardly an inconspicuous pair. Dukey in his calf-length, belted mink trench coat, boots, and huge shades. And Bosco Sam, a camel-hair-coated, three-hundred-pound man with an attitude problem.

'Fuckin' park,' Bosco Sam complained. 'Only place a deal can get it on any more.'

'Here's the action,' Dukey said, as they strolled in front of the monkeys. 'Word's on the street you're about ready to dance with the Crowns. You and them make sweet soul music while Frank Bassalino gets the short ones plucked. Beautiful. No sweat. But how would it grab you if *I* did the plucking? Frank, the brothers, Enzio. The whole Bassalino bag of shit.'

'You?' Bosco Sam said, starting to laugh.

'Jesus! You sound like an elephant farting!'

Bosco Sam heaved with even more laughter.

'Listen, man,' Dukey continued. 'I ain't layin' no shit on you, you hear me talkin'? I'm serious. For the two hundred thou – you're out of it. Your hands are clean. There'll be no heat knockin' on *your* door. Nobody's gonna know 'bout our little deal 'cept you an' me. Am I reachin' you, bro?'

'Yeah,' said Bosco Sam thoughtfully. 'Yeah . . .'

'It'll be cool. Keep up the pressure 'til it blows. An' you with a powdered fuckin' ass nobody can suspect.'

Bosco Sam started to laugh. 'You still cut it. Big fuckin' star, but you still foxy as Puerto Rican tail!'

408

'Hey – I'll throw in a song or two at your daughter's wedding.'

'The kid's only ten.'

'So I'll be around when I'm needed. How about it? We all set to jive or what?'

'Yeah, I'll give you a shot at it. Why the fuck not? We go back a long way. Just remember – you give me results or no deal. Understood?'

'Right on.'

'Who you gonna use?'

'I got my own ideas.'

Bosco Sam spat on the ground. 'If you're smart you'll use Leroy Jesus Bauls. He'll cost you, but that black motherfucker don't know no fear, that's why we call him Black Balls!'

One of the monkeys let out a loud screech.

'Shit!' exclaimed Bosco Sam. 'That fuckin' monkey just pissed all over me!'

'It's lucky,' Dukey said, managing to keep a straight face.

'It better be,' Bosco Sam grumbled. 'Or your bones gonna be *dead* fuckin' bones.'

CHAPTER 12

Lara's effect on Nick was slow but lethal.

They met again at the party Jeanette and Les threw for her, and then again at a screening of the new Dustin Hoffman film.

Lara was seeing Sammy Albert, fighting him off because to get involved with him sexually was a diversion she did not need. It was at her suggestion that Sammy invited April and Nick to dinner at the Bistro.

Confident that this was the night, Sammy was in a buoyant mood.

Lara put on her Yves Saint Laurent black velvet jacket, cut man's style, and underneath a high-necked blouse in black chiffon which, when you looked closely, was see-through. Underneath she wore no bra, and the effect was incredibly sexy because as she moved, the jacket moved too, exposing her, and then falling back into place.

'Now you see them, now you don't,' Sammy announced proudly at the beginning of the evening.

Nick and April started to fight half-way through dinner, a whispered argument no one was supposed to hear, because above all April would never blow her image by revealing a jealous streak.

The champagne Sammy had insisted on was beginning to have its effect. 'For God's sake get your eyes off her bloody tits!' April hissed angrily at Nick.

Nick, who had been making a concentrated effort *not* to look, was insulted. 'Cool down, April,' he muttered. 'Don't make a fool of yourself.'

'Cool down,' she mimicked. 'Just *who* do you think you're talking to, little man?'

'I'm talking to you, and goddamn it – you've had enough.' He gripped her wrist as she lifted her glass.

Furious, she tried to shake free, and the champagne spilled down the front of her dress.

'Oh, dear.' Lara was the first there with a napkin, dabbing it dry. 'I don't think it will stain.'

'It's only an old rag,' April said, recovering her composure and shooing Lara away. 'Nick, dear, you're *so* clumsy.' She turned her back on both of them and began to talk to Sammy on her other side.

Lara glanced at Nick and smiled sympathetically. He grinned back, allowing his eyes to drop briefly to her breasts. If he was going to get accused he might as well do it.

She was still looking at him, her green eyes probing and interested.

He felt a sudden uncomfortable tightness in his pants, a feeling he had long ago learned to control. Christ, this girl was really something, she was getting to him in no uncertain way. In the year he had been with April he'd only taken chances twice. Once, on a business trip to Vegas, a faceless showgirl with incredible legs. The other, a redhead he'd met at the beach on one of his rare afternoons off. Neither of the girls had known who he was, or anything about him. That way there was no risk of April ever finding out.

'Let's go to The Discotheque,' Sammy was saying.

'Yes, marvellous idea,' April agreed, downing another glass of champagne.

Nick didn't try to stop her. Tonight it was her problem, let her get good and boozed up. She would be sorry in the morning.

There was more champagne at The Discotheque, and Lara noticed that even Nick was drinking, something she had never seen him do before.

She danced with Sammy, and was embarrassed by his convulsive, almost obscene way of moving. One thing about European men, Prince Alfredo especially – they knew how to keep their cool on the dance floor. Sammy hopped about like a baby elephant jerking off.

When she sat down, April invited her to accompany her to the Ladies' Room. She went, because half the initial battle was remaining friendly with the ageing movie star.

'I think you're right, darling,' April observed, studying herself in the mirror. 'Look at my dress, all dry and not a stain in sight.' She produced a lethal tube of scarlet lipstick from her purse and jammed it on, going above and below her natural lip line as a series of studio make-up artists had taught her to do.

They stood side by side, observing themselves in the full-length mirror. April could easily have been Lara's mother, but she didn't realize this. As far as she was concerned her reflection was just as smooth and youthful as the girl beside her.

'Isn't Sammy a darling boy?' she commented. 'Such fun. I do hope you realize how lucky you are.'

'Lucky?' Lara questioned, brushing her hair.

'Well, of course, darling. Sammy's *very* much in demand, and I can see he's absolutely crazy about you.'

Lara smiled slightly, sensing what was coming next.

'Real men are few and far between in this town.' April hiccuped elegantly. '*I* should know, I married four of them.' More lipstick. 'Now take Nick, for instance. He's good looking enough, but what does he have to offer, darling? There's more to it than just being a good fuck. Confidentially I need a little more from a man, you know what I mean?'

Lara nodded. 'Yes, I know what you mean.' She knew exactly what April meant – stick with Sammy and keep your hands off my Nick. He's taken.

Leaning forward April examined her teeth closely in the mirror, removing any tell-tale lipstick stains. 'I adore your blouse, darling, you must tell me where you bought it. Of course, Nick's not a man for boobs, he's a leg man.' April hoisted her skirt exposing still perfect legs. 'Although I doubt very much if he'd allow me to wear a top like that. He's really very prudish. It's the Italian side of him, you know.' She stepped back, liked what she saw, and added, 'Ah well, back to the champagne.'

Lara lingered in the Ladies' Room. April didn't have to tell *her* about Italians, the only time they were prudish was if you were their wife.

She wondered if Nick wanted to marry April. The woman was still good looking for her age, and then there was the fame thing. April Crawford was a name that had once been right up there with Lana Turner, Ava Gardner, and the other famous Crawford. That had to be the attraction.

Lara sighed; she knew quite a bit about Nick, but there was still plenty to find out.

By the time she returned to their table April was dancing with Sammy, while Nick sat alone.

'Hi.' Sliding into her seat she shrugged off her jacket allowing him the full view.

He looked. He couldn't help himself.

'It's hot, isn't it?' she said, although there was no reason to make an excuse.

'Very.'

They locked stares, holding the look for several beats too long.

'Would you like to dance?' he asked.

'Yes.'

They got up and he took her by the arm steering her to the small, tightly packed dance floor. The Stones were at full shout.

Facing each other they went through the ritualistic moves. He was a good dancer, tight, controlled and at ease. The sounds were too loud to talk. Across the floor Sammy Albert and April Crawford made fools of themselves. Suddenly the music changed and Isaac Hayes was singing 'Never Can Say Goodbye'. It was slow, throbbing and sensual.

Nick stared at her again, his brown eyes intent and moody. He pulled her slowly towards him, his nails digging into her bare flesh under the black chiffon.

Lara shivered slightly, this man was dangerously good looking. When she was close to him she felt the proof of his attraction, and for one short moment the music, the feel of his maleness, it all combined to make her want to forget everything, and just be with him. Surrendering to the feeling she pressed close against him.

'Hey, baby, I don't have to tell you how I feel,' he muttered. 'No – I don't have to tell you – you know – you knew from the first time we saw each other.'

Managing to push him away a little she shook her head.

'I've got to see you,' he said urgently. 'How about lunch tomorrow? We could meet at the beach, some-where quiet where no one would see us.'

'Wait a minute.' She took a deep breath, pushing him away completely. They stood in the midst of the swaying dancers. '*I* can see you any time,' she said challengingly. '*I'm* not tied down.'

He pulled her back into a tight embrace. 'Listen, baby, you know my scene with April. She's a great lady. I wouldn't want to hurt her.'

'Then don't,' Lara replied crisply, back in control.

'Ah, come on,' he said. 'You feel the same way I do, I *know* you do. If I was to slide my hands under those tight pants of yours I could prove it to you – you'd be –'

She cut him short, her green eyes wide and appealing. 'Nick, I'm not arguing. Let's go home now. You say goodbye to April and I'll kiss Sammy on the cheek. Then I'll take off my tight pants for you and—'

'Hey, you're beginning to sound like a bitch.' He was angry.

Her eyes gleamed. 'What's the matter? Don't you like it when I'm honest? If we both want each other so much, what's the big hang-up?'

'You *know* the hang-up,' he groaned.

'Yes, I think I do, and I'll tell you something, Nick, it's all yours.' She walked off the dance floor and rejoined April and Sammy at their table.

With a jolt she realized for a moment she'd almost lost control. What a stupid thing to do. Purely physical.

'Having fun?' April asked tensely.

Lara grabbed Sammy's arm. 'Not nearly as much as I'm going to. Right, Sammy?'

He couldn't believe his luck. The ice queen was finally thawing. 'You'd better believe it, honey. They don't call me action man for nothing!'

CHAPTER 13

The only day Beth saw Frank Bassalino was on a Sunday. It appeared to be the only day he spent at home. Weekdays he was up and away before anyone was awake, returning late in the evenings after the household was asleep. But Sundays he spent with his children. Early in the day he took them to the park, then home for a huge lunch of various pastas that Anna Maria spent the morning preparing. In the afternoon he played with them, absorbing himself in their interests. Cars and trains with the two boys, perhaps a game with his six-year-old daughter – his obvious favourite – and complicated building stacks with the two-year-old.

He was a good father, if you could call devoting one day a week to his children being a good father.

Anna Maria was a placid, almost stupid girl. She had no particular desire to learn English. Frank and the children conversed with her in Italian, and since they were her whole life, what was the point in learning to speak to other people? She spent her days baking, sewing and writing letters to her family in Sicily. It was a rare day when she left the house.

Beth found the children to be well behaved and easy to manage. She gave them an hour's coaching in English a day, and they seemed to enjoy it, even the little ones. There wasn't much else to do. The older children went to school, and the two-year-old slept in the afternoons.

After two weeks she met Cass. 'I don't think it's going to work,' she said despairingly. 'I never get to see him. And when I do he doesn't even notice me.'

Cass had always thought Beth wasn't the type to be involved in the revenge. She agreed. 'It's a crazy idea anyway. You should get out. We'll find someone else to take care of Frank.'

Beth thought longingly of the commune, her own child, Chyna, and her boyfriend Max. It was tempting to say yes to Cass, pack her things and leave. But that would be admitting defeat, and she wanted to accomplish just as much as the others. She had to.

'I'm not quitting,' she said firmly. 'I'll get to him somehow. How are Lara and Rio making out?'

'Everything takes time,' Cass replied evenly, wishing she had Margaret to turn to for advice. 'I'm meeting Dukey tonight. I'm sure he's going to agree with me about you. Honestly, Beth, you shouldn't be involved.'

'Why not?' Beth's face flushed.'Don't forget I'm Margaret's sister. *I* want to do something just as much as the others. And I can – you'll see.'

416

Cass sighed. 'You aren't cut out for this. I said so from the beginning.'

'Well, I'm involved now,' Beth said stubbornly. 'And I have no intention of stopping until the job is done.'

That evening Beth waited. She put on a long white cotton nightdress, frilled and virginal. Then she brushed her straight blonde hair loose. She looked very young and appealing.

The bedroom she occupied overlooked the front of the house, and she waited patiently by the window. At two in the morning a car drew up with three men inside. Frank and another man got out and walked over to the front door. Once Frank was inside his bodyguard returned to the car, and after. a few moments it drove off. Frank was safely home.

Beth remained at the window, her mouth dry with anticipation. She knew Frank's routine so well. First he would go to his dressing-room where he changed into his pyjamas and robe. Then into the big, old-fashioned kitchen where he made himself coffee and toast.

Another car moved slowly past the house, its headlights dipped, two men inside. Frank seemed to have bodyguards to look after the bodyguards.

Still she waited, not moving, shivering slightly. What if she went to the kitchen and he wanted her? What then? She didn't know how to manoeuvre people, pull the strings. She wasn't like Lara or Rio.

Frank Bassalino was a hard, strong man. How *did* one destroy a man like that?

Thoughts of Margaret drifted through her head. And of Enzio Bassalino – the man who'd ordered Margaret to be assassinated.

Beth knew she had to avenge her sister's death. And she knew exactly what had to be done.

417

Frank was brooding and thoughtful. There was trouble all over. The cops were tightening up, more money or further harassment. The Crown gang were causing a disturbance, something would have to be done about those sons of bitches. On top of everything else, Enzio was driving him crazy, phoning to complain about this and that. The old man must have spies everywhere. Enzio Bassalino was supposed to be retired, why the fuck didn't he keep his nose out of business that wasn't his any more?

There was also the protection problem. Several restaurants and clubs under the 'security' of Frank Bassalino and his organization were being leaned on to put their faith in other directions. There had been a few unfortunate incidents, and the owners of certain establishments were beginning to wonder why they should pay protection to Frank Bassalino, *and* the cops, and *still* get hit.

Frank suspected a black group headed by narcotics' king, Bosco Sam, was behind the trouble.

Rumour had it Bosco Sam had big plans for muscling in on Bassalino and Crown territories.

Frank had sent out word he was prepared to meet Bosco Sam, to discuss things.

In the meantime the clubs and restaurants were persuaded it was in their best interests to keep up their payments. It was a problem Frank was confident he could deal with on his own.

At home there was Anna Maria with her belly so swollen a man couldn't even get a good fuck any more, and Frank didn't like to go elsewhere. The last time had been bad. Esther's place, a new girl. Esther *knew* what he was like, so he figured the hooker would be prepared. She was a black-eyed girl, full breasted, and meaty thighed. He'd turned her over and rammed it to her from behind. A slow count of ten, then wham – he'd pulled her head back and started to slap her, squeezing her breasts, hands paddling her buttocks.

As he got rougher the whore began to struggle and fight back. He enjoyed this action until she started to scream. Her nose was bleeding and the whole thing was a mess. The bitch was yelling for the cops, and it took Esther some time to calm her down.

Frank left, angry and moody. It hadn't been satisfactory. That had been two weeks previously and now he would have to make do with Anna Maria.

Ah, in the beginning his wife had been so sweet. Ripe and lovely. Young and untouched.

As he was thinking this, Beth entered the kitchen. She was like a dream come true.

'Excuse me, Mr Bassalino,' she said, in a low voice. 'I didn't realize anyone was up. I couldn't sleep and thought I would make some warm milk.'

'Warm milk is for old maids,' he said slowly. Christ! He'd never realized how delicate and pretty she was.

With a nervous laugh she took the milk carton from the fridge.

He watched her as she bent to take a pan from the cupboard and began to pour the milk into it. She wore no make-up. He liked that. Women who plastered on the gunk always reminded him of hookers. Hot, dirty tarts in black bras and garter belts. The kind his father liked. The kind his father had introduced him to when he was thirteen years of age.

'The job workin' out?' he asked.

'Yes, thank you, Mr Bassalino.' She concentrated on stirring the milk, a curtain of fine blond hair falling across her face.

'The kids treatin' you OK?'

419

'Yes, they're lovely children.' She turned to look at him, and he got a whiff of virgin skin.

At that moment Beth knew everything was set. If only she could go through with it and hide her revulsion.

'Uh . . . you're a nice-looking girl,' he said. 'How come you're hidin' away watchin' someone else's kids?'

'I enjoy leading a quiet life, Mr Bassalino.'

'You do, huh?' He stared at her reflectively.

The milk began to boil. Beth watched it bubble and froth to the top of the pan until it finally cascaded over the top and on to her hand.

She screamed out in genuine pain.

'What the f—' Frank started to say. Then he saw what she'd done and smothered her hand in great globs of butter.

'I'm sorry.' She stared at him with very blue vulnerable eyes. 'I guess I wasn't concentrating on what I was doing.'

They were close, so close that the very smell of him made her want to run. Instead she forced herself to lean even closer.

Without warning he picked her up, holding her under the arms the way you lift a child, and commenced to kiss her – slowly at first, and then stronger, harder.

She didn't say anything, allowing her lips to stay dry and closed, puckering them only slightly.

'Christ!' he exclaimed. 'You're so light, like one of the kids. Shit! You don't even know how to kiss. How old *are* you, anyway?'

She was a captive in his arms. He had such enormous strength she felt he could crush her to bits if he wanted to.

'I'm twenty,' she whispered.

'Have you ever had a man?'

Valiantly she attempted to push away from him. 'Mr Bassalino – please – you're hurting me. Let go.'

He released her abruptly. 'You know what I want to do?' he said thickly. 'You know what, honey?'

She nodded, lowering her eyes.

There was no stopping him now. 'We'll go to your room,' he said gruffly. 'Nobody's gonna know. You ever done it before?'

He was hoping she would say no. He hadn't had a virgin since Anna Maria. In fact, the only other women he had been with had all been prostitutes.

'I'm not a virgin,' she said, the rehearsed lines flowing easily. 'Once before, when I was very young – only twelve, my stepfather came to my room. He was drunk. I didn't understand what he was doing. Later I had a baby. There's been no one since.'

Frank digested this information silently. It appealed to him. One time with a drunken relative, it hardly counted. And only twelve at the time.

He slid his hand beneath the bodice of her nightgown.

'Mr Bassalino, I can't.' Her eyes were wide with fear. 'Your wife, the children, it's not right . . .'

'I'll pay you,' he said, watching her shrewdly. 'One hundred dollars – cash. How about *that*?'

Shaking her head she said, 'I don't think you understand. I do find you attractive, but the circumstances are wrong. I'm employed by you. I have your trust and your wife's. If we – well you know – how could I face myself tomorrow?'

He was impressed with the girl's honesty. He didn't come across many people who had scruples, it made a refreshing change. However, it still didn't solve the problem of what he had for her. 'How about if I fire you?' he suggested.

'That's a silly idea. Besides, I need the job.'

He was fascinated by her soft blond hair, virgin hair. He had an urge to wrap it around his feet – other things. He wanted her now. Nobody got away with refusing Frank Bassalino.

'What do you want?' he asked thickly. Experience told him there was always a price.

'Nothing,' she whispered. 'I knew when I first saw you I shouldn't have taken the job. You're the first man I sensed was different. I knew you'd understand.' She paused, playing him like a fish. 'You're also the first man I've felt anything for.' Her eyes were downcast. 'But you're married. So it's impossible.'

'Nothin's impossible,' he said, wrapping her up in his big arms again, and smothering her with kisses, while his hands roamed over her body.

She struggled – a futile act, he was even stronger than the men who'd raped her.

Exhaustion overcame her and a feeling of relief. It would happen soon, it was what he wanted, and it was exactly what she had planned.

She hardly noticed him carrying her to her room. All the while he was mumbling, 'It's gonna be all right. Nobody's gonna know.'

She was glad she'd smoked a joint earlier, it had certainly taken the edge off things, made her as relaxed as she could be under the circumstances.

Roughly pulling off her nightgown, he locked the door and struggled out of his clothes.

'I'm not going to hurt you,' he promised, crawling all over her. 'It won't be like before. You'd better believe it.'

Recoiling from the weight of his body she shut her eyes as he pushed her legs apart. And then she felt him, and the tension slipped away and she almost smiled.

Frank Bassalino was endowed with no greater gift than a ten-year-old boy.

CHAPTER 14

Leroy Jesus Bauls stood motionless at the door to the restaurant. His hard cinnamon eyes flicked slowly over the occupants, finally coming to rest on one man sitting at a corner table.

The *maître d'* was walking towards Leroy, his mouth open, ready to say there was no room. It was a fancy restaurant, and they didn't encourage blacks, even if they were well dressed and expensive looking, like Leroy.

But before the *maître d'* could reach him, Leroy had placed the parcel he was carrying on the floor, given it a swift kick in the direction of the corner table, and turned and left.

The *maître d'* scratched his head in a puzzled fashion and started towards the parcel.

On television later that night there was a full report of the incident. The Magic Garden, a popular Manhattan restaurant, had been blown apart by a bomb. Fourteen people were dead, twenty-four injured. The police were working on several leads.

'Bull*shit*,' muttered Leroy Jesus Bauls, walking over and switching the television off.

'What did you say, hon?' a black girl of startling beauty asked. She was in her mid-twenties, with curled auburn hair and almond-shaped brown eyes.

'Nothin',' Leroy replied. 'Nothin' to interest you.'

'Everything about you interests me,' she whispered, nuzzling up behind him, stroking his hair.

Impatiently he shook her off. How nice it would be to

find a girl able to keep her hands off him.

Leroy was twenty-two. Six feet, slight of build but extremely strong. Straight features, perfectly symmetric, inherited from his Swedish mother. Dark brown skin, inherited from his Jamaican father.

He was always dressed impeccably. Suits, vests, silk shirts. Even his socks and undershorts were made of the purest silk.

Leroy favoured black as a colour, in clothes, women, cars and furniture.

His mother had given him the taste for expensive things. His mother had also turned him off white people for life.

'How about catching a movie tonight?' the girl asked. 'We could go to the late show. I'm not working tomorrow, so—'

'I don't think so, Melanie,' he said. '*I* have to work later.'

'What do you do?' Melanie asked curiously. She had known him for three weeks, slept with him for two, and still knew nothing about him except that he had a nice apartment, plenty of money and was interesting to be with.

'I've told you, don't be nosy,' Leroy said, his voice flat. 'I do ... uh ... things that wouldn't interest you – deals, business matters.'

'Oh!' She was silent, then, 'What time do you have to go out?'

'Later.'

'I could stay, keep the bed warm. I don't have to be up early, so if you liked I could stay all night. Yes?'

'Yeah – some other time though.'

Melanie's mouth tightened into a thin line. She was very beautiful and unused to turn-downs. 'You've got

another girl,' she accused. 'That's it. You're going out to
see someone else.'

He sighed. They were all the same. They all wanted
to own you. Why couldn't he find a woman who would
keep her cool? He always chose very carefully. No hookers, junkies, or hustlers in any sense. He went out with
black models, actresses, singers. Melanie, for instance,
had recently been on the cover of *Cosmopolitan*, and
the girl before her was a runner-up in the Miss Black
America competition.

'Don't blow it,' he hissed, as she turned on the tears.
'It ain't gonna work. Your lovely eyes gonna get all red
and runny, and that I don't like.'

'Shall I stay then?' she questioned tearfully.

Leroy shook his head. 'I told you. Didn't I tell you? I
got business to conduct.'

CHAPTER 15

Rio attracted freaks the way a bitch in heat attracts dogs.
They clustered around her in thrilled little groups, clad
in outlandish clothes, high on anything that happened
to be around, gossipy, bitchy.

Rio didn't mind. She could get it together with anyone
as far as having a warm, generous relationship was
concerned. She looked for the good in everyone, and if
she didn't find it, she looked again.

Straight men were her only difficulty. Like Larry
Bolding, for instance. She found they were all full
of such ridiculous hang-ups, dishonesty and bullshit.
It turned her off. She became feline and hard in their
company.

Rio had never been to London before, but she had friends anxiously awaiting her arrival. There was Peaches, the gloriously stunning blonde model who had once been a man. And Perry Hernando, a gay Mexican singer who prowled London every so often looking for new talent. Rio had known them both in her Billy Express days.

They came to her rented apartment accompanied by a host of others. They brought champagne with them and smoked some incredible grass supplied by a middle-aged American lady in low-cut black. Then in cars and taxis they took Rio triumphantly to Tramp, the only place to go in London according to Peaches and Hernando.

It was exactly where Rio wanted to be. Tramp, she'd found out, was the club where Angelo Bassalino put in a nightly appearance with his lady of the week.

After some deep-dish research she knew most of his movements and habits. At the moment he was currently screwing a bit-part actress, also a married woman with four children and a rich husband, and a female blackjack dealer from one of the casinos where he worked.

Angelo Bassalino liked women. Any shape, size or colour. He was not particular.

Rio had no set plan of action. She was confident that whatever she wished to do was possible. She knew people, and she knew she was able to get into their heads if she wanted to. It would be easy deciding what had to be done to destroy Angelo.

She wished she could have dealt with all three of Enzio Bassalino's sons – Frank, Nick *and* Angelo. It was her plan. She should never have told anyone, she could have done it alone without any help. What did Lara and Beth know about beating someone mentally, reducing them to a wreck, finding the one chink and pressing, pressing until it gave way?

426

Bullshit! They knew how to get a guy in the sack and that was it. Not like Margaret, she could have done it. Margaret was capable of anything.

Rio remembered their first meeting. It was winter, and so cold she could recall how she'd first thought of setting her apartment building on fire. An insane thought, but at the time she was ready for any way to kill herself.

What a way to go! One big glorious blaze. But then she'd thought about all the other people living there, and what use would a goodbye note be for Larry Bolding if it went up in flames? She wanted him to suffer. Her plan was to ruin him and his whole stinking political career.

She had made her face up very carefully, an extravaganza of exotic colour. Then she'd put on a long red Halston dress. After all, she was a superstar – she certainly wasn't going to creep out.

She was high. A little acid to help her on the ultimate trip. By three o'clock in the morning she was ready to go. First some incredible sounds on the stereo – loud, then she'd used the razor that Larry kept at her place, he didn't like electric ones.

She slid the fresh blade out and cut a deep line along the inside of her right wrist, then the other. It didn't hurt, the sudden gush of blood was beautiful, it matched her dress.

She was laughing. It was the best she'd felt for months. No hang-ups, no worries, no anything.

She was still laughing when she passed out, the blood pumping out of her cut wrists on to the pure white carpet.

It was all hazy after that. Margaret's face, very close and concerned. A feeling of movement, of being carried. Voices – muffled and far away.

And after that the awakening – how many days later? Two? Three? Margaret Lawrence Brown sitting at a table writing, her long black hair propped back from a strong face by tinted glasses.

Rio couldn't move. She was in a strange bed in a strange room and her arms were bandaged up to the elbows.

'Hey,' she managed, causing Margaret to look up at her, a direct confrontation stare. She wore no make-up, and her face was not beautiful, not even pretty. But it was a face of such enormous warmth and attractiveness that Rio was immediately drawn to her. It was a strange feeling, because what the hell, she didn't even want to be in the world any more.

Margaret smiled slightly and got up. Tall, small-bosomed in a loose T-shirt and Levi's. 'I guess you're going to make it,' she'd said in a gravelly voice. 'It didn't look like it for a while, but I had a feeling you'd survive. I'm Margaret, I live next door and I happened to get blasted out of bed by your musical choice. Since you're usually so quiet, I came over to investigate. You would have made a devastating picture for the newspapers – the red dress and the blood and the white rug. It was almost a shame to save you. Only think about it – you can't pull that kind of shit over a guy!' Margaret had shaken her head in disbelief. 'Larry Bolding's an asshole. Baby, I don't even know him, but I'm here to tell you he's a prick. And we do not – I repeat do *not* – kill ourselves over pricks.'

Margaret never lost any time in making a point.

Rio stayed with Margaret in her apartment for two weeks before moving back to her own place. She learned more in those two weeks than she had in a lifetime.

Margaret was that rare exception, a truly selfless person. She wanted nothing out of life except to do good for others. She gave her time, her energy, her money, to any cause she found worthy. And she had a biting furious anger at the way women were treated as second-class citizens. She wanted to change things and unlike most people she didn't just sit around talking about it, she went out and did what she could.

In the dim recesses of Tramp Rio recognized Angelo Bassalino when he came in. She looked him over with a strong and steady gaze. He was with a skinny little blonde.

Rio had no plans to waste time, so she walked directly over to his table and sat herself down.

'Hey, Angelo,' she said tauntingly. 'What's all this shit I hear about you being the best fuck in town?'

CHAPTER 16

Enzio Bassalino placed three phone calls. In order of importance he spoke to Frank in New York first.

'I'm thinking of coming in,' he stated. 'How's the climate?'

Frank realized his father was not referring to the weather. 'The same,' he replied, his voice guarded. He knew for a fact that the FBI had a tap on his phone.

'I'll come in anyway,' Enzio growled. 'The usual hotel, the usual set-up – arrange it.'

'It's not the right time.' Frank tried to keep the irritation out of his voice. Why did his goddamn father always have to interfere?

'I want to see the grandchildren.' Enzio was stubborn.

'At the same time we can clear up some other matters. You know what I mean?'

'Yeah. I know what you mean.' Frank knew exactly what he meant. He meant the panic that was going on over the bombing of the Magic Lantern restaurant.

Frank had everything in hand. He was calling meetings and finding out hard facts. He didn't need any help.

At first he had thought it was Bosco Sam, or maybe the Crowns. But the information he'd collected pointed against them.

Tomassio Vitorelli, Frank's counsellor, had been meeting an informant at the Magic Lantern the night the bomb had exploded. Unfortunate for poor Tomassio.

'OK, so arrange it. I'll be in tomorrow,' Enzio said impatiently. 'International, three o'clock. Tell Anna Maria to start cooking.' He hung up, well aware that Frank was annoyed. Enzio knew his eldest son thought he could handle everything himself. But what was wrong with a little insurance? What was wrong with Enzio Bassalino showing his face in New York?

Enzio had found out the Crown gang were trying to move in on several Bassalino territories. They weren't succeeding, but they were causing certain 'problems'. What with that and the protection business, he knew it was time he paid a visit. He was sure with him in town those problems would soon cease. Perhaps a personal meeting with Rizzo Crown would fix things, they went back many years together, so why not?

Finished with Frank, he telephoned Nick in Los Angeles. 'What's happening?' always his opening question.

Nick gave him a short rundown.

'Fine, fine.' Enzio coughed and spat into an ashtray on his desk, a habit that did not endear him to his staff. 'I'm going to New York tomorrow, it might not be a bad idea for you to fly in for a couple of days. We'll have a family meeting.'

'Why?' Nick didn't like leaving the Coast. He didn't like his sun-tan suffering for even one day.

'It might be advisable,' Enzio said. 'I'll let you know.'

'Jesus . . .' Nick muttered.

'What's the matter with you?' Enzio boomed. 'Can't you leave the old broad for two days? What's she got, a direct line to your balls?'

'If it's necessary I'll be there,' Nick said, giving in without a fight. Maybe a trip to New York wasn't such a bad idea. It just might be the perfect opportunity to get something together with Lara that April couldn't find out about.

'OK, OK, I'll let you know,' Enzio said, hanging up.

Nick was a stupid boy. Any man was dumb if he let a woman tie his balls together. Enzio had always prided himself on being very clever about the female sex. A piece was a piece and there was plenty about. Use them before they use you had always been his motto. Once they became clingy and demanding, that was the time to get rid of them.

Mary Ann August wriggled into his study. Clad in her customary bikini with puffs of teased blond hair, she stood silently picking off her nail polish until he said a curt, 'Yeah? What is it?'

'Alio's here,' she singsonged. 'Out by the pool. He wants a sandwich and the cook's out. What shall I do?'

'So make him a sandwich,' Enzio said irritably, delaying his call to Angelo.

'What kind?' she asked blankly.

'How the hell do I know? Ask him.' Mary Ann was beginning to piss him off, sometimes big boobs were not enough.

'There's cheese, I guess,' she said vaguely. 'Or cucumber. Do you think he'd like cucumber?'

'What am I? A chef?' Enzio stormed. 'Get outta here, ya dumb broad. I gotta place a call.'

Mary Ann left quickly. She knew when to make herself scarce.

It would have been nice, Enzio mused, if Rose had not gone insane and locked herself away. An old-style wife was irreplaceable. A woman who knew her position in life and kept it. It would have been far more convenient to stash his mistresses in separate apartments, visiting them only when necessary, putting up with their ridiculous chatter only when he had to.

But it was too lonely without anyone. He needed to share his bed. Sometimes he had nightmares, dreams from which he awoke shaking and cold around the heart. At those times he stretched out for human contact, he desperately needed the security of another body nearby.

Enzio worried about his health. What if his heart should fail and no one was near? He had suffered one attack three years before. The doctors had assured him he was fine now, better than before.

Still . . . What did doctors know? He didn't trust any of them.

It wouldn't be a bad idea, he decided, to replace Mary Ann in New York. Her time was almost up.

Phoning London he was aggravated because he could not get hold of Angelo. His son wasn't at the Casino, nor his home. The boy's out screwing, Enzio thought with a snort. He smiled, the proud father. At Angelo's age he'd been just the same.

Ah . . . at Angelo's age he'd had the world by the balls. Prohibition, Chicago, a different kind of time, a world of crazy excitement and thrills. Once, the Bassalino name

432

had rated alongside Capone, Legs Diamond, O'Banion. Enzio sighed with pleasure when he remembered the early days with Alio by his side. It was all so different now, everything hidden under a cloak of legitimacy. Crime was getting dull.

Enzio chuckled, and strolled out to the pool still laughing. He wondered if Alio would remember the time they'd tried to bribe the chef of their favourite Italian restaurant. They'd wanted him to put arsenic in an arch rival's soup. The chef had refused and fled the city, and to this day Enzio still missed the coward's incredible meatballs.

CHAPTER 17

They met on the plane like conspirators. Nick warily checking the first-class section for friends of his or April's. Only after he'd done this and found all was clear, did he condescend to join Lara.

She was dressed all in white and looked ravishingly beautiful. He decided the risk was well worth taking, even though she'd steadfastly refused to meet him in Los Angeles, giving him an ultimatum – her or April.

There was no way he could possibly choose. He was going to *marry* April. Lara had turned up at the wrong time. Sure, he wanted to get her into bed, but he wasn't prepared to risk his future, and his future was most definitely April Crawford.

Enzio had suggested the New York trip at just the right moment. Nick mentioned to Lara he had to go, and hinted she should come too. Surprisingly she'd said yes.

'April mustn't find out,' he'd warned, and for a change she'd agreed with him.

'We'll do it your way,' she'd said calmly.

Over the weeks they'd enjoyed an ongoing flirtation – bumping into each other at parties, restaurants and clubs. The more he'd seen of her, the more he'd wanted her. Now he was going to get his wish.

He had the situation well covered. They'd arrived at the airport separately, boarded the plane separately, and they would disembark separately. Who could possibly find out they were travelling together?

Lara had her own apartment in New York. Nick planned to stay at the hotel with Enzio. He figured New York was a big place, you could get lost there. It wasn't a nosy little city like Los Angeles where you couldn't even take a piss without everyone knowing.

All he wanted was a chance to be with Lara without the anxiety of April catching them together. One or two days should be long enough to get her out of his system. It was just sex, pure unadulterated lust. Yeah, she was gorgeous, and well connected in her own way, but she wasn't April. April Crawford was a star. Something he had no intention of forgetting.

Frank was a demanding man. After the first night he came immediately to Beth's room as soon as he arrived home. It was always late, and Anna Maria slept soundly.

He silenced Beth's objections, reassuring her that his wife was a heavy sleeper and would not wake up.

Beth accepted him in the dark old-fashioned room above the kitchen. She accepted his kisses and embraces, the fumbling way he made love. In spite of the revulsion he produced in her, she felt sorry for him. Frank Bassalino stood for everything she loathed, and yet there was a certain loneliness in the man that caught her sympathy. Maybe it was the cruel joke nature had played on him, it made him vulnerable. It also explained why he needed a girl like her, a girl he thought was inexperienced, and therefore could make no criticism or comparison.

She lived up to his expectations. She was soft, warm and appreciative, feigning a childlike innocence that seemed to fascinate him.

He bought her little presents. One night a cheap charm bracelet, the next a pound of strawberries which he proceeded to eat.

He was a selfish lover, satisfying himself and forgetting about her. It never took him very long, a five-minute routine which didn't vary. He liked her to be in bed waiting. He insisted she wore her long white nightdress. First he would fondle her breasts for a few minutes, then suck at her nipples until he was ready to mount her. A few thrusts and it was over.

By the end of the week he was already talking of finding her an apartment.

By the end of the week she had already planned how she would arrange to have Anna Maria discover them together.

Lara called Cass as soon as she arrived at her apartment in New York. 'I'm making progress,' she said. 'April should find out about us in the morning paper.'

'Are you sure you're all right?' Cass asked anxiously.

'Perfect,' Lara assured her confidently. 'Once April discovers he flew here with me – he's out. The woman is too proud to accept seconds. The funny thing is I haven't slept with him.' She paused. 'How's Beth?'

'I don't know. I spoke to her a week ago and she seemed disturbed. I want her to quit. I told her so but she won't listen. I'm worried.'

'Yes, she's so young.' Lara thought with concern of the sister she hardly knew. 'I think we have to insist that she drop out of the whole thing. After all, she does have a child at the commune, and the important thing is to persuade her that little Chyna needs her more than our crazy scheme.'

'You're right,' Cass agreed. 'I'll try and make contact.'

'And how about Rio? Any word from her?'

'A wire saying SUCCESS ASSURED. The agreement was to touch base every Wednesday. If I can't reach Beth by tomorrow I'll go to the house and pretend I'm a relative.'

'Good,' Lara agreed. 'Enzio Bassalino is in New York. That's the reason I'm here.'

Cass sounded alarmed. 'God, I hope Dukey doesn't find out, he's always muttering about there only being one way.'

'Killing's too good for him,' Lara said, surprised at her own coldness. 'Our way is best.'

She hung up, walked into the bathroom, brushed her luxuriant mane of hair, and touched up her make-up.

She looked tired, and she was worried about Beth. Her younger sister was such an innocent, so unworldly. Beth had been stuck away in a commune all her life, and now she was stuck in a house with a dangerous hood. Cass had to get her out, there was no question about it.

Next Lara thought about Nick. She was supposed to hate him, but it wasn't that easy. The funny thing was that instead of hating him she found she liked him – a pure natural like that had nothing to do with money or position or title. God! It would certainly make everything a lot easier if she didn't. Still, she had a job to do. And with Beth out of the picture it was more important than ever.

Frank arrived at the hotel with Golli and Segal. They accompanied him everywhere, they were his protection, his insurance. The way things were going in New York there was big trouble everywhere. Only the previous week one of his chief 'executives' had been gunned down in the middle of Manhattan. He was taking no chances, Golli and Segal were worth the exorbitant money he paid them each week.

Enzio had used the hotel many times before and his security arrangements were as usual. The entire third floor was inaccessible except to members of his immediate entourage. Even Frank had to use the complicated passwords, although all the men Enzio travelled with had known Frank since he was a baby.

Enzio did not believe in new faces. He kept a permanent army of twenty-five men who had been with him many years, and were always on call. Frank had argued with him many times over this. 'They're old guys, what can they do for you if there's trouble? They can barely carry a gun any more, let alone use it.'

Enzio laughed in his face. 'These "old guys" as you call them are tougher and smarter than any of the punks you have around. I *know* I can't be got to – do you have the same security?'

Frank felt safe enough with Golli and Segal, they were young and fast, he'd seen them in action.

Father and son greeted each other warmly, kissing and hugging in the Italian way.

Enzio patted Frank on the shoulders, standing back to survey him. 'So, you look OK,' he announced. 'How's the little girl? She about ready to pop again?' He was very fond of his daughter-in-law.

437

Frank nodded. 'Anna Maria's fine. She's looking forward to seeing you.' But his thoughts were not of his wife. His thoughts were of Beth.

'An' the bambinos? They excited to see their old grandpop?'

'Yeah, pa. Dinner tonight, Anna Maria's making your favourite – spaghetti, meatballs, the works.'

'That's good.' Enzio paused, his face becoming serious. 'I'm most troubled by the reports I've been hearing.'

Frank turned, staring out of the window. 'Everything's under control,' he said, his voice uptight.

'I wonder if Tomassio Vitorelli would agree with you,' Enzio replied mildly, adding more harshly, 'we're not gonna fuck around on this, Frank. I'm not here to get my rocks off.' He frowned. 'No use talkin' now. We'll discuss it tonight after dinner, when Nick is here.'

'Sure.' Frank managed a smile. 'Sure, poppa, everything's gonna be OK.'

CHAPTER 18

Dukey K. Williams was pleased. The hit on the Magic Lantern restaurant was a success. It had disposed of Tomassio Vitorelli, a big man in the Bassalino organization. And the bombing had put the fear of God into other restaurants and clubs who didn't want the same treatment. Let the Bassalinos start to sweat. It was a good beginning.

Leroy Jesus Bauls was also pleased. The hit had been his idea.

Dukey K. Williams had come to him.

Dukey K. Williams was prepared to let him do it his way.

Dukey K. Williams was going to lay a lot of bucks on Leroy. Mucho, mucho big bucks.

Yeah, things were sweet for a guy who had started out with everything against him.

Leroy's Swedish mother was a hooker, and his black father a pimp. As soon as he was able he'd left home. His parents were dead as far as he was concerned, and it wouldn't bother him one bit if they actually were.

Good looking at an early age, he never had any trouble finding a bed to sleep in. If he wanted to he could have followed his father's profession, there were plenty of offers. But Leroy had no desire to be beholden to any woman.

Instead he joined a street gang, and cruised with them for a while. It was small stuff, rolling drunks and old ladies, knocking off neighbourhood stores. By the time the profits were split up they were practically non-existent. Leroy knew he had to move on to better things.

He decided that narcotics was the business for him. Once or twice he'd smoked pot, tried acid twice. Neither did anything for him. That was good. The thing to be when dealing with drugs was cool, and definitely a non-participant.

He'd seen what drugs did to people, the way it affected their looks, and he wanted none of that. But pushing was another bag of shit, pushing could lead to a lot of money.

Leroy was young, good looking, and a convincing talker. He picked out the area he wanted to operate, and with a small stake from a friend, went into business.

Soon he found he was stepping on toes. The space he'd picked was already fully covered. They warned him off. They thought he was some punk kid, easy to handle. He bought a gun with his first week's profits and waited.

There were three sets of toes he was stepping on. Within a month all three of them were dead, shot. Leroy wrapped his gun in plastic, weighted it with rocks, and safely laid it to rest at the bottom of the river.

With his fifth week's profits he bought himself another one. He was sixteen years old.

For a year he concentrated solely on dealing, working on his own with good sources of supply. He stashed his money away, and kept his gun handy. Nobody bothered him. His reputation preceded him. He kept to his own area, and didn't get in anyone's way.

He lived alone in a rooming house. Never went out except on business, and rarely spent any money. By the end of a year he'd saved a substantial amount. Enough to buy a car, a whole new wardrobe of clothes, and rent a decent apartment.

His first purchase was a black Mercedes. Next he had several black suits custom made for him. And then he furnished his apartment with a lot of expensive black leather couches and chairs.

He looked older than seventeen.

Leroy found that to maintain his new life style he needed even more money. So he employed two friends of his to work his space, and moved on to new territory.

Within days he received word that Bosco Sam wanted to see him. Bosco Sam's toes were too many to step on and Leroy knew it, so he paid him a visit.

They came to an arrangement. Leroy was to keep to the area he already had, and instead of moving in on Bosco Sam's action, Bosco Sam would throw a couple of things his way that would bring him a lot more money than hustling drugs.

Leroy liked the idea. More bucks for less work, and he still kept a couple of guys working for him.

In the first year Bosco Sam gave him three contracts to take care of. Three hits. Leroy executed them all without a hitch.

Leroy was moving up. He was getting himself a reputation, and it was doing him nothing but good.

Now, four years later, Leroy Jesus Bauls was top man in his profession. He had long ago moved out of the drug scene.

He had used his spare time to study explosives, electronics, computer bombs. There was nothing he didn't know how to do, from blowing up a plane, to planting a bomb in a bank that he could detonate three weeks later.

Leroy Jesus Bauls was a free-lance hit man. The best.

He had a reputation for taking risks, and every risk he had ever taken paid off. Leroy was riding high.

Now he waited. Dukey K. Williams would let him know when to move again, and when he did, Leroy was ready.

CHAPTER 19

Angelo's apartment in Mayfair was small. A living-room, kitchen and bathroom. He'd splashed out on the bedroom. The walls were draped with leopard and tiger skins, the floor was carpeted in three-inch-thick fur, the ceiling was a kaleidoscope of different coloured mirrors. Naturally the bed dominated. It did everything electrically, from turning around in a slow circle, to producing television, stereo, or coffee at the touch of a button.

441

Angelo was proud of his domain. 'Hot, huh?' he boasted to Rio.

She dismissed her surroundings with a glance. 'Get yourself a water bed, baby,' was her only comment.

They were both stoned. After Rio's initial introductory remark to Angelo, he'd lost no time in getting rid of his blonde companion and joining up with Rio's group. She was immediately cool, palming him off on Peaches, while making rude comments about cocky Italian studs.

As usual Rio was the centre of attention, outrageous in whore's shoes with five-inch heels which raised her six-foot height to ridiculous proportions. She towered over everybody, her sinewy body undulating on the packed dance floor in a revealing dress tied and swathed around her body. Silver bangles jangled half-way up both her arms, and fertility symbols jostled and moved around her neck. Her make-up was extreme, while her long black Indian hair was coiled up and hidden under a purple Afro wig.

She danced with everyone, generating sexuality and excitement at high-level voltage.

Angelo was content to hang around and watch. He had no doubts that later she'd go home with him.

He sat back and enjoyed the show, remembering a few years earlier. New York. At the time he'd been working for his brother Frank, and one day he'd been sent over to Billy Express's house to deliver a package. 'Personally,' Frank had said. 'Make sure you give it to him *personally*.'

Billy Express was not home, and Angelo had been told to wait. He hadn't enjoyed being treated like a messenger boy. It pissed him off. But then he heard the noises, unmistakable noises, and he went to investigate, soft-footed in the white sneakers he always chose to wear.

The noises came from a room next to the study where

he'd been told to wait. Opening the door a crack he'd peered in.

Rio Java and a Chinese man were performing on the floor. She was naked, spread-eagled, and above her the Chinese posed very still while she groaned loudly. Occasionally the Chinese man moved, grinding himself deeply into her, withdrawing and then remaining motionless until the next short stab. It was driving Rio mad, until suddenly she'd clutched at him, locking her long legs around his neck and screaming with complete abandon.

Angelo had closed the door quickly, feeling more than horny. As soon as he'd delivered the package to Billy Express he'd hurried over to Carita's house and dropped another load.

'You bin' here four times this week,' Carita had complained. 'I told Frank you could have two freebees a week. Whadda ya think I am for chrissake? I'm running a business, not a friggin' charity!'

The memory had always remained with Angelo. And now Rio Java was in London, in his apartment, and he was just as horny as the day he'd delivered the package to Billy Express.

Rio stretched, touched a strap or two, and with a couple of deft moves her dress fell off. Underneath she wore nothing except hooker shoes and the purple wig. She was very thin, almost bony, almost flat chested, with incredible black extended nipples. In underground movie circles her nipples were famous, having been photographed by Billy Express from every angle. In fact, her nipples were almost as famous as Andy Warhol's Campbell's soup can.

Angelo hurriedly stripped off his clothes, anxious to keep up. Then he lowered the lights to a red glow and flicked on a James Brown tape.

Rio's eyes swept over him, lingering on his most important asset. 'Is that it?' she asked with an amused laugh.

Angelo grinned unsurely, not quite certain what she meant. She couldn't possibly mean he was underendowed. He had a good solid hard-on. Usually he received nothing but admiring 'Oohs' and 'aahs', not short derisive laughs.

'Well now, *little* boy,' she said mockingly. 'Where would you like to begin?'

Angelo approached her, silently wishing she would take her shoes off. Without the goddamn shoes they would be more or less the same height. As it was the shoes gave her an advantage he didn't like. They made him feel small.

Rio moved her body in time to the music, parting her legs, swaying back and forth to the funky sounds of James Brown's 'Sex Machine'.

'Hey,' he said, 'take your shoes off.'

'But, honey-pie, I *looove* my shoes,' she sighed in an exaggerated Southern accent. 'They make me feel *reaal* big and mean. All the better to eat up naughty *little* boys like Angelo Bassalino.'

He gripped her by the waist.

'Show me your stuff, super-stud,' she drawled.

They moved together.

'Get up – get on up – get up – get on up – get up – get on up – stay on the scene – get on up – like a sex machine.' Rio sang along with James Brown, while Angelo's grip tightened and he managed to move her over to the bed. She was still singing as he pushed her back – 'Get on up,' she chanted, 'get up – get it together – right on, baby.'

He mounted her, and before he knew what was happening she stretched her long legs straight out, trapping him inside her, and with one movement she twisted her pelvis up, and the pressure was so great, so incredibly tight, that he came at once.

She started to laugh, loud mocking laughter. The whole thing had only taken a few seconds.

'Hey, baby baby,' she crooned. 'What are you – a rabbit?'

She dissolved with more laughter while Angelo withdrew and tried to puzzle out what had happened. All he'd done was moved inside her and that was it, a vice-like grip on his manhood that pumped it all out of him in one fell swoop. Jesus! What was going on here?

Rio rolled across the bed. 'How long's the intermission?' she complained, throwing off her purple wig and shaking her long, shiny black hair free.

To his credit Angelo was hard again. He prided himself on his control, knowing he could go for hours if it was required. Mind over matter, that was the secret. And his mind had probably been dwelling on the first time he'd seen her.

He moved over her breasts with his tongue.

'Let's fuck, baby,' she said briskly. 'I'm here for action. We can worry about tongue jobs later.'

She rolled on her stomach and he entered her from behind. When he was good and in she drew her legs together and raised herself a few inches. Again there was that incredible sensation, a tightness so relentless he couldn't stop himself from coming. And it was a great come, a beautiful happening that no amount of mind over matter could stop.

'Jesus!' she exclaimed angrily. 'How long is it since you've been laid?'

Angelo was exhausted. He lay back on the bed in a daze, closing his eyes. Five minutes of sleep and he'd feel strong again.

445

James Brown sang 'It's A Man's Man's Man's World.'

Angelo slept.

Grinning to herself, Rio got up and slipped into her dress. It was a satisfying start.

Jamming on her wig, she danced around the room in her hooker shoes humming softly to herself. Then in brown lipstick she wrote on the bathroom mirror *HONEY* YOU'VE *GOT* TO BE KIDDING!!

She let herself out without disturbing him.

CHAPTER 20

Mary Ann August was delighted Enzio had decided to bring her to New York with him. She would never admit it – well only to herself – but she found Miami tediously boring. It wasn't so much Miami, but the fact that she wasn't allowed out on her own, and the people who came to the house were all old. And then of course there was the woman peering out of the window all the time. It was very unnerving to have a pair of crazed black eyes following you everywhere.

'Who is it?' Mary Ann had asked in alarm when she'd first arrived.

'Forget it,' Enzio had warned her. 'Just ignore it, an' *never* let me catch your ass near that room. You understand me?'

Mary Ann knew enough not to question him any further, but that didn't stop her speaking to the maid who took meals into the room twice a day.

The maid was Italian and frightened to talk, but gradually Mary Ann pieced together the story. The woman was Enzio's wife. She was a mental case, and never left her room.

Mary Ann was scared, but as the weeks drifted into months, she forgot about the crazy, ever-watchful eyes and pretended they weren't there. It was kind, she reflected, that Enzio let the old bag stay and had not shoved her into an institution.

Mary Ann planned to do lots of things in New York. She wanted to buy new clothes, see all the Broadway shows, and eat at the best restaurants.

Enzio had other ideas. Upon their arrival he shut her in the hotel suite and told her to stay there until he said otherwise.

They had arrived in the morning, now it was seven in the evening, and Mary Ann was bored, hungry and fed up.

She sat pouting on the bed, legs crossed, china-blue eyes glued to a quiz game on the television.

At first she didn't hear the knock on the door, and she was quite startled when Alio Marcusi walked in.

'Oh, it's you,' she said, her voice sulky. 'Where's Enzio?'

Alio smiled. He had showered and put on his new blue suit. His few remaining hairs were plastered down with a shiny pomade.

Enzio had given him the word. Mary Ann August was out. There was a position for her in Los Angeles.

Enzio always allowed Alio a turn when he was finished with a girl. It had been that way for thirty years. Sometimes they objected. Those were the ones Alio liked best. At his age it was difficult getting it up under normal circumstances.

'He won't be coming,' Alio said mildly. 'I have a message for you, my dear.'

447

CHAPTER 21

There were candles on the table at Frank Bassalino's house. His children, washed, scrubbed and clad in their best clothes, sat straight backed at the table. Frank had given up his place at the head to his father, and settled himself on Enzio's right. Anna Maria nervously faced her husband.

Nick was there, laughing and joking with the two younger children. He'd wanted to spend the evening with Lara, but Enzio had insisted he attend the dinner, and his father was not a man you argued with.

He'd arranged to meet Lara later. She hadn't minded, merely smiled and said, 'I understand, Nick. Family is family.'

April would have ranted and raved for a week.

'Hey,' Enzio roared. 'Anna Maria makes the best spaghetti in town. You're a lucky man, Frank, you know that, huh?' He paused, belching loudly. 'Of course, *I* could give her a few hints about the sauce. A little more garlic, stronger wine . . .'

Anna Maria giggled timidly.

Frank glanced at Beth. She had entered the room to assist the youngest child with his food. Her long hair was tied off her face, and she looked pale. He wondered how quickly Anna Maria would fall asleep tonight, and how long before he could be with Beth.

A nerve throbbed in his cheek. There would be business to discuss after dinner, it could turn out to be a lengthy evening.

After dessert and coffee Enzio sent Anna Maria and the children from the room. 'Men's talk,' he explained with a wink, sipping from a small glass of Sambuca.

When he began to speak his eyes fixed firmly on Frank. 'It doesn't take long,' he said sourly, his good humour evaporating, 'for the word to get around when you got no balls.'

'What?' Frank jumped, feeling anger and frustration flood through his body.

'In our business, somebody throws a hit on you, you shove it right back at 'em. You don't fuck around. No way.'

'I've been lookin' to find out who's responsible,' Frank replied, his voice a surly mutter.

'Fuck that!' Suddenly Enzio was screaming. 'Who gives a shit 'bout who's to blame? What you do is pile some action on *all* the fuckers – you'll hit the dirt with one of 'em. Huh? Listen to an old man, Frankie boy – Don't let nobody shit on you. 'Cos if you do, we'll all end up under the pile.'

Lara prowled around her apartment like a stranger. She hated the draped paisley fabric ceiling, the matching walls, the small round table with a collection of interesting miniature boxes.

She loathed the exotic plants climbing up the antique-mirrored hall. She couldn't stand the zebra throw rugs, the brown leather couches.

Her apartment had been designed by a decorator, there were no personal touches. About the only place she felt at home was the bathroom. Here, among the rows of make-up, atomizers and brushes, she could relax.

The apartment had been put together with a view to looking sensational in the fashion and beautiful home magazines. And indeed it did. Lara had spent more time being photographed in it than living there.

She decided that when the whole business with Nick was over she would sell it. It was pointless to surround oneself with somebody else's idea of good taste.

When *would* the whole business with Nick be over? Wasn't it just beginning?

Sometimes she felt so confused. Was the revenge going to work? If April Crawford left Nick, was it going to affect him *that* much? And after she'd consoled him for a few weeks, when *she* dumped him, what then? Even if he was destroyed, how was that really going to punish Enzio Bassalino?

She gave a deep sigh. At the time Rio's revenge had sounded perfect. But now . . . well, she wasn't so sure any more. Maybe Dukey was the one with the right ideas.

Slowly she dressed to meet Nick at Le Club. A black jersey snake of a dress with no back. A jewelled choker from Afghanistan. Bracelets of thin beaten silver halfway up her arm.

Tonight was the night. Take Mr Nick Bassalino home to bed and keep him there until he read the morning gossip columns. The longer it took for him to call April, the better.

Another sigh. Margaret wouldn't have approved of what they were trying to do. Margaret would have been ashamed of them resorting to sex to get what they wanted.

The phone rang. She picked it up.

'Lara? Lara, is that you?' The anxious voice of Prince Alfredo Masserini.

'Oh, Alfredo. How did you know I was here?'

'I call you every day,' he said indignantly. 'Every day I try. Every day no answer. How you think I feel?'

'I'm sorry. I had to fly out to the Coast. I just got back.' She wasn't sorry at all. The break was delightful.

'But Lara, Lara,' he accused, 'you could have phoned me.'

'I said I'm sorry,' she snapped.

'Now I have you, so we forget it.' The Prince sensibly realized arguing was not going to get him anywhere. 'You want I come there?'

'No.'

'So you fly to me then. Tomorrow. I meet you at Rome airport, then together we go to Gstaad for the backgammon. Yes, my darling?'

'No, Alfredo. I have business to finish.'

'Ah, Lara, my beautiful. You make me very wild.'

'Give me a few more days. I'll join you in Gstaad.'

'How many days?'

'Don't pin me down. Phone me tomorrow.'

She hung up quickly, ignoring the phone when it immediately began to ring again. Alfredo had been a spoilt Italian Prince all his life, it would do him good to strike out for once.

Besides, she didn't want to be late for Nick.

CHAPTER 22

Angelo called Rio ten times before he finally reached her.

'Hey,' he said, 'about the other night.'

'No apologies,' Rio said with a deep, throaty laugh. 'I understand, I'm a *veree* understanding lady.'

'Maybe we can get together tonight?'

'Honey, understanding I may be, but you and I just don't swing at the same pace.'

'Hey – the other night was a mistake,' he explained.

'That's not usually the way I am. I don't want to boast, but—'

She cut him short. 'You're a sweet horny little guy, and great for teeny boppers and cute little bunnies who want some fast action – and I *do* mean fast – action. But sweetheart, you and I are in a different league.'

Angelo felt his whole reputation was at risk. 'I can explain about the other night. It was—'

She interrupted him again. 'Yeah, baby, it certainly was.' And then she cut him off.

He threw the phone down in disgust. How dare that great big freak put him down like this. He wanted to see her, to prove his manhood. It was a slight to have her think of him as a sexual failure. Shit! He was a *great* fuck. Countless women could confirm that. He could go for hours. He had incredible control.

Picking up the phone he dialled his married lady friend. 'Come on over right now,' he commanded.

'I can't, one of the children is sick,' the woman apologized.

He slammed the phone down. Was he losing his touch?

Next he reached his female croupier friend. She arrived within the hour and he rushed her into bed, giving her controlled action and countless orgasms for two hours. She screamed and moaned her appreciation. He found he couldn't come himself. He was still hard when he threw her out.

He phoned Rio again.

'Wow, you're a very anxious *little* boy,' she said mockingly. 'I don't like anxious guys. You know something, honey? It *really* turns me off.'

'Can I come over?' he asked, hating himself for begging, but consumed with the need to prove himself to her.

She consulted her watch, it was six o'clock. 'OK. Be here in five minutes.'

As soon as she put the phone down she went out.

Angelo hurried over, and then waited outside her rented apartment for an hour constantly pressing the buzzer. Naturally there was no reply which really pissed him off. Just who did the bitch think she was?

Finally he settled himself into a nearby bar and had a few drinks. Every fifteen minutes he phoned her, getting no answer.

He consumed several Scotches. Normally he didn't drink much, grass was his scene. But tonight he needed something.

By the time he arrived at the casino he was unsteady on his feet and belligerent. Eddie Ferrantino took one look and sent him home.

He called up another girlfriend and met her at Tramp. Rio was there, surrounded by her so-called friends.

'You're a fuckin' bitch,' he hissed at her.

'And you're a lousy lay,' she hissed back.

'Listen lady – come home with me now and you'll eat your words,' he insisted, forgetting about his girl-friend.

'It's not *words* I'm interested in eating,' she said with a mocking grin.

'It's not words you'll get,' he mumbled, wishing he was sober.

'Let's go,' she said briskly.

They took a taxi. Rio flung off her clothes as soon as they entered his apartment.

Angelo realized he'd made a mistake. The booze had made his body limp and his mind groggy.

'Well?' She faced him, hands on hips, legs spread. 'Get your clothes off, lover. Let's *see* what you can do.'

She stripped him herself. He couldn't summon a hard-on if his life depended on it. Humiliation overcame him.

Laughingly she jeered, 'Call Momma when you grow up to be a *big* boy. OK, babe?'

And with that she dressed and left.

CHAPTER 23

It was late by the time Nick was through at his brother Frank's house. There were problems on top of problems. And a lot of talk. Nick didn't feel he was that much involved. Things were running smoothly for him in California, the inside killings and take-overs in New York didn't really concern him.

'*Putan!*' Enzio spat at him when he said as much. 'What happens here today happens there tomorrow. You think you're protected by some fuckin' guardian angel? Balls!'

Both Enzio and Frank were mad at him because he had flown in with no bodyguard.

'You don't *move* in New York unless you're covered,' Enzio had bellowed, and Frank immediately agreed. They'd dismissed the car and chauffeur he'd rented at the airport and replaced it with a black Cadillac sedan and two of Frank's men.

Nick couldn't help wondering how Lara was going to feel about a couple of heavies stationed outside her front door when they were together.

He arrived at Le Club late. Lara was with a group who fortunately he didn't know. To his annoyance she introduced him. He wished she hadn't.

Glancing around, he couldn't spot any familiar faces. What a relief! Anyway, it wasn't like he was *alone* with Lara. How could anyone think they were together? He'd even arrived after her.

Relaxing slightly he decided she looked more beautiful than ever. Immediately he wanted to touch and hold her. Why waste time? He was sick of only being with her at parties and discotheques.

'Why don't we get out of here, beautiful lady?' he suggested in a low voice, touching her leg under the table.

'You just got here,' she chided gently. 'It's rude.'

'Listen.' His grip tightened on her leg. '*I* don't give a damn. How about you?'

'Don't you?' She sounded amused. 'My, how the climate changes your attitude. Shall we dance?'

He didn't feel like dancing. He just wanted to be alone with her.

Reluctantly he allowed himself to be pulled on to the dance floor where she pressed against him. Once again he felt the excitement, and the promise of what was to come.

The hell with April. He was free to do what he pleased. He wasn't married yet.

There was an Italian restaurant called Pinocchio's in New York that reserved a king's welcome for Enzio Bassalino whenever he was in town. It was a family concern. Mother, father, two daughters and a son. They anticipated Enzio's needs, and on any evening he dropped by nearby tables were only given to people he personally agreed to.

At one such table sat Kosta Gennas. A small, sweating man, with blackened teeth and gnarled skin. It seemed incongruous that he should be sitting with the three most attractive girls in the room.

Kosta chewed on the end of a stubby cigar and sucked at his Scotch through a special silver straw.

No one at the table spoke. The girls, three different kinds of beauties, stared vacantly ahead. They all had old-fashioned, teased hairstyles, though each one had hair of a different shade. They were all big of bosom, long of leg.

Kosta Gennas jumped up abruptly when Enzio Bassalino entered the restaurant.

Enzio nodded briefly at him as he passed his table. But it wasn't until an hour later that he summoned Kosta to join him. 'I like the look of the blonde,' Enzio said. 'What's her story?'

'She's nineteen years old,' Kosta replied quickly. 'A lovely girl, hard worker, only been with us two months. She was married to some bum, and when he split on her she decided there were smarter ways to make a living. We was saving her to send to Brazil, she'd be a sensation there. Then, when I heard you was lookin', we hung on to her.'

'Is she clean?' Enzio asked, getting straight to the point.

'*Is she clean?*' Kosta echoed in amazement, his furtive eyes darting around in surprise at Enzio's six or seven male companions. 'He asks me if she's clean. Would I ever—'

'Enough,' Enzio interrupted sharply. He didn't like Kosta Gennas, never had. But Kosta had the best girls, and he always knew exactly which ones would please Enzio the most. 'Send her over,' he growled. 'I'll see for myself.'

The girl wobbled across the restaurant on ridiculous stiletto heels. She stood by the side of the table grinning foolishly until Enzio indicated she should sit beside him.

When she was seated he looked her over carefully.

She had a pretty pointed face, dominated by jammy, wide red lips. Blue-shadowed grey eyes, a smattering of freckles she'd endeavoured to conceal, and from what he could see – a perfect body.

'What's your name, dear?' he asked kindly, patting her in a not-so-fatherly way on the knee.

'Miriam,' she whispered, in a breathy Marilyn Monroe voice.

'Well, Miriam,' he said, his eyes greedily devouring her ample cleavage. 'How would you feel about comin' to stay in my house in Miami?'

Anna Maria set her alarm clock for six a.m. every day. Then, heavy with child, she would stumble in the dark to the kitchen, where she liked to sit and drink warm, sweet tea, and watch the morning grow light.

Anna Maria had never trusted anyone else to make her children's breakfast. She enjoyed doing it herself. Mixing the hot, lumpy porridge. Heating the bread. Setting out the home-made plum jam. By seven, when they all appeared, she always had everything ready.

Anna Maria was a strong girl, but after four pregnancies her legs were feeling weak, her belly stretched almost beyond control. She was hoping the birth would be soon. Frank went off her when she was pregnant. He never touched her, and avoided looking at her. Not that he said anything, but she knew, and it saddened her. After all, Frank was the one who wanted many children.

Anna Maria struggled into her robe. She was exhausted, hopefully today would be the day. It was a strain entertaining Frank's father. There had been so much extra cooking to do, preparing all his favourite dishes. And the children always became more excitable than usual, while Frank himself was surly and gruff.

It seemed as if she'd just got into bed, and now it was another day. Wearily she plodded into the kitchen, switched on the light, and stared with a sense of stunned shock at her husband.

Frank was crouched over Beth whom he had spread-eagled across the kitchen table. His face was creased with concentration, and his breath short. He was dressed, but Beth was naked, a crumpled white nightgown lying on the floor by her feet.

Anna Maria's hand fled to the crucifix she wore around her neck, and her eyes wide with shock she began to mumble in Italian.

'Jesus Christ!' Frank bellowed. He was nearing the moment of climax and in no mood to be interrupted.

Beth wriggled out from under him. It was too late for him to stop. With a roar of fury he came all over the kitchen floor. The final insult.

'You fuckin' bitch,' he screamed at Anna Maria. 'What the hell you doin' spyin' on me?' His face was red with rage.

Anna Maria turned to run, but it was too late. Frank was after her, his arm raised in uncontrollable anger. He struck her across the face twice. The second time she fell to the floor.

'Bitch!' he yelled, standing over her with his arm raised, ready to give her more punishment.

Beth could not believe what was happening. She hadn't meant it to be like this. When she'd altered the time on Anna Maria's alarm clock, she'd fully intended Anna Maria would discover them together. But she hadn't realized Frank would turn into a screaming madman.

For a moment she was paralysed. And then the full realization of what he was doing to his wife hit her. With all her strength she threw herself at him, trying to

458

hold back the angry blows now raining down on Anna Maria.

He shoved her away.

'Stop it, Frank. *Stop it!*' she screamed. '*You're killing her!*'

Suddenly he seemed to realize what he was doing. Abruptly he stopped and began to groan. 'Oh, my God. Oh Jesus! What have I done?'

Anna Maria lay very still. For a moment Beth feared she might be dead. But she listened and heard faint breathing, and without a word to Frank she rushed to the phone and called an ambulance.

Frank was crying and trying to cradle Anna Maria in his arms when the ambulance arrived.

'She fell down the stairs,' he told the ambulance attendants. 'I couldn't save her. She fell.'

The two men exchanged glances. They'd heard that one before.

Then Anna Maria started to groan. Horrible loud animal groans.

'Please! Get her to the hospital quickly,' Beth said urgently. 'I think she's starting to have the baby.'

CHAPTER 24

Leroy Jesus Bauls watched the ambulance pull up at Frank Bassalino's house in the early hours of the morning with hardly a flicker of interest showing in his flat eyes. He was chewing gum, slowly, methodically. Now he took the gum from his mouth, squeezed it into a tight, hard ball and rolled it between his fingers.

How easy it would be to lay a hit on Frank Bassalino.

One carefully aimed shot between the eyes, it would be a cinch. By the time the two goons who were apparently his protection reacted, Leroy Jesus Bauls would be long gone.

Frank Bassalino was a far easier target than the old man. Enzio Bassalino knew what protection was all about, and wherever he went he made sure he was always surrounded and shielded. The trouble was, he protected himself in the old-fashioned way. Somebody should tell him, Leroy thought, with a wide yawn.

It was a shame there was nothing to be done right now. But he'd studied his homework, and if the occasion arose, if Dukey K. Williams gave the word for the final hit . . . Well, he was ready.

Leroy dropped his chewing gum to the ground. He had work to do. The Bassalinos were proving to be a stubborn family, but they would learn . . . Eventually.

Later that morning Leroy walked slowly towards the van he had stolen. He wore cheap clothes with SAMSONS LINENS written across the T-shirt he had on. Once in the van, he jammed on a black leather cap and yellow-tinted shades.

With a tight smile he imagined he could hear the witnesses now. 'Yeah – a black boy – about twenty something – tall – skinny – how the hell do I know what he looked like – he was *black*.'

'Sure, sure. We all look alike, baby,' he muttered to himself. '*Beee-oootiful!*'

He drove the van carefully. It wouldn't do to have any kind of accident.

Barberelli's was a large Italian restaurant and bar situated on a main street. Pulling the van up outside, Leroy got out. Collecting a large laundry basket from the back of the van, he carried it inside.

A girl was sitting behind a cash register adding up bills, while a wizened old man beat at the floor listlessly with a broom.

'Morning,' Leroy sang out. 'Samsons Linens, fresh delivery. Anything to go?'

The girl looked up vaguely. She had only worked there a week. 'I don't know,' she said. 'Nobody's in yet. You'd better leave it on a table.'

'Sure.' Whistling, he chose a table by the window. The old man kept on sweeping. 'I'll drop by tomorrow,' Leroy said cheerfully.

'OK,' the girl replied, uninterested.

Still whistling, he departed.

Leroy was three blocks away when he heard the explosion. It gave him a strange, almost sensual jolt of pleasure.

Carefully he extracted a new piece of gum from the pack, and even more carefully he drove the van to his next stop.

Manny's was a night-club, and the front was all closed up. Leroy took another laundry basket from the van and made his way around the back. There was an open door, but no one around.

Leroy began to whistle as he carried the basket past several dirty-looking dressing-rooms, across the dance floor, and placed it on a table.

He was starting to perspire slightly, the basket was heavy, and there wasn't that much time. He was cutting it close.

Quickly he turned to leave, and as he did so the door to the Ladies' Room swung open, and a sharp voice said, 'Hey, boy, what you think you doin' here?'

Leroy stopped and smiled. 'Samsons Linens,' he said politely.

A fat old black woman waddled into sight. Obviously she was the cleaner. With her was a small, bright-eyed black child.

'We don' deal with no Samsons Linens,' the old woman said with an impatient snort. 'So's you all kin git that basket outta here fast as you got it in. Unnerstand me, boy?'

He glanced at his watch. *Shit!* A voice screamed in his head. *Shit! Shit! Shit! Be smart and get your ass out.*

But something made him hesitate. He couldn't leave them. They were his people.

Jesus! What was the matter with him? Was he getting soft?

'Well, Ma'am,' he said calmly. 'If you'll be kind enough to step outside with me, maybe you can tell that to the driver, 'cos he ain't gonna listen to me.'

The old woman viewed him suspiciously, then she said to the child, 'You stay here, Vera May. Don't you touch nothin', you hear?'

Christ! Now he was really sweating. Time was running out and what could he do? Tell the truth? No, the old crone wouldn't believe him. Anyway, there wasn't time.

On impulse he scooped the kid up and started to run back the way he had come in. The child began to yell.

Leroy glanced behind him. Waving her arms in a panic the old woman careened after them.

In his head he began the countdown – *sixty, fifty-nine, fifty-eight.* There was no time to take the van now. The van would have to go up with the rest of the building. *Forty-five, forty-four, forty-three.* Outside at last.

'Shut up,' he muttered to the screaming kid. The old woman would be out soon. Get at least a block away.

He ran down the street clutching the child, and behind him he heard the old woman screeching, 'Stop that man, stop him – he's got my Vera May, my baby!'

462

Passers-by turned to look at him, but nobody tried to detain him. This was New York, people were not stupid.

At the corner he paused, any second now.

He placed the child on the pavement. 'You stay right here,' he commanded.

In the distance he saw the old woman getting closer.

Without hesitating he sprinted off in the direction of the subway entrance, annoyed at his own foolishness.

Within seconds he heard the explosion. Glancing back he noticed the woman and kid were together, frozen in shock, while people around them ran back towards the noise.

Ducking down the stairs to the subway he went straight to the Men's Room where he got rid of the Samsons Linens T-shirt, the hat and the shades.

It had been a good morning's work. It would certainly scare the shit out of the Bassalino family. And Dukey K. Williams would be more than pleased.

Leroy was satisfied. Nobody could beat him when it came to doing things right.

CHAPTER 25

Angelo didn't know what it was. It was a feeling that twisted his gut and stayed in his head. Rio Java. Rio Java. All he could think about was Rio Java.

Was this love? he thought to himself bitterly.

This couldn't be love, this nagging, persistent obsession.

Rio Java was not a beautiful woman, she wasn't even a particularly young woman. She was just a freak. A tall, randy, Red Indian fuckin' freak.

He made up his mind to forget her.

Enzio phoned from New York to inform him there was trouble all over, there had been certain threats. It was best that Angelo didn't go around unprotected.

'Aw, c'mon,' Angelo bitched. 'Nobody's gonna come after me.' His father talked like an old gangster movie.

'Read the newspapers, you dumb little cocksucker, there's hits happenin' everywhere. You're my son, so that makes you a target. I'm havin' the Stevestos assign a man to you.'

Angelo groaned, 'Listen—'

'No, *you* listen,' Enzio said coldly. 'I'm gettin' reports of you being drunk, bumming around. Straighten your ass or I'll haul you back here. You want that?'

Angelo swallowed an angry reply. He liked it in London. The more distance between himself and his family the better. 'OK, OK. I'll get myself together,' he promised.

'You'd better,' Enzio warned.

A man called Shifty Fly was commissioned to protect him. It infuriated Angelo that he had to be followed and accompanied everywhere.

Shifty Fly looked like his name. He was small, with watery, darting eyes, and a thin, downturned mouth. Under the crabby grey suit he wore rested a shoulder holster and concealed gun.

'This is a joke,' Angelo complained to Eddie Ferrantino.

Eddie's cold eyes flicked over Angelo, marvelling yet again that this bearded asshole was Enzio Bassalino's son. 'Just do as your father says, be a good little boy, huh?'

Fuck the 'little boy' jazz. Angelo was sick of it. First Rio and now Eddie. Who the frig did they think they were?

He took out his various girlfriends and gave it to them regularly. There were no complaints.

He forced himself not to contact Rio. She was a bad scene, and even he knew enough not to ask for more.

He couldn't hold out. He called her.

'Hey, Rio, this is Angelo.'

'Angelo who?'

Bitch! 'Angelo Bassalino.'

Her voice was cool. 'Let me see now, I don't think I remember an Angelo Bassalino . . .'

He laughed, full of false bravado. 'Stop kidding around. I thought you might like dinner.'

'I *always* like dinner. In fact I have it every night.' A long pause. 'Do *you* have it every night?'

'Yeah.'

'Then why don't you run off and have it now.'

She hung up on him. The bitch hung up!

He sent her flowers, something he had *never* done. She sent them back when they were dead with a short note, 'Hey – isn't it funny – does everything you handle turn limp?'

He found that although he was able to service all his girlfriends, it was virtually impossible for him to reach a climax. He remained hard as a rock, ready to go for ever, never reaching the final destination. It was causing him great physical discomfort. When the hard-on vanished he was left with a pain in his gut that lasted all night.

Apart from that aggravation, there was Shifty Fly always close at hand. Foul mouthed and slimy he trailed Angelo everywhere.

Rio was pleased with the way things were going. She'd always possessed the power of grabbing men sexually. Larry Bolding had been one of the few exceptions, and that was because he was shit scared of his wife, political career, and spotless reputation.

Boy, could she blow the whistle on his spotless reputation.

It was days since she'd returned the flowers to Angelo. Now the time was ripe. Picking up the phone she called him.

Angelo groped for the receiver in his sleep. 'Yeah?' he said in a muffled voice.

'Listen, stud,' she said. 'Don't you think it's about time I taught you how to *really* get it on?'

He was silent, trying to gather his thoughts.

'Last chance, sweetheart,' she said mockingly. 'So why don't you get your fine ass over here quick, an' I'll show you tricks you ain't *never* gonna forget!'

By the time he was properly awake she'd hung up. It was past midnight. Throwing on some pants and a shirt he ducked out the back entrance. This was one scene Shifty Fly wasn't going to be following him to.

CHAPTER 26

Lara paced her living-room smoking agitatedly. It was early, light was just beginning to seep through the darkness. New York was taking shape outside.

Why did I ever become involved? she thought.

Nick was asleep in the bedroom. *Why did it have to be Nick?*

Her hand shook slightly as she dragged on the cigarette, realizing that she didn't want to take it any further. Nick was not responsible for things his father did. Dukey K. Williams was right, and Rio with her insane plans all wrong. Much as she had loved Margaret, her sister was dead, and no amount of revenge could bring her back. If Enzio Bassalino *was* the man responsible, then let Dukey deal with him in the way he wanted to.

Oh God! How had she ever got into this? A few hours earlier she and Nick had left Le Club.

'Your place or my hotel?' he'd asked intently.

Light headed from too much champagne she'd replied, 'My place.'

They'd started to kiss in the car, all over each other like a couple of high-school kids.

'Baby, baby, you make me crazy,' he'd said, guiding her hand to the bulge in his pants that lent truth to his statement.

For a moment she'd been overcome with guilt – because she was enjoying his touch, and there was no way she was supposed to enjoy it. But once they reached her apartment, her guilt melted away in his arms as he ripped the nine hundred dollar black dress off her, and made love to her on the floor.

Later he'd carried her into the bedroom, and it had happened one more time before she'd fallen asleep.

Now she was awake, pacing up and down like an agitated cat.

Was it possible to fall in love with someone you were supposed to hate?

'How about some coffee, princess?' Nick walked into the living room, startling her. He was naked. His body lean, hard and tanned.

Wrapping his arms around her he hugged her close, and slowly began pushing her négligée off her shoulders, sliding it down her body.

With great anticipation she leaned her head back – all the better to catch his kisses. It had never been this way with anyone before, this pure physical pull. There had always been reasons why she'd gone to bed with men. Hard-hitting, down-to-earth reasons.

With Nick it wasn't like that. Oh, there was a reason all right. But it didn't matter any more, it wasn't important.

He lifted her easily and carried her back to the bedroom. 'You, lady – are beautiful. I mean *really* beautiful. You know what I'm sayin'?'

Yes, she knew what he was saying. She also knew that soon the morning papers would arrive. And how would he feel then?

Beth stayed with the Bassalino children. She felt sick and scared. If anything happened to Anna Maria's baby it was all her fault, and that didn't bear thinking about.

Frank phoned in the morning. His voice sounded funny. 'Pack up and get out of there,' he instructed her harshly. 'Do it *now*. I don't want to find you around when I get back.'

'Is everything all right?' she asked anxiously. 'The baby?'

There was silence for a moment, and then Frank's voice cold and loud. 'Get the fuck out of my house, you whore. An' don't leave no forwarding address, 'cos if I ever set eyes on you again I'm gonna kill you.' He slammed the phone down.

Beth recoiled in shock. It was over. Whatever it was it was over. She was free. Now she could go home.

With an unsteady hand she picked up the phone and dialled information, obtaining the number of the hospital.

'I'm enquiring after Mrs Frank Bassalino. She was admitted early this morning. I'm a relative. Is she doing OK?'

The operator's voice sounded apologetic. 'I'm sorry, we cannot give out information over the phone.'

Of course not, she thought bitterly.

Hurrying to her room she packed her few things. Minutes later she stepped outside the house. Relief swept over her. Soon she could return to her daughter Chyna, and the commune. But first she had to find out about Anna Maria.

A bus dropped her half a block away from the hospital. She was terrified of bumping into Frank, but her fear was overcome by a desperate need to know.

'Mrs Bassalino died at eight a.m.,' a nurse told her. 'Complications with the position of the baby, and other things . . .' The nurse trailed off. 'Are you a close friend? I think Doctor Rogers might like to speak to you.'

'And the baby?'

'Everything possible was done, but I'm afraid . . .'

Beth turned and ran.

The nurse started after her. 'Please wait, if you can help us at all—'

Beth kept running. She didn't stop until she reached Grand Central Station where she bought herself a ticket home.

Before boarding the train she phoned Cass. 'I guess it's what you all wanted,' she said bitterly. 'But how does it help Margaret? It certainly doesn't bring her back, does it?'

CHAPTER 27

They were making love.

'You're getting better all the time.' Rio finally threw a compliment his way. 'Maybe I was wrong about you.'

Angelo rode the wave. He was in control. Like a car

469

that has been perfectly tuned he crested each bump and hill and didn't falter.

The Stones mumbled hornily on background stereo. It was early evening and things had been going successfully all afternoon.

'Let's take a break for food,' Rio announced. 'I've got a friend who'll bring over anything we want.' Rolling away from him she lifted the phone.

Angelo lay back triumphant. He could go as long as she wanted him to. King Stud.

'Yeah, you can bring Peaches,' Rio purred into the receiver. 'I'm certain there's plenty to go around. Sure. See you soon. Bye.' She flopped back on the bed. 'Food's on its way. How about an appetizer, babe?'

Angelo thought about phoning the casino to let them know he wasn't coming in tonight, but what the hell, it would only bring Shifty Fly running to station himself outside, and who needed that?

'I'm ready,' he said confidently.

'Great!'

Rio liked popping ammis. Soon she was breaking open another glass vial and forcing it under his nose.

He breathed in deeply, feeling the effect down to his toe-nails.

'You know, you're not too bad,' she murmured, sliding across his body, straddling his neck with her long legs. 'But Jesus Christ your beard is itchy!'

Enzio paced the private room at the hospital, his face a grim mask.

Frank sat in a chair, his head buried in his hands.

Enzio muttered in Italian, occasionally throwing words of contempt in his son's direction.

Dr Rogers entered the room. He was a weary, bespectacled man with receding hair, and a slight build.

Enzio clapped him on the shoulders. 'Doctor, we know you did all you could, you mustn't blame yourself.'

Dr Rogers shook Enzio's hand away. 'I don't blame myself,' he said indignantly. 'Not at all, Mr Bassalino.' He turned to glare at Frank. 'I'm afraid that poor girl was very badly beaten. The baby had no chance, it was—'

'She fell down the stairs,' Frank interrupted, stone-faced. 'I told you that before. She fell.'

'Mr Bassalino, your wife's internal injuries were not consistent with falling down stairs. She was beaten, and *that's* what will have to go on the death certificate.' His voice was full of barely concealed disgust. 'I'm sure there will have to be an enquiry.'

Enzio approached the doctor. 'Are you a family man, Doc?' he asked, very friendly.

'Yes,' the doctor replied shortly.

'Pretty wife? Nice kiddies?'

'I don't see what this has to do—'

'Plenty,' Enzio said. 'As a family man you can understand the occasional little tiff. Y'know what I mean – lovers' quarrel – that kind of thing. Happens all the time, don't it, Doc?'

'What has this got to do with anything?' the doctor asked stiffly.

'Well, y'see, my boy – he's a man suffering. Now you wouldn't wanna make it any worse for him, wouldja, Doc?'

'Mr Bassalino, I have a duty to perform.'

'Sure you do, an' believe me, I'm not trying to stop you. I think you doctors do a wonderful job. And yet you're underpaid. It's shockin'. A crime really. I mean here you are workin' your asses off, an' what do you get? Hardly enough to keep your wife looking pretty.' Enzio took a beat. 'You know what I mean, huh? I'm an old man, but I still appreciate a pretty face.' A meaningful pause. 'It would be a shame if your wife lost hers.' He fumbled in his pocket, producing a wad of bills carelessly held together with an elastic band. 'Here's a thousand dollars, Doc, somethin' to help you out.'

Dr Rogers hesitated as Enzio thrust the money towards him.

'Take it,' Enzio said, his voice mild. 'Keep your wife pretty.'

By the time the papers were delivered Nick had fallen back to sleep.

Lara scanned them quickly. In the gossip column of one was the item she had known would be there. The writer – a bitchy woman columnist – had put it together as only a bitch could.

> How does glamorous star of the forties, still frisky April Crawford, do it? Married four times, those in the know say she is about to take el plungo five with handsome thirtyish Nick Bassalino, a Los Angeles businessman. However, someone should tell Nick, for when last seen he was boarding a plane for New York with gorgeous, beautiful Lara Crichton, a stunning jet setter of twenty-six. Last report had them dancing cheek to cheek among other things at New York's chicest discotheque, Le Club.

There was a picture of Lara taken in Acapulco for a *Harpers Bazaar* layout looking incredible in a one-piece white swimsuit. There was also a picture of April leaving a film premiere. She looked tired.

Oh well, Lara thought ruefully – goodbye April. The movie star would never stand for Nick making a public fool of her.

What now? Where did it leave her and Nick?

472

It wasn't fair. She hadn't known it would be like this. She hadn't counted on actually falling in love.

Was one night of incredible sex, love?

Maybe, maybe not. He was so different from all the other men she'd known. He was masculine and sexual. There was nothing phony about Nick Bassalino. He was just as he was.

Angry at herself she took the paper in the bedroom and tossed it at him. 'You're not going to like this,' she said flatly. 'And I think it's going to make April mad as hell.'

Rio fixed fantastic drinks. Rum, brown sugar, eggs, cream, Benedictine, all mixed together in the blender. When the doorbell rang she told Angelo to stay in bed, she would get it. Naked except for the stiletto heels she always liked to wear, she marched off.

What with the amyl-nitrate poppers, the sex, the couple of joints they'd smoked, and the heavy rum drink, he felt pretty tired. Pleasantly so. Christ, she couldn't object to him falling asleep now. There would be no more name calling, he'd proved himself at last.

He closed his eyes, feeling strange, almost suspended. More than being stoned, it was like his mind was leaving his body and drifting over to the corner to watch him.

That was funny. That was *really* funny, and he started to laugh. Soon he realized his laugh wasn't coming out of his mouth, it was coming out from all over, his nose, ears, even his ass. The thought only made him laugh more, and the more he laughed the more peculiar sensations overcame him.

He noticed a lot of people crowding into the room. Nice smiling faces who appreciated his laughter.

Everyone began to take off their clothes and as they did so the clothes floated around the room in slow motion. Angelo was too exhausted to sit up. He was enjoying himself. He was having such a *great* time.

'Hey, baby.' Rio's face swam into focus very close to his. 'You remember Hernando and Peaches, don't you, babe? They *both* think you're *reaal* special. They *both* want to meet you.'

Her voice saying 'meet you' echoed and echoed around the room until it sounded like an Indian *mantra*.

He nodded. Immediately his head seemed to leave the rest of his body and ricochet up to the ceiling.

Hernando began laying strong hands on him, caressing his sex, taking it in his mouth.

Angelo groaned with pleasure. His penis felt bigger than his body. His body was nothing.

Peaches was exquisite, a fine-boned Slavic face with thick blonde hair. She was pushing Hernando away and taking over.

Somewhere Rio's laughter hung heavy in the air.

They turned him over and Hernando mounted him and he knew it was a man forcing his way inside, but it didn't matter, it didn't matter at all. In fact, it was fantastic. Peaches was taking him in her mouth at the same time and he thought he was reaching a pinnacle of eternity, and the actual coming was an explosion that rivalled with the atomic bomb. Pow!! Great mushroom clouds. And he drifted off into the deep sleep he had been waiting for.

CHAPTER 28

Nick argued impatiently with April Crawford's maid on the telephone in Lara's bedroom. 'Now come on, Hattie, I *know* she's there. Tell her again, I *have* to talk to her, it's *very* important.'

Hattie lowered her voice. 'Mr Bassalino, it's just no good. She is locked in her room and won't speak to anyone.'

'You're sure you told her it's me?'

'*Especially* you she won't talk to.'

'Oh, shit, Hattie, you know what she's like. I'll try and get a plane back today. How many bottles has she got in there with her?'

'*Mr Bassalino!*' Hattie exclaimed in shocked tones. She had been with April nineteen years and still refused to admit her employer drank.

'Keep an eye on her, Hattie, explain things to her, tell her not to believe everything she reads in the papers. I'll see you tonight.'

Lara, hovering outside, marched briskly into the room. 'Well,' she said, forcing a smile, 'that's it then, is it?'

'What?' he said shortly.

'Running back to momma's arms, huh? I do hope she'll forgive you for being bad.'

He shook his head sadly. 'Lara – Lara. I'm surprised at you.'

He's surprised *at me!* she thought angrily. Jesus, she'd really been acting like a naïve idiot. Blinded by a great-looking guy with a fantastic body and one night of wild sex. She'd expected he might *want* to stay,

475

but the only thing on his mind was running back to April.

'When are you leaving?' she asked flatly.

'I don't know, I have to call my father.'

'Oh, I see. Can't go unless daddy gives the word. Well, if he says you have to stay another night, shall we have a repeat performance? After all we're both here, it would be foolish not to take advantage.'

'Listen,' he said, getting off the bed, still naked. 'Don't talk like a cunt, it doesn't suit you. You knew what this was going to be. I never lied to you about me and April. I *love* April Crawford. I'm going to *marry* her.'

'You insulting bastard!' She was close to tears. 'Just get dressed and get the hell out.'

He shrugged. 'If it means anything to you, last night was Wonderland.'

'And I was Alice, a naïve little girl. Thank you, Nick. You sure made me grow up in a hurry.'

He tried to take her in his arms but she pushed him away.

'When are you coming back to Los Angeles?' he asked.

'Never. Does that make you feel more secure?'

'If we're careful we can still see each other.'

She laughed bitterly. 'God, Nick, I don't believe you! In one breath it's how you love April Crawford and you're going to marry her. And in the next it's when will you see me again. Well let me tell you, Nick Bassalino. You won't – not ever.'

He shook his head. 'Don't count on it, baby. Just don't count on it.'

Golli and Segal arrived at the hospital and escorted Frank home. 'Whatever you do, don't leave him,' Enzio warned. 'Stay with him at all times.'

476

Enzio made all the arrangements for the funeral. He had spoken to Anna Maria's family in Sicily. Her mother and sister said they would fly in for the funeral.

Enzio was sick to his stomach. Frank was a bitter disappointment. Beating a pregnant woman was a terrible thing to do. A sin. But thank God it had happened while Enzio himself was in New York and able to deal with matters so there would be no disgrace brought upon the family.

Still, he'd never expected anything like this from Frank, his eldest, and he'd thought most dependable, son. God would surely punish him for such a violent and sickening act. Enzio firmly believed in the power of the Almighty for a certain things.

What a morning. News of the bombings at Manny's and Barbarelli's had reached him. He was sure Bosco Sam was behind it. A show of strength was needed, but Christ, what strength could you show to a bunch of crazy maniacs who walked around in broad daylight blowing up places?

Enzio knew there had to be an answer. There had to be, or the whole Bassalino organization's reputation would be at risk. Who was going to pay protection for no protection?

All morning he'd been trying to reach Angelo in London. It was yet another worry he didn't need. Angelo hadn't shown up at the casino, and somehow he'd managed to disappear without his bodyguard. Out getting laid of course.

Once more the overseas operator told him there was no reply from Angelo's number. He knew what he would do when he got hold of him. Bring the horny little bastard home for Anna Maria's funeral, and keep him home. No more screwing around in London. Angelo's place was with his family where they could

477

watch him. Maybe he'd put him to work for Frank again.

Finally Nick arrived at the hotel.

'What took you so long?' Enzio snapped. 'You shoulda come to the hospital.'

Nick was distressed. 'I only just heard,' he said. 'What happened?'

Enzio grimaced sadly. 'An accident. She fell down the stairs.'

Nick looked incredulous. 'Fell down the stairs? How? Where was Frank?'

'He was sleeping. She was pregnant, clumsy on her feet. It was a tragic accident.'

'God! I can hardly believe it. Anna Maria was such a sweet kid . . .'

'And you?' Enzio bellowed. 'Where the fuck were you all night? When I need you, no one can find you.' He shook his head. 'Don't you have no sense, Nick? These are dangerous times.'

'I called the hotel soon as I got up,' Nick said defensively. 'Then I broke my balls rushing over here.'

'You broke your balls last night,' Enzio commented dryly. 'At least it's good you can forget about the old broad you screw in Hollywood. But hey – no time for talk now, you go to your brother's house and stay with him.'

'I gotta be getting back to the Coast, without me things can start—'

'Enough!' Enzio shouted. 'I don't understand my children. Your brother loses his wife – *your* sister-in-law. There should be grief, respect. But no, you mumble about getting back to the Coast. What kind of brother are you? Get over to Frank's house an' sit with him. You can plan on stayin' here until after the funeral.'

'When's that?'

'Don't question me!' Enzio screamed. 'Get out of here.' His heart was bouncing around, a sign of over-exertion no doubt.

What had he done to deserve three idiot sons?

CHAPTER 29

Dukey K. Williams accepted the news of the bombings calmly. He congratulated Leroy.

Later he visited Cass. 'I'm leaving the apartment soon,' he told her.

The apartment he'd shared with Margaret held too many memories. He had to forget about the past. Remembrances of Margaret were making every day painful. When her death was avenged, he wanted to be ready to move on.

Cass told him about Anna Maria Bassalino, and Beth's sudden return to the commune.

'Pull the other two out,' he warned harshly. '*I'm* takin' over now. I'm doin' it my way, and I don't want them around, screwin' things up.'

'What are you going to do?' Cass asked, alarmed.

'It's better you don't know,' he replied.

Back home he called his manager. 'Let's get the show on the road again. I'm gonna be ready to work sooner than you think.'

His manager was delighted.

Next he called Leroy. 'Why don't we cut the overture an' get down to business. I want this over. Start with Frank at the funeral for his wife, an' then take care of the house in Miami. No more waiting. Put your plan into action. The money will be ready when you are.'

479

'It's as good as done,' Leroy replied. He didn't make idle promises.

CHAPTER 30

Angelo had trouble forcing his eyes open. With a supreme effort he managed it and blinked several times. His eyes felt crusty and bloodshot. Serious hangover eyes.

For a moment he was completely disoriented, and then he remembered where he was. He was alone on Rio's bed in her apartment. The curtains were closed, and he had no idea if it was night or day.

His body ached, and there was an uncomfortable, unfamiliar feeling about his backside.

'Jesus Christ!' He sat up slowly, gingerly. What the hell happened to him?

He clearly remembered coming to her apartment, and Rio greeting him. He remembered the fantastic sex scene they'd had, and the ammis, the pot, the drinks. Then everything went blank. One long – how long? – great big blank.

It must have been the drinks. Those thick, creamy, rum concoctions Rio had dipped her fingers in and fed him with. They'd knocked him out.

Where was she anyway?

Unsteadily he got up, aware of the difference in his body, beginning to be much more aware of how it must have happened.

He had to take a piss, and groped his way into the bathroom.

Scotch-taped to the mirror were six colour Polaroids,

leaving him in no doubt as to what had happened. In case he was not convinced, Rio had written across the mirror in bright red lipstick – RIGHT ON BABY! I ALWAYS KNEW YOU WERE A FAG.

With mounting horror he stared at the Polaroids. They showed him with a plumpish, dark man, and a beautiful blonde girl. Only she wasn't a girl, she couldn't be a girl, because in spite of her breasts she also featured a formidable penis.

Angelo had always feared men getting close to him. He hated being touched by them. Even a friendly back pat irritated him. All his life he'd scrupulously avoided any male contact. And now this.

In the pictures he was smiling, laughing. He actually looked like he was *enjoying* it.

Panic overcame him. God Almighty! If anyone *saw* these pictures. If his *father* should see them. Holy shit! It didn't bear thinking about.

Hurriedly he ripped the offending Polaroids off the mirror and tore them into small pieces, flushing the bits down the toilet.

He took a deep breath. With the evidence gone he felt calmer.

What was he worried about anyway? He wasn't gay, half of the women in London could testify to *that*.

Jesus! It was that bitch Rio's fault. She'd spiked his drink and had her fun. Where was the cow?

He searched the apartment. It was empty. She must have planned the whole sick scene.

Well, he wasn't going to let her get away with it. He would think of *some* form of retaliation to blow her cool.

With Nick gone, Lara was keyed up and agitated. Things had worked out the way she'd planned, but what if April took Nick back? It wasn't a likely prospect, but what if she did? Then all her scheming and planning would count for nothing – a useless waste of time.

Maybe. Maybe not. Was it useless she'd finally met a man who could make her feel emotions other than how big his bank balance was, or what kind of title he held?

Was it useless she'd fallen in love for the first time ever?

None of it mattered. Whatever the outcome, she didn't care to be involved any more. And she certainly never wanted to set eyes on Nick Bassalino again.

For insurance she decided to call Prince Alfredo in Rome or wherever he was, and summon him to fetch her. And then she would phone Cass and tell her it was over.

Decision made, she felt better. Or did she? Nick Bassalino was on her mind, and he wasn't going to be that easy to forget.

Nick went to Frank's house. The children were whiny and noisy.

'Where's the nanny?' he asked.

'Gone,' Frank mumbled. He was drinking neat whisky, hunched in a chair, his eyes bloodshot, his appearance unkempt.

'Jesus, Frank, I'm sorry about everything . . .' Nick trailed off. He'd never been very close to his older brother. When they were kids Frank used to beat the shit out of him. Frank had always been the biggest and the strongest and he'd never let Nick forget it.

Nick wandered into the room where Golli and Segal were watching television. It was such a depressing house. Old and worn. It was a house that must have looked the same twenty, even thirty years previously. He thought with longing of his own place in Los Angeles. Big and spacious. White and modern. Then he thought of April's rambling mansion, with the lake in the garden, and the swimming pool in the living room. California was the only place for him. He enjoyed the climate, the people, the whole relaxed way of living. You could shove New York. Dirty pavements and uptight people. Everyone white faced and hustling, scurrying around like guests at a rat-fuck.

He went upstairs and placed another call to April. It was the same story. She refused to speak to him. He told Hattie he was delayed, and why. 'Be sure to tell her why,' he emphasized. Christ, April was liable to think he was hanging around to be with Lara.

Thinking of Lara, it had been nice, she was a very lovely lady. But beautiful girls were a plague in Los Angeles. You fell over them everywhere you went. April Crawford was an original, and Nick was confident she would forgive him once he explained there was nothing to it. Lara just happened to be on the same plane – coincidence – it could happen to anyone. And April, better than anyone, understood about the gossip columns – pure hokum – nobody ever believed the garbage they printed.

Yes, Nick was sure everything was going to work out fine.

Restlessly he wondered what Lara was doing. Would she hang up if he called her?

He wasn't about to risk finding out. Nope. Best to forget her.

He'd wanted her. He'd had her. End of story.

Christ, it was going to be boring, hanging around the house with Frank.

'Hey, Segal,' he yelled downstairs. 'How about a game of poker? Any cards around this mausoleum?'

CHAPTER 31

Mary Ann August woke up in Los Angeles. She couldn't remember much about getting there; after Alio Marcusi had slobbered all over her, there had been another visitor, a woman called Claire.

Mary Ann could remember being frightened and telling Claire that when Enzio found out what had happened there would be plenty of trouble. Claire had laughed, and called her honey. 'Don't worry, honey, Enzio knows all about it. He wants you to come on a little journey with me.'

Then Claire had stuck a needle into her arm, making her groggy and docile, and she had dressed and left the hotel with Claire, and there had been a car journey, then an airplane, another car trip, and after that a house, a room, and sleep. Now she was awake.

She got up and took stock of her surroundings. She was in a bedroom, a plain room with olive green walls and shuttered windows. The shutters wouldn't open, nor would the door.

She peered at herself in a mirror. Her teased hair was sad and straggly. Her make-up streaked and faded.

Nothing annoyed Mary Ann more than not looking her best. Searching for her purse she found it on the floor. Painstakingly she applied fresh make-up and redid her hair. When the the two jobs were finished, she finally allowed herself to wonder where she was, and what was going on.

During her six months with Enzio, Mary Ann had acquired quite a few possessions. Jewellery, clothes, a mink coat, and of course her latest acquisition – the full-length chinchilla.

She was thinking of those things now. They were her protection when Enzio finally got tired of her. They would buy her a decent future so she wouldn't have to go back to dancing around naked on a stage for a living. She would kill rather than lose her possessions.

The woman Claire came into the room. She was fortyish and slim, slightly masculine looking.

'I don't understand,' Mary Ann said in her best baby-girl voice. 'Where's Enzio? Why does he want me here?'

Claire shrugged. 'He figured you needed a change, honey. He knows I have lots of nice friends here in LA, and he thought you'd enjoy meeting some of them.'

'Why didn't he tell me?'

Claire put her arm across Mary Ann's shoulders. 'Enzio told me one of your best qualities is that you don't ask a lot of silly questions.' She narrowed her eyes. 'You're a very pretty girl, but that hair-style will have to go.'

'Enzio likes my hair this way,' Mary Ann said stubbornly.

'Get used to it, kitten. Enzio won't be around for a while.'

'What about my things? My clothes and jewellery? My fur coats?'

'Don't worry about them,' Claire replied easily. 'Enzio's having them sent. Be a good girl and cooperate with me – that way everything's gonna turn out OK.'

Dumb as she was, Mary Ann was slowly beginning to realize that all was not well.

CHAPTER 32

Shifty Fly saw Angelo safely aboard the big jumbo jet bound for New York. 'Don't think it hasn't been fun, Yank,' he sneered.

'Listen, man,' Angelo said. 'Why are you so uptight? I understand you've got your job to do. Only thing is – you're not too good at it.'

Shifty Fly glared at him. He'd had a right dressing down from Eddie Ferrantino for allowing Angelo to give him the slip.

'Don't wait around on my account,' Angelo continued. 'I'm not going anywhere.' Leaning back in his seat he shut his eyes, hoping that by the time he opened them Shifty Fly would be gone. He was.

The day had been a fuck-up. Screaming from every direction. Enzio in New York. Eddie Ferrantino in London. Christ knows what he was supposed to have done. Free, white, and over twenty-one, he'd shacked up with a broad and not told anyone where he was. Terrible thing. A crime.

'Would you like to order a drink, sir?' asked the stewardess. She was pretty in a plastic, groomed sort of way.

Normally he would have imagined screwing her, but his head was so full of other things he hardly noticed her. 'Just a Coke,' he said.

The two seats beside him were empty, and that pleased him. Later he hoped to be able to lie out and sleep. He needed the rest.

He was apprehensive about seeing his father. Enzio was sure to scream about the way he looked. He hadn't even had time to get his hair trimmed and it was now as long and thick as a rock star's.

If only he could tell Enzio Bassalino to go fuck himself. But he couldn't. He knew he couldn't. Yet he wasn't sure *why* he couldn't.

As the big jet taxied down the runway, Angelo allowed himself to think about Rio. She was some woman, the sort of woman who would stand up to someone like Enzio. One thing about Rio Java. She was an original. She did her own thing.

On the other hand, she was a sadistic bitch. And he wasn't happy about her hyping his drink and involving him in her orgy with her own personal band of perverts. Just who exactly did she think she was dealing with? He wasn't some schmuck off the street.

He wondered if she would call him. His fast departure for New York had to surprise her. Maybe she would think he was running away. From what? He had nothing to run from. So some guy had made it with him. Big fucking deal. Most men had at least one homosexual experience in their lives.

But when he thought about it, his skin began to crawl, his stomach to churn, and a helpless excitement crept through his body. Deep down he knew, although he wouldn't admit it, that it was something he would want to try again.

Lara went to Kennedy Airport to meet Prince Alfredo Masserini. She had called him, told him she needed him, and although in the middle of a backgammon tournament in Gstaad, he had promised to fly to her side at once.

She'd decided to meet his plane because she had to keep occupied. Too much thinking was driving her crazy. Nick Bassalino was on her mind with a vengeance,

487

and she didn't know how to forget him.

Prince Alfredo should be able to make her forget.

Sure, a mocking inner voice told her.

At the airport she bumped straight into Nick.

They stared at each other for a moment of complete surprise, then Lara smiled the hurt out of her eyes and extended a hand for her customary European hand-shake. 'Are you returning to Los Angeles?' she asked politely, silently adding *and April.*

'No.' He shook his head. 'My brother's coming in from London, I'm meeting him. What are you doing here?'

'Uh . . . I have friends arriving from Europe.' She didn't know why she hadn't said my fiancé, Prince Alfredo Masserini, a Roman Prince, not a miserable half-breed Yankee Italian like you.

Twenty-four hours previously they had been in bed together. Now they stood like polite strangers.

Nick peered at his watch. Lara glanced around in the faint hope she might bump into someone else she knew. Someone who could rescue her.

'I guess I'd better check on the plane, see if it's on time,' he said. 'What flight are you meeting? Give me the number and I'll check that out too.'

She handed him a piece of paper with scribbled details.

'Wait here,' he commanded.

As soon as he'd gone she had an insane desire to run. How childish. Wrapping her lynx coat tightly around her she stood her ground.

He returned shortly. As he approached she noticed women watching him. He was the sort of man you looked at twice. You almost recognized him. Was he an actor, a singer?

'We're meeting the same plane,' he announced. 'De-layed two hours. Want to go to the airport motel and make crazy, incredible love?' He was smiling slightly. A joke?

She smiled back, coldly. It was a joke she didn't appreciate. 'I don't think so.'

'Pity.' He was in control. 'You look very beautiful, like you've done very beautiful things lately.'

'How's April?' she asked, briskly changing the subject.

'Great,' he lied. 'Everything's fine. She understands it was nothing but gossip.'

'But it wasn't,' Lara pointed out.

He laughed uneasily. 'Yeah, sure. *You* know that and *I* know that, but *we* aren't telling, are we?'

She enjoyed the moment, mocking him with her green eyes. 'Aren't we?'

He gripped her firmly by the arm. 'I'm buying you a drink,' he announced. 'We can't just stand here for two hours.'

'I'm going back to the city,' she said crisply. 'I've decided not to wait.' Damn Alfredo for making the connection that put him on the same plane as Nick's brother.

'Then you've got time for a drink first.'

She wanted to say no, turn and run, get out of his life. But her body begged to stay next to his, and her body wouldn't move.

Taking her arm he led her to a nearby bar and sat her in a corner booth. She ordered champagne and orange juice. The cocktail waitress looked at her as if she was some kind of nut, and then turned her attention to Nick, giving him a suggestive wink.

'I probably won't be able to get back to the Coast for a couple more days,' he remarked, 'so if you're going to be around maybe we could—'

'Maybe we could what?' she interrupted icily. 'Have a few more secret interludes? A little bit of fun on the side that April won't find out about?'

'You didn't object yesterday.'

'Yesterday I had no idea you were going to turn to jelly as soon as you saw our names together in a newspaper.'

'I told you the truth about me and April. I haven't been keeping secrets. But that doesn't change the way you turn me on. You *know* you turn me on. And it's the same for you, isn't it?' He took her hand in his and held it tightly. 'We've got something goin' together, so don't fight it, lady. Just relax.'

How easy to agree with him. Two or three more days of incredible sex. And then what?

'You meet your friends,' he was saying, 'I'll meet my brother, we'll get that over with, and then later I'll come by your apartment. Nobody has to know, only you and me. This way we're all winners. What do you say?'

Her mind was racing. Nick Bassalino needed to be taught a lesson, he was too sure of himself by far.

She hesitated for only a moment.

'C'mon, Lara,' he urged. 'Do you have a spare key to your apartment?'

Revenge was sweet. 'Yes, as a matter of fact, I have,' she said, fumbling in her purse.

CHAPTER 33

It wasn't fair to blame Beth, Frank reasoned. It wasn't her fault Anna Maria had caught them together. Beth was a good kid, genuinely sweet and concerned. He'd called her a whore. She was probably destroyed. He regretted his phone call telling her to get out. It was stupid. He needed her now, more than ever. The children needed her. How many girls like Beth were there around? Not many, he could vouch for that. The day of the innocent girl was over. They were all hookers and hustlers out for what they could get.

He wanted Beth back. But how was he supposed to find her when he couldn't even remember which employment agency sent her? He had all of them checked out, but none of them seemed to remember her. At her interview she'd brought references. References he hadn't bothered to check, because he'd liked her at first glance. Now he found himself in the frustrating position of not knowing where she was, or any more about her than her name was Beth.

He put people in charge of tracking her down, knowing she would have to register with the employment agencies if she wanted another job. Meanwhile, because of his own stupidity, he could only sit and wait. And sitting and waiting meant thinking, and he did not like the thoughts that crowded his head. So he drank, and drinking meant a sweet oblivion that only hit him after a full bottle of Scotch, and being drunk meant he couldn't work.

Enzio gave strict orders to Segal and Golli not to let Frank out of their sight, and to keep him at home. There would be time enough after the funeral to pull Frank back into shape.

In the meantime Enzio took over. First he met an old friend, Stefano Crown. Stefano was sympathetic, he too was having trouble with new organizations trying to muscle in.

'What's your solution?' Enzio asked.

Stefano Crown shrugged. He was younger than Enzio by fifteen years, and still kept complete control of his business empire. 'Maybe I give 'em a piece of action, bring some of 'em in,' he said.

Enzio spat his disgust on the floor. He'd experienced

trouble with Stefano Crown before. The prick was getting soft. 'You give 'em some, they want more. You give 'em more, they want it all.'

'I run legitimate businesses,' Stefano said, stroking his chin. 'Last week they blew up two of my supermarkets. Whaddaya think that means? I can't have the ordinary jerks too shit scared to drag their asses to work in the mornings. Last week thirty-three of my employees quit – *thirty-three*. Word gets around. Soon I'll have 'em all takin' off. Then what'll I do when there's no one to run the beauty parlours, garages, supermarkets, huh, Enzio my friend?'

Enzio spat again. All Stefano Crown was concerned about was his legitimate front. Fuck that. Things were so different from the old days.

'You go with 'em, you get no help from me,' he said roughly. 'I have other plans, better plans.'

Stefano shook his head. 'I don't want no more trouble. I can't afford it. I'm a man who pays my taxes. A businessman. What does Frank want to do?'

'Frank,' Enzio sighed. 'Frank has other things on his mind. You heard about Anna Maria?'

Stefano nodded. 'Shockin' tragedy. I feel for you an' the family.'

'The funeral's tomorrow. It would be a sign of respect if you attended.'

'Of course I'll be there.' Stefano extended his hand. 'No hard feelings, Enzio?'

'Not at all,' Enzio replied evenly. 'You do it your way. I do it mine.'

Later that day Stefano Crown was shot in the head as he was about to enter an apartment building on Riverside Drive.

'It's a terrible thing when a man can no longer move

492

freely in this city,' Enzio said with feeling when he heard.

Alio Marcusi, who was with him at the time, merely nodded.

CHAPTER 34

'Hey Angelo baby, you're looking good, *really* good, brother.'

Angelo and Nick hugged tightly, genuinely pleased to see each other.

Angelo scratched his beard ruefully. 'I guess the old man's going to pop a few buttons when he gets a load of this.'

'Well, you are a bit hairy,' Nick admitted, 'but nothing that good a barber can't take care of.'

'Forget it,' Angelo said quickly. 'I like it. It stays.'

'Sure,' Nick agreed. 'I'm not the one that has to kiss you.'

Angelo looked at him sharply. Was there a snide meaning to that remark?

'How was the flight?' Nick asked cheerfully. Bumping into Lara had made him feel great. 'Were the stewardesses pretty? Word filters back you were quite a stud in London, but then you always were a horny little bastard.'

'You *and* me, bro,' Angelo said with a wide grin.

'Hey,' Nick reminded, 'remember the time you were shacking up with that hot starlet – the one with the pink Cadillac – and her boyfriend beat the shit out of you?'

'Yeah. How could I forget?'

'Trouble with you is you always got caught. A boy-friend here, a husband there. I'm amazed you survived, asshole!'

Angelo nodded his agreement.

Nick grabbed his arm. 'Come on, let's get moving. Enzio's waiting to see you. By the way, take no notice of the armed escort, he's got some crazy idea we make good targets.'

Angelo glanced around, observing two men close by. The bodyguard contingent. They followed Angelo and Nick out to the car and got in the front.

Nick took no notice of them, but Angelo couldn't help feeling uncomfortable. He preferred Shifty Fly to a couple of anonymous hoods who looked ready to pump a bullet into anyone.

'So what's going' on?' Angelo questioned, as soon as they were safely in the car. 'Why was I dragged back here so fast?'

Nick stared out of the window, his expression serious. 'You heard about Anna Maria?'

'No, what? Did she have the baby? What is it this time?'

'She's dead,' Nick said stonily. 'She fell down the stairs at the house.'

'What?' Angelo screwed up his face in disbelief. 'Fell down the stairs? Are you shittin' me?'

Nick shrugged.

'Hey, did Frank beat up on her? Did that lousy sonofabitch—'

'Shut up.' Nick nodded towards the men in the front seat. 'We'll talk about it later in private.'

'Jesus!' Angelo exclaimed. 'I always liked Anna Maria. What do *you* think really went on?'

'Accidents happen,' Nick said non-committally.

'Yeah, especially around Frank.'

*

494

Enzio waited at Frank's house. Frank was in the kitchen holding on to a bottle of Scotch, with Golli and Segal close by.

Enzio sat with Alio in the living room. Two of his men were stationed near the back door, another two at the front, and a further couple of men were sitting in separate parked cars outside.

Enzio had decided he couldn't be too careful. Especially now, with Stefano Crown's son bent on revenge. The young blood seemed to think that Enzio was in some way responsible for his father's death.

'Nothing to do with me,' Enzio proclaimed, hurt and angry that Georgi Crown should even suspect him. 'It was those pieces of shit Stefano wanted to bring in as partners.'

Georgi Crown didn't believe him. The Crowns had already opened negotiations with certain black groups, so it would hardly be to their advantage to put a bullet in Stefano Crown.

'I think Georgi Crown needs a rest,' Enzio remarked mildly to Alio. 'Arrange it. Oh, and also my friend, please see that a wreath is sent to Stefano's funeral on behalf of myself and family.'

Enzio felt better than he had in years. Life in New York was fast and exhilarating. Miami was boring for a man who had always lived such an active life. Fuck all the Bassalino rivals. Enzio was giving them a taste of their own medicine.

After her drink with Nick, Lara returned to the city, confused, filled with mixed emotions, and furious with herself for having got mixed up in the whole bizarre business. She stopped by Cass's apartment on the way.

'You look lousy,' Cass said bluntly.

'I feel worse,' Lara replied, fixing herself a drink.

'You heard then?'

'Heard what?'

Cass brought her up to date on the Frank Bassalino story. 'Beth's gone back to the commune. She sounded pretty bad on the phone.'

'I wish I'd seen her,' Lara replied wistfully, wondering why Nick had not mentioned anything about his brother's tragedy.

'I thought we could visit her in a week or two.'

'I'd like that. Just tell me when.'

Cass nodded. 'I don't know what's happening with you and Nick, but I heard from Dukey, and he wants you all out. I think he's right. It's getting too crazy.'

Lara wasn't really listening. 'I can't be involved any more,' she said, shaking her head.

'I know,' Cass agreed. 'That's what I just said. Let Dukey do it his way. I'm not sure what he has planned, but whatever it is, I don't think it's safe to be around the Bassalinos. I'm going to contact Rio and tell her.'

'She'll probably be arriving in New York at any moment. Nick was meeting his brother, Angelo, at the airport. He never mentioned a word about his sister-in-law.' She laughed bitterly. 'I guess it's time for me to return to my former life. You know, fun and games with the jet set. Back to the high life. What do you think, Cass? Will I still fit in?'

'If that's what you want,' Cass said evenly. 'What happened with Nick Bassalino?'

'Nothing important.'

Back at her apartment she studied her face in the bathroom mirror. She seemed to look different, only she didn't know why. *Ugly, I look ugly*, she thought.

So what good had it all done? Nick appeared to be as resilient as ever. And were they supposed to be glad that Frank Bassalino's wife was dead, along with his unborn child? Carefully she took off her make-up, then just as carefully she applied more. She did it three times before she was satisfied. It kept her from thinking too hard.

Finally she sat in a chair staring at the front door waiting for Prince Alfredo.

'You little punk!' Enzio spat, clapping Angelo round the shoulders, kissing him on both cheeks. 'You *still* look like a fuckin' communist!'

Angelo joined in the laughter that followed. His father had been saying the same thing to him for years.

'Good to be home, huh?' Enzio said. 'It's nice to be with the family in times of trouble.'

'Yeah, sure,' Angelo agreed half-heartedly. If there was any trouble he wanted to be long gone.

'You seen Frank yet? I want you to go to him, pay your respects.'

Nick went with Angelo to find Frank. Their older brother was sprawled half asleep in the kitchen.

'Hey, Frank, I'm sorry 'bout things,' Angelo mumbled.

Frank grunted.

'Shit, this house is depressing,' Angelo muttered in a low aside to Nick. 'I hope I'm not supposed to be staying here.'

'No, you're at the hotel with Enzio. Anna Maria's mother and sister are arriving later, they're going to be here with Frank an' the kids.'

'How long does the old man expect *me* to hang around?'

'I don't know,' Nick said. 'The funeral's tomorrow, then pop has some half-assed idea that we go to Miami for the weekend and see Rose. He wants us out of the city. Personally I just want to get back to the Coast.'

Angelo scratched his beard. 'Hey – you ever wished you were born an orphan?'

Nick laughed. 'Every fuckin' day, little brother.'

497

'You look wonderful,' Prince Alfredo Masserini said, kissing Lara on both cheeks. 'You have not changed, my darling. You are still the most beautiful woman in the world.'

'It hasn't been that long,' she commented.

'Too long,' he said accusingly. 'I have missed you. You have made me look foolish to my friends. All the time they tease me, make jokes. Lara has left, they say.' He clicked his tongue disapprovingly. 'Your family business has taken you far too much time.'

'I'm sorry,' she said quietly.

'It is good you are sorry,' he replied pompously, loosening his tie and examining his handsome face in a wall mirror for the wearisome signs of travel. 'I think now you will not run off like that again.'

Jesus, he was full of himself! 'No, I won't,' she agreed. 'I guess it was important at the time, but now . . .' She gestured towards the kitchen. 'Are you hungry? I can fix you bacon and eggs.'

'Peasant food, my darling. We shall dine out.'

'I thought it might be better to stay in.' She moved closer to him. 'It's been so long.'

He was flattered. 'You have missed me, Lara?'

'Yes,' she lied.

'A lot?'

'More than you'll ever know.'

Later Alfredo slept. Lara lay beside him in the big bed. She was wide awake, staring into the darkness.

He did nothing for her. He made her feel empty, used. With Nick it had been so different. So very right.

498

She wondered if Nick was going to turn up. A quick glance at the bedside clock told her it was late, and she hoped he wouldn't come. It had been stupid of her to give him her key. Such a petty form of revenge.

Prince Alfredo snored offensively. It was very annoying, the noise prevented her from sleeping.

Later she did sleep fitfully, and she had no idea Nick was in the apartment until he switched the bedroom light on and pulled the bedclothes roughly off her and Alfredo. Still half asleep she managed a weak 'Hello, Nick.'

Outraged, Prince Alfredo sat up and furiously demanded, 'Who is this person, Lara?' As he spoke he reached for his pure silk underpants.

'You really win the prize,' Nick said, shaking his head and staring down at her. 'Jesus Christ, you really do.'

She didn't try to cover herself, merely returned his stare.

Prince Alfredo flung on a paisley dressing-gown. 'What do you want?' he asked, his voice becoming high pitched and out of control.

'There's nothing I want here,' Nick replied sourly, throwing her front door key so it landed on her stomach. 'Nothing worth having. Nothing worth paying for.'

'Cover yourself,' Prince Alfredo shrieked at Lara.

'Hey – bud – no problem. I've seen it all before,' Nick said coldly. 'Every quivering high-class-hooker inch of it.'

'I don't understand—' Alfredo whined.

'Nor do I, buddy boy, nor do I.' Nick turned to leave, but Prince Alfredo decided it was time to assert his manhood, and grabbed him by the sleeve of his jacket.

Nick shook himself free.

'Have you slept with her?' the Prince demanded.

Nick's eyes were ice. 'Back off, fucker, before I lose my temper,' he said roughly.

Alfredo grabbed him again. 'You will answer my question!'

With one easy movement Nick smashed his knee into the Prince's groin. At the same time his fist connected with the royal nose. Alfredo was out for the count.

Lara didn't move.

Nick paused for a moment and glanced at her. He went to say something, thought better of it, and abruptly left.

Frank couldn't sleep. He refused to go to bed, all he wanted to do was sit in a chair in the kitchen guzzling from a bottle of Scotch and occasionally dozing off. It had been that way ever since the accident.

Nobody said anything, they left him alone. Enzio had attempted several times to engage him in conversation about business activities, but after a while he'd given up. 'When the funeral is over you'll pull yourself together,' he'd muttered. 'A few days in Miami. You'll spend time with your mother, Rose. It'll do you good.'

Like hell he'd go to Miami. He wasn't going anywhere until they found Beth.

Anna Maria's mother and sister arrived. It was fortunate they did not speak English. After a short greeting they left Frank alone, and that was the way he wanted it. Alone with his thoughts, his plans for the future. Family business did not enter his mind, let Enzio worry about all that crap.

He thought he might take a vacation, go to Hawaii, or Acapulco. Somewhere far away where he could be alone with Beth.

After the funeral he would find her, he had no doubt of that.

Nick left Lara's apartment in a fury. How could she have screwed him like that? What kind of a woman was she?

He went to the best whorehouse in New York. He needed *something* to calm him down.

They put out the red carpet for him. Nick Bassalino. Enzio's son. Frank's brother. It was almost like a visit from royalty.

The madame herself, a Scandinavian lady, with big boobs and a girlish face, offered to serve him personally. He declined her invitation and chose a sour-faced redhead instead. The woman kept their encounter on the impersonal level he wished for. It was not satisfactory.

Afterwards he was so pissed off he got good and drunk on straight brandy.

Finally he went back to his hotel, booked a call to April Crawford in Los Angeles for early morning, and slept fitfully.

The call came through while he was still asleep. He held the phone to his ear and listened to the long distance ringing while he tried to open his eyes. His mouth felt like lead shit.

Faithful Hattie told the operator Miss Crawford was not at home, so he spoke to Hattie.

'Hey, Hat, what's happening? She's not *still* mad, is she?'

'Haven't you heard, Mr Bassalino?' Hattie sounded embarrassed.

'Heard what?'

'Miss Crawford and Mr Albert were married yesterday.'

He was silent.

'Mr Bassalino, are you there?' Hattie asked in a worried voice. 'I *told* Miss Crawford she should have let you know.'

Nick put the phone down, his face tense. He called the desk and had them send up the newspapers, and there it was in black and white. Proof positive.

Las Vegas. Monday.
April Crawford and Sammy Albert.
April Crawford took husband number five today in a quiet ceremony in the garden of Stanley Graham's *Hi-Style* Hotel. Sammy Albert, thirty-year-old star of *Road Job*, *Tiger* and *Prince California*, was the lucky man. His only comment on the twenty-year age difference was, 'April is a real lady, a class act. Her age is of no interest to me.'

Nick threw the paper on the floor in disgust. Jesus Christ, but April was stupid. Any woman who would marry a juvenile super-stud like Sammy Albert was out of her fucking mind. She must have done it in a fit of jealous rage, that was the only feasible explanation.

He couldn't believe it. April and Sammy! It was a bad joke.

He was angry, and yet at the same time – in a strange way he was relieved. Now that he didn't have to answer to April he was free.

And now that he was free maybe he could do something about Lara.

CHAPTER 36

Leroy Jesus Bauls did not smoke, it was bad for your health, and Leroy never did anything that was bad for his health.

He was still at a loss to explain his behaviour at Manny's. What a stupid fucked-up thing to have done, getting the old lady and the kid out. So it had turned out all right, and that was fortunate. But it had meant taking unnecessary risks, and that was not his bag.

Never again, he vowed. If anyone got in his way in the future it was their problem.

Once again he wore his errand boy clothes as he sat in the parked van a block away from the entrance to the cemetery. A lesson Leroy had learned early in life was that a black in New York could hang around anywhere as long as he dressed the part. Wear something sharp, and stand on a street corner, and the cops were there in no time, hustling you, moving you on. Stand there like a janitor holding a broom, and you were on your own, nobody noticed you.

Leroy was parked in a prime position, the perfect spot to watch the limousines as they arrived in a long, dark, sober parade. His shades were fitted with special telescopic lenses, so recognizing the mourners was no problem.

He noted that Enzio Bassalino was taking no chances. Enzio was surrounded by his men, old cockers in shiny suits with stealthy, darting hands.

Nick and Angelo Bassalino arrived in a car together. They too were surrounded by protection as they waited on the sidewalk for Anna Maria's mother and sister who came in the next car with the children.

Leroy sat perfectly still, watching, noting every detail.

He was good at waiting, the first words he could remember being spoken to him when he was a kid were, 'You sit still and wait. Y'hear me? Just wait.' His mother repeated that phrase to him every day when she left him outside hotel rooms. It was only when he was big enough to peek through keyholes that 'he realized why she wanted him to wait.

Frank Bassalino arrived. Leroy's knuckles slowly whitened as he gripped the steering wheel hard. It was the only sign he gave that Frank was the one he'd been waiting for.

Eventually they all disappeared into the cemetery grounds, the family, relatives and friends.

A group of four men remained outside. They split into twos, and stayed each side of the gates, their eyes ever watchful.

Leroy did not move for ten minutes, then he got out of the van, opened up the back, and took out a giant wreath. Slowly he carried it down the street towards the cemetery.

One of the men blocked his path at the gate. 'Yeah? Whacha want?'

'Special delivery for the Bassalino funeral,' Leroy said solemnly.

'Leave it here.'

'Sure.' He deposited the wreath on the ground, fumbling in his pocket for the receipt book. 'Sign here, please.'

The man scrawled an illegible signature.

Leroy hesitated, as if waiting for a tip. 'You want I should take it through?' he asked. 'I was given instructions it had to be left graveside.'

'Just leave it where it is.'

Leroy shrugged. 'It's your funeral,' he muttered under his breath as he walked back to the van.

Exactly six minutes later the four men standing by the cemetery gates were blown to pieces.

Leroy, now parked three blocks away, heard the explosion clearly. He waited for half a minute, and then walked back to view the chaos, carrying a brown paper parcel.

Police sirens screamed through the air, a crowd was gathering.

Leroy found it was easy to place his package on the front seat of Frank Bassalino's limousine. The chauffeur had left the car and was among the crowd by the cemetery gates. The line of parked limousines was deserted. Leroy realized if he'd so desired he could have left a package in each car. But that wasn't the way Dukey K. Williams wanted it.

Within minutes Enzio and his sons came rushing out. There was so much confusion, women were weeping and screaming, and the crowd was growing by the minute.

Leroy strolled casually off, the first part of his job successfully accomplished.

CHAPTER 37

Angelo could feel the fear in his stomach, a tight, burning knot of pure terror.

They had been standing by the grave when they heard the explosion. Instinctively he dropped to the ground, burying his head in his hands.

Jesus, what a fucking noise! What was he doing here

505

anyway in this maniac city when he should be safely in London?

Nick dragged him up. 'Stay easy,' he warned. 'Don't panic. Act like a man, for crissake.'

Enzio was already sending people to find out what was going on.

Within minutes they were back with the bad news. A bomb.

Immediately Enzio took command. 'Go to the cars. Keep alert. Stay in groups. Golli, Segal, hold on to Frank. Nick, look after Angelo.'

Frank appeared to be unaffected by the explosion. He had started the day drunk, and with the help of a flask in his back pocket he planned to finish the day drunk.

'Go straight to the airport,' Enzio instructed. 'Don't stop by Frank's house or the hotel.'

No one argued. With bombs going off around them a weekend in Miami seemed like a good idea.

'I'll take Frank with me,' Nick said.

'No, you stay with Angelo,' Enzio insisted, noticing how white faced and shaken his younger son was. 'Golli an' Segal will take care of Frank.'

Nick didn't argue. All he wanted was to get the fuck out of there before the cops arrived. Let Enzio deal with the police, he was the one with enough connections to wire a building.

They bundled into cars. Angelo slumped back on his seat. 'Those guys,' he mumbled. 'Those poor goddamn guys . . .'

'Why don't you thank your skinny balls it wasn't you,' Nick said grimly. 'It was probably meant to be.'

'Me?' Angelo was incredulous. 'Why me?'

'You, me, Frank. What difference, we're all Bassalinos.'

506

Angelo nodded helplessly. Yes, they were all Bassalinos, and that meant anyone warring with Enzio automatically included his three sons.

'Who do you think did—?'

'Listen kid, I don't want to talk,' Nick interrupted. 'Sit back and relax, turn on or something, but leave me alone, I've got some thinkin' to do.' He closed his eyes. All day long he'd been trying to get his thoughts straight, and it wasn't easy. For someone who didn't drink he had one sonofabitch of a hangover. The business with Lara had really turned him over. Jesus, she'd planned it, *wanted* him to find her in bed with that Italian piece of shit.

She was a bitch. A prize bitch.

And yet. . . .

He hoped he'd damaged the guy.

He wished he'd damaged her.

And as for April Crawford – she and Sammy Albert together would soon be yesterday's news. If he *really* thought about it they deserved each other.

Lara Crichton was something else. When the trouble was over and he could concentrate, he was going to have to do something about her. She was too special to let escape.

'I don't know why I couldn't have stayed in London,' Angelo complained, interrupting his brother's thoughts.

Before Nick could reply they both heard the explosion. It came from behind.

The car with Frank in was behind.

CHAPTER 38

Prince Alfredo Masserini had suffered a broken nose. 'I will sue that man for every dollar he has,' he ranted from his private hospital bed, his perfect Roman nose encased in a plaster cast.

'You don't know who he is,' Lara remarked calmly.

Prince Alfredo swore hotly in Italian, then, 'Lara, you are being a very stupid girl. I thought perhaps there was a future for us together, but now ...' He shrugged, trailing off.

Lara got up from the chair beside the bed and nodded. 'You're right Alfredo. You really are.' She walked towards the door. She'd had enough of him and his whining. News of April Crawford's surprise marriage to Sammy Albert was all over the newspapers. What was Nick doing? Thinking? Was he destroyed?

'Where are you going?' Alfredo demanded imperiously.

She shook her head. 'Paris, maybe. Acapulco. I don't know.'

'You wait here a few days,' he said, condescendingly. 'I will forgive you. We go somewhere together.'

'Ah, but I don't want to be forgiven,' she replied, her green eyes bright. 'I'm not a child, Alfredo. The truth is I'm sorry about your nose. I'm sorry about everything. It's just best we don't see each other again.'

'Lara!' He was shocked. 'What do you mean? I have waited these last months, I have made certain plans for us. My mother, she look forward to meeting you. We ski first, then on to Rome where I will present you to my family.'

'No,' she said firmly. 'It's over.' She left the room hardly listening as he burst into a stream of angry Italian.

As she walked down the corridor she felt completely blank. Nothing mattered, nothing at all. She was very tired, and the only thought that appealed to her was to climb into bed, bury herself beneath the covers, and sleep. Maybe for days.

She wished the impossible. She wished she had Margaret to talk things over with.

Outside she climbed into her chauffeured car and closed her eyes. 'My apartment,' she instructed the driver.

'The city's goin' mad,' he informed her. 'There's hoodlums runnin' wild blowin' each other up. It ain't safe drivin' no more.'

Lara wasn't really listening. She was already drifting into sleep.

There was no body to identify. No body to bury. Frank Bassalino had been blown into a thousand little pieces. Two people innocently standing near the car were killed, many more were injured as the blast blew out all the windows in nearby office buildings and shards of glass came showering down.

Nick didn't hang around. He took it all in at a glance and knew Frank had no chance. Thinking quickly, he hauled Angelo out of their own car, and holding him tightly by the arm, marched him away from the wreckage.

Angelo was too shaken to talk. Nick moved fast, they were three blocks away when several police cars zoomed past.

When Nick was sure they weren't being followed, he hailed a cab and told the driver to get them to the airport as speedily as possible.

'Somebody's going to get his balls sledge-hammered for this,' he said at last. 'And *I* am gonna do it. *I'm* gonna cut his fuckin' balls off and string them up for salami.'

Angelo was a nervous wreck. 'Who did it?' he asked, trying to keep the fear out of his voice.

'We'll find out,' Nick replied grimly. 'We always find out. Nobody gets away with killing a Bassalino.'

'You're beginning to sound like Enzio.'

'I hope so, little brother. I really hope so.'

Rio Java flew into New York and saw the head-lines.

She went straight to Cass's apartment. Dukey was already there. 'Did *you* arrange it?' she asked.

He made a vague gesture. 'Maybe I did, an' maybe I didn't. We're not the only ones who want to see the Bassalinos go down.'

'Well, don't touch Angelo, he's mine. Understand, brother?'

'Sure,' he agreed. 'If you get to him first.'

'I don't have to get to him. I just want to destroy him. Isn't that supposed to be the plan?'

Dukey nodded. 'That was before. Things are different now.'

'What do you mean – things are different now?'

'Let's just call it a little racial problem, and leave it at that.'

'Racial problem my ass!' she exploded.

'Listen,' he said angrily. 'You had your chance, an' you blew it. Now it's my turn.'

'Oh,' she said coldly, 'you mean I'm supposed to drop everything on account of what *you* say.'

'Clever girl.'

'Don't call *me* girl, asshole.'

'Beth and Lara are already out,' Cass interrupted

quickly, looking to avoid a fight. 'I think Dukey's right, Rio.'

Rio turned on her. 'Oh, do you? Well fuck you, too.'

Dukey's eyes were hard and cold. 'Shame you're not black.'

'I'm multicoloured, it's more fun.'

'You're just pissed you can't play any more of your mind games.'

'I can do what I like, Dukey. And don't you forget it.'

He nodded in agreement. 'Sure, babe. Only don't do it near the Bassalinos, 'cos your long, skinny multicoloured ass gonna get blown all the way to hell an' back. OK, babe?'

CHAPTER 39

Mary Ann August smiled at Claire, and Claire said, 'Honey, you've really surprised me, things are working out fine. Mr Forbes was very pleased today, and for Mr Forbes to be pleased – well, that's really a compliment.'

'He promised he'll be back soon,' Mary Ann said, stretching her arms above her head, so the short, white nightgown she wore pulled up, exposing a fine matting of pale coffee-coloured pubic hair.

Claire's eyes wandered down to take a peek. No trouble with this one. Some girls were born to be whores.

Mary Ann flopped back on the bed parting her thighs. 'Gee, Claire, I wish I could take a walk,' she said innocently. 'I'm really cheesed about being shut in all the time. I need fresh air.'

'Next week,' Claire promised.

Mary Ann pouted. 'You *can* trust me, I'm not going to run off. I *like* it here. I like you . . .' She threw her captor a long, lingering look.

Claire moved nearer to the bed. 'You're a smart girl. No trouble. A girl like you can make a lot of money if you want to. Now that we've fixed your hair, you look so pretty.'

Mary Ann smiled. 'Enzio wouldn't like it this way.'

Claire sat down on the bed, and casually ran her fingers up Mary Ann's leg heading towards the fuzz. 'Enzio's not going to have to like it, is he?'

Mary Ann giggled, spreading her legs apart. 'Are you a dyke, Claire?' she asked, licking her lips.

The pressure of Claire's fingers hardened. 'I've seen too many pot bellies and limp hard-ons to be anything else.' A pause. 'Have you ever tried it?'

Mary Ann giggled again. 'Mr Forbes couldn't make me come. I told him a little head would do the trick, but Mr Forbes said that was *my* job.'

Claire bent down slowly, her eyes bright. 'Mr Forbes must be out of his mind.'

Mary Ann sighed and lay back, ready to enjoy the ministrations of Claire.

Five minutes passed. Soon Claire was thoroughly engrossed in the task at hand.

Carefully Mary Ann reached under the bed and got a firm grip on the chair leg she'd hidden there earlier. She then raised her upper body until she could see the top of Claire's close-cropped head. She moaned, causing Claire to increase her efforts. Then slowly, so as not to disturb anything, she raised the chair leg and smashed it down heavily on Claire's head. Once, twice, three times.

There was blood as Claire slumped to the floor, and Mary Ann was sorry about that. But she certainly had no intention of being locked up and forced into the life of a prostitute. Oh no. Oh dear me, no. Not Mary Ann August. Not after she had worked hard and put up with Enzio Bassalino for all those months. She had jewellery, clothes, and two fur coats. She had possessions worth money, enough money that if she sold them she could go back to the small town in Texas she hailed from and buy herself a nice little business. A boutique perhaps, or maybe a beauty parlour. She had known her time with Enzio was not a permanent thing and planned accordingly.

Dressing hurriedly, she took money and keys from Claire's pocketbook.

Mary Ann August had possessions, and sonofabitch, she was going to get them.

CHAPTER 40

By the next day the house in Miami was buzzing with activity. There was a meeting in progress.

Enzio sat behind his desk, his eyes red rimmed, shoulders slumping heavily. Beside him stood Nick, doing most of the talking, words coming hard and fast.

Enzio appeared to have aged ten years as he listened to his middle son, occasionally nodding to let the room crowded with men know he was in agreement with everything Nick said.

Angelo hunched in a chair nearby. He was scared, and it showed. His face was white, and his hand was unsteady as he gulped mouthfuls of Scotch from a large tumbler. What he really needed was to get good and truly stoned. A few joints would calm him down and stop the shaking.

Only he couldn't turn on in front of Enzio. His father didn't approve of drugs.

Nick was surprisingly cool as he issued instructions. He wanted information and he wanted it fast. He offered a ten-thousand-dollar reward for the right information.

When the meeting was over the men dispersed.

'Rose . . .' Enzio mumbled. 'For Christ sake, somebody's got to tell her.'

Angelo buried himself in his drink. His mother scared the shit out of him. She always had. Frank was her favourite, and Nick seemed to make out OK, but to Angelo she'd always been crazy Rose.

'I'll tell her,' said Nick, saving Angelo any excuses. He could communicate with his mother if she was in a good mood. Sometimes he was even able to get her to summon up a faint smile from her otherwise dead face. 'I'll go see her now.'

Rose sat in her usual chair by the window, gazing out.

Nick crept up behind her and squeezed her shoulders. 'Ciao, mama.' He was shocked at how thin she seemed.

Rose looked up at him without a flicker of surprise, nodding slightly, even though it was over a year since she'd seen him.

'I'm sorry it's been so long, mama,' he said. 'But you know how it is. I've been busy out on the Coast. You look great, you really do.'

Nick could remember his mother before she had locked herself away. He recalled her startling beauty, vivacious personality, and the way she used to make friends so easily.

He also remembered the night it all happened. He was sixteen and out on a date. When he'd returned home, Alio met him at the door and told him his mother was sick. 'You're to stay at my place tonight,' Alio had said. 'Angelo and the nanny are already there.' Alio hadn't even let him into the house to get his tooth-brush.

For two weeks he wasn't allowed home, and when he finally was, he found his mother had locked herself away, refusing to speak to any of them. She kept up her silence for several years, until Enzio moved them all to the Miami mansion. There she staked out her room overlooking the pool and never emerged, although she did deign to speak to her sons occasionally.

'Frank's dead,' Nick blurted out. 'It was an ... accident.'

Rose spun around and stared at him. She still had the most magnificent eyes he'd ever seen. They could burn a hole in you they were so deep and bright. Her eyes spoke for her, they begged him to tell her more.

'Uh ... I don't know much. He was in a limo. There was an explosion. ...' He put his arms around his mother. What more could he say?

'Enzio,' she muttered. 'Basta!'

And then there was silence.

CHAPTER 41

'Strike, before they strike back.' Those were the orders Leroy Jesus Bauls received from Dukey K. Williams. Which was why he was now on the road to Miami. It was a long drive, but it would have been too dangerous to fly with the equipment he needed. All the security at airports today, luggage being searched and people being frisked. He wouldn't have got anywhere near a plane.

His black Mercedes roared down the highway at a steady pace. Leroy was completely at ease, his mind clear and able to deal with the job ahead.

He'd thoroughly inspected Enzio Bassalino's mansion a few days previously before the family arrived. Enzio was in New York, so the grounds had not been as closely guarded. With no family present it had been a relatively simple matter to gain access to the house posing as a telephone engineer. The oldest trick in the world, but once the telephone went dead it always worked. Cut the lines, wait twenty minutes, then appear. 'Telephone engineer, fault reported on your line.' Guards check the phone, check his phony credentials, and nod agreement that he can come in. At first someone follows him everywhere, but then they get bored and he's on his own. Ready to do whatever he wants. He'd set the house up exactly as he wanted it. Only the finishing touches were needed.

He was well aware of the guards at the gates, the alarm systems, the dogs.

It was an exciting job, a challenge, and Leroy looked forward to challenges.

Mary Ann August bought a black wig. It was long and covered her blondness nicely. Next she purchased jeans, a T-shirt, a man's shirt and tinted glasses. Hurrying to the Ladies' Room she washed off her make-up, and put on the new clothes. When she emerged she looked like a different girl.

A cab took her to the airport, where she bought a ticket for Miami.

She was extremely jumpy. There had been a lot of money in Claire's purse and she was sure that someone would come after her if just for that. But they wouldn't find her – she didn't even recognize herself in the mirror.

After buying a selection of magazines, she boarded the plane.

Nick was in charge. The old man had gone to pieces, his age suddenly and surprisingly catching up with him.

Angelo sat around, restless and manic, until Nick finally got one of the boys to fix him up with a couple of joints to calm him down.

After the meeting, Nick phoned Los Angeles to check on business. Everything seemed OK. He had good people working in LA. Men he could trust.

He kept on thinking about Lara. April was a distant memory. So he wasn't going to be Mr April Crawford. Big Deal. So what?

The old man was resting, and Angelo was playing cards out by the pool.

Nick called the gate. No problems. He'd put an extra man out there. Now there were three of them on constant alert, and no one was allowed through unless they got his personal OK.

The Bassalino family was under fire, and Nick was taking no risks.

Picking up the phone he dialled Lara in New York. He couldn't help himself.

She took her time answering.

'Listen, lady. You're lucky I didn't kill the sonofabitch,' he said threateningly. She didn't answer, so he added, 'If I catch anybody in bed with you again, their number is up. Do you understand what I'm sayin'?'

'You broke his nose,' she said quietly.

'Yeah? That's a shame.'

'It's not a joke, he'll probably sue you.'

'I'm shakin' in my boots.'

517

'Why are you calling me?'

'I wanted to.'

She was ridiculously pleased to hear from him, and yet she couldn't just give in and fall into his arms because April had married Sammy, and Nick was now on the loose.

'I'm in Miami,' he said. 'I want you to go straight to the airport an' catch the next plane here. We have a lot of talking to do.'

Breathlessly she said, 'Are you crazy?'

'Yeah, I'm crazy,' he replied recklessly. 'Crazy about you. I need you here, Lara. It's got nothing to do with April and Sammy. I want you. Don't let me down, baby.'

'I can't, Nick, I—'

'Don't fight it, sweetheart. We belong together, and you know it. I'll have a man at the airport to meet you – he'll bring you straight to the house.'

She felt light headed. He needed her. He wanted her. 'OK,' she whispered. What the hell, she'd never made a spontaneous decision in her life. Now was the time to take a risk and do something just for Lara.

Before she changed her mind she began throwing things into a suitcase, humming softly to herself, until suddenly Cass's words hit her. Words she hadn't really listened to before were now very clear in her head.

'Let Dukey do it his way. I'm not sure what he has planned, but whatever it is, I don't think it's safe to be around the Bassalinos.'

She experienced a moment of panic. Quickly she phoned Cass. 'What did you mean when you said it's not safe to be around the Bassalinos?' she asked urgently. 'What does Dukey plan to do?'

'I don't know,' Cass replied. 'I guess he's going to finish off—'

'Finish off *what?*'

'I don't know.'

Slamming the phone down she tried to reach Dukey. There was no reply at his apartment.

Oh God! She had to get to Nick, tell him the truth, and warn him.

Finishing her packing she called down to the doorman to find her a cab.

Miami was her next stop. And as quickly as possible. There was no other way of warning him.

Sitting in her room Rose Bassalino brooded. She had no tears left to cry for her oldest son. Her tears had all been shed many years before.

It was Enzio's fault of course. Everything was always Enzio's fault. Basta! Bastard! Big man with a big cock.

He had taken Frank away because he knew Frank was her favourite.

If she closed her eyes she could picture in vivid detail that night so many years ago when Enzio and his men had sliced Charles Cardwell to death in front of her. Like a piece of beef they had sliced and carved and hacked.

Animals!

And all the while Enzio had held her, his hands on her breasts, his body stiffening with excitement.

Rose stifled a scream as the memories came crowding back. She stared out of her window. The pool was still there, the grass, the trees. She had trained her mind to go blank, shut out everything, concentrate on the scenery. Over the years she had even managed to ignore Enzio's succession of whores.

Today it didn't work. Today the sun-drenched garden and bountiful greenery did nothing to calm her.

Rose Bassalino was not crazy. She was as sane as anyone. But to hang on to her sanity she had shut herself away, and now she could feel the fury building in her body, a fury giving her new strength.

For her children's sake she had remained in her room for years. It spared them the agony of what she might do if she ever returned to the real world.

Now it didn't matter. Frank was gone. And it was Enzio's fault.

Rose stood up and stepped away from the window.

She knew what she had to do. Her mind was clear for the first time in seventeen years.

CHAPTER 42

'Angelo – it's the telephone for you.' Alio strolled out to the pool to tell him.

'For me?'

'Yeah – a woman.' Alio was not interested.

Angelo put down his cards. Nobody knew where he was. He picked up the phone beside the pool.

'You little prick,' a familiar voice said. 'Running away ain't gonna get you but *nowhere*, baby!'

He recognized her voice immediately. It wasn't difficult. 'Rio. How did you find me?'

'I *smelt* you out, baby.' She laughed. 'We still friends?'

He relaxed. 'Yeah, but I want to talk to you.'

'To me.' She paused. '*And* my friends?'

'Listen, that was strictly a one-time scene.'

'Sure, sure. And you hated it – right?'

Once again he experienced the same excitement as he'd known that time in her apartment. 'I don't go that route,' he said slowly.

'Oh, *come on*,' she replied mockingly. 'This is *me* you're talking to. And I am right here at the Fontainebleu with two divine *new* friends who are *aching* to meet you. Shall we come to you, or will you sashay your *nice tight* ass over here?'

His throat was dry and constricted. 'I can't see you today,' he said weakly. Nick had given strict instructions that nobody was to leave the house.

Her voice purred raunchily over the phone. 'But Angelo, baby. I am naked and horny and I *never* take no for an answer. My friends are naked and horny and very *very* willing to do *anything* your little heart desires. They are also *very* impressed with your advance publicity, I showed them the pictures – pictures I'm sure you wouldn't want Daddy to see. So come on over *now*, baby.'

He had wanted to go and now he had to go.

The only problem was getting out.

The only problem was getting in.

More than anyone Mary Ann August realized how heavily guarded the Bassalino mansion was. She had lived there all those months and she knew Enzio's stringent methods for keeping strangers out.

However, she was banking on the fact that she wasn't a stranger. She was Enzio's girlfriend, his mistress, and as far as everyone was concerned she had gone to New York with him just over a week before. And it was perfectly logical that she'd come back with him. She didn't think Enzio would have bothered to announce the fact he was sending her away. He'd obviously told Alio, had him do his dirty work, but apart from that – well, she was sure she knew him well enough to know he kept things to himself.

Mary Ann August had a plan. It was risky. But with luck and guards she knew on the gate, things might just work out.

'I'm going to the airport,' Nick said.

'Hey, I'll go with you.' Angelo saw a way out. Drive to the airport with his brother and then get conveniently lost.

'No.' Nick shook his head. 'You stay here and take over from me. There's no way of knowing what their next move is.'

Angelo hesitated. He didn't want to argue with Nick, but then again he was desperate to get out.

Nick was already on his way to the door. Angelo decided to hang back. It would probably be simpler to split when Nick wasn't there anyway.

'Sure, I'll take care of everything,' he said. 'You can depend on me.'

CHAPTER 43

Enzio awoke around five. His bedroom overlooked the pool, and when he got up he walked over to the window and gazed out for a while.

He felt old and tired. Feelings he wasn't used to. Age was a sonofabitch. In two months' time he would be seventy years old. Frank was only thirty-six, and the bastards had murdered him, a man in his prime, a Bassalino.

Enzio swore to himself, a slow murmuring of never-ending curses. A prayer of obscenities.

He would have liked to have gone to Rose, she was the only one who could possibly understand the pain he was going through.

But it was impossible. Rose had sworn never to talk

to him again, and he knew his wife. She would try and punish him for the rest of his days. Not that he let it bother him. She was lucky he hadn't thrown her out.

Perhaps he should visit the girl he'd imported from New York – the one Kosta Gennas had brought him – what was her name? Mabel, no, Miriam, that was it, Miriam. She had been sent to the house and installed in the usual room, but so far he'd not visited her.

'Filth!' With a sudden show of anger he spat on the floor. They were all filth, these women he could buy. Besides, he could summon no sexual interest. At his age it was becoming more difficult.

He lay once again on his bed. Maybe he would sleep some more, perhaps he would feel better in a while.

Images of Frank as a child kept flashing before him. They'd called him Frankie, and the kid was a tough little monkey. He remembered the day Frankie lost his first tooth. The day he learned to swim. The time he beat up a boy at school twice his size. Oh, that had made Enzio so proud! When Frankie was thirteen he'd taken him to his first girl – an eighteen-year-old hooker. Frankie had performed like a man. From that day on they'd called him Frank.

Enzio chuckled, although his eyes were filled with tears.

The door to his room opened quietly. For a moment he couldn't quite make out who it was standing there. Then he recognized Mary Ann August, with her blonde teased hair, small red bikini, long legs and large breasts.

'Hi baby sweetie pie,' she said, smiling nicely.

He grunted, struggling to sit up. Hadn't he sent her away? Hadn't Alio dealt with her?

Mary Ann swayed towards the bed. 'How's mommy's big bad man?' she cooed, at the same time undoing the tie on her bikini top, allowing her breasts to tumble out.

Enzio's mind was muddled, Alio must have screwed up. Anyway, so what? Mary Ann August was just what he needed now. She knew what he liked, his fads and fancies.

Suddenly he wasn't an old man of nearly seventy, he was a Bassalino, a stud.

Reaching the bed, she leaned over him, her breasts dangling tantalizingly over his face. He opened his mouth and attempted to cram an obliging nipple in.

She giggled, and began fiddling with his clothes.

He closed his eyes and sighed as he felt the erection beginning.

His mouth was full of her when she shot him precisely and silently straight through the heart.

CHAPTER 44

Angelo left the house soon after Nick. It was easy. Just walk out, climb into his old souped-up black Mustang, drive to the gates, wave at the guards as they let him through. Easy. After all, he was a Bassalino too, so who dared to stop him?

He switched on the radio. Bobby Womack. Loud and clear. Great. He felt good, a little high, just enough. Frank's death had completely unnerved him. A fucking bomb right in the middle of New York, that was one hell of a way to go. But he couldn't pretend he was heartbroken. OK. Sure. So Frank was his brother. But he'd always been a mean bastard. There had never been any love lost between the two of them.

The thought of seeing Rio again filled him with elation. *She* was sending for *him. He* wasn't phoning *her*, grovelling for a chance to prove himself. She'd tracked *him* down, and flown to Miami especially to see him.

He put his foot down a little harder on the accelerator. Mustn't keep her waiting. Rio was not a woman to keep waiting.

He turned the radio louder. The disc jockey was talking in rhyming slang, jazzing his audience up for James Brown. The Man. Sexy Sexy Sexy.

Angelo couldn't help laughing aloud. James Brown reminded him of his first scene with Rio. 'Sex Machine' had been the record then. He turned the radio up full volume so the sound flooded all around him in a deafening roar. Revving the engine he shoved his foot down to the floor.

'Rio baby,' he shouted. 'Here I come!'

He failed to see the red light ahead. The car plunged through the junction and smashed straight into the side of a massive oil tanker.

Angelo was killed instantly, but on the car radio James Brown sang on . . .

CHAPTER 45

'Hey.' Nick gripped her by the arms and stared intently into her green eyes.

Lara smiled. 'You came to the airport yourself.'

'I couldn't wait any longer. Jesus! Has anyone ever told you you're the most beautiful woman in the world?'

'I love you, Nick,' she said simply. 'That's why I came.'

'Hey, here's a lady who says it like it is.' He kissed her. 'I love you too, princess. You got any suitcases?'

She nodded. 'One.'

He took her hand, holding it tightly as they walked through the terminal to wait for her luggage.

'Listen to me,' he said, 'there's so many things I want to tell you.'

'There's plenty I *have* to tell you too, Nick.'

'OK. So we have all the time in the world, don't we?'

'We certainly do.'

He stopped walking, pressed his hands around her face and kissed her, a long slow kiss. 'It's so great to see you. When we get back to the house, you'll meet my family. They're not like other people's families. It's all very heavy at the moment. I'll explain later. Right now I just want you near me. Is that OK with you?'

She nodded. It was fine with her. Thank God he was all right. Soon she had to warn him about Dukey, tell him the whole story. And when he knew, what then? Would he still want her? Or would that be it?

She sighed deeply. If they were going to have a relationship the truth had to be told.

'There's my suitcase.' She pointed out her Vuitton bag.

Nick signalled a porter and they set off for the car.

CHAPTER 46

Mary Ann August left Enzio's room quietly. Outside his door was the suitcase she'd packed neatly with her possessions. She'd found everything where she'd left it, and encountered no problems getting past the guards. All she'd had to do was stroll through the grounds in her red bikini as if she still lived there.

She wasn't sure why she decided to shoot Enzio. It had all seemed so easy, the little gun he'd given her for her own protection was still in her jewellery case. And he was such a cold bastard. Leaving her in New York. Sending Alio along to take his turn. Shipping her off to a whorehouse in Los Angeles as if she were less than nothing. Keeping all her things.

Now that it was done she started to shake.

What if she couldn't get away?

What if someone *found* him before she could escape?

She hurried down the hallway, and to her horror, just as she was about to pass his wife's room, the door opened and the crazy woman called Rose appeared.

Rose Bassalino *never* left her room. Mary Ann had lived in the house for months, and she knew the door was *never* opened.

Rose stepped into the hallway and they faced each other. She had wild, matted black hair, and penetrating insane eyes.

Mary Ann shuddered as the woman smiled at her – a strange, far-away smile. And then Rose Bassalino lifted the knife she was carrying and taking Mary Ann by surprise she plunged it into her stomach.

Mary Ann slid silently to the floor. Rose drew the long knife out of the girl's body and continued along the hallway until she reached Enzio's room.

He was asleep in bed, the covers drawn tightly around his chin.

Rose began to laugh as she plunged the knife into him.

Plunge, laugh, plunge, laugh.

It was the same knife he'd used so many years ago to murder Charles Cardwell.   A strange and wonderful justice.

CHAPTER 47

It was nearly five when Leroy parked his Mercedes some distance away from the Bassalino mansion. He was beginning to feel tired, it had been a long day.

Stepping from the car he stretched, at the same time taking stock of his surroundings. There was no one around to observe him. He'd taken care of most of the work on his last trip.

Opening the trunk of his car he took out a small canvas holdall, opened it and scanned the contents. Finally satisfied, he set off for the house.

'We've been sitting here for ever,' Nick complained. 'Goddamn traffic.'

'Calm down,' Lara said, squeezing his hand.

They were crawling along a three-lane highway, every lane slow moving.

'It usually takes no more than fifteen minutes to the house,' he said impatiently, lighting up a cigarette. 'Today we'll be lucky to make it in an hour.'

He knew he should have waited for Lara at the house, it was stupid to have left. Things could be moving, information might be coming through, and he should be there.

'It seems like there's some kind of accident up ahead,' the driver said. 'Looks like a bad one. Once we're past it'll be clear.'

'Take the next turn off,' Nick instructed. 'I know a short cut.' He squeezed her hand back. 'We'll soon be there, baby.'

*

Leroy strolled towards the gates of the Bassalino mansion, pausing several yards away.

One of the guards stepped out of the security gate-house and watched him warily.

Very slowly Leroy reached into his blue canvas bag.

'Yeah?' the guard started to question, his hand tightening on a pistol stuck in his belt.

In one fluid movement Leroy produced a hand grenade from his bag, deftly removed the pin, and flung it at the guardhouse, throwing himself flat on the ground. Seconds later the earth shook from the explosion.

Leroy counted to five, jumped up, grabbed his bag and ran past the flames into the grounds of the main house. Running fast, he dodged and weaved through the trees.

He could see the mansion. The front door was open, and men were racing out with guns drawn. Lots of dumb white motherfuckers. They didn't know what hit 'em.

Under the cover of the tall trees, Leroy managed to get to the back of the house. Nobody spotted him. The assholes didn't even think to let the dogs loose. Even if they had, he was prepared.

Stealthily he made his way over to a back window. It took him less than a minute to dig up wires he'd buried on his last visit. Connect them, set the timer. Preparation. That was the secret. What a fucking brilliant scheme!

Get moving, he thought to himself, never cut it too fine.

He started to run from the house doing a fast countdown in his head.

Zero. One. Two. Three. Four. Five.

Keep on running.

Six. Seven. Eight. Nine. Ten.

POW! The first explosion, and at intervals of five seconds, more explosions all around the house just as he'd planned it.

Suddenly, with a leaden feeling in the pit of his stomach, he realized he'd made one fatal mistake. He realized it when he saw the pack of ferocious German Shepherds heading in his direction.

His blue canvas bag. He'd left it on the ground by the back window, and in it was the fresh steak he'd brought to keep the dogs happy.

'Shit!' Leroy uttered.

It was the last word he ever spoke.

CHAPTER 48

Cass Long was alone when she saw the news on television.

Her first reaction was of an almost satisfied shock, until the full horror of the event overpowered her as television cameras hovered in a helicopter above the wreck that had once been the Bassalino mansion.

The scene was one of devastation. Fires were still burning, while police and firemen swarmed all over the place. A row of blanket-covered victims was lined up beside the swimming pool.

'It has not been established,' the newscaster said, 'how many bodies are still to be recovered from the house. However, authorities seem certain there are more to come.' The newscaster paused as further information was relayed to him. 'It appears that a series of bombs was placed around the house, triggered to go off at short intervals. We will have more news on that later.

530

The owner of the Miami mansion – Enzio Bassalino – was a well-known underworld figure in Chicago in the late twenties, along with his contemporaries Al Capone and Legs Diamond. In recent years Mr Bassalino has lived in seclusion and retirement at his house in Miami with—'

Cass clicked the television off. For a moment she stared at a framed photograph of Margaret hanging on the wall.

It was time to take up Margaret's work again. Time to go out in the world and try to achieve some of Margaret's goals.

Cass knew exactly what to do.

CHAPTER 49

Lara would always remember the fear and the panic of that afternoon with Nick. They were less than minutes from the house when the explosions started.

'What is it?' she'd asked fearfully. There was a noise like long rumbling peals of thunder.

'Jesus Christ!' Nick yelled. 'Move this fucking car!' he screamed at the driver.

As they drew closer they both saw smoke and flames coming from the house. 'Stop!' Nick instructed urgently. 'Turn the car around and take her back to the airport. Fast. Put her safely on a plane.'

Jumping from the car, he ran towards the house. It was a nightmare scene.

'Nick!' she screamed after him. 'Be careful. Oh, God! Be careful.'

He didn't hear her, he'd vanished into the smoke, and the driver was already turning the car around and racing off in the other direction.

'Nick,' she cried out in vain. 'Oh, Nick, I love you.'

The driver followed his instructions. He took her to the airport and put her on a plane to New York. She was too numb to argue.

When she arrived she went straight to Cass's apartment. Rio was already there.

'Have you seen the news?' Cass asked.

Lara held her breath. 'What exactly happened?' She knew it was something terrible.

'Dukey scored,' Rio said without emotion. 'He had someone burn the Bassalino mansion down. They're all dead. So much for our efforts.'

'Dead?' Lara asked blankly. 'How do you know?'

'It's all over the television,' Cass said grimly. 'Nobody had a chance. The house was surrounded with explosives. It was a death trap.'

Shortly after that, Dukey arrived, smoking a big cigar. He smiled at everyone. 'This is a celebration,' he said triumphantly. 'We did it my way.'

'*Your* way,' Rio said, her voice filled with disgust. 'You make me want to throw up.'

'Results,' he boasted. 'That's all that counts.'

'You cold bastard!' Lara said, fighting back tears.

He puffed on his cigar. 'Why don't you call me a *black* bastard – isn't that the kind of name calling people like you do?'

'You've got no conscience.'

'Oh, and I suppose you have? Fucking a guy is OK if it works out. But my way is shit.'

'Your way is murder,' Rio pointed out.

'They murdered Margaret,' he countered.

'All those innocent people . . .' sighed Cass.

'Fuck it, girl,' Dukey said. 'Margaret was worth every one of them ten times over. An' let me tell you a little

532

fact of life – there's nobody innocent involved with the Bassalinos.'

Cass shook her head. 'You don't understand, do you? Margaret wouldn't have approved of any of this. All she'd have wanted was her work to be carried on.'

'Get real, Cass. *I* wanted revenge. And *I* got it. Every one of those Bassalino bastards dead. Every mothafuckin' one.'

'How do you know?' Lara asked flatly.

'Because *I* took care of it, sugar. I took care of it good.'

Lara returned to her apartment. Nick was dead and she was through crying, there were no more tears left. Why hadn't she warned him in time? It was all her fault.

She didn't know what she would do now. Everything seemed so hopeless.

When her phone rang she was tempted not to answer; it was probably Prince Alfredo, and she couldn't deal with him right now.

On the fourth ring she changed her mind. Listlessly she said, 'Hello.'

'Princess? Is that really you? Thank Christ you got out in time.'

Relief and joy swept over her. 'Nick! You're safe!'

'I can't talk. It's a mess here. I'm with the cops now. Jesus, Lara – my mother, my father, my whole family . . .' He started to choke up.

'Let me fly back. I want to be with you.'

'No. I'll call you again tomorrow. Just wait for me, sweetheart. You're all I've got.'

'Nick . . . There's a lot of things I have to tell you. . . .'

'Not now.'

'When?'

'Soon, baby, soon.'

*

She never did tell him. Somehow she couldn't summon the courage. He came to fetch her in New York and they flew back to California together. A few days later they took off for Hawaii where they were married in a simple private ceremony. The only person she confided in was Beth, safely back at the commune and happy to be reunited with her little girl and boyfriend, Max.

'I don't know how it happened, but it did,' Lara told her sister over the phone. 'And I'm not telling the others,' she added defiantly. 'Let them find out for themselves.'

Beth didn't lecture or judge. 'The Bassalinos have been punished more than enough,' she said quietly. 'I hope you and Nick can find happiness.'

'We will,' Lara said confidently. 'We're going to move to Italy and start afresh. Nick wants to and so do I. When we're settled will you visit us?'

'You bet!' Beth replied.

CHAPTER 50

Bosco Sam and Dukey K. Williams met at the zoo.

'I ain't truckin' with you past those goddamn monkeys again,' Bosco Sam complained. 'I'm still smelling monkey piss every time I wear my damn coat.'

Dukey laughed.

Bosco Sam glared.

'So, what's goin' on?' Dukey asked. 'Lay it on me, bro', 'cos I gotta be at rehearsal two hours ago. Little blond number held me up.'

'Dukey, boy, we had a deal.'

'Right on. Ain't nobody arguing that fact.'

Bosco Sam produced a Hershey bar from his coat pocket, and carefully peeled off the wrapper. 'Deal was I forget the two hundred thou – and you arrange the hit on the Bassalinos. Right?'

Dukey nodded.

'OK, Frank Bassalino I give you. But the others? C'mon Dukey, who're you shittin'?'

'Hey, man – Enzio was the important one. Leroy did a great job.'

'Leroy Jesus Bauls got his ass chewed off by a pack of fuckin' wild hounds. What was left of him his own mother wouldn't recognize. The cops showed me the photos. I got *very fine* connections with the police.'

'So?'

'So the word is that Enzio was got at *before* the house blew. Someone shot him through the heart an' sliced him up with a butcher's knife – just for kicks. You gettin' the picture?'

Dukey licked his lips. 'No, man, I'm not.'

'Angelo Bassalino got his in a car wreck. Nick Bassalino's back in LA. I reckon that still leaves you one hundred and fifty thousand in my debt.'

'Don't fuckin' lay this shit on me, man,' Dukey said angrily. 'You can't possibly mean—'

'I'll tell you what,' Bosco Sam interrupted. 'With interest we'll call it a straight two hundred thousand. Two days, my man. I'll give you two days. An' that's generous of me.'

'Come on,' Dukey groaned. 'You're full of shit. This ain't fair—'

'Fair? I've been very fair with you. I don't have to tell you what happens next. Two days is generous.'

'You fat fuck!' Dukey exclaimed. 'You jealous asshole. You'll get your money.'

Bosco Sam nodded. 'Sure I will, Dukey boy. Cash. An' I want it by six o'clock tonight.' Abruptly he shoved the rest of the chocolate bar in his mouth and walked away.

Dukey began to sweat.

There was no way he could get two hundred thousand together by six o'clock. No way.

CHAPTER 51

'The man who comes to you with his dick hanging out may want to make it with you, but does he want to work next to you? Does he want to see you get paid the same money for the same job he's doing? Hey – what about the guy in the street who undresses you with his eyes, fucks you with his mouth to his friends. Is he your equal, baby? Well? WELL?'

The crowd of women, joined by a few males at the rock festival, screamed their agreement.

'Hey, sisters – you want to be put down by a race of male pigs for ever? *Old* pigs with racist, chauvinistic, biased, old-fashioned views on *every* single thing that affects women in America today.

'To them we are pieces of ass. Look pretty, have the kids, but baby – stay home or you'd better stay quiet.'

Rio Java was speaking between appearances of rock groups. With her frizzy purple hair and sequinned make-up, she looked like a rock star herself.

In one year she had become as dedicated and intense as Margaret Lawrence Brown ever was. And her following was just as large. In fact, she attracted an even wider group of supporters than Margaret, as even the freaks liked her.

'One day I'm going to be President,' she'd told anyone who would listen. 'And I'm going to expose the whole stinking corrupt mess that politics represents.'

'For a start,' she told her friends, 'I'm exposing that sonofabitch Larry Bolding. He ain't gonna be chasin' *nothin'* when *I* get through with him.'

Larry Bolding, her ex-lover, the politician with the clean-cut image, blonde elegant wife, and two perfect little kiddies, was running as a Presidential candidate.

Rio held both arms straight up above her purple hair and made fists of her hands.

'Strike out, sisters!' she shouted. 'Strike out!! We are going to get what we want. We are going to be EQUAL in every way!'

The crowd whistled and screamed approval.

Rio felt the bullet hit her. She stood very still. She smiled. And the crowd spread out before her whistled and stamped and screamed.

'Strike out!' Rio managed. But then the blood bubbled up her throat and out of her mouth in one life-taking gush.

CHAPTER 52

The house in Connecticut could only be approached by passing through electric gates, and then undergoing the scrutiny of two uniformed guards with pistols stuck casually in their belts.

Dickson Grade passed this scrutiny easily. He was a precise-looking man in a dark business suit. He wore rimless glasses on small brown eyes, and his hair was combed neatly back.

He approached the big house, holding a slim leather briefcase tightly by his side.

A uniformed maid answered his ring. 'Good afternoon, Mr Grade, sir,' she said respectfully. 'Mr Bolding is out by the pool.'

Dickson Grade nodded, making his way through the house to the patio which led out to an Olympic-size swimming pool.

Susan Bolding greeted him. She was a most attractive woman, with straight fair hair pulled firmly back in a French twist. Her shapely figure was concealed beneath a loose silk shirt and tailored white trousers.

'Hello, Dick.' She smiled, kissing him lightly on the cheek. 'What can I get you? A drink? Tea? Coffee?'

Dickson smiled politely; he found Larry Bolding's wife extremely appealing, but when you were Larry Bolding's personal assistant you sat on thoughts like that and did nothing about them.

'Coffee, please, Susan. Where is Larry?'

'Exploring the garden in search of weeds, I think. Honestly, Sunday is the only day he gets time to relax. And you know how he loves his garden.'

'I'll go find him.'

Dickson walked down a side path until he discovered Larry Bolding playing softball on the grass with his children.

They greeted each other, and then Larry sent the children off to find Mommy. He was a tall, clean-cut man in his early forties. Craggy good looks combined nicely with a deep masculine voice and a politician's firm handshake.

'Everything is under control,' Dickson said. 'A perfect operation.'

Larry Bolding glanced around to make perfectly sure they were alone. 'Is she – dead?' he asked in a low voice.

Dickson nodded. 'And nothing to connect it with us. You're in the clear. Oh, and rest assured, the right people will be dealing with her personal effects.'

Larry Bolding sighed, and patted Dickson on the shoulder. 'It was the only way, wasn't it?' he questioned.

Dickson Grade nodded agreement. 'The only way.'

If you have enjoyed *The Love Killers*, you will want to read all of Jackie Collins' bestselling novels available in Pan. Here is an extract from the opening pages of *Rock Star*.

Saturday, July 11, 1987
Los Angeles

It was a perfect, cloudless Los Angeles day. The Santa Ana winds had driven off the smog, and Saturday, the eleventh of July, dawned crisp and clean, settling into a seductively lazy heat.

Kris Phoenix awoke early. Unusual for him, but he had flown in from London the previous afternoon and gone straight to bed. Fourteen hours later he surfaced in his over-sized California King bed, in his over-sized palatial Bel Air mansion, and rolled over to find that his Los Angeles girlfriend, Cybil Wilde, had joined him sometime during the night. Fortunately for her, she had not tried to wake him. Sex was great, but woe betide anyone who came between Kris and his jet-lag.

Cybil slept on, her nineteen-year-old body smooth and naked, long, honey-blonde hair fanning out around her wholesomely pretty face.

Cybil Wilde was a highly paid, extremely visible commercial model. Not quite Christie Brinkley, but on her way. Recently she had appeared on the cover of *Sports Illustrated* in a revealing one-piece swimsuit. Now the offers were pouring in, but Cybil never accepted anything without deferring to Kris's superior judgement. And he preferred having her at home – whether he was there or not.

He debated waking her – after all, it was several weeks since they'd seen each other. Then he remembered the concert tonight, and decided he could wait. Astrid, his London live-in, had not exactly let his motor idle. In fact, Astrid was a maniac in the sack, she never left him alone.

Astrid, the clothes designer. They'd met four years ago in Paris, when his manager hired her to design some leather pants for him, and she'd ended up feeling a lot more than the material. At twenty-eight, Astrid was nine years older than Cybil, but she had the requisite long blonde hair and knock-out body, plus she was Danish, and everyone knew about Scandinavian women.

He liked his women blonde and long-legged, with big bosoms and an amiable disposition. What more could any man ask?

Silently Kris stepped from bed, making his way into his black-mirrored bathroom. Fortunately he'd managed to stay sober on the flight from London. It was amazing the difference it made – he actually felt like a human being. And on close inspection in the mirror above his marble sink, he actually looked like one.

Kris Phoenix was thirty-eight years old. He had intense, ice-blue eyes, longish, dirty-blond hair subtly streaked by the sun (and if the sun wasn't around, an English hairdresser called Spud took care of it), and rakish good looks. Neither tall nor short, he hit a comfortable five feet ten inches – and since taking up weight training he was all dynamic body power and rippling muscles. Hardly Arnold Schwarzenegger – more Bruce Springsteen fused with Mick Jagger.

Kris Phoenix was a rock star. A very famous rock star indeed.

In fact, some said, Kris Phoenix was a rock legend.

All that talk never bothered him. As far as he was concerned he made music, sang songs and played a mean guitar. So did a lot of other guys. Kris reckoned he had a hold on reality. Just because he divided his life between two fantastic mansions, made millions of dollars a year, owned seven cars, and kept two beautiful live-in females, it didn't make him any different inside. He would always – deep down – be plain Chris Pierce from Maida Vale, London. There was no getting away from the fact that his mother once scrubbed other people's floors, and his stepfather drove a bus.

'Ohh ... my ... God! You ... are ... *sooo* ... sexy!' Cybil barefooted her way into the bathroom, and it wasn't only her feet that lacked coverage. 'I've really *missed* you, Kris!' she sighed, throwing her arms around him.

Suddenly, Astrid the maniac began to fade from his thoughts.

'You too, kiddo,' he replied, kissing her warm, inviting lips.

She rubbed her full breasts against his bare chest, knowing full well what *that* would do to him.

One snag. Sex was *out* on the day of a performance. Only somebody should tell the massive hard-on growing in his pyjama pants.

Regretfully he pushed her away. 'Leave it out, Cyb. Y'know the rules, and tonight's that goddamn private gig for Marcus Citroen.'

Snaking her arms around his waist, she rocked him back towards her. 'How about a private gig just for me?' she whispered in her best sexy voice. 'After all, I *am* asking nicely. And I promise I'll be good.' A meaningful pause. '*Very* good.'

There was no way Kris would break his rule. And nobody – not even the gorgeous Cybil Wilde – could make him. On the day of a performance he was like a fighter entering the ring: he needed every ounce of his precious sexual energy. Not one drop got spilled until it was all over.

'Later,' he promised, disengaging himself and moving purposefully towards the shower.

Cybil pulled a disappointed face.

'I said later, luv,' he repeated, flashing his famous crooked grin as he stepped under the icy needles of water and grabbed a bar of lemon soap.

Lathering his chest he decided the shower felt good. Freezing water. Freezing out the old sexual urges. Making him feel alive and alert, ready for anything.

Anything except a private performance for Marcus son-of-a-bitch Citroen.

Coldly Kris reflected on how much he loathed the powerful record magnate.

And with dull resignation he realized there was nothing he could do about it.

Not yet, anyway.